The Exchange

By the same author

Time To Act: A Mercenary Tale
published by Minerva Press 2000

Vertical Challenge: A Harrier Encounter
published by Book Guild Publishing 2007

Island Of Vengeance: A Story of Revenge
published by Raider Publishing International 2010

Sparkle of Death: A Tale of Revenge
published by Raider Publishing International 2012

Learn more about the author at his website:-
www.anthonyjbroughton.co.uk

The Exchange
A Story of Deceit

Anthony J Broughton

Copyright © 2014 Anthony J Broughton

The moral right of the author has been asserted.

Apart from any fair dealing for the purposes of research or private study, or criticism or review, as permitted under the Copyright, Designs and Patents Act 1988, this publication may only be reproduced, stored or transmitted, in any form or by any means, with the prior permission in writing of the publishers, or in the case of reprographic reproduction in accordance with the terms of licences issued by the Copyright Licensing Agency. Enquiries concerning reproduction outside those terms should be sent to the publishers.

All characters in this publication are fictitious and any resemblance to real people, alive or dead, is purely coincidental.

Matador
9 Priory Business Park
Kibworth Beauchamp
Leicestershire LE8 0RX, UK
Tel: (+44) 116 279 2299
Fax: (+44) 116 279 2277
Email: books@troubador.co.uk
Web: www.troubador.co.uk/matador

ISBN 978 1783062 829

British Library Cataloguing in Publication Data.
A catalogue record for this book is available from the British Library.

Typeset by Troubador Publishing Ltd
Printed and bound in the UK by TJ International, Padstow, Cornwall

Matador is an imprint of Troubador Publishing Ltd

CONTENTS

	Acknowledgements	vii
	Characters	ix
1	The Meeting	1
2	The Wait	11
3	Bad News	19
4	Robbery	32
5	Closing In	38
6	Motive	48
7	Rescue	57
8	Interrogate	70
9	Cannes	76
10	Choice	87
11	Getting the Picture	97
12	An Evening Out	106
13	The Search	122
14	Deadline	131
15	Delay	140
16	The Deal	149
17	The Party	156
18	An Offer	167
19	London	177
20	Arrival	184
21	The Unexpected	201
22	A Nasty Surprise	207
23	Following On	219
24	Camp West	228
25	Passport Home	239
26	Escape	244
27	Smash and Grab	255
28	Final Fling	272

ACKNOWLEDGEMENTS

I would like to thank Jane and Bernard Adsett for their enthusiastic comments and encouragement when reading my books, and Pauline and Quentin Gilpin for their assistance. I would also like to thank my cousin Gladys Scott for being such an inspiration to me, and my wife Linda for giving me the time and space to indulge in my favourite pastime of writing.

CHARACTERS

SUZIE DRAKE, ex-mercenary, co-owner of SMJ Boatyard Ltd

MIKE RANDLE, ex-mercenary, co-owner of SMJ Boatyard Ltd, partner of Suzie Drake

SIR JOSEPH STERLING, diplomat troubleshooter in FO for security matters

DI COLIN BROOKE, Detective Inspector in Special Branch

JIM & JENNY STERLING, son of Sir Joseph Sterling & his wife, co-owners of SMJ Boatyard Ltd

ROY KELLY, small time Irish thief

KATHERINE BOYD, Nelson's Building Society employee

DI MAIDLEY, Detective Inspector in charge of the boatyard robbery

MAGGIE HAINES, Katie Boyd's school girlfriend

SIR JEREMY PENDLETON MBE, millionaire playboy.

HENRY, Sir Jeremy Pendleton's chauffeur

MR ROGER MILES, Roy Kelly's solicitor

DI JAMES ROLLINSON, Chatham police chief

MURPHY O'CONNOR, murdered Irish politician

GILES HARMAN, rival boat builder

RAY TEAL & JOHN GREEN, DC's in Metropolitan Police Special Branch

MR WAINWRIGHT, building society employee

DC JAKE SMITH, Chatham policeman. PC LOUISE JORDAN, Chatham policewoman

OWEN SUTTON/OLIVER STATHAM, arms dealer

REG, foreman at SMJ boatyard. GEORGE, Reg's helper

MR LASSITER, Jeremy Pendleton's agent

MR GORRINGA, President of Jetuloo.

GENERAL ABOTTO, Camp West commander

MR FENNER, Kelly's probation officer.

ROBERT WESTON, Diplomat in Karuna

1

THE MEETING

In the Medway town of Chatham in Kent, the high street thronged with a multitude of shoppers and tourists, all pushing their way along the packed pavements. Some were visitors, enjoying the experience of a new setting, while others were going about their business or perhaps dashing to an important meeting.

The weather had been kind to everyone this year by producing a longer than usual summer for a change. Now, in late September, the sun had cooled from the heady, scorching days of July and August, but the temperature had continued to hold up well. Many of those in the bustling crowds still wore light or sleeveless tops and were determined to extract the last drop of sunshine to help them keep their much-sort-after suntans well into the autumn and winter, or longer if at all possible.

Few people took any notice of the bright yellow van parked in one of the numerous side streets that spread out from the main thoroughfare. It carried the familiar local electricity supplier's logo and address in red letters blazoned along the sides. Sat in the vehicle was Roy Kelly, a man of below average height, who was a small-time thief. He was about to commit a very different kind of theft, after he had succumbed to a beguiling woman who he had met while trying to burgle her house.

A scraggy looking man with a heavily lined face, he used his skills, acquired by years of petty thieving, to steal from unoccupied houses. His *modus operandi* was to break in, pocket as much of his victim's cash, jewellery or any small item that he could easily remove and sell, and get out quickly. He chose houses carefully and selected ones that offered a modicum of seclusion at the rear, allowing him to jemmy open a window without prying eyes watching his lawbreaking activity. Once inside, he took what valuables he could grab in only a few minutes, and retreated before either he or the theft could be discovered.

On the previous Friday afternoon, shortly after two o'clock, Kelly had wandered up and down a cul-de-sac street while he checked out the large detached house with the nameplate above the door stating that it was *The Red House*. It was covered in ivy and had an inviting side entrance to a garage. Assured that nobody was watching, he slipped down to the side entrance and put his shoulder to the gate. It took little force for him to tear away the screws fixing the bolt in place, and he was in. With his jemmy he prized open the back window and entered the house. It was as he suspected, empty, and he crept up the carpeted stairway to the bedroom where jewellery was usually to be found. Rummaging through the dressing table drawers, he discovered some rings and necklaces – items that were easy to sell. Things were going well for him when he stiffened abruptly at a noise that came from below. Frozen to the spot, he listened as the front door slammed shut and footsteps tramped up the stairs. His heart suddenly began pounding much faster as he searched in vain for somewhere to hide. The owner had returned unexpectedly and came straight into the bedroom that he was ransacking.

'What the hell do you think you're doing in my house?' the buxom woman angrily shouted, her face reddening with rage.

Kelly dropped the jewellery he was admiring and sidled towards the door. 'Let me out and I won't hurt you,' he bluffed.

'Hurt me! You'll be lucky to get out of here alive,' she growled.

Kelly had no intentions of hurting her; robbery with violence carried a much stiffer penalty, and he knew it. He rushed at her, hoping to shove her aside and make his getaway, but found her tougher than he had expected for a woman. She slapped him across the face, knocking him to the floor.

He looked at her in amazement. 'Right! Now I'm angry,' he blurted, attempting to frighten her by waving his jemmy.

Rising from the floor he charged head down at her. Nearby on the bedside table, sat a lamp. The woman grabbed it and crashed him over the head as he charged in, smashing the lamp to pieces and knocking Kelly into senselessness, despite the blow being slightly softened by his cloth cap. Blackness engulfed him; he dropped his jemmy, sank to his knees and slumped to the floor.

Gradually, the darkness that became his world for a few moments began to lighten as Kelly flicked open his eyes. By the time he had regained his senses, his eyes were open wide with amazement on discovering that the woman was attending to the wound on his head, despite his threats and his attempt to burgle her house.

'I haven't rung the police – not yet,' she told him, watching his eyes to see what effect the comment had on him.

As a man on remand, Kelly was pleased that she had not rung them, and it brought a calmer look to his face, which she recognised. He was acutely aware of the authority's willingness to unhesitatingly send him back to prison if he was caught perpetrating the smallest misdemeanour, let alone if he continued to break into houses and commit robbery again.

He glanced at her full figure and the tantalising glimpse of cleavage that showed above the scooped neckline of her blouse. She was aware of his eyes discovering her body and his thoughts mentally imaging how she looked undressed.

'Why are you doing this?' he asked, in his gentle Irish accent, wincing at the pain he suffered as she bathed the lump on his head, which had now begun to swell and change colour.

'You were about to take my jewellery, I couldn't let you do that.'

'The insurance would cover it. You live in a nice big house and don't look as if you're short of a bob or two.'

'Not true. My husband hangs on to all the money. Now, if you'd broken into his safe and were taking his valuables that would have been different.'

Creasing his brow, Kelly suggested, 'I don't have enough brains to crack a safe open, and I suppose your comment means that you don't care very much for your husband?'

'Clever boy,' the woman said. 'You look like a much nicer man than my husband, even if you do burgle houses for a living.'

'I don't usually do this,' lied Kelly, 'but my wife and kids are hungry and we've got no money and no food,' he stated, trying hard to elicit sympathy for his plight from the woman who had strangely not reported his attempted burglary.

'I don't think so,' she replied. 'You don't look like the sort of man who is married with kids.'

Kelly's face coloured. This was a clever woman who could read him well. 'What do you want, lady?' he asked, surmising that his continued freedom probably depended on what she wanted, and whether he was willing to agree to it.

'I knew we could approach this sensibly. What I need, is a man who is not afraid to take what he wants.'

'Oh! And what is it that I want?'

'How about an equal share of £100,000 … and me?'

Kelly was shocked. 'You mean you'd let me share a bed with you?'

'I would.'

Kelly's heart started to race at the thought of having such a voluptuous looking woman, even before he had considered what he could do with that amount of money. He had never had such a forthright offer made to him before. He studied this woman's face. She was attractive; a lot more attractive than any other woman who had befriended him since his teenage years. She spoke quite eloquently, a sign of a good education thought Kelly, unlike the torrid school years that he had endured, and was pleased when they came to an end at the age of fourteen. She was at least ten years younger than him, and could be no more than thirty-five he judged, though he was the first to admit that he was not very good at telling people's ages, especially women.

He again glanced at her figure. She had a delightful figure, with ample breasts that he would love to get his hands on. Never in his wildest dreams did he ever consider that he would get the chance to share a bed with a woman as desirable as her. The thought excited him, though he was not so stupid that he did not realise there would be a price to pay. He wondered what that price was, for such a glorious gift.

'So, what do I have to do get this money, and have a gorgeous woman like you willing to let me take her to bed? Rob the Bank of England?'

The woman giggled, 'Don't be silly! Not at all, nothing as drastic as that.'

'Even so, it must be something pretty horrendous.'

'All I want you to do is help me to get away from my nasty husband. He treats me like a slave, and beats me if I don't do exactly as he says.'

'That's not very nice, and I sympathise with you if it's true, but why don't you go to the authorities, or to some other group that helps wives who are battered by their husbands?'

'I've tried that and got nowhere. He is a very convincing man, and tells them I am making it all up.'

'Show them the bruises.'

'He is careful to hit me where it doesn't show very much and if it does, he tells them I fell over. I have to put up with the mental torture as well. No, he is making my life a misery and I have to get away from him. To do that, I need money and a friend who's willing to help me.'

'If it's sympathy you want, I can give you that, but I don't have any money and why would you want to let me sleep with you anyway?' he asked, glancing at her shiny wedding ring.

'I work part-time in a building society. Jeffery, my husband, is the manager and works there full time. I know the routine, when there is a lot of cash about, and being on the inside I can give you details about when to rob the place.'

Suddenly, a more sinister reason became apparent to Kelly, and one that scared him. 'I ... don't know about that,' he hesitated. 'I've never robbed anything but houses before. And I've only burgled them when they are empty, or at least I thought they were empty,' he said, fingering the lump on his head.

'I can help you, and if you do this little job for me, I will be *ever so* grateful, just like I said I would,' she encouraged, smiling at him in her most friendly manner.

'Little job?' he muttered. 'What's your name?' asked Kelly, while he considered her proposition.

'Katherine Boyd, but you can call me Katie. What's yours?'

'Roy Kelly, but you can call me clumsy.'

'Clumsy! Why?' she giggled.

'Any burglar worth his salt wouldn't let a woman catch him in the act and knock him out cold with a table lamp.'

'Don't be silly! I do get a bit aggressive when it comes to the few worthwhile things I possess. That probably comes from having to put up with the domination I suffer from my husband. So, what do you say? Will you take me up on my offer?'

'What happens after we've robbed the building society?'

'You take the cash back to your place, I leave the society later on and meet you at your home to split the cash, then after all the fuss has died down, we fly off to sunny climes. Do you have a current passport?'

'Yes, an Irish one.'

'Good. We could live a life of laziness and basking in the sun, or if you wanted to, you could take your half and do whatever you want.'

'It sounds risky to me.'

'Not at all. We can make sure that your face is covered, and I can give you all the information you'll need. I'll be there to hand you the money, though of course I don't want the police to know that I'm involved.'

It all sounded too good to be true.

'And that's all I have to do, take the money and run?' Kelly asked.

'There is one other thing, but that can wait until after we've got to know each other better,' Mrs Boyd said, undoing the buttons on her blouse and slipping it off.

She wore a black lacy uplift bra, which supported her breasts and enhanced the look of her figure and cleavage. She allowed Kelly to pull the straps down and release her ample bosoms. They were the most magnificent breasts he had ever seen, except for those in the magazines he had bought and regularly drooled over. If nothing else came of this association, at least he will have had one unforgettable interlude with a willing, voluptuous woman.

With quivering hands and a pounding heart Kelly removed his coat, a garment in a poor state, which had seen better days. He kicked off his shoes and undid his belt. Mrs Boyd removed her underwear and stretched out on the bed. Kelly was more than ready, slipped between her thighs and entered her straight away, before she could change her mind.

He felt that glorious feeling in his loins, a feeling which had eluded him ever since he was a teenager. He grabbed her breasts with both hands, eager to extract every sensation of euphoria that flowed through him. His tongue savoured her nipples and he had barely started to thrust when the unparalleled excitement caused him to immediately ejaculate. Wanting to relish the moments for a lot longer, he held on tightly to Mrs Boyd's plentiful bosoms while he nuzzled his face in them. This was an experience that he did not want to end.

'You got a little bit over excited, didn't you?' declared Mrs Boyd, pulling herself free from his grip.

'Yes, I'm sorry about that. The thrill was too much for me. It's been a long time since I've stuffed a woman, and never one as lovely as you.'

Mrs Boyd cringed at Kelly's crude expression of intercourse, but smiled. 'I'm sure it will last longer and be much better for you the next time we make love,' she said, eager to keep her fish on the hook.

She adjusted her bra, slipped her arms into her blouse, but left the buttons undone as an enticement. Kelly looked pleased at the thought of a repeat encounter.

'When will that be?' he enquired, hopeful that it would be soon as he buckled up his belt.

'It won't be long,' she assured him. 'I have to find out when my husband is not around. It wouldn't do for him to catch us.'

'It certainly wouldn't,' said Kelly, jolted into awareness of a potential problem that could end his enjoyment of this newly found sexy partner and inflict even more bodily harm on him.

'What is you telephone number?' she asked.

'I don't have a phone.'

'No telephone?'

'No.'

'Or mobile?'

'No.'

'That's unusual.'

'When you live alone as I do, you don't need one.'

'I see. So, as I surmised, you're not a married man with kids.'

'No, you were quite right,' conceded Kelly, his face colouring once more.

'Where do you live then?'

'In a basement flat, near the top of the hill in St Mark's Road, almost opposite the church.'

'Yes, I know where that is. What's the number?' asked Mrs Boyd, knowing the area was a poorer part of the town, populated by blocks of flats and Victorian houses which had been converted into flats.

'Number 63B. The entrance is around the side and down some steps. It's only a one bed flat with a kitchen, living room and bathroom, but it's clean – more or less,' Kelly said, hoping that Mrs Boyd might consider visiting him if her husband's presence made it difficult for them to meet at her house.

'I'm sure it is, Roy. Tell me, have you ever handled a gun?'

'A gun? Why do you ask?'

'Well, you can't very well go into a building society to rob it, if you haven't got something to threaten the teller with, now can you?'

'No, I suppose not. I hadn't thought of that.'

'So, have you ever fired a gun?'

'Not for a long time. Not since I was an angry teenager in Northern Ireland,' he admitted.

'Have you killed anyone?' Mrs Boyd asked, in a rather excited manner, recalling the continual media reports of troubles that had occurred there for many years.

'No, I don't think so.'

Disappointment was written all over her face. 'Nevertheless, you know how to handle one?'

'Yes, I do,' he said, remembering his youth and the troubles he had witnessed in the province, and took part in against the British Army and the police.

Barely a day went past without an incident of one sort or another occurring. Sometimes it would be a bomb that went off, often killing more citizens than soldiers – their intended target. At other times it would be a shooting, generally at an army checkpoint where other soldiers or civilians would end up dead. Riots were frequent, and often vehicles or premises were set alight, bringing firemen as well as police and soldiers to the scene, all to be attacked with whatever weapons were handy.

Kelly was lucky. At least he had survived those torrid times; more lucky than his father was. He had blown himself up with a home-made bomb that was intended to destroy a pub that the soldiers frequented. It was a terrible accident, but Kelly never admitted that to anyone. As far as he was concerned, his father's death was the fault of the British soldiers, and he had repeated the story to so many people telling them that they had shot him, that he almost came to believe it himself.

Since those frantic scary days he had mellowed, and although the province was now mainly peaceful, jobs were still hard to find, and like so many others he ventured to the English mainland to find work. As an unskilled man the only employment he was offered were labouring jobs, which a man of his stature and build found hard to maintain. Working on a building site was hard; thieving was much easier, so began his life of crime and the start of his prison sentences, the last of which he had finished less than six months previously. He decided not to tell Mrs Boyd that he was obliged to report to his probation officer every week, she may not like that, and he wanted to keep in her favour and not do anything to upset their new relationship.

'Have you been back to Ireland lately?' she asked.

'Yes, I went there after … that is, I spent a couple of months there earlier this year in May and June. Just a little holiday to see my sister and her husband. The weather was very good, and the sun shone all the time. I enjoyed seeing the old country again. It's true what they say – the grass there is definitely greener.'

'I understand that's because it rains a lot in Ireland.'

'Not at all. It rains just as much here in England.'

'Perhaps. I think you'd better leave now. My husband will be home soon and he wouldn't like it if he found you here.'

Shoving his feet into his shoes, Kelly grabbed his cloth cap and coat from the bedside table, and gingerly put the cap on his head. He took a last longing look at Mrs Boyd's cleavage before she fastened her blouse buttons.

'How will you contact me?'

'I'll come to your flat, or put a note through the letterbox telling you when it's safe to come here.'

'Okay. I'll hear from you soon then.'

Mrs Boyd smiled, but did not answer. Kelly crept down the stairs, an act he did automatically when in other peoples' houses, opened the front door, glanced furtively around to check for passers by, and took the step down into the street. He pulled his collar up even though it was a warm day, and shuffled out of sight, watched all the way from an upstairs window by a smiling Mrs Boyd.

2

THE WAIT

In Chatham over the following week, Kelly remained in his basement flat for most of each day, worried that if he went out for any length of time he might miss the lovely Mrs Boyd and not be able to repeat the delightful favours she had offered to him.

On Mondays he was scheduled to visit his probation officer, Mr Fenner, and although he considered not keeping the appointment, he finally decided that he dared not miss it. Mr Fenner was a grumpy looking almost bald man with a long chin, who was a stickler for all ex-convicts in his charge to arrive on time, and was not slow to admonish those who dared to turn up late. Kelly dreaded to think what he would say if he missed his appointment altogether. Nothing short of being almost dead would satisfy as an excuse for not turning up.

When he arrived, Mr Fenner asked him the same old questions about his behaviour that he replied to the week before. Was he looking for work? Was he keeping away from other crooks and criminal activities? Kelly gave the same old answers, saying that he had reformed, was going regularly to the job centre and not burgling houses. He tried to hurry the interview along, but his probation officer became suspicious.

'Do you have another appointment to go to?' Mr Fenner asked.
'No. Why do you ask?'
'You seem to be in more of a hurry this week.'
Kelly hesitated, had an idea and stated, 'Well ... the lady at the job centre did say there was the possibility of a suitable opening becoming available this week, and I didn't want to miss it,' he lied.

'Good. In that case, I think we've finished, so you can go. I'll see you next week at the same time. Perhaps you'll have better news about employment by then, and don't be late.'

Kelly hurried home and was disappointed that Mrs Boyd had not left him a note, and during the next few days was beginning to wonder if she ever would. To his delight she knocked on his door on Friday afternoon. He had tidied up the flat, especially the bedroom, and had high hopes that she would still be willing to let him indulge in his sexual fantasies with her.

'Do come in err … Katie. I was beginning to think you'd given up on me.'

Mrs Boyd stepped through the doorway, which lead straight into the old fashioned kitchen. It looked tired with the off-white paint peeling from the cupboards and walls. The whole room was badly in need of redecorating, and Mrs Boyd had a horrified look on her face when she entered, but hid it from Kelly.

'Given up on you? No, Roy. Why would I do that? I like you and we have an arrangement that is to both our benefits, but I have to be careful of my husband. If he suspects that I'm going out for anything other than to do the shopping, he gets very jealous and beats me.'

'You don't have any shopping with you,' Kelly remarked.

'No, I have to call in at the supermarket on the way home, so I can't stay very long.'

Kelly's heart sank. 'So, you won't be … that is … we won't …'

'No, I'm afraid not; not today. I'm going first to see a friend of mine this afternoon – a girl friend. I knew her at school and she's asked me to drop in on her for a chat about old times.'

'I see,' Kelly said, lowering his eyes in disappointment. 'Would you like a drink?' he asked.

'A cup of tea would be nice,' stated Mrs Boyd, sitting at the Formica covered kitchen table.

While he brewed the tea, Kelly remained quiet. Mrs Boyd realised he was disappointed that she was staying for only a short while, and not allowing him to repeat his sexual desires with her. The whistle on his kettle started to blast out its shrill when the water began to boil, and Kelly threw in one teabag and filled the teapot.

'I'll be free next Tuesday and my husband will be away all day. He's taking part in some seminar or something up in London, so we wouldn't be disturbed. You could visit me then, if you want to,' she suggested, intent on keeping him happy.

'If I want to,' said Kelly. 'Christ! I've done nothing else this past week but want to,' he said, handing Mrs Boyd her rather weak cup of tea in his best china.

He only had two cups and saucers that were not chipped or cracked, and were the only ones that remained from a set that he had stolen a long time ago.

'Sugar?' he asked.

'Not for me, thank you.'

Kelly spooned in three tablespoonfuls into his cup. 'You get used to taking sugar when you're in … in Ireland,' he hastily added.

The hesitation was noticed by Mrs Boyd, who had already guessed about Kelly's past, but she said nothing. It was the reason she had chosen to befriend him, that and the obvious lack of a woman's touch, which showed in his general demeanour and the state of his clothes.

They drank their teas, sat at the kitchen table. Mrs Boyd took only a few sips before she rose and gave Kelly a quick kiss on the cheek.

'Don't go getting into any trouble and get yourself arrested,' she said, subtly trying to suggest that he should curtail his housebreaking activities for the time being.

He understood the suggestion. 'Don't worry about that. I won't do anything that is likely to stop me from visiting you again next week.'

'Good. Then I'll see you next Tuesday at about two o'clock. Give me a ring first to make certain that the coast is clear,' she said, handing him a piece of paper with her telephone number typed on it.

Kelly looked at the piece of paper. 'I will,' he replied, trying to remember where the nearest telephone box was that had not been vandalised. He held the door open and watched the lovely legs of Mrs Boyd as she climbed the steps and disappeared from view.

At least, she had come back and had not forgotten him. He was pleased about that, if rather disappointed that he had not been able to get her into his bed, though the promise of more delights was still on the horizon.

★ ★ ★

Each day dragged by very slowly for Kelly, before the following Tuesday finally dawned. He had watched the days and hours tick slowly along until the moment to see Mrs Boyd finally arrived. As she suggested, he rang her first from a telephone outside the local railway station. He was half expecting to hear her make another excuse and say that something else had cropped up to prevent his visit. She did not, and he was delighted to get the all clear to attend their tryst. He was instructed to enter by the back door, after making sure that the neighbours did not see him. As a burglar, he was used to sneaking around furtively and blending in with the background.

He arrived at *The Red House* in good time and checked carefully to make certain that he complied with her wishes to remain invisible to the neighbours. He wanted nothing to stand in the way of his desire to repeat their first sexual experience.

The back door was unlocked this time and Kelly did not have to climb in through the window, as he had when attempting to burgle the house on his last visit.

'Do come in,' Mrs Boyd said, smiling at him.

He followed her up the stairs to the bedroom, and noticed for the first time the freshly polished smell in the house, and the abundance of antique furniture, or at least what seemed like old furniture to him. Mrs Boyd was obviously house-proud and she and her husband had collected a house full of well-made heavy furniture. Too heavy for a simple thief like him to take any notice of. Grab what you can carry and get out quickly, was his motto.

'The bathroom is there,' she pointed out, 'if you want to freshen up first. I'll be in this bedroom.'

'Why should I want to freshen up first,' thought Kelly, but decided he would wash his hands anyway, even if he did not understand why.

When he entered the bedroom, Mrs Boyd was waiting for him perched on the end of her bed, wearing a dressing gown. 'I've left my under things on. I thought you might like to remove them from me.'

'Yes, I would,' enthused Kelly, his eyes opening wide and his heart beating fast at the expectation of the enjoyment he was about to receive.

Unfastening the belt, Mrs Boyd opened her dressing gown and Kelly looked at her bruised body with horror.

'What on earth has happened to you?' he questioned.

'My husband beat me, again.'

'Why?'

'I went to see Maggie Haines, an old school friend, last week. We got chatting and I didn't realise what time it was. I rushed to get the shopping done, but got home late, after my husband had returned from work. He didn't believe that I'd been with another woman, so he punched and kicked me to tell him where I'd really been,' Mrs Boyd said, with tears starting to dampen her eyes. 'It was horrible.'

'The bastard! I'd like to kill him, beating up on a defenceless woman like you.'

Mrs Boyd seized on the comment. 'Would you do that for me? That's what I want you to do. It's the only way we can be rid of him for good.'

Kelly was startled. 'You mean … that you want me to kill him?' The incredulity in his voice was very apparent.

'Yes, I do. Then we will be free to be together all the time.'

'I don't know about that. Killing someone is not a thing to take lightly,' said Kelly, who was now shaking for a different reason.

'I realise that, and if there was any other method for us to take, I would use it.'

Kelly shook his head. He though that robbing a building society was bad enough, but murder – that was a different matter altogether, and carried a very long prison sentence if you were caught.

'You do want us to be together and have lots of fun in bed, don't you?' asked Mrs Boyd, playing on Kelly's infatuation of her, or at least of her shapely body. She unfastened her bra to let Kelly feast his eyes on her buxom figure once more. He did, and the sap began to rise in him.

'Of course I do, but I hadn't figured on murdering anyone. It won't be easy.'

'I can help you,' she said, guiding him to sit beside her on the bed.

'Help me! How?'

'The building society that I work in is very small. There are only two customer windows. My husband will be serving at one of them and I will be at the other. There are no other employees in the building. I will make sure that you are given the cash, and as you are about to leave I will sound the alarm by my husband's window. You will get annoyed at this, and turn and shoot him before making your escape. It takes the police eight minutes to reach the building society, plenty enough time for you to make your getaway.'

'Do they have cameras there?'

'Yes, but don't worry, I will give you a mask to put on, nobody will be able to recognise you.'

'Except when I'm standing in the doorway and take it out of my pocket.'

'Ah! I've though about that. You will wear a woolly hat that has a rolled up rim. When you get to the building society, you simply bow your head and roll down the rim of your hat to cover your face before opening the door. It will already have holes cut out for your eyes and mouth, and will come down to your chin. Nobody will see your face.'

'Very clever,' said Kelly, uncertain whether the idea was practical.

'I will make sure that the open and closed sign is hanging on the door. All you have to do is turn it over to read closed and slip the catch down on the door. That way, everyone will think the place has just closed and nobody will disturb you during the robbery.'

'So that's why you asked me if I'd ever handled a gun. You've been planning this all along, haven't you?'

'After I met you, yes. It's lucky for us that you are such a versatile man,' Mrs Boyd said, boosting Kelly's ego.

'And what about the gun? I don't have one.'

'As fortune would have it, the lady friend I visited last week knows a man who can get you one. Apparently, he was an old boyfriend who ditched her for a younger woman. She was unhappy about the way he did it, but told me that he was getting into heavier stuff, drugs and crime etcetera, so she was becoming afraid of where it might lead to anyway. I've got his telephone number, so you could ring him and say that Maggie is a friend and she gave you his telephone number.

Considering the problems, Kelly tried hard to find an obstacle that Mrs Boyd had not though of, and which would free him of making a decision that scared him more than anything else had in the last twenty years.

'How do I get away afterwards? The police are bound to block the area off when a murder has been committed.'

'You are going to borrow a van and will drive away.'

'Borrow a van?'

'Yes, you do know how to drive, don't you?'

'Yes, but I don't have a current licence.'

'Never mind that. On the outskirts of town, the local electricity board have their headquarters. They have a yard full of large and small vehicles, and there are no security guards on patrol. The gates are always left open to allow the vans back in after the men have finished work. There are cars parked in there all day. On Fridays the men only work until lunchtime, and leave the keys in the ignition and go home for the weekend. I've watched them.'

'You seem to have thought of everything.'

'Yes, I hope so. When the police arrive at the building society, I will have to play the grieving widow for a while and join you abroad on holiday a little later.'

'Abroad? That's different to what you said before.'

'Yes, I thought about it and I've decided that it would be better for both of us.'

'Where abroad?'

'Across the Channel, in France. I have a friend who has a holiday home in Normandy. She's told me it will be empty for a month and I can use it whenever I want to. I'll book you a ticket on the ferry from Dover later that evening. You can make a smart getaway before the police have even begun to figure out what has happened. After the robbery, I'll explain that I want to get away to recover from the horror of seeing my husband shot dead. Meanwhile, you can rest in France for a while and I'll join you when I can. What do you say?'

'I'm not sure. It sounds like you've got everything covered, but I don't speak a word of French.'

'Most of the locals know some English and lots of English people live there as well. You will manage okay. It will only be for a short while.'

'And when do you plan for me to make this robbery?'

'Next Friday, just before closing time. We shut early on Fridays, at 2 p.m.'

'Let me consider it for a while,' suggested Kelly, thinking that it would be the answer to his prayers to skip abroad, have money and a lovely sexy woman by his side, and almost better than that, he would get rid of his aggravating probation officer. He was a fastidious man and a pain in the neck. Mr Fenner was very strict about Kelly seeing him on time every single week, and refused to be flexible about anything. It would give Kelly great delight to annoy him by simply disappearing from sight and leave him wondering where he had vanished to.

'Okay? Treat me gently, won't you?' said Mrs Boyd, slipping out of her dressing gown. She knew the best way to keep Kelly interested was to let him act out his sexual fantasies with her, and she was desperate for him to help her.

He grabbed her buxom breasts. Cupping each one with a hand he eagerly pressed his face into them and kissed her nipples.

'Gently,' Mrs Boyd implored. 'I'm a bit fragile at the moment still.'

Kelly obliged, and as Mrs Boyd suggested, he removed her underwear and was happy to let her sit on top of him to avoid any pressure on her bruised body. It was ecstasy again and allowed him to feast his eyes on her bouncing breasts at the rise and fall of her body as they engaged in their union. The encounter lasted only a short while longer than Kelly's first experience with her. It did not bother him though, he pushed all thoughts of the building society robbery to the back of his mind, and enjoyed the most unbelievably delightful time of his life with the woman of his dreams.

# 3

BAD NEWS

Beneath a dark sky, the guard switched on his torch, looked at his watch for the fourth time in the last ten minutes, and noted the hour was a few minutes before 1 a.m. It had been a warm day, but was followed by a cool evening that brought a chilly night breeze blowing in from the river.

A red Ford XR3i screeched to a halt in the yard, and its occupant jumped out and slammed the car door shut. A figure approached, lit by the umbrella of a dim tungsten glow from the security lamps that hung on the nearby workshops, and spilled over the jetty towards the two motor yachts moored at the waters edge. The guard aimed the beam of his torch on the man ambling towards him across the yard of SMJ Boatyard Ltd, a boatbuilding company situated in Hamble Marina on the southern Hampshire coast.

'Wotcha Pete. I thought you were going to be late for a minute,' the first guard, said.

'Nah, not me, Barry. I've timed it just right. I wanted to see the football highlights before I left. It was a good match, and United won two nil.'

'Oh thanks! I set the freeview machine to record it, so I could watch it before I go to bed. There's not a lot of point now that you've told me the score.'

'Sorry, Barry. I didn't realise you stayed up that late to watch TV. I though you were tired and went straight to bed when you got home,' Pete said halting beside him, his features appearing quite frightening, cut by deep shadows from the upward beam of the torch on his face.

'Not me. It takes a while for me to wind down. So, I have a beer and watch the tele' for an hour or two.'

Pete turned and stared into the darkness along the jetty where the two yachts were moored. 'I thought I heard something. Did you?'

'Nah,' replied Barry, staring into the darkness.

He shone his torch up and down the concrete walkway, across the two yachts and listened to the water gently lapping against them at the jetties edge, nudging them into the quayside.

'There's nobody there. You ain't getting jittery about noises again are you? It's probably just the sound of the water.'

'I guess so. This job gives me the creeps sometimes, wandering around in the dark, especially after you've gone and I'm on my own.'

'Before I go home, let's go back to the office and have a nice cup of tea,' Barry stated, putting an arm around Pete's shoulder and guiding him in the direction of the main building.

'That sounds like a good idea.'

Before either realised what was happening, Pete lurched forward as a silenced pistol spat its deadly piece of lead into his back, and in the blinking of an eye another bullet tore into Barry. He fell to the ground alongside his colleague. Both were still alive, but unable to comprehend what had happened to them.

A shadowy figure stepped from one of the motor yachts, stood over the bodies and pumped another bullet into the head of each man to make sure they were dead. A second man approached them.

'Nobody said anything about a couple of guards being here, and I don't like getting mixed up in murder.'

'Don't start going soft on me now. I didn't know that either, but now it's taken care of, we can get on with the job we were hired for.'

★ ★ ★

In their cliff top house on the southern English coast on the outskirts of Bosham Hoe in West Sussex, partners Mike Randle and Suzie Drake completed their morning showers. They had worked up a sweat on their jog along the nearby beach before showering, getting dressed and trooping down to the kitchen for breakfast.

'Friday again and the end of another week,' stated Suzie. 'We've not had a great deal of response yet for all our efforts at the Southampton Boat Show a few weeks ago,' she complained.

'We've a few orders trickling through from the show, and we had a lot of interest in our work, especially from the new luxury motor yacht we've built for Jeremy Pendleton. I'm sure it will pay dividends in the long run. People don't want to hurry when spending a lot of money on a boat. I'm sure that business will pick up again soon,' declared Mike.

'I hope so. At least the trials went well on the yacht, and all the work has just about been completed.'

'Yes, I'm pleased to see the job finished; it's been quite a headache. We've got one working day left to make the final checks before we have a lazy sail down to Cannes tomorrow morning to hand the yacht over to Pendleton,' Mike stated.

'We don't want to be late, it'll take us at least three days to get there and there's a hefty penalty clause to pay if the delivery is not made by noon next Tuesday,' reminded Suzie.

'We could have finished the yacht a lot sooner if Pendleton's agent, Mr Lassiter, hadn't been so finicky about checking every single stage of the build, and insisting on so many minor changes that weren't really necessary,' argued Mike.

'Yes, but after delivery we can invoice Pendleton for the final half of our payment.'

'True, the boatyard needs that cash urgently. We don't want to have to pump more money into the business if we can help it. It'll only set Jim's dad wondering where it all came from again.'

'I get the sneaky feeling that he already knows really.'

'You may be right but, as long as he's willing to let it rest, we should do the same.'

'I guess you're right.'

'Work on the yacht's been taxing. It took a lot of effort to get all the components delivered on time in order to satisfy Pendleton's requirements, especially with him hanging around you a lot of the time. He's tried hard to impress you with his wealth and importance, and still wants to get you into his bed, the creep.'

'Stop worrying about him! He hasn't succeeded and anyway, I hear that he's not been in this country for the last few weeks.'

'Oh! So where is he, and how do you know that?'

'Mr Lassiter told me. Pendleton's been sunning himself in the south of France, in Cannes, playing the roulette wheel and waiting for the yacht to be delivered. He's got a permanent mooring there and is staying at *The Metropolitan Hotel*, mixing business and pleasure. That lot must cost him a fortune.'

'Lucky him, he can afford it,' Mike stated.

Mike Randle and Suzie Drake were ex-mercenaries in their mid-thirties, who had given up soldiering and now owned SMJ Boatyard Ltd along with their friends Jim and Jenny Sterling. A little over a year earlier they had secured an order to build a luxury motor yacht for millionaire playboy Jeremy Pendleton against tough opposition, much of it from Harman's Boatyard, a rival boat builder from a yard in Devon. A good deal of their success in gaining the order, was due to Pendleton's strong desire to get the very attractive Suzie, and her slim athletic figure, into his bed for his personal sexual gratification; a feat which his wealth, charm and good looks had allowed him to succeed with many other females. Afterwards, he would discard them in his quest to entice others into his bed. The number of attractive women seen hanging on his arm had given him the reputation of being a man who was a good lover. With charm, attractive impish looks and more money than most people saw in their lifetime, he was a magnet that continued to entice many beautiful women to his side. His attempts to draw Suzie into his net had helped SMJ Boatyard to win the motor yacht contract.

Pendleton was eager to add Suzie to his list of conquests by using the contract as bait, but failed in his prime objective at the last hurdle when she and Mike were called to go abroad on business. Even after the contract was signed with their boatyard, Pendleton continued his attempts to get Suzie into his clutches. His reasoning was, that because she and Mike were not married, he was entitled to look on Suzie as a free woman and fair game for his lustful approaches; not that he allowed a wedding ring on a woman's finger to stand in the way of his many conquests.

His association with SMJ boatyard had also brought Pendleton more into contact with the father of their partner Jim Sterling. Sir Joseph Sterling was a Whitehall troubleshooter for the government on security matters. He was one of many influential people whose friendship Pendleton was cultivating in order to help him impress those who mattered. His efforts were rewarded when he finally received his knighthood, and was now Sir Jeremy Pendleton MBE, an added fillip that he used to influence more women, normally to good effect.

Mike and Suzie were sat at the breakfast table in their kitchen, unusually situated at the front of their house facing towards the ten-foot outer wall and the coast beyond. Mike read the newspaper as he and Suzie crunched through their toast and sipped their orange juice. The hands on the kitchen clock moved up to the hour and the radio announcer was beginning to read the eight o'clock news when the telephone rang. Suzie answered the call to a very animated Jenny Sterling on the other end of the line.

'Suzie, something terrible has happened.'

'What is it Jenny? What's all the excitement about?'

'I've just arrived at the boatyard,' she blurted out between sobs. 'Pete and Barry, the two security guards, have been shot dead and Pendleton's yacht is missing. Reg rang the police when he got here and saw what had happened, they've just arrived.'

'Oh, my God! That's terrible. Mike and I will leave straight away. We'll see you in about half an hour,' she said, jamming the telephone back on the wall mounted receiver.

The concerned look on Mike's face turned to anger when he heard the news. 'What bastard's done that?' he cried, quickly swallowing his drink and snatching a slice of toast. He grabbed their car keys and gizmo to open their electronic gates as they bundled through the front door.

The wrought iron gates to the driveway of their house, clanged shut behind them as their Aston Martin DB9 roared along the coast road towards the M27, and on to their boatyard at Hamble Marina. On the way, they discussed the consequences of the murders and theft. They quickly realised that, apart from the horror of having two employees killed, the theft could severely damage, and possibly even bankrupt the boatyard if the perpetrators could not be caught and the yacht found in time to deliver it by the contract date, unless Jeremy Pendleton could be persuaded to relax the penalty clause, a gesture that they knew he was unlikely to agree to.

After arriving at the boatyard in the shortest time ever, their DB9 swept through the archway into the yard and screeched to a halt behind Pete's aging Ford XR3i, waiting lifelessly for an owner who would not return. Mike and Suzie hurried to the water's edge where the police were talking to Jenny and Reg, the boatyard foreman. The workmen were standing around, shocked at what had happened and discussing it in lowered tones. Some puffed away nervously on their cigarettes as they watched the proceedings. They all knew how important the yacht was to the yard, and now wondered how safe their jobs were if the yacht could not be found and delivered on time, giving Jeremy Pendleton the opportunity to evoke his penalty clause.

Jenny rushed over and she and Suzie hugged each other as tears flowed from both of them. 'This is awful,' Jenny blurted.

A plain clothed policeman approached Mike, who had wandered over to glance at the blanket covered bodies of his two guards.

Holding up his warrant card, the 6' 2" gangly policeman stated, 'I'm Detective Inspector Maidley. I'm in charge of this investigation.'

'Mike Randle, and this is Suzie Drake,' he said, she and Jenny approaching. 'We're co-owners of this boatyard,' he added extending his hand. 'Have you learnt anything about this unbelievable murder and robbery?'

The policeman shook Mike's hand and nodded to Suzie. 'No, not yet. We've not had time to assess anything other than the obvious. It looks as if there were two suspects who stole the boat. The forensic boys might be able to give us a better idea of what happened when they get here. They shouldn't be very long. All I can tell you is, the two guards were each shot in the back and the head, and probably knew very little about it. And of course your boat is missing, which at the moment I am assuming is the reason they were shot.'

'I'll take Jenny into the office and make us all a strong cup of tea,' interrupted Suzie. 'We're both very upset at Pete and Barry's murder. While I'm there, I'll ring the office staff and tell them not to come in today, though I think most of them are already here or on the way.'

'Yes, good idea,' agreed Mike.

'What are you going to do about the men, send them home?' she asked.

Mike looked at the inspector.

'I need to ask them a few questions first, then they can go,' he agreed.

'Okay,' said Mike. He turned to Suzie. 'Tell the boys to wait in the reception area and see if they want a cup of tea, and ask Reg if he'd come and see me, please love.'

'Okay. Would you like a cup of tea, Inspector?' offered Suzie.

'Yes, please, Miss. I didn't get time to have one before I got the call to come here this morning. White with two sugars please.'

Suzie half-smiled and left, arm in arm with Jenny, their eyes red with the tears that each had shed.

'Is the boat worth a lot of money, Mr Randle?'

'Just a few tens of millions, Inspector.'

The detective inspector blew a silent whistle.

'The motor yacht is a very expensive, specially commissioned craft that is due for delivery to Jeremy Pendleton; that is Sir Jeremy Pendleton MBE, in a few days time in the south of France. We've been working on her for over a year. The second half of the payment is due on delivery, so if we don't get her back in time to make the deadline, the yard could be in serious financial trouble.'

'I see. I assume that you have insurance?'

'Yes, but have you ever tried getting several million pounds out of an insurance company in a hurry, Inspector?'

'I see what you mean. Do you or your co-directors have any enemies that you know of; perhaps someone who may have a grudge against your boatyard and want to bankrupt it?'

'No, I don't think so. We are in a competitive business of course, but it's not cutthroat. I imagine the yacht was stolen purely because of its value, and the guards were in the way of preventing that.'

'I can't see any cameras covering the area, are there any?'

'No, there aren't. It's something we've talked about, but never got around to installing.'

'That's a pity. With boats worth that amount of money, I'd have thought it was an obvious deterrent to have.'

'With a man on guard each night, we didn't think it was necessary. After this, I'll see they are fitted.'

'You said a man on guard, not two men, why?'

'They take … that is, they took turns to cover the night shift. Last night Barry was on from 6 p.m. to 1 a.m. Pete was to take over from 1 a.m. to 8 a.m. this morning.'

'So, as they were both here and killed, I think we can safely assume they were shot at around 1 a.m. this morning,' the inspector calculated.

'That seems likely.'

'I'll need details of their addresses and next of kin.'

'I'll ask Jenny to get them for you,' agreed Mike.

'Were they armed in any way?'

'No. We don't ask our guards to carry any sort of weapon. We didn't think it was necessary, and hoped that it would discourage any violence against them.'

'I see. Was either of them married?'

'Barry wasn't and Pete was divorced. That's why they didn't mind the unsociable hours quite so much.'

The inspector nodded. They both looked round at the flash from a camera, as the police photographer took pictures of the dead men and surrounding area. Mike looked at the bodies of his two men and inwardly swore that he would track down whoever did this and exact revenge, however long it took.

Reg, the boatyard's foreman, a man in his late fifties with a leathery looking suntanned face, due to him working out of doors much of the time, came over and spoke with them.

'This is a terrible thing, Mr Randle,' he croaked, finding it difficult to hold back his anguish and hardly daring to look at the bodies.

'Yes, I know, Reg,' he replied, putting a friendly hand on his shoulder. 'Was the stolen yacht tanked up?'

'No, there was only a small amount of fuel left in her. If they want to take her any distance they'll have to get some diesel very quickly.'

'Have you checked our tanks to see if any is missing?'

'I've no need to. We're down to the last drop after running extensive trials on the yacht over the last couple of weeks. A load is due to be delivered by tanker first thing this morning. It should arrive here any time now.'

'Hmm, that might help us. Where's the nearest terminal for getting the fuel?' asked the inspector.

'There are many boatyards on the Hamble that have fuelling pontoons. They could have filled up at one of several places along the river,' Mike replied.

'Right. I'll get someone to start checking them out. If they had to stop for fuel then we might get lucky and find a witness who can give us a description of them,' said the inspector, wandering over to a police sergeant to give him instructions.

While the inspector was out of earshot, Mike asked, 'All the equipment is installed and working on the yacht, isn't it Reg?'

'Yes, it is. We've tested all the electronic wizardry that Mr Pendleton wanted fitted. Everything's working fine.'

'That means the anti-theft GPS tracker should be working then?'

'That's right! Because of the horror of what's happened here, I'd forgotten all about that. It's installed, but not activated yet. If you know what the code is, you can use the transponder on our motor yacht *Quester* to activate it. Then we can use her GPS system to pinpoint the stolen yacht's position,' said Reg, turning to see a tanker, carefully negotiated through the archway and pulling into the yard. 'That'll be our diesel arriving.'

'How quickly can you and the boys have *Quester* checked, fuelled and ready to leave?'

'Give us a couple of hours or so. The lads will pull out all the stops to help you catch those bastards. I'll get her filled up with diesel straight away now the tanker's arrived.'

'Fill up the spare tanks as well, please Reg. If they are planning to take our yacht abroad, we may need all the fuel we can carry.'

'Okay.'

'Is there power aboard?'

'Not at the moment. Give me a few minutes, I'll soon get that fixed.'

'Good. Let me know when that's ready, then I'll see if I can locate our missing yacht, and say nothing to the policeman.'

Reg nodded.

Mike scurried off to the main building of the boatyard, pushed his way through the glass front doors into the crowded lobby, which fell silent at his entrance. The men looked at him with sadness in their eyes and he nodded in return. No words were spoken and none were needed. They all understood the shock and sadness that engulfed them all. Mike took the wooden stairs to the general office. He thumbed through the specification for Pendleton's, as yet unnamed yacht, and found the information he was searching for.

'Ah, here it is,' he mumbled to himself, pulling out the tracker information sheet.

Returning to the yard, Mike was approached by Reg.

'The electrical shoreline connector is now fitted and switched on to give power to *Quester*.'

'Thanks Reg.'

Mike dashed aboard the sixty-foot long motor yacht that had sophisticated electronic guidance equipment installed that was capable of activating the GPS tracker on the stolen vessel.

In the wheelhouse Mike punched the tracker code into the transponder, it beeped, confirming that the receiver had been located and the transmitting signal turned on.

'Great! It's working,' stated Mike, noting the latitude and longitude. He skipped down the steps into the cabin, grabbed a chart and marked in the coordinates.

'Right, let's see where our murderers are taking you to.'

Suzie appeared with a cup of tea in her hand. 'Reg told me you're going to use the GPS tracker to locate them. That's assuming they haven't ripped it out,' she said, handing Mike the cup.

'Thanks.' He took a sip. 'It's not as easy as that. The tracker is well hidden and enclosed in a strong box, welded in place and with a combination lock. If you don't know where to look for it, it's damn difficult to find. The tracker's working okay. I've activated it, and I'm checking the location now,' he stated, marking a cross on the map. 'That's where they are at the moment, in the English Channel heading west towards the Atlantic. If they left shortly after 1 a.m., they haven't travelled very far, so they probably stopped for fuel and they don't appear to be in any hurry. They're close to the French coast. My bet is they're going to turn south and sail down towards the Med.'

'Do you think we should tell the inspector?'

'No. Now they're out of English jurisdiction, it could take years of legal wrangling to get them brought back, assuming we can catch them up and find out who they are. If we want to get the yacht back, we'll have to go after these scumbags ourselves. Reg and the boys are getting *Quester* ready to sail.'

'How long will that take them?'

'Two to three hours at least.'

'I'll dash back home and get our things. Knowing that they've shot our guards in the back, I'd say we're dealing with ruthless men; we'll need to be armed.'

'Yeah, that's good thinking. I'll keep track of them until you get back. Drive carefully,' said Mike, pulling the car keys from his pocket.

Suzie grabbed them and gave him a kiss on the cheek. 'Better get some food aboard. We don't know how long it's going to take us, and don't forget to grab the ownership papers. We'll need those if we manage to get her back and can motor on to Cannes.'

'Yeah, right,' he agreed, watching Suzie jump ashore and head for their car.

Mike dashed across to the office and into the reception area. Most of the men were still standing around drinking cups of tea or coffee, and discussing the night's events.

Mike had a quiet word with Jenny. 'Would you please ring the local supermarket and arranged for a variety of food, several bottles of red wine and a couple of bottles of whisky to be delivered straight away? Suzie and I are going to chase after those bastards in *Quester*.'

'How are you going to find them?'

'I've activated the GPS tracker aboard her. I can see where they're heading, but I don't want the inspector to find out what we're planning. He might not understand and may try to stop us.'

'Okay. I'll get the food ordered straight away. How much do you want?'

'Enough for about a week for two people.'

'Right.'

'And when you've done that, could you please get the inspector a copy of Pete and Barry's details. He'll need them to notify their next of kin.'

'Okay. I'll go round and see them myself afterwards.'

'Good idea. Thanks.'

Jenny tramped upstairs to the main office, to carry out her tasks, and was glad to have something to do. Meanwhile, Reg and several of his men were preparing *Quester* for the voyage. Inspector Maidley had noted the increased activity and was curious to know what was happening. He approached Mike, walking across the yard, back towards the yacht.

'Are you planning to leave us?' he asked.

'Suzie and I have a lot of friends who work along the Hamble River. We're going to scout around and ask if anyone noticed something unusual this morning. We may get lucky.'

'Good. Be sure to let me know if you discover anything.'

'Of course,' said Mike.

A couple of hours later, the deep throaty roar of the DB9 signalled Suzie's return with their belongings. Mike stepped ashore to meet her, anxious to avoid explaining to the inspector why they were taking personal items aboard. Having successfully negotiated that, the inspector started to wonder what was happening when the supermarket van arrived and the contents were loaded aboard the yacht.

He tackled Mike. 'I couldn't help noticing that you are having quite a lot of food and drink taken aboard your boat,' he said suspiciously.

'We need to check out the yacht. We want to make sure that nothing was touched last night. We're stocking it up for a customer, who's due to rent it from us later today for a boating holiday. Despite what's happened, we don't want to disappoint them. Suzie and I will take it for a short run to make sure everything's working okay, while we're out asking about our intruders,' Mike lied.

'Oh, I see,' said the inspector, not sounding totally convinced.

Foreman Reg watched the inspector return to the area where the men from the forensic lab had pitched a cover around the bodies. Other policemen were busy meticulously combing the area for clues.

Reg stepped aboard *Quester*. 'She's fully fuelled up and ready for you to leave whenever you want,' he told Mike.

'You'll probably have to make excuses for us to the inspector when he realises that we're not returning.'

'Don't you worry about that. I can take care of any questions he asks. You just get those bastards.'

'We will,' said Mike, looking at Suzie.

She nodded in agreement. 'We'll keep in touch with you by radio and let you know how we're progressing,' she told Reg. 'Meanwhile, we're counting on you and George to keep an eye on things around here. Jenny was very upset, so I rang Jim to give him the news and suggested he cancels his London meeting and takes her home for today.'

'Okay. We can handle everything. Don't you concern yourself about anything.'

Suzie smiled, patting him on the arm.

'Good luck,' Reg said, stepping ashore.

Mike fired the engine up and *Quester* pulled slowly into the Hamble River, watched by both Reg and the inspector, and headed towards the open sea.

4

ROBBERY

Roy Kelly looked at the stolen watch on his wrist and resigned himself to carrying out a robbery that he was not sure he wanted to do, and a murder that he was certain he did not want to do. Both actions were prompted by the considerations that Mrs Boyd offered him in the way of a financial reward and the freedom to enjoy her sexual enticements – an offer that was like nothing he had ever received before, and one he found unable to refuse. She had assured him that everything was arranged and nothing could go wrong.

Dressed in white overalls and a woolly hat, both provided by Mrs Boyd, Kelly looked a strange sight as he slammed the door shut of the stolen electricity van, parked in a side street close to the building society. He was following the instructions where to park the vehicle and how to find the building society that she had impressed upon him. Kelly had walked the route several times, nervously fingering the gun in his pocket. He kept his head down and hurried along towards Nelson's Building Society. The branch was situated in a quieter street, away from the main shopping area, where fewer people roamed along the line of the dozen or so shops, one other building society and a bank.

Wandering past the building, Kelly glanced through the glass windowed door and noted that no customers were present. He looked at a clock on the building society wall, showing the time as 1.55 p.m. – the time he was instructed to begin. The date was also shown as Friday 13th; was this an omen he wondered, trying hard to ignore the pace of his racing heart beat and the butterflies churning away in his stomach? Though it was not raining the sky was grey and overcast, reflecting the mood that Kelly could not shake himself free from.

This was a small building society, which had, as Mrs Boyd had taken pains to point out, only two teller's windows. Kelly walked back to the entrance porch and peered over the top of the half frosted window. Mrs Boyd was perched on a chair behind one window and behind the other was a man, who Mrs Boyd had told him was her husband, and who to Kelly's mind, had a mean look on his face. He looked the type to beat up a woman!

Pulling the band down from his woolly hat and the gun from his pocket, Kelly pushed his way through the door into the building society, turned the sign on the door to closed and slipped the catch down, locking it shut behind him.

Waving his gun at the two tellers, Kelly declared, 'No heroics now, like setting off the alarm, or I'll shoot. Give me all the cash you've got and put it in this bag,' he demanded, pulling a supermarket plastic bag from his pocket and shoving it through the access hole towards Mrs Boyd.

His voice crackled with nervousness and his hand was visibly shaking. Mrs Boyd put on a frightened look, mainly for the camera, and opened her money drawer ready to hand over the cash. The man beside her looked belligerent and aggressive, he appeared ready to cause trouble.

'You get out of here right now and take that gun with you,' he demanded.

Kelly stepped closer and pointed the weapon at the teller as he stood from his seat behind the glass fronted counter.

'Give me all the cash you've got or I'll blow you to kingdom come,' he stated, as ruthlessly as he could in his Irish accent, which had become stronger with the adrenaline rush that was coursing through his body, sending his heart rate and pulse so high that he though he might explode.

'Get lost! I'm not giving you any cash. You're not going to shoot me to get your hands on a measly few thousand pounds. That amount is not worth risking a life sentence for,' the man bellowed.

Kelly was perplexed. This man was certainly trouble. This was not supposed to happen.

'I think he means it,' stated Mrs Boyd, trying to help the situation along the path she desired. 'Perhaps we should give him the money. There's no point in getting us killed for it; it's not even ours,' she said, grabbing a handful of money from her drawer.

'Not on your life!' stated the man, pressing the alarm bell, immediately sending out a loud ringing noise from a box on the outside wall, alerting everyone within one hundred yards. 'The police are on their way here now, so you get out,' he shouted, pointing at the door.

For a moment Kelly panicked, as did Mrs Boyd, who began to look a little flustered. Things were not going as planned. What should he do now? Kelly looked at the contorted expression on the man's face and suddenly pictured all the bruises this nasty individual had inflicted by beating his wife – the sexy wife that he now adored and wanted.

Beneath the mask, the look on Kelly's face hardened, he gritted his teeth, pointed the gun and made one more demand, 'Give me the money you evil bastard or I will shoot you.'

'Not a chance,' the man spat. 'The police will be here any second now and they will soon sort you out.'

Confusion ran through Kelly's mind. What should he do next? His strongest instinct was to turn and run. He half turned away when a further verbal tirade was hurled at him.

'Go on run! If I had a gun I'd shoot you - you horrible little Irish thief,' the teller yelled, waving a fist at him.

Kelly's screwed up his face with anger. Similar taunts flashed through his mind from his troubled days in Northern Ireland when he was a youth. This man was nasty and intolerable. It is no wonder that Mrs Boyd wanted to get away from him. He turned back, levelled the gun, pointed and pulled the trigger.

The blast from the weapon was deafening in the small room as the bullet shattered the glass and the recoil shoved Kelly back on his heels almost knocking him over. Mrs Boyd squealed as shards of glass peppered her and she ducked, falling to the floor below the counter. The bullet struck the man squarely in the chest, catapulting him into his seat. He overbalanced and crashed backwards into a filing cabinet that stood behind him at the rear of the counter. His eyes were wide with incredulity at the miscalculation he had made; a mistake that looked likely to cost him his life.

Blood spurted from the wound in his chest, he slid, with his body shaking violently, to the floor beside Mrs Boyd. She let out an ear piercing scream at the horror before her eyes and fainted, collapsing in a heap next to the twitching body of the man.

With the smell of cordite hanging heavy in the air, Kelly span on his heels, rammed the gun in his pocket and grabbed the door handle. He pulled hard, but the door remained shut. The woolly hat he was wearing as a mask had slipped down his face, obscuring his view. He swore and pulled it back up to see the door handle. He suddenly remembered that he had slipped the catch down to lock the door, and he flustered trying to twist it back to get the door open. The deafening alarm bell was clanging away and several people had stopped in the street to stare. Eventually, Kelly released the catch, threw the door open wide and charged out, pulling up the rim of his stupid woolly hat that had slipped yet again, preventing him from seeing where he was going.

He had taken no more than three paces towards his getaway van, when a fist slammed into his face, sending him reeling back on his heels. His whole world turned into a dream, sounds disappeared down a long dark tunnel and blackness swirled before his vision and finally engulfed him. Kelly crumpled to the ground unconscious. A few moments later, he began to recover and slowly emerged from his dream like state; voices echoed in the distance as if spoken from far away. Consciousness dawned on him. He felt his arms held tightly behind his back and his woolly hat mask had been torn off. His nose, broken and bleeding, was pressed against something hard.

'You stay where you are and you won't get hurt any more,' an unfamiliar voice told him, swirling in the background of his mind.

As his jumbled thoughts came back to reality, his eyes opened and he started to comprehend what fate had befallen him. With his face jammed against the pavement, Kelly was unable to see anyone, and the man had a tight grip on him with his knee pressed hard into his back to keep him pinned to the ground.

A badly shaken Mrs Boyd had revived from her fainting spell and staggered to the building society entrance with blood running down her face from cuts, caused by the flying glass. A man hurried to help her. She looked in horror at the predicament Kelly was in, and realised immediately that his capture was the last thing she wanted. She knew that the police would arrive at any moment, and wondered if she could trust him not to implement her in the robbery and shooting when they questioned him. He was infatuated by her, so she hoped so, but had no way of being sure.

'I'm an off-duty policeman ma'am. Have you rung the station?' the man asked, while keeping his stunned captive firmly pinned to the pavement.

'Err, no, I haven't,' she hesitatingly replied, her arm held by the man helping her.

'Then please do so straight away.'

'The alarm automatically rings at the ambulance and police stations. They should be here within eight minutes.'

'Good.'

Mrs Boyd looked at the blood seeping from Kelly's nose, colouring the pavement. 'Was it necessary to injure him that way?'

'I heard a gunshot, so I didn't want to take any chances. I retrieved a firearm from his pocket. Was anyone else hurt?'

'Yes, the other teller was shot. I think he's dead.'

Gasps of horror came from the small crowd of passers by who had stopped to stare at the event. The volume of police and ambulance sirens wailing in the distance, increased as they sped along the high street and neared the scene. A few minutes later a police car screeched to a halt and two policemen jumped out.

'I didn't expect to see you here, Harry,' said the driver.

'I heard the alarm ringing and apprehended this man coming out of the building society with a mask over his face. He had this gun in his pocket,' he said, holding the weapon up. 'I believe he's shot someone,' explained the off-duty officer.

The policemen took the weapon and handcuffed Kelly. He dragged him to his feet and shoved him into the back seat of their car. Kelly watched in bewilderment as an ambulance with paramedics arrived. They rushed into the building society, guided by the arresting policeman. A local newspaper reporter and photographer had reached the scene and Kelly turned his face away from the photographer's camera flashes, as the man strived to take his picture through the police car window.

The teller was badly wounded, but still alive. He was brought out on a stretcher, with the paramedic holding a drip bag aloft. He was rushed to the local hospital where he underwent an emergency operation to remove the bullet. Policemen cordoned off the area to keep the swelling crowds of curious onlookers away.

Kelly, with blood on his face and down his white overalls, glanced at the blood spattered face of Mrs Boyd being attended to by a paramedic in the back of their ambulance. She glanced at him as the police car began its journey back to the station with its prisoner, their eyes met, but a changeless expression held their faces as Kelly was driven away.

5

CLOSING IN

The motor yacht *Quester* left the Hamble River, glided into Southampton Water and sailed on past the Isle of Wight heading out into the English Channel. At the helm was Mike and Suzie piloting her. They were in hot pursuit of the thieves who had stolen the yacht that their boatyard had built for Jeremy Pendleton; thieves who had also ruthlessly killed their two boatyard security guards.

Co-owning and running a boatyard had taught both Mike and Suzie a great deal about life on the water, and had enabled them to become competent navigators and pilots. SMJ Boatyard Ltd had a small but steady list of customers worldwide, which required them to be able to expertly navigate their vessels to deliver them anywhere on the globe. This had quickly become an essential skill they had to master, and electronic equipment had made this task much easier.

As they moved into the English Channel, Mike continued to watch the progress of their stolen yacht using the on-board GPS tracking system.

'They're still heading towards the Med,' he informed Suzie.

'Can we catch up with them? After all, Pendleton's motor yacht is fast.'

'Yeah! Two 1400hp diesel motors means she's capable of nearly twenty knots, but with a brand new motor yacht, they may want to take it easy on the engines, because they certainly aren't using anything like full speed, unlike us.'

'That could be good for us.'

'Yes, I reckon we can catch up with them, but I'm not sure how long it will take us, probably a couple of days at this rate. If they pull into port anywhere, we'll close on them a lot faster,' suggested Mike.

'Hmm, if.'

'At least they're heading in the right direction. If we can get the vessel back, then we'll be well on the way to delivering it to Cannes.'

'If – again,' said Suzie.

'Ye of little faith,' muttered Mike.

Suzie looked at him and smiled. 'I'm sure you're right.'

'Jeremy Pendleton rang the boatyard this morning while you were collecting our things. He said that if we don't deliver the yacht to his berth in Cannes by the agreed delivery date of next Tuesday, he'll be exercising his rights under the late delivery clause to demand compensation.'

'Did you tell him about the robbery?'

'No. I didn't want to tell him that his pride and joy has been stolen. I'll leave that until later, just in case we can't get the yacht back in time.'

'I hear that he's a ruthless businessman. Remind me, how much compensation is it?' asked Suzie.

'A lot! It could almost bankrupt us.'

'Perhaps we can persuade Jeremy to extend the delivery time after he hears what's happened. After all, it won't be our fault if we can't deliver his new toy on time.'

'You might be able to, by charming him,' said Mike. 'He's been attempting to get you into his bed ever since he first met you, he might see this as a good excuse to press you into his clutches.'

'He might, but he hasn't succeeded so far.'

'More by luck than anything else, and it won't stop him trying.'

'Probably not, but all the time he's keen on staying friendly with us, we have a chance to get more orders from him or his rich friends.'

'True,' Mike agreed.

'Why does he want the boat delivered to Cannes?'

'So that he can have a very lavish party with lots of friends, in order to show off his wealth and name his new toy.'

'That's nice,' Suzie remarked sarcastically. 'It also explains why he didn't want us to fill in the name plate on the yacht.'

'Right. It's going to take at least a day or two to catch up with our killers, so now we're well out to sea, you could do some last minute sunbathing,' Mike suggested.

'That's an idea. It's a nice sunny day, so I might as well while we're chasing along. I didn't bring my costume, but that shouldn't matter while we're out here at sea.'

Mike knew that Suzie's idea of sunbathing was to go topless and although he continued to admire her athletic figure every time he got the opportunity, he never tired of gazing at her naked features. Suzie duly obliged and stretched out on the deck of *Quester* in the briefest of flimsy knickers.

Their motor yacht was a modern craft, equipped with the latest electronic gadgets, which enabled Mike to set the yacht on automatic pilot and spend more time eyeing Suzie's naked figure than watching the controls – a pastime he gladly indulged in.

Speeding along, close to 17 knots for the rest of the day and throughout the night, their motor yacht made good headway. Meanwhile, Mike and Suzie slept a restless sleep, allowing the automatic pilot to keep them on course, and the radar to warn them of any possible collision.

Morning arrived, with Mike checking their position before waking Suzie and bringing her a cup of tea in bed. He placed it on the bedside table.

'Good morning. Sleep well?'

'I was a bit restless, but yes, okay thanks.'

'Yeah, me too.'

'You were a bit hot last night, Randy.'

'That just shows what one day at sea can do for you,' Mike declared.

'Especially when I'm laying around topless most of the time.'

'That might have had something to do with it,' he conceded.

'Are we any nearer our quarry?'

'I checked the tracker. We're a lot closer to them than I thought we'd be at this stage, so I guess they must have stopped for the night.'

'Perhaps they don't know how to use the automatic pilot?' Suzie suggested.

'Perhaps. Or maybe they're simply not expecting anyone to follow them. I wonder where they're going.'

'Do you think they have a buyer already lined up for the yacht?'

'You mean was it stolen to order?'

'Don't you think that's a possibility?'

'Yes, I do. It's a very expensive, state-of-the-art motor yacht that a lot of people would love to get their hands on. We saw that at the motor show, and perhaps our thieves saw it there too.'

Suzie sat up and reached for her cup of tea, revealing her naked figure. Mike reached out, caressed her breast and got a slap on the hand for it.

'Work now, play later,' said Suzie. 'We've got to reach that yacht before they get into port or we'll have a lot of legal wrangling trying to get her back, especially as we don't even have a name for her. And, Jeremy Pendleton won't pay us until we deliver it and the ownership papers to him.'

'Right. I'll get back to the wheel.'

'And I'll get breakfast, once I finished my delicious cup of tea.'

Mike gave Suzie a kiss and departed to the pilot house. The radio squawked into life – it was Reg from the boatyard.

'How are you progressing, Mr Randle?'

'We're doing quite well and catching up with our quarry, Reg.'

'Good. That copper was a bit annoyed when he realised you weren't coming back, but by then he knew there was nothing he could do about it.'

'He'll get over it.'

'I smoothed things over with him and I think he understood why you did it.'

'Good, well done.'

'His men did find the pontoon where our stolen vessel was refuelled. He's got a description of the three men involved, but it was very vague.'

'Three men?'

'Yes. He was told that one man looked like a sailor and seemed to know what he was doing, while the other two weren't dressed for a sea journey and looked more like business men in suits.'

'Two killers to steal the yacht and one man to pilot it, by the sounds of things.'

'That's what I thought.'

'Okay, thanks Reg. I'll contact you later if there's any more news.'

Suzie joined Mike twenty minutes later carrying their breakfast on a tray.

'Reg phoned to say there were three men involved in the robbery. One a sailor and two who were definitely not.'

'The two killers?'

'That's what we reckon.'

'That would seem to rule out the likelihood of them not knowing how the automatic pilot works.'

'Yeah.' Looking puzzled, Mike stated, 'They seem to have stopped twenty-five miles or so off the Portuguese coast, near Porto. The coordinates are the same as when I checked them first thing this morning.'

'Perhaps they are late sleepers,' Suzie suggested.

'Or perhaps the yacht has a problem, or worse still, perhaps they've damaged the engine. Of course, they might have arranged to meet their buyer there. Whatever the reason, we should be able to catch sight of them by this evening if they stay where they are.'

Mike and Suzie kept a close eye on the yacht's position. It slowly moved a few miles further south, before doing an about turn and returning to the same position.

'I can't make out what they're up to!' exclaimed Mike. 'Whatever it is, it's giving us the chance to catch up with them.'

By early evening, *Quester* was fast approaching the stolen yacht, which was sitting near the horizon, bobbing up and down on the waves, but not making any headway.

Mike pulled back the throttle levers and reduced *Quester's* speed. 'They've either broken down or they're waiting for a contact. That's the only reason I can think of to suggest why they've hardly moved all day,' Mike declared, edging their vessel closer, and taking a look at the darkening sky. 'You'd better get dressed and be prepared for a fight. The light's starting to fade, so we'll need to keep our eyes peeled.'

'Okay. We know they're armed,' stated Suzie, 'so, I'll check the weapons and get them ready.'

'Good idea,' agree Mike.

Quester closed in on the stationery yacht. Emerging with a Heckler and Koch MP5 sub-machine gun and two handguns, Suzie handed Mike one of the handguns, which he stuffed in his belt at the back.

'I'll stay hidden,' Suzie said, jamming the other handgun into her belt and dropping to the floor in the pilot house, cradling the sub-machine gun.

Easing back the throttle, Mike slowed *Quester* to a few knots as they came in close to the stolen yacht. A rough looking heavy set man, wearing a suit appeared and moved to the rail.

Mike leaned out of the pilot house. 'Is everything okay?' he shouted across.

'Yes, we've no problem,' was the reply, in an accent that Mike couldn't place immediately.

'He said 'we', so there's more than one of them still aboard,' Mike whispered to Suzie, crouching low.

'I thought you might have a problem as you don't seem to be making any headway,' Mike shouted back.

'No, it's okay. We're just taking a rest for a while.'

'He sounds Spanish, or maybe Portuguese,' whispered Mike.

Suddenly another man, similarly dressed, appeared from below deck holding a sub-machine gun and started blasting away at Mike. Holes peppered the pilot house, smashing the glass window. Mike ducked, rammed the throttle lever forward and accelerated the motor yacht away. Suzie stood up and sent a volley of shots across in reply, which made both men duck and prevented any more bullets flying their way. *Quester* sped into the distance.

'What did you have to go and do that for?' the first man asked. 'They were only asking if we were okay.'

'Didn't you recognise their boat?' was the reply.

'No. It's starting to get dark. It looked like any other boat I've seen.'

'That figures. Well, I did. It was moored alongside this one at the boatyard. They must be from the same place that we stole this one from. I don't know how, but somehow they've managed to follow us.'

Mike sped *Quester* off to a distance of 1,000 yards away, turned the vessel around to face the killer's yacht and cut the engines. 'Are you okay, Suzie?'

'Yes, I'm fine. They must have recognised our yacht.'

'Yeah, seems likely. I hope you didn't damage our expensive yacht with your volley of shots.'

'Of course not! I fired high. We don't want a lot of bullet holes in it. Jeremy Pendleton would not be pleased.'

'Good. The question is what do we do next?' asked Mike, staring back at the vessel through his binoculars.

'Well, as they didn't want any help we must assume there's nothing wrong with the yacht,' suggested Suzie.

'And if that's the case, it means they must be waiting for someone to contact them, probably from the mainland. Let's take a look at the map and see if anywhere nearby looks likely.'

'Okay.'

'Wait a minute, they're on the move,' stated Mike. 'And it looks as if they're heading this way.'

Gunning the engines, he jammed the accelerator handles forward, turned *Quester* around and sped off towards the southern horizon. The stolen motor yacht chased them for almost half an hour, but with Mike's skill at the wheel, bobbing and weaving *Quester* and with darkness rapidly overtaking them, the thieves were unable to get close enough to hit them with gunfire again.

'Whoever's at the wheel of that vessel, doesn't know much about piloting it,' stated Mike. 'With the power they've got, they should have caught us up long before this.'

'Lucky for us! Perhaps their sailor's not used to that type of motor yacht in the gloom.'

Despite gaining on them slowly, the thieves gave up and turned their vessel around.

'They've turned back, Mike,' stated Suzie, cradling the submachine gun, ready for the fight that looked imminent.

Mike glanced back and slowed *Quester* to a halt. 'They probably only wanted to chase us off. I still reckon they're waiting to meet someone to hand the vessel over to them, probably to the culprits who organised the theft.'

'So, what's next?'

'We're not giving up that easily. We wait, and keep them in our sights,' he said, spinning the wheel round, and turning *Quester* to follow them.

They shadowed the yacht back to the area, close to where they were chased from, but kept their distance. They remained far enough away to not be easily seen in the gloom.

'They've stopped again,' said Mike, checking the GPS tracker, 'and we're back where we started from – more or less, except they've stopped about five nautical miles south of where they were before.'

'Do you think they know how to use the onboard GPS and radar?' Suzie asked.

'From what I saw of them, neither looked like the seafaring type, so I doubt it, unless their sailor's still aboard.'

'They've got this far okay. That suggests he must be aboard, and at least have an idea of how to pilot the boat and navigate.'

Looking up at the sky, Mike said, 'It'll be completely dark soon. We could leave our lights off and try sneaking closer to them. I need to get aboard if we're going to have any chance of getting the vessel back.'

'That's true, but it's easier said than done. They'll be on the lookout for us now.'

'Yeah, right.'

'I caught a brief glimpse of something in the water just a moment ago,' remarked Suzie. 'I saw a reflection of it from the moon. What's that over there in the sea?' she said pointing.

'I can't make it out, but there definitely something floating out there,' Mike declared, focussing the binoculars on an object bobbing up and down in the water.

Wrenching the wheel round, he manoeuvred the yacht towards the spot and stopped along side.

'It's a body!' he declared.

They caught the body using a boat hook and hauled it aboard. Mike laid the man out on the deck.

'He's been shot twice in the back. And, from the state of him, I'd say it was very recent.'

'There's no one else around here except those men in the stolen yacht. Do you think he was their pilot and navigator?'

Mike checked the body over. 'Yes, I do. This bloke looks like a sailor. Look at the tattoos on his arm. An anchor; a mermaid; the name of a ship. I'd say he was definitely the pilot of our stolen yacht, and when he got them to the rendezvous point they had no further use for him, so they shot him in the back and dumped the body overboard.'

'Just like they shot poor Barry and Pete.'

'Yeah, exactly. That must be why they sailed south for a few miles, then turned back to their previous spot. They didn't want the body floating alongside them. I though it was a strange move to make. Now we know why.'

'So, the jokers who are aboard now may not know how to use the radar to check their position.'

'Right, and that's why they weren't very adept at manoeuvring the yacht when chasing us and didn't want to pursue us very far …'

'Because they were worried they may not be able to find their way back in the gloom to the right spot to meet their buyer,' Suzie finished.

'That's right. And they probably don't realise they're a good five or six miles off course.'

'So their buyer may have a job finding them.'

'Right. That could give us the breathing space we need.'

'Are we going to board her then?'

'It's the only way to get her back. We'll sneak in close and I'll row the last part in the dinghy. You stay piloting *Quester* and be ready to come riding to the rescue like the 7th cavalry with guns blazing, should I need it.'

'That's a bit histrionic, but I know what you mean.'

'I think it's best for us to wait about another half an hour until it gets completely dark.'

'Good idea.'

'Then you can manoeuvre us around to come in from the east. That way we won't be silhouetted against the sunset horizon. I'll change into my dry suit; it's black and will help me to blend in with the dark.'

'Aye, aye Captain,' Suzie said, saluting with a smile.

'I've still got time to teach you not to be so cheeky,' Mike said, chasing Suzie as she ran below deck shrieking.

He caught her up in the bedroom, pushed her on to the bed and started kissing and petting her. She responded and soon, all their problems were forgotten for the moment, as Mike eagerly thrust into their lovemaking.

6

MOTIVE

Roy Kelly was brought from the cells at Chatham Police Station to the interview room, and questioned by the police about his attempted robbery of Nelson's Building Society, and the shooting of a teller at the branch earlier that afternoon. His clothes had been removed and he was now wearing an overall, which he though strange as it was very similar to the one they had made him take off. The police doctor had examined him and cleaned the blood away from his face before submitting a report, which stated that in his opinion Kelly's mental and physical health were good, but that he had sustained a broken nose when tackled by the off-duty policeman.

When questioned by the police, Kelly refused to say anything. After his fingerprints were taken, it was not long before his police record was discovered and details of his life of petty crime were unearthed.

His probation officer, Mr Fenner, was summoned, and Kelly had to face the indignity of hearing him tell the police that he was a no-good individual and how, as his probation officer, he was not surprised to learn that it had come to this. He painted for them, a picture of a man who had a history of petty crimes, was not sensible enough to find a proper job, and who was always going to be on the wrong side of the law.

Kelly sat quietly at the desk in the interview room and waited for the inevitable barrage of questions that he was sure to face. His nose hurt like hell and he could not help fingering the shape of this unfamiliar lump in the middle of his face. He imagined that he was scarred for life.

Detective Inspector James Rollinson, the man in charge of the case, entered the room accompanied by DC Smith. They sat opposite Kelly, and after starting the tape recorder and stating who the occupants of the room were, the inspector outlined the facts of the robbery that they were aware of.

He asked Kelly, 'What made you chose that particular building society?'

Kelly remained silent.

'What prompted you to make the change from your usual *modus operandi* of housebreaking?'

Still no answer.

'And why did you turn to the dangerous habit of carrying a gun?'

He received no answers and continued, 'Where did you get the gun from?'

'What gun?' Kelly defiantly replied.

'The one taken from your pocket, and confiscated by the off-duty policeman. The one that we have both a video recording and forensic evidence of you shooting the teller with. That gun.'

'No comment,' Kelly maintained.

DI Rollinson was a seasoned police officer with over thirty years experience in the force, and had witnessed other stubborn suspects many times before. His square jaw, lined face and thinning hair gave him the firm and resolute look of a man who took his job seriously, but did not let it frustrate him. Kelly's obstinacy neither surprised nor fazed him. He was unable to get any further information about anything connected with the robbery out of him. Kelly refused to utter another word.

Finally Rollinson asked, 'Do you have someone to represent you?'

'Represent?'

'Yes, a solicitor to represent you. You will need one. You are in a lot of trouble. Do you know someone who will handle your case for you?'

Kelly shrugged his shoulders. 'Err, no, and I can't afford one.'

'Then it is my duty to see that one is appointed for you, and will be paid for out of taxpayers' money. Mr Royston Donahue Kelly, you are charged with the attempted robbery of Nelson's

Building Society this afternoon and the shooting of a teller there. Anything you say …'

Kelly sat, not listening to the formal charge read out by the policeman. He had heard it all before. His thoughts turned to Mrs Boyd and the short-lived, but wonderful time he had experienced with her. He was determined to protect her name and keep her out of the clutches of the police, and wondered how she was and hoped that her injuries from the flying glass had not badly hurt her.

DI Rollinson completed the formal charge of arrest, and he and the DC left the room. Rollinson returned a short while later accompanied by a different man.

'This is a solicitor, Mr Roger Miles. He has been appointed to act on your behalf,' Rollinson stated.

Kelly's eyes flicked across to momentarily look at Miles, but silence prevailed.

The solicitor was in his early thirties, clean-shaven, but with a well worn look about his craggy face, making him look older than his years. Much of this was due to the heavy workload he had to undertake defending many clients who had fallen foul of the law, and were unable to afford their own solicitor. He carried a large briefcase and sat opposite Kelly. DI Rollinson, and the policeman who had been standing guard at the door, left the pair of them to discuss their business in private.

The solicitor formally introduced himself to Kelly, took out a notebook and began, 'I have been apprised of the situation by DI Rollinson, who tells me that you are refusing to say anything. If you don't cooperate with them, the police will prosecute you for robbery and attempted murder, and you will spend a very long time in prison,' his solicitor warned.

'Attempted murder?' questioned Kelly.

'Yes, the building society teller is not dead. I understand that he has undergone an emergency operation in hospital and is critically ill, but still alive, so far.'

'So, I didn't kill him?'

'No, though I understand that he is likely to be paralysed.'

'Paralysed, you say?'

'The bullet went through him and lodged near his spine. If he recovers, he will probably spend the rest of his life in a wheelchair.'

'At least he won't be able to beat up Mrs Boyd,' thought Kelly. That pleased him.

'Robbery and attempted murder are very serious charges, Mr Kelly.'

'They can't do me for robbery,' stated Kelly.

'And why not?'

'Because I didn't steal anything. The bugger wouldn't let me have the money. All he did was yell at me and tell me to get out, and said if he had a gun he'd shoot me and I was a horrible little Irish thief. That angered me a lot.'

'So you shot him?'

'Something like that.'

Miles drew in a lungful of air. 'I could plead temporary insanity and say that you were driven to shoot the man by his outburst of insults. I haven't seen the building society video yet, but it should show that he was goading you. If it does, then we may have a case to claim for mitigating circumstances, though I have to say that your past record, and the testimony of your probation officer doesn't help.'

'Huh! He wouldn't say a good thing about any one of his parolees if his life depended on it,' asserted Kelly.

'Even so, his testimony carries weight. I think I'll ask the inspector to show me the building society recording straight away. It could be vital evidence that shows something in your favour as well as condemning you. I'll look at it and we'll discuss the matter afterwards,' he stated, slamming his notebook shut.

'What about my nose? That policeman smashed me in the face without warning and broke it. I didn't see him coming, and didn't try to fight him; he just smashed me in the face. He didn't need to be that violent.'

'Perhaps not, and you could try suing him for it, but under the circumstances, I don't think it would help your case very much. In fact it may harm it.'

'Huh! That's justice for you,' Kelly complained.

Miles disappeared for half an hour to view the security video recording. Kelly was taken back to the cells, and afterwards returned to the interview room to be confronted by his solicitor once more.

'Well, Mr Kelly. I can confirm that the video recording does show the teller was shouting and waving an angry fist at you. Unfortunately, there's no sound with it to hear exactly what was being said, but his manner and fist waving clearly shows that he was communicating very angrily with you. I'm sure that we can use that in your defence.'

'I suppose that's something.'

'You have still been charged with attempted robbery and attempted murder. I may be able to get the murder charge amended to aggravated assault, assuming the teller doesn't die.'

'How long will they give me?' Kelly asked.

'It's difficult to say. If we get a good judge and jury, and they accept your plea of being goaded into committing a rash act on the spur of the moment, then you might be lucky enough to get away with eight to ten years, if the teller doesn't die. And if you behave yourself in prison, you could be out in about four or five years time.'

'That's no so bad.'

'Of course that also depends on you giving your full cooperation to the police on this matter and …'

Kelly sat passively listening to his solicitor drone on, while his mind wandered to thoughts about Mrs Boyd once more. He again hoped that the flying glass that had cut her lovely features was only superficial and that she was not badly injured. He thought about the wonderful sexy time they could have spent together if things had worked out as they had planned. Now, he was facing a long time in prison without her and would only be able to recall memories of her buxom features and the thrilling experience he had enjoyed from her for such a short while. He was drawn back to reality by Mr Miles repeated questioning.

'Mr Kelly, are you all right?'

Kelly snapped back to the real world. 'Yes, I'm sorry. I was thinking about the woman teller and wondering if she was okay. She was hit by flying glass, you see.'

'Oh! I see. Well, I'll enquire about her condition when I speak to Detective Inspector Rollinson in a moment. Are you ready give him a statement?'

Kelly thought for a moment before replying, 'Yes, I'll make a statement.'

Miles and Kelly had spoken for almost an hour about the case. Miles looked at his watch and said, 'It's getting late. Tomorrow morning Detective Inspector Rollinson will need to ask you some more questions and when he does, I of course will be here to represent you, and guide you in what you should and should not admit to. I'll be sitting next to you, so look at me and I'll prompt you on each question. Is that perfectly clear?'

'Yes, thank you. It's clear.'

'Then if you've nothing else to tell me, I'll sort through my notes and will see you tomorrow morning, after I've told the inspector that you will be ready to make a statement in the morning.'

Resigned to his fate, Kelly nodded his agreement. He was in a bad situation and had to face the fact that he might have to spend many years of his life in prison. At least Mrs Boyd would not have to put up with her bullying husband any more, and he would make sure the police remain unaware of her involvement in the robbery. She was the only good thing to come into his life lately, and he was prepared to protect her. After all, there was no point in both of them having to serve a prison sentence. If he got out in four or five years time, perhaps she would be waiting for him and be very grateful that his actions prevented her husband from beating her any more, and because he had kept her name out of it. That was a warming thought for him to cling on to.

Kelly was returned to the cells to spend his first night in custody for more than six months. He wondered what Mrs Boyd was doing that evening instead of making plans to take the ferry to France, or perhaps she had gone anyway; unlikely he thought. No doubt she would like to go now, but realised that if she did, suspicion that she was involved in the robbery would immediately fall on her. Kelly wished he could let her know that he would keep her involvement in the robbery a secret, so that she did not have to worry about it.

★ ★ ★

In the local hospital, where Mrs Boyd had been detained for the night to keep her under observation, much to her annoyance, her friend Maggie visited to see how she was. Mrs Boyd was on edge, wondering if Kelly would keep her secret safe, or whether the police would get the information from him by either persuasion or trickery. She wondered what would happen if the charge against him became murder, and he would be facing a much longer sentence. That would put more pressure on him to talk. The worrying thoughts went round and around in her mind, with no clear answers emerging to quell the turmoil they caused her. The following day or two would reveal what the situation held for her. In the meantime, she thought about the risk of staying at home, and considered making a break for it and fleeing. Mrs Boyd spent much time on the telephone seeking advice from a friend, and spent a reluctant and restless night pondering her options.

★ ★ ★

In the afternoon of the following day, Saturday, Mr Miles revisited the interrogation room with the inspector. Kelly was already waiting for them and wondered why they had delayed the meeting until late that afternoon before talking to him again, instead of in the morning as he was originally told. He was soon to find out.

DI Rollinson sat on the opposite side of the table to Kelly, with DC Smith beside him. Mr Miles sat next to Kelly and a policeman stood by the door. The inspector started the tape recorder, announced the time and date, and details of who was in the room.

'I am sorry that we were unable to speak with you this morning, as we had originally intended, but new information has come to light,' the inspector began.

'New information,' thought Kelly. 'Have they discovered the truth about Mrs Boyd,' he wondered.

'Now, Mr Kelly, I have to ask you once again where you got the gun from?' the inspector asked.

Kelly looked at his solicitor who nodded, confirming that as agreed the previous evening, his client should answer the questions he indicated.

'I met a man a few days ago in a pub and bought it from him. That's all I want to say about it.'

'We need more information than that, Mr Kelly. What is the name of the man who sold it to you, how did you get his name, and in which pub did you meet him?' asked the inspector, in a tone of voice designed to convey the importance of the answers.

'No comment,' answered Kelly without checking his solicitor's opinion.

Rollinson raised his eyebrows and sucked in a lungful of air. 'If you don't tell me, then you are likely to face the rest of your life in prison.'

A look of shock crossed Kelly's face.

'Why? What's the significance attached to this gun?' asked Mr Miles, aware that something else more important had prompted the inspector to delay their meeting and make the comment, but yet to find out what that was.

The inspector looked at both men, flipped open a folder on the desk before him and adjusted his glasses. He read a few lines and slowly gave his reply.

'Forensic tests were carried out on the gun retrieved from Mr Kelly and the bullet removed from the building society teller. The report of their findings came in early this morning. It was so unexpected that I asked them to do the tests again to confirm the results. That is why we've had this delay. The tests were confirmed to be correct, and have revealed that the gun was used in the past - for a murder.'

'Not by me,' Kelly interrupted getting to his feet. 'I only got it a few days ago, like I already told you.'

Mr Miles prompted him to sit back down.

'You are Irish, are you not, Mr Kelly?' the inspector said.

'Yes. What of it?'

'So, you return to Ireland from time to time?'

Kelly looked at his solicitor who nodded. 'I do. What are you driving at?'

'Do you recall the recent murder of the prominent Irish politician, Mr Murphy O'Connor?'

'Yes, I do. That was some months ago. Surely you don't think that I had anything to do with that?'

'It may have been months ago, but the murderer, or murderers, so far have not been identified and brought to justice. Forensics has matched the bullet from your gun to one taken from the body of Mr O'Connor, and enquiries have shown that you were in the province at that time.'

'It's true that I was on holiday in Ireland then. I'd recently got out of prison and had nowhere to go. I wanted to get away for a while. I went to visit my sister and her husband in Belfast to relax. I didn't kill O'Connor.'

'Your gun is the one that was used to assassinate him with, you were there when he was killed, and you have used the gun again in a robbery, which might yet end in the death of another man.'

'I didn't use it again. I've never fired that gun before,' shouted Kelly again rising from his seat, frustration boiling over in him.

Mr Miles put a hand on his shoulder. 'Please sit down, Mr Kelly. Try to keep calm.'

'Calm! You lot are trying to fit me up with a murder that I didn't commit.'

'That's no so, Mr Kelly. We merely want to get at the truth. The facts we have so far, make you a prime suspect for O'Connor's murder,' said Rollinson, 'and with your latest journey to the wrong side of the law, I would say that you are in a great deal of trouble, Mr Kelly, and should cooperate fully with us if you want to avoid getting in so deep that you cannot get out.'

'I think I should have another talk with my client, in private,' Mr Miles stated.

Rollinson nodded. 'Yes, of course, Mr Miles. Only don't take too long about it. Special Branch has been informed of the discovery, and their officers will be arriving here first thing on Monday morning to speak with Mr Kelly. He'd better have more to say than 'No comment' to them.'

7

RESCUE

In the Atlantic Ocean close to Portugal, and after waiting an hour until the sky had turned from a brilliant blue through charcoal grey to almost black, *Quester* was manoeuvred towards the stationary yacht that was stolen from SMJ Boatyard. Mike donned his dry suit and slipped his knife into its scabbard. He clipped a small radio transmitter-receiver to an inside pocket, a microphone next to his throat and placed an earpiece over his right ear, allowing communication with Suzie to let her know what was happening. He grabbed a rope and tied one end to a small grappling iron.

Mike twisted tape around the prongs of the grappling iron. 'I don't want this to make a noise when I throw it over the railing,' he told Suzie.

'Hmm, I hope that works. If they hear you, you could be in trouble.'

'I'll have to take that chance.'

He was now ready to sneak board the yacht.

'Be careful,' implored Suzie, giving him a kiss. 'We know these men are capable of cold blooded murder, so don't go trying any heroic stuff.'

'I might be a bit rusty, but I still know how to take care of myself. I'll shout help if I need you.'

Suzie smiled. 'I've taken us as close to them as I dare. They're only a couple of hundred yards away, and as we're running without lights and the sky is quite cloudy, I think it's safe to assume they haven't seen us.'

'Okay, good. I'm sure they would have let us known by now if we'd been spotted.'

Mike gently lowered the dinghy over the side and set off across the divide of water that separated him from the stolen yacht. Clouds rolled slowly across the sky, blotting out the crescent shape of the quarter moon, darkening the already murky scene. He paddled carefully on the calm Atlantic Ocean, rising and falling with the gentle swell of the water, his eyes fixed on his target to detect any sign of movement.

Visible by the light issuing from below deck, a man appeared at the railings smoking a cigarette as he searched the horizon. Mike stopped paddling and waited, his dinghy gently tossing from side to side. He stared at the dark shape stood on the deck and his heart rate increased at the added danger. Pacing around the stern of the vessel and seeing nothing, the man flicked his cigarette end into the water and disappeared below as he lit another cigarette. Mike breathed a sigh of relief and Suzie lowered her machine gun. Paddling on, Mike edged towards the yacht.

The cool night air and vast expanse of water filled his nostrils with an expectant chill, as if a prelude to the calm before a storm. He reached the bow end of the yacht, and Mike's dinghy gave a gentle bump as they touched.

Watching through binoculars, Suzie could barely make out the shape of Mike in the dark. Clouds drifted away from the moon, on their never-ending journey across the heavens, allowing a small glimmer of light to fall on the constantly ebbing water. Suzie caught a glimpse of Mike as he lobed the padded grappling iron over the handrail, hauled himself up the side of the yacht and vaulted on to the deck. The first part of his objective had been successfully achieved. The next few minutes were the most dangerous and would decide if their plan was going to work.

'Right, I'm aboard. Everything's okay so far,' Mike relayed in a whisper, carefully dropping the grappling iron back into the dinghy.

With his work on the motor yacht plans from first conception to final design, and watching the craft take shape in the workshop, Mike had an intimate knowledge of its layout; essential knowledge that he was now about to put to good use.

'There doesn't seem to be anyone on guard,' he whispered, quietly sneaking towards the pilot house and cabin entrance at the stern of the yacht. 'They must think that we've been chased off.'

A shaft of light beamed skywards up the steps from below deck, where Mike could hear the faint sound of voices and laughter.

In the cabin below, two men smoked while they chatted and watched the television. 'I'd better take another look and see if they're in sight yet, they're very late,' the first guard said, rising from the comfortable settee and stubbing his cigarette out in the ash tray.

He tramped across the soft luxuriously carpeted floor, up the wooden steps, across the deck to the rail and searched the eastern approach. With no sight of his visitors he took a quick tour around the yacht's perimeter, looking out to sea. Mike dropped to one knee and hid in the shadows near the entrance. He held his breath, conscious that the man might see *Quester* or the dinghy. Mike drew his commando knife from its sheath strapped to his leg, prepared to silence the man should he become aware that something was wrong. The guard's eyes scanned the far horizon in a direction that he was not expecting to see the vessel they were waiting for, but made a check to see that all was clear. He came full circle to his starting point and stood at the stern rail watching, waiting and glancing at his watch every few seconds.

While he stood searching the vastness of the inky sea, Mike sheathed his knife and crept down the steps, taking them one at a time. In the tastefully furnished vast cabin lounge sat the second man, resting with his feet on the settee, while engrossed in a television programme. Mike tiptoed down to the last step and halted as the guard suddenly burst into laughter at the comedy show he was watching. Edging forward, Mike bent low and crept behind the settee. He drew his knife and was about to silence the guard when a shout came from above.

'There's a boat on the horizon and it looks to be coming this way,' yelled the first guard down to the cabin, after seeing distance lights from an approaching vessel.

Mike froze for a moment, and remained hidden behind the settee.

'Okay,' replied the second man rising from his seat. 'I hope it's the right one this time and not that interfering couple from the boatyard.'

The guard moved towards the steps, then stopped when he saw damp patches of footsteps leading down to the cabin. He turned to see the dry suit clad figure of Mike, their eyes met and he immediately jerked open his jacket to grab the gun strapped in its holster under his left arm. In one quick movement, Mike threw his commando knife underarm with deadly accuracy, a method he had practised in his days as a mercenary, and one that he had used before to good effect.

The Fairborne–Sykes knife cut through the air and buried its way deep into the man's ribs. He let out a cry as the expression on his face changed to one of fear, the gun slipped from his grasp and dropped to the floor. With a contorted look and a curse on his lips, the man staggered, sank to his knees and slumped sideways to rest on the bottom step.

'One down, one to go,' Mike relayed to Suzie.

'There's another vessel approaching, Mike,' Suzie warned.

'Yeah, okay. I heard it.'

Retrieving his knife, Mike picked up the gun and glanced up the steps to see if the other guard had heard anything. The roar of the approaching motor vessel masked the sounds of the scuffle and increased in volume as it came closer. The still night air carried the resonance of its engines far into the night. With no movement from above, Mike dragged the body and hid it behind the sofa. He checked the gun and gingerly made his way back up the steps, treading quietly. At the top, he glanced across the deck and saw the guard standing by the rail with his gun drawn, waiting for the vessel that was fast approaching from the north.

Without turning the man said, 'It looks like our visitors all right. I wonder why they're so late.'

With the vessel now close, Mike could not tackle the second guard without being seen, giving away an advantage the darkness had afforded him. He was also curious to know who he was up against, and how many of them there were, before starting a fight or frightening them away.

'The other vessel's coming alongside,' Mike whispered.

'Yes, I see their lights,' replied Suzie, staring through her binoculars. 'It's too dark for me to make out any detail. This must be the boat they've been waiting for, and I guess must be from the person who hired them to steal our yacht. I wonder if that person is aboard.'

The throaty roar of the vessel's engines were throttled back, and the motor yacht bumped alongside. A line was thrown aboard. The guard grabbed the rope and secured it to a cleat on deck. A wiry man, with a heavily lined angular face, deep set eyes and thinning hair, flanked by two minders, stepped across.

Mike peered at the man with incredulity written over his face.

'So, guess who's stepping on to this yacht,' Mike stated, with intrigue running through his voice.

'I've no idea. Who is it?'

'It's Mr Giles Harman.'

'What! Harman?' Suzie could hardly believe what she was hearing. 'The boss of Harman's Boat Yard?'

'The very same person. Because he lost the yacht contract to our boatyard, it seems that he's decided to steal the vessel instead. Well, I've got something to say about that. There's a big surprise in store for you, Mr bloody Harman.'

'You be careful, Mike,' Suzie implored. 'How many of them are there?'

'Harman and two minders have come across. There's a pilot on their boat, but he's stayed in the pilot house.'

Harman stepped onto the yacht and tackled the guard with a stern look on his face. 'You're miles off course. It's taken us several more hours to reach you. Why is that? I assigned a seaworthy pilot to guide you.'

'We had a small problem. Two people from the boatyard followed us,' said the guard, holstering his gun.

Harman looked concerned. 'Oh! How do you know they were from the boatyard?'

'Ignacio recognised their boat. It was moored next to this one.'

'So, who were they?'

'A man and a woman, and they were armed.'

'That sounds like two of the boatyard owners, Mike Randle and Suzie Drake. They're ex-mercenaries and nobody's fool. What happened to them?'

'We chased them off,'

'Are you sure they're gone? They're not the sort to give up easily.'

'They're gone! We chased them for miles and saw them off, that's why we're a bit adrift of where we should be. Unfortunately, we'd already got rid of the pilot and had to take a guess about where we should wait. We're not sailors and don't know how to steer a boat to an exact spot in the middle of all this bloody water.'

'But you know how to kill people, don't you?' Harman said angrily. 'I asked you to steal this yacht and deliver it to me. Nothing was said about killing the pilot or the people at the boatyard to get it here.'

'We had no choice, they were guarding the boat. You didn't tell us the boat was guarded.'

'I didn't know. In any case, you could have knocked them out and tied them up.'

'That's not sensible, it's too risky. They might be able to identify us,' said the guard.

'And what about the pilot you got rid of?'

'He could identify us as well.'

'So can I.'

'But you're in this up to your neck. You can't inform on us without putting yourself in the dock. We're only doing what you asked us to.'

The four men turned towards the cabin as Mike stepped forward. Standing in his black dry suit, outlined against light streaming from the cabin below, with a gun in one hand and a commando knife in the other; he looked a menacing figure.

'Randle!' exclaimed Harman. 'So you chased them off, eh?'

'Everybody stay exactly where you are. No sudden moves now,' Mike warned, thrusting the gun towards them to reinforce his intentions.

The guard immediately went for his holstered gun, but was not nearly quick enough. Mike pulled the trigger and his weapon spat out a single bullet that dug into the man's chest. The force of the shot catapulted him backwards as the bullet tore into him.

'That's for what you did to my guards,' spat Mike, pulling the trigger once more.

The guard was propelled into the railings, toppled over the side and crashed down into the sea between the two vessels. A fountain of water cascaded into the air as his limp body plunged into the ocean.

'Some people never learn,' Mike declared. 'And that's the price they pay for killing my men.'

'Neither of my minders are armed,' Harman stated, taking a step towards Mike with his hands raised.

'Neither were the men who were guarding this motor yacht at my boatyard. That didn't stop them being shot in the back,' Mike spat.

'I heard shots. What's going on, Mike,' Suzie relayed to his earpiece.

'Everything's under control. Come across, Suzie,' he confirmed into his microphone.

Harman stopped in his tracks and wondered what Mike was up to. 'That must be a signal to the lovely Suzie Drake. I know you used to be a soldier. I see that you've lost none of the killing techniques you learnt in the army.'

'That was a long time ago, when I was in the paras, but the skills remain. And, it's just as well they do when I have to deal with murdering scum like the last two you hired.'

'The last two?' repeated Harman.

'The other guard's in the cabin below. Both of them have paid the price for murdering my men.'

'I didn't want anyone to get hurt. You must believe me. I simply asked for this yacht to be stolen for a buyer I have in the Gulf States,' pleaded Harman.

'The Gulf States! I would have thought that your buyer would have enough money to purchase a yacht like this one.'

'I'm sure he could, but he didn't want to wait the year or more it would take my boatyard to build another one.'

'So that's the reason why.'

'That's the reason he asked if I could get it for him, and I told him that I could.'

'Then it's a pity you didn't take more care over the men you hire to do your dirty work.'

'I will – next time.'

'There isn't going to be a next time for you.'

'We'll see about that.'

Harman motioned his men to go below to the cabin. 'Check the other man.' He looked at Mike. 'I assume that you consider yourself above murdering unarmed people and won't shoot my men?' he asked.

The question remained unanswered as the two men cautiously passed Mike and disappeared to the cabin below.

'What do you intend to do about me and my men?' asked Harman.

'I don't know yet. What is the penalty for hiring murderers and stealing a yacht?'

Harman's men appeared carrying the guard's body. Harman tipped his head towards the side of the yacht and his men carried the body to the rail and threw it overboard with Mike protesting, but unable to stop them.

'You'll have a job finding either of the bodies in the dark. And as to your question, my men and I are here answering a distress beacon that was fired into the air a short while ago. We came alongside because we thought the yacht was in trouble. As there are no longer any witnesses to the contrary, thanks to you Mr Randle, you will have a hard time proving that I had anything to do with the stealing of this vessel.'

Suzie brought *Quester* alongside and jumped aboard carrying a sub-machine gun. Mike tied their boat up.

'Giles Harman!' she exclaimed, in a surprised tone of voice. 'I wouldn't have believed it if I hadn't seen you for myself. Are you all right, Mike?'

'Yes, I'm fine. Mr Harman's the rat who hired the two gun happy thieves who killed our men and stole the yacht.'

'That's something you'll never be able to prove,' retorted Harman. 'And as my business here seems to be finished, I'll bid you and the lovely Miss Drake farewell,' he said, turning to re-board his yacht, closely followed by his two men who released the line and backed slowly away while they kept their eyes on Mike and Suzie.

Mike thought about putting a bullet in Harman and raised his gun. Suzie grabbed his arm.

'No, Mike. He isn't worth it. We'll get our revenge some day.'

Their motor yacht burst into life, backed away and circled around. The revs were increased as it pulled away when suddenly, one of the guards produced a sub-machine gun and let loose with a volley of shots, peppering the side of Pendleton's motor yacht with bullet holes. Mike and Suzie dropped to the deck, thinking for a moment that he was shooting at them. His intentions became clear very quickly as Diesel started to pour into the sea from the fuel tanks.

Harman waved and laughed. 'You'll have a job to deliver the yacht on time now,' he yelled, as his vessel accelerated into the night. 'I'm sure Mr Pendleton will have included a late delivery clause attached to your contract, as he always does. With any luck, your boatyard will be out of business, and out of my way very soon.'

'The bastard! Quick, bang the spotlight on and turn it towards them,' Mike said, watching the vessel fade into the darkness.

Suzie flicked the spotlight switch on and swivelled it toward Harman's motor yacht as it sped away. Mike ran to the side, levelled his gun, held on tightly with both hands resting on the railing to steady himself, and pumped four bullets at the fast disappearing vessel.

Despite thinking that he was far enough away in the dark for him not to worry, Harman saw four holes appear in his motor yacht, just above the waterline, and fuel began to seep out.

'Let's see how he likes some of his own medicine,' Mike stated.

Suzie watched the vessel disappear into the blackness as the engine started to cough and splutter. 'What a bastard he is! I hope he's adrift for hours.'

'Fortunately for us, in this vessel there's another fuel tank on the starboard side,' said Mike, stepping into the pilot house to check the gauges. 'That tank is nearly empty and the port tank is emptying fast. We'll have to dock somewhere and get more fuel and have the holes patched up if we want to make the delivery on time.'

'Can we use some of the diesel in *Quester's* tank?'

'I'm afraid not. There's no way for us to pump it out of one tank into another.'

'That's a pity. I hate to think of Harman getting away with stealing our yacht and making us late for the delivery. Can't we prove anything against him?' she asked. 'It might help us to persuade Jeremy Pendleton to give us more time.'

'No, not really. It's our word against his.'

'What happened to the guards?'

'They're both dead, and now thanks to Harman, their bodies are in the drink, so that's our proof gone. But we can still tell Jeremy Pendleton what happened. Now he's got his knighthood and is probably quite influential, I'm sure he'll want to do something about our cocky Mr Harman. Especially when he hears who tried to steal his very expensive luxury motor yacht, and put holes in it to try stopping us from delivering it to him on time.'

'Do you think we should tell him about that? We could say that the delay is because he ran the motor yacht out of fuel.'

'No, I don't think that would work and anyway, he would expect us to pull into the nearest port to restock with Diesel.'

'I guess you're right. And talking of Jeremy Pendleton, he's heard that his yacht was stolen and has repeated his threat to ask for compensation if it's not delivered as agreed.'

'That's more or less what I expected. He's not one for giving away favours – not that kind anyway.'

'That's probably why he's got a lot of money,' suggested Suzie.

'We've got to get the repairs done quickly. It may show, however good a job the boys make of it, but at least we've rescued the yacht. If we can get it patched up quickly, there's still a chance that we can deliver it on time. That'll disappoint him again, won't it?'

'I certainly hope so.'

'How do you know that he's heard about the robbery?' asked Mike.

'Reg called me on the radio while you were killing all our witnesses.'

Mike gave Suzie a, 'that's not very fair' look.

She recognised it and responded, 'Only kidding. I'm pleased that you've managed to get the yacht back without getting yourself shot, and made sure that the perpetrators paid for killing our guards.'

'So am I. Reg must be working late.'

'I think he's sleeping at the boatyard, waiting to hear from us about our progress in catching Pete and Barry's killers. He's really upset about it, and about losing the yacht that he's worked so hard on over the last year. He's really proud of the finished vessel.'

'We'd better call him and give him the good news and the bad news. I'll tell him we need him and George to get out here as quickly as possible to repair the holes.'

Jumping aboard *Quester*, Suzie said, 'I'll contact him now. How do you want to arrange everything?'

'Give Reg our position and tell him I'll be sailing down towards the Med, because we can't afford to lose any more time. I should be able to make it to Gibraltar; they've got good facilities there for repairing ships and boats of all sizes. Reg and George can fly to Spain and contact me when they arrive. If we can get the repairs done quickly, I'll have the motor yacht refuelled and make a dash for Cannes. Tell Reg to ask Jennie to book the flights.'

'Okay. Can I help?'

'I don't think so. Much as I don't like the idea, it would be better if you took *Quester* straight to Cannes and informed Pendleton about what's happened, and try to get his agreement to extend the delivery time, even if it's only for a few hours. Tell him I'll get there as quickly as humanly possible.'

'He may complain about the damage to the boat and refuse to accept it.'

'I doubt it. I'm sure he will have invited a lot of influential people to his yacht who are expecting him to throw a big party, and he won't want to disappoint them. Tell him he can bring the yacht into out boatyard later, whenever it suits him, and we'll repair it properly at our expense if he's not satisfied. I'm sure he'll want to keep in contact with you for as long as he's got a good excuse to.'

'What are we going to do about the body we fished out of the water?'

'Oh! I'd forgotten about him. I heard Harman tells his thugs that he'd supplied them with a pilot and one of them said they'd got rid of him, that's why they were out of position.'

'So, our suspicion about him was correct.'

'Yes. You'll have to tell the police in Cannes that you saw the body floating in the water and fished him out.'

'What about the other two bodies, can we find them?'

'It's doubtful in the dark, and we don't have the time to waste searching for them. Even if we found them, trying to explain to the police how I came to knife one and put two bullets into the other might prove to be a bit tricky. I could end up in prison.'

'I guess so. I'll contact Reg,' Suzie said, stepping into *Quester's* pilot house.

Mike checked the charts and the GPS to calculate the direction they needed to set, before stepping across to join her.

'I could almost feel the delight in Reg's voice when I told him that you'd killed both the men who murdered Pete and Barry,' Suzie related.

'Well, I hope he doesn't go bragging about it to too many people. I don't relish the idea of having to explain to the British police about what we've done either.'

'I asked Reg to be discrete, so I'm sure he will. He and George will fly out straight away.'

'Good. We must get on our way soon and say goodbye for a while, so would the very attractive female piloting the motor yacht *Quester*, care to come aboard the JP luxury floating bonking boat and partake of a cuddle?'

Suzie laughed. 'You'd better not say that to Jeremy Pendleton when we see him, however, it would be nice to christen the vessel properly before we hand it over, Randy. Do we have time?'

'We'll make time. You ought to get some rest before you set out for Cannes, anyway.'

'Rest doesn't sound like what you have in mind.'

With the two yachts tied together, Mike and Suzie used the opulent shower that was big enough for five people and made love before taking a nap in a king size bed in the master bedroom.

After a few hours rest, Suzie said goodbye to Mike, boarded *Quester* and cast off. They set course for the Mediterranean Sea, with Mike using the last remaining fuel in the bottom of the tank as economically as possible until it ran out, before he was obliged to hoist the sails. Suzie waved goodbye as *Quester* sped off into the distance ahead of him. The next twenty-four-hours would be crucial for both of them and their boatyard.

8

INTERROGATE

Roy Kelly found himself detained at Chatham Police Station after he botched an attempt to rob Nelson's Building Society, and spoke for a long time with his solicitor, Mr Miles. He was anxious to avoid involving Mrs Boyd or any of her friends in the attempted robbery if possible, but with the O'Connor murder hanging over him, he was now staring at a much longer sentence than the four or five years he had previously expected to receive. They sat in the bleak interview room with Kelly biting his nails, showing signs of the turmoil his mind was going through.

'If you don't give the police the information they are seeking, they will try to pin O'Connor's murder on you, and you will not see the light of day again for perhaps twenty years or more,' his solicitor warned.

His graphic statement frightened Kelly. He had been in prison several times, but never more than one or two years at a time, and only for petty robbery. This was a completely different set of circumstances for him to face, and one that he was uncertain how to cope with and yet still keep the woman he was besotted with, free from blame.

'Supposing I agree to tell them who I got the gun from. Would that get the police off my back for the political assassination?' he asked.

'Possibly. One thing is for certain, if you don't tell them, you will remain their prime suspect and in deep trouble.'

Kelly thought about the man who had sold him the gun. Mrs Boyd had told him that he was an old boyfriend of her schoolmate

Maggie, and had ditched her for a younger female. Could he chance giving them his name, and if he did, would he talk if the police grabbed him? That could lead the trail back to Mrs Boyd. Kelly decided that he had no choice in the matter and would have to risk it, or he would rot in jail for an eternity and never see his delightful paramour again.

'I'll give the police the name of the man who sold me the gun, if they agree to drop all the charges against me,' Kelly said.

'I can't see them doing that,' his solicitor maintained, 'but I'm sure they will drop the charge of murdering Mr O'Connor if the information you give to them proves to be reliable. I'll also try to get them to reduce the charge of attempted murder to one of attempted robbery with grievous bodily harm through temporary insanity because of the antagonistic nature of Mr Wainwright. That carries a lesser sentence.'

'Mr Wainwright!' exclaimed Kelly.

'Yes, Mr Wainwright, the teller you shot. You look surprised,' Miles stated.

'Umm … It's the first time I've heard what his name was. It makes shooting him more real somehow,' bluffed Kelly, his mind in greater turmoil at the name.

His thoughts were racing, trying to think of an explanation to the bombshell that Miles had inadvertently dropped on him. Had he shot the wrong man? Had Mrs Boyd's husband found out what they were planning and deliberately swapped places with Wainwright? If so, he could be beating Mrs Boyd black and blue right now. Kelly's mind was in a state of confusion, which Miles had noticed.

'Are you quite sure that you are all right, Mr Kelly?' he asked. 'You look to have gone quite pale.'

'Yes, thank you, I'm fine. The idea that I could be blamed for shooting O'Connor has left me feeling shaky. I'm a bit light headed that's all.'

'I'll bring you a drink of water,' his solicitor said, 'and ask the inspector to join us.'

Water was not what Kelly felt like drinking. Whisky was nearer his mark, but he realised that making such a suggestion was unwise and simply said, 'Thank you.'

Miles left to collect the water and to recall the inspector.

DI Rollinson along with DC Smith returned with Miles. He handed the glass of water to Kelly, who took a sip and put the glass down on the table. The inspector returned to his seat, restarted the tape and made the usual opening comments.

'Mr Kelly will now make a statement about where he got the weapon from that he used in the attempted robbery of Nelson's Building Society on Friday October 13th at around 2 p.m.,' he announced into the microphone.

'Are you dropping the political murder charge?' Kelly asked.

'We have not charged you with that yet, and if the information you supply us with concerning when and where you purchased the gun from proves to be accurate, then we won't be bringing a charge against you for that crime,' DI Rollinson stated, choosing his words carefully.

Licking his lips, Kelly thought for a moment. The room sank into a time of quiet stillness, the only sound coming from a barely audible squeak issuing from the tape recorder as the cassette wheel slowly span round.

Kelly though about what he would say, took a deep breath and began. 'I was given the name and telephone number of a man who could sell me a gun. I only intended to use it to frighten the tellers, not to shoot anyone,' he pleaded.

'Yes, I understand that. Who gave you that information and what was it?' Rollinson asked.

'The man who sold me the gun was named Oliver Statham, and I was given a note of his mobile telephone number to ring. I called him and we arranged to meet in a local pub.'

'Who gave you the telephone number, and do you still have it?'

'I'm not prepared to say who gave it to me, but there's a copy of his number in my wallet. We met in 'The Admiral's Arms' on the outskirts of town.'

'Yes, I know the pub.' Rollinson looked at the constable who was standing by the door. 'Ask the duty sergeant to get Mr Kelly's belonging and bring them here,' he instructed. 'And ask Louise to run the name Oliver Statham through the system to see if we have anything on him.'

The policeman nodded and left the room.

'Go on, Mr Kelly. When did you get the gun?'

'The day before the robbery.'

'Thursday 12th October?'

'Yes. I copied the telephone number down in case I lost the piece of paper with it on. Statham said he wanted that when I met him.'

'He wanted the paper with his mobile number on?' asked Rollinson.

'Yes, that's right. He asked me to bring it with me when I met him as proof of who I was.'

'That seems a little strange. Was it hand written?'

'Yes.'

'That could explain it. He wanted to retain the proof of who wrote it, so that he could destroy the evidence to prevent you proving you ever had it. He probably didn't expect you to make a copy of it.'

The policeman returned to the interview room holding a box, which he placed on the table.

'Show me,' the inspector said.

Kelly pulled off the lid and opened the cardboard box containing the few personal belongings he had on him when he was arrested. He pulled out his wallet, searched through it and extracted a piece of paper.

'Mr Kelly has handed me a piece of paper from his wallet with a mobile telephone number on,' Rollinson explained into the recorder, looking at the paper. 'The number is 00553138007.'

He gave the paper to the constable. 'Get Louise to check this number out as well, please.'

'Yes, Sir,' the constable replied, taking the piece of paper and exiting the room once more.

'What happened when you met this man?' asked the inspector.

'We sat in a corner booth. He asked me for the piece of paper and put it in his pocket, then passed me a package wrapped in brown paper. He told me not to open it until I got home, then he got up immediately and left. I finished my drink and went home. When I got there, I opened the package and the gun was in it, wrapped in a piece of cloth.'

'Did he ask you for any money for the gun?'

'No.'

'Didn't you think that was strange? After all, guns cost money.'

'I didn't really think about that. I was too worried about having a gun in the flat.'

'Any particular reason for that?'

'Yes. My probation officer sometimes pays me an unexpected visit. If he saw the weapon, he'd send me straight back to prison.'

'I see. I'd like you to give us a description of this man, Statham, and look through a book of local criminal mug shots to see if you can recognise him.'

Kelly nodded. Gave them a description and the book was brought in. He scanned through the pages, but was unable to find anyone who resembled the man he met.

PC Louise Jordan returned to report her findings to Rollinson. 'We've nothing on an Oliver Statham, Sir. The mobile telephone was apparently purchased by a Mr John Jones a week before Kelly said he met Mr Statham. It was a pay as you go phone and has not been used since Thursday October 12th. The address given by the purchaser is a false one.'

'The 12th. That was when Mr Kelly said he met the man in the pub. Where was the mobile purchased?' Rollinson asked.

'Liverpool.'

'Liverpool! That looks like a dead end then. Okay, that's all for now, Mr Kelly. I've got a few enquiries to make. We'll talk again later,' Rollinson said, stating the time and turning off the recorder.

He returned to his office and Kelly was taken back to the cells.

Rollinson spoke with DC Smith. 'Contact the Liverpool police will you Jake, and have them email a list of known and suspected arms dealers in their area to us. We might get lucky and find out who our Mr Statham really is.'

'You don't think that's his real name then?'

'No, I'm sure it isn't. There's something not right about all of this. It doesn't hang together properly somehow. It's an odd situation that I can't put my finger on yet, but I will.'

★ ★ ★

The following morning a list of suspects from the Liverpool Police came by fax for DC Smith at Chatham Police Station. He checked the list over, but no obvious suspect showed up.

That afternoon, the telephone rang on his desk; he snatched it up, 'Yeah, Smith,' he answered.

After listening to the caller he returned the telephone to its cradle and entered the office of DI Rollinson.

'Governor, I've just had a telephone call from a guy at British Airways. I rang him this morning and asked him to check the names on the list I got from the Liverpool mob, against their list of passengers leaving the country in the last two weeks. It seems that an Owen Sutton booked the first flight out to Nairobi on Saturday morning, and his name is on the Liverpool list of possible arms dealers in their area.'

'Owen Sutton? That's the same initials as Oliver Statham. Crooks sometimes like to do that, it helps them to remember what name they're using. It could be a coincidence, or it could be our man. Ask them if they've got video cameras at the booking-in desk will you, Jake? If so, get a copy and we'll show it to Kelly to see if he can confirm if it's the same man. If he picks him out, it'll go a long way to confirming his story of how he got the gun.'

9

CANNES

After recapturing Jeremy Pendleton's luxury motor yacht and killing the thieves that Giles Harman had hired to steal the craft from their boatyard, Mike had a clean-up job to do. It was important to get the inside of the vessel back to a pristine state before handing it over to the new owner, and the carpet showed a few traces of blood that were spilled after Mike had killed the guard and placed his body behind the settee. The blood was difficult to remove, and when he had cleaned it up as best he could, Mike moved the settee a few inches back to cover over the stain.

'That should do it,' he muttered to himself. 'I doubt if Pendleton will even notice it.'

Reg and George had boarded an aeroplane to fly to Spain on the following morning, a Sunday, and travelled on to Gibraltar to join Mike and make the necessary repairs to the bullet holes caused by Harman's gun-happy guards. After the Diesel ran out, Mike sailed the yacht into Lisbon to refuel. He had set his sights on reaching Cannes before the handover deadline, but knew it was a race against time.

Strategically located at the entrance to the Mediterranean Sea, Gibraltar offered a natural port for Mike to head towards in order to have the repairs done. The seafaring tradition in Gibraltar produced repairing, bunkering and a variety of ship services that became the mainstay of their shipping industry, and was conveniently located on Mike's journey to Cannes. He headed for the port there, and at eight o'clock on a bright Monday morning he was joined by Reg and George. Follwing their inspection of the damage, the repairs were started straight away – there was no time to lose.

* * *

While Mike oversaw the repairs, Suzie pressed ahead piloting *Quester* to that French Riviera tourist attraction, in order to explain to Jeremy Pendleton the events surrounding the loss and recapture of his yacht. She also needed to explain why repairs were necessary, and why Mike may be late delivering his luxury yacht to him. This was a task that Suzie was quite looking forward to. She had already crossed swords with Pendleton in the past, and had experience of his reputation for taking advantage of any situation in order to have his way with any woman who took his fancy and get her into his bed. On the occasion of their previous encounter, he was unable to achieve his objective and Suzie was pleased to elude him at the last moment, before she was obliged to succumb to his charms.

Now, she might have to consider turning the tables on him, by using the knowledge that he wanted her, to prevent him enforcing the late cause in their contract. She intended to make use of his desire for her, knowing that the final outcome at worst would entail her giving in to Jeremy Pendleton's quest to satisfy his sexual urges with her body. This was a similar situation to one that she had faced in the past, and Suzie then was able to divorce her feelings from what her body was subjected to. And though she had not disclosed it to Mike, she was curious to know how accurate Jeremy Pendleton's reputation as a good lover really was, and whether he could live up to expectations, if and when it became time to deliver.

By late afternoon on Monday, the day following the recapture of their yacht, Suzie had piloted *Quester* into a berth at the riviera resort of Cannes and radioed Mike with her progress.

'I've arrived in Cannes, Mike. This is not a place visit unless you've got a pocket full of cash. They charge a fortune here to berth your yacht. How are things going in Gibraltar?'

'Not too bad. Reg and George are cracking on with the repairs. They're doing a great job, and I doubt if Jeremy Pendleton would be able to tell that a repair has been done at all.'

'Good. When do you expect to be finished and ready to leave?'

'By later tonight with any luck. I should be able to join you some time tomorrow. I'll have a better idea exactly when, after the repairs are finished.'

'Right. I'll let Pendleton know he will get his motor yacht as planned. I've got to ring the police now to tell them about the body we pulled out of the drink.'

'Okay. Take it easy. I'll see you tomorrow.'

Suzie rang the local police to inform them she had fished a body out of the water. Two police cars and an ambulance arrived at the quayside amid a flurry of wailing sirens, which seemed over the top to her for checking on a dead body. The sailor was removed to the morgue, and Suzie was asked to accompany the officers to the police station to give a statement.

At police headquarters she was escorted to the second floor, where the chief of police showed Suzie into his office, in a modern police station situated on the outskirts of Cannes. After waiting in his office for over half an hour, she was subjected to a barrage of personal, as well as relevant questions. The policeman gave the impression that he was uncertain whether to believe her story or not. Suzie said nothing about Pendleton's yacht, or what the real purpose of her visit to Cannes was for. She did not want to have to explain about the robbery at their boatyard or the fact that Mike had killed two men while retrieving their vessel.

'I've told you, I came across the body purely by accident and fished it out of the sea off the coast of Portugal, somewhere off Porto,' Suzie told the police chief, a man in his mid-fifties, who had thinning hair, was overweight and had a round, suntanned face with a pencil thin moustache above his thick lips.

'Why did you not hand the body over to the Portuguese authorities?'

'Because I was on my way here to meet someone and didn't want to be delayed. The man was dead, and the body was in international waters, so I didn't see any need to rush to the nearest port, which would probably have delayed me for some time.'

'Who are you here to see?'

'A friend. He is holidaying here at the moment.'

'Ah! A male friend,' he said in a knowing tone.

'Yes, a friend,' replied Suzie, aware of the inference that he was drawing.

'My men have found weapons aboard your boat, including a handgun. I'm told the man was probably shot with a handgun.'

'That's for my protection, and you've no right to go snooping around my yacht.'

'Where murder is concerned, I have every right. When somebody brings in a body with two bullet holes in their back, I have a right to be suspicious and ask as many questions as I like. Your gun is being checked to see if the bullets match those taken from the victim.'

Jumping out of her chair, Suzie proclaimed, 'I didn't kill him and I resent you suggesting that I may have done so.'

'Our checks have shown that you used to be a mercenary; so killing is not new to you. Sit down and shut up, or I will have you taken to the cells to cool off while I await the test results.'

'I gave up being a mercenary years ago, and now I'm a co-director of a boat building business and help to run it. I do not kill innocent people,' snarled Suzie.

'So you say.'

'Am I under arrest?'

'You are helping me with my enquiries.'

'In that case, I want to make a telephone call,' demanded Suzie, realising that she was becoming more ensnared in the situation and may not after all, get the chance to explain to Jeremy Pendleton about the robbery and recapture of his motor yacht, before the delivery deadline.

'You can make your telephone call later.'

Suzie was fuming and banged on the chief's desk. 'I demand to make a telephone call right now. That is my legal right.'

The police chief stood up. 'Right. I've had enough hassle from you.'

He beckoned to one of his men from the outer office who

opened the door, leant into the room and held on to the door handle while he waiting for instructions.

'Take this … lady, to the cells for holding until I call for her.'

'Yes, Sir,' he said, stepping into the room.

The officer clutched Suzie by the right arm. She grabbed his wrist with her left hand and twisted his arm behind his back in one quick movement, preventing him from taking further action.

'I am not a criminal and resent being treated like one.'

The chief waved more men to come to the aid of his officer, and Suzie was pounced on by three more policemen. After flooring one with a right hook, she was overpowered, dragged to the basement kicking and struggling, and bundled into a small cell that was not much bigger than a cupboard. The door was slammed shut behind her. An ugly looking jailer, with thick lips close-cropped hair, tattoos on his hairy arms and wearing a dirty white vest covered with holes, locked the door and clipped the ring of keys to his belt.

'We don't often get a woman in here,' he proclaimed as the other policeman left, nursing the bruises they had received in their struggle with Suzie. 'You look like you've got a nice pair of tits. I could make it more comfortable for you, if you behave,' he stated, reaching through the bars and grabbing the corner of Suzie's blouse, tearing it open. She often dressed without a bra and wore a loose fitting blouse, especially if the weather was warm, as it was in Cannes. The torn blouse revealed much of her breast and cleavage. The jailer's eyes lit up in anticipation.

'This could be an interesting interlude to your plans, and if you're good I won't need to bruise you,' he maintained, holding on to the edge of her torn blouse.

Forcing his attentions on Suzie was a mistake he came to regret. Before he realised what had happened, Suzie grabbed his wrist, bent it back and yanked him towards the cell. His head crashed into the bars with such a force that it dented them. His eyeballs rolled to the top and he slumped to the floor. Reaching through the bars, Suzie lifted the keys from his belt and unlocked the door. A lump began to swell up on the jailer's head as Suzie grabbed his arm, dragged him into the cell and dumped him on the floor.

'That'll teach you to be a smart arse,' Suzie hissed, locking the cell.

On the jailer's desk was a telephone. Suzie asked the operator to ring *The Metropolitan Hotel*, one of the most expensive hotels close to the marina, and the one that Suzie knew Pendleton was staying at. When the call was answered she asked to be connected through to Jeremy Pendleton's suite. The telephone rang.

'Come on, Jeremy,' Suzie whispered, anxious for the telephone to be answered before anyone else arrived to interfere.

It continued to ring and Suzie began to despair of anyone answering it. Eventually the receiver was picked up.

'Yes,' said a grumpy voice.

'Jeremy, I hope I haven't interrupted anything ... delicate,' Suzie said.

'Hello, Suzie. Nothing's too important for me not to talk to you,' he replied, recognising her voice straight away. 'To what do I owe this pleasure? My yacht's not due to be delivered until tomorrow,' he asked, untangling himself from the arms of the woman sharing his bed.

'I arrived in Cannes a short while ago to talk to you about your yacht, but had to speak to the police first about a body I fished out of the water ...'

Pendleton was livid when Suzie told him what had happened to her, and said he would be at the police station in a few minutes. He jumped out of bed and dressed immediately.

'Who's Suzie?' asked the woman.

'A gorgeous woman, who I can guarantee is better than you in bed.'

The woman pouted. 'Well, if that's all you think of me, then I'll be off.'

'Goodbye,' announced Pendleton, striding from the bedroom as he donned his jacket. He shouted for his minders and chauffer to accompany him, and gave instructions for the bedroom to be cleaned and tidied immediately.

In the police station, Suzie wandered back up to the police chief's glass panelled office, swirling the jailer's keys around her forefinger –

like a cowboy twirling his gun. She sauntered past the look of amazement on the faces of the other policemen, many of them still nursing cuts and bruises, and dropped the cell keys on the chief's desk.

'I think these belong to you,' she said.

His face was blazoned with anger. 'How the hell did you get out?' he demanded, banging a fist on his desk.

'I needed to make the telephone call that I'm entitled to, and I have, as you will shortly find out.'

He stood up. 'Who to? Who did you ring, and why are you here in Cannes?'

'I'm here to meet *Sir* Jeremy Pendleton MBE,' said Suzie, trying to make her visit sound as important as possible.

'Sir Jeremy Pendleton MBE, the millionaire playboy who has a string of beautiful women trailing around after him?'

'That sounds like Jeremy.'

The police chief scoffed. 'Huh! Why should a man like him be interested in a skinny, ex-mercenary female like you – even if you do have a pretty face?' he stated, glancing at the depth of cleavage that was showing above the rip in her blouse.

Suzie pulled the torn fabric to cover herself up.

'You'll soon find out? He'll be here in a few minutes, and I'm sure that Jeremy will have something to say about the treatment you've subjected me to. He tells me that he's a good friend of the Mayor. That should make for an interesting discussion about police methods the next time they meet.'

Much of the colour drained from the police chief's face. 'Perhaps you'd like to sit down while I check on those results,' he sheepishly stated. 'And I'll see if I can get someone to find you a new blouse.'

'Don't bother,' Suzie declared. 'I want Jeremy to see what your jailer tried to do to me. Do you normally allow him to molest your women prisoners?'

The police chief barked out his orders from his doorway to a policeman in the office, 'Get me those test results – now.'

He closed the door, turned the speed of the fan standing in the room to maximum, and sat down. 'I do not condone prisoners being mistreated, especially women. 'I will have words with the guard,' he stated, taking a tissue from a box on his desk to wipe his brow.

'I should wait for a while if I were you. He'll have more than just a headache when he eventually wakes up.'

The police chief looked dumbstruck. He could hardly believe that such a skinny looking woman could knock out the brutish man that his jailer was.

Shouting and commotion came from the main office. Suzie turned to peer through the glass window and saw Jeremy Pendleton and two of his heavy guards striding towards the chief's office, and unseen she allowed the torn piece of blouse to fall away. The door was flung open and Pendleton barged in.

'What's going on here?' he demanded of the chief, glancing at Suzie.

'Oh, Jeremy, thank you for coming,' Suzie responded, knowing his affection for her would make him even angrier, and playing on it.

She stood to face him. He looked at the torn, open blouse, now showing most of her breasts.

'What happened to you?' he demanded to know.

'The prison guard tried to rape me.'

'What!' He turned to face the chief. 'I'll see that the Mayor hears about this. You'll be lucky if you've still got a job pounding the beat when I've finished speaking to him.'

'It's all a mistake,' the chief blubbed. 'Miss Drake brought in a body, and I needed to detain her until I could confirm that her story about how she found it was correct. I did not realise that she was a trusted friend of yours, Sir Jeremy,' he pleaded.

'You could have, if you'd allowed me to make my telephone call, as I asked,' stated Suzie.

The chief's face went red as he acknowledged the comment with a crooked smile.

A policeman pushed his way into the office. 'The gun is not the one used to kill the sailor,' he declared, waving a piece of paper in the air.

'Just like I said,' Suzie reminded. 'I found the body in the water. He'd already been shot.'

'You are free to go,' the chief directed.

'I want my guns and anything else your men have taken from my yacht returned, and I want them today.'

'I'll see that it's done,' he said, bowing his head.

'You've not heard the last of this,' Pendleton threatened, putting an arm around Suzie's shoulder and ushering her out of the chief's office.

The chief grabbed another tissue from the box and wiped his perspiring brow before dumping his ample frame into his chair. Looking at the bunch of keys left on his desk, he grabbed them and shouted for his officer.

He threw the keys at him as he entered the office. 'Take these back to the cells and see what's happened down there,' he instructed.

The officer nodded and made his way down to the underground guardroom, where he found the jailer still lying unconscious locked in one of his own cells, with a lump the size of an egg on his forehead.

Outside the police station, Pendleton guided Suzie into his Rolls Royce. She recognised Henry, his chauffeur and nodded to him. He smiled and the Rolls effortlessly moved off.

'I'd like to go back to my yacht in the marina,' she told Pendleton.

'You've had a bad experience and your blouse is torn. Come back to the hotel with me, have a shower and change. I will get some new clothes delivered to the room for you, and then we can check your yacht.'

'Thank you, but I'd rather get my own clothes and check the yacht straight away to make sure everything is okay. The police have searched it, and I don't trust them to leave it in the same state as they found it,' replied Suzie, aware that Pendleton was doing all he could to help, and which he knew would leave Suzie in his debt. It was a debt that he may try to make use of, and which could unwittingly be to Suzie's advantage.

'Of course. To the marina, Henry,' he instructed.

Amid the hundreds of vessels tied up in the marina, many of which were owned by millionaires, Jeremy Pendleton's Rolls Royce purred its way along jetty and stopped alongside *Quester*. He and Suzie stepped out of the car to a fresh, salty breeze wafting in from the sea, mixed with a hot sun blazing down.

'That's a glorious smell, don't you think?' he asked Suzie.

'Yes. It's a lot better than the smell of that jail. It reminds me of when I was a child in Portsmouth. I used to watch the fishing boats arrive and unload their catches on the dockside. There was one fisherman who would always let me have a lobster or a codfish, or something. I think he felt sorry for me after he caught me trying to steal one. He realised that we were very poor, probably by the clothes I wore, and guessed that we couldn't afford to buy the fish. I wonder what happened to him,' mused Suzie. 'He'll be an old man by now, if he's still alive.'

Boarding *Quester*, Suzie and Pendleton went below and stopped in their tracks. The yacht was in a shambles. All the cupboards had been turned out onto the floor, and everything was left lying where it had been thrown, including Suzie's clean clothes.

'The bastards! Look what they've done. Next time I find a body in the sea, I'm going to leave it there, if this is what happens when it's reported to the police.'

'I'll get someone to tidy it up and get the clothes cleaned. You come back to the hotel with me and get freshened up. I insist that you accompany me to dinner tonight.'

'In a restaurant or in your hotel room?' questioned Suzie, recalling the last time she dined with Pendleton at his home and nearly ended up in bed with him.

He laughed, also recalling that time. 'This time you can choose the venue.'

'Any restaurant that you select will be acceptable to me.'

'Very well. I'll arrange it straight away.'

'And you promise to let me return to *Quester* to sleep tonight?'

'I don't make promises that I may not be able to keep,' he suggested.

'Of course, I think we know each other by now.'

'Good. Henry can drive us to the hotel, and you can explain to me what is happening about the delivery of my new motor yacht. I understand that it has been stolen?'

Stepping back into Pendleton's Rolls Royce, Suzie knew that when she told him delivery of his new vessel was likely to be late, it was not going to be the news that he wanted to hear. His motor yacht naming party would be an embarrassment without the vessel, or if he had to cancel it at the last minute. Suzie had to soften the blow and try to persuade him to allow Mike more time to reach Cannes. It could be quite a challenge, and promised to be an interesting evening.

10

CHOICE

In a Whitehall office, tastefully furnished and decorated in the Victorian style, which echoed the period of the building's construction, sat Sir Joseph Sterling at his large oak desk. An ex-diplomat with a charming manner, his sharp mind and eloquent speech made him the ideal candidate to fill the job of troubleshooter for the government on matters of high police importance and security, including antiterrorist measures.

Now past the age of sixty-five, he continued to hope that a suitable replacement would soon be found who could step into his shoes, thus enabling him to retire to a cottage in the countryside. So far, his hopes had all been in vain.

His son, Jim Sterling, had married Jenny Jones, a delightfully attractive long-legged female with a curvy figure and piercing black eyes, who was born in England to Jamaican parents. They had met after she was seconded to Sir Joseph's office to carry out undercover work, and the pair had an immediate attraction to each other. Over the following twelve months their romance blossomed, and they were married.

A few months before they met, Jim Sterling had become the fortunate winner of several million pounds on a rollover jackpot from the National Lottery. Along with his wife Jenny, they purchased a boat building business with their friends Mike Randle and Suzie Drake. This purchase enabled all of them to take up a more sedate style of life, in which they were better able to control their time by taking overall responsibility. This allowed them to delegate much of the work to the two dozen or so staff they employed, relying heavily on their foreman Reg, and his helper, George.

Now, in his London office, it had come to Sir Joseph's attention that the murder weapon used to kill a prominent politician in Northern Ireland had been recovered, and he asked Special Branch Detective Inspector Colin Brooke to investigate. He had become both a working colleague and a friend, having built up a mutual relationship with the policeman over several years, after his collaboration on a number of assignments that Sir Joseph was involved with.

DC's John Green and Ray Teal were selected to accompany Brooke to Chatham, in order to carry out the interviews of Roy Kelly. The pair had worked successfully with Brooke in the past and they all got on well together. Both the DC's were hoping for promotion soon and were eager to make a good impression whenever the opportunity arose.

Motoring from their London headquarters on a bright Monday morning, the trio's car swept into the Chatham Police Station car park and drew to a halt. Brooke and his two DCs wandered into the reception area of the recently refurbished police station, which was erected in the nineteen-thirties, and soon found themselves ushered into the office of Detective Inspector Rollinson.

His office was small, and dominated by an extremely cluttered desk and several filing cabinets stacked against the walls. Diplomas, for numerous awards and commendations that Rollinson had gained over the past thirty years as a policeman, hung on the only vacant space on one wall. The office overlooked the heavily used main road, and only a small top window was open to keep the noise of traffic down to a tolerable level.

Brooke introduced his DC's to Rollinson and there were hand shakes all round. Although nearing the end of his career as a policeman, Rollinson was still very involved with all that occurred on his patch. His and Brooke's grips were strong, as both men discovered when shaking hands. Rollinson was almost six-foot tall, a few inches shorter than Brooke, and had a face that was heavily lined reflecting his strong character.

After the introductions, Rollinson asked his visitors, 'Would you like a cup of tea?'

Brooke looked at his two DC's who both nodded. 'Yes, please. That would be most welcome.'

Rollinson open his door and spoke to a woman PC in the office. 'Louise, be a love and get us all a cup of tea, please.'

She nodded and Rollinson returned to his desk. He motioned the men to sit on the three chairs that faced him, placed there when he learned that three officers were about to arrive that morning.

'Can you give us a brief outline of what's happened so far, and what progress you've made in finding out where this gun came from?' Brooke asked.

Easing himself to a comfortable position on his desk seat, Rollinson stated. 'There was an attempted robbery and shooting in a local building society last Friday, and we've caught the man involved. He is Roy Kelly, a small time Irish crook, who in the past has stuck to burgling houses and is on probation at the moment. We are holding him for the attempted robbery and shooting of the building society employee, and also of possession of the gun he used. He insists that he bought the weapon recently from a man he met in a pub.'

'I presume that's the weapon we've subsequently discovered was used to kill Mr. O'Connor?' asked Brooke.

'Yes, that's right.'

'So, do you think we have our political murderer? If we do, then we are to inform him of his rights and escort him back to London for further questioning,' disclosed the DI.

'I have my doubts that he's the man you are looking for,' Rollinson stated, in a slow, but confident voice.

'Why?'

'Firstly, because he doesn't seem the type,' he replied, holding up his hand to prevent the obvious question being asked, 'though I agree that looks can sometimes be deceptive, but I don't think so, not in this case.'

'And secondly?'

'And secondly, because I think he's telling the truth when he says that he bought the gun only a few days ago. I've been in this game for a long time and like most of us, I have an instinct about what rings true and what doesn't. Kelly is very scared. He realises that he's in a lot of trouble and could be looking at a long stretch. I think he is likely to be telling the truth.'

'Hmm. Do you have any concrete evidence to support his claim?'

'No, not directly as yet, but a known arms dealer, with the same initials as the man Kelly says he met in the pub to buy the weapon from, left London Airport for Nairobi the day after Kelly was caught trying to rob the building society.'

'That could be a coincidence.'

'True.'

'What's the dealer's name?'

'Owen Sutton.'

Brooke glanced at Teal and Green to assure himself they were listening carefully and taking notes.

'The name doesn't ring a bell with me.' Brooke turned to Teal. 'Check that name out will you please, Ray.'

'We've run it through the police computer and come up empty,' Rollinson stated.

'Special Branch has access to a wider range of information, so if you don't mind I'll still have it checked out.'

'Of course.'

'Is there a telephone I can use,' Teal asked Rollinson.

At that moment PC Jordan, an attractive woman police officer opened the door and brought in a tray holding four cups of teas and a bowl of sugar.

'Well done, Louise. Could you give DC Teal a hand please?'

'Yes, of course, Sir,' she replied smiling at him.

Teal grabbed his cup of tea and followed her to the outer office.

'What was the name of the man with the same initials that Kelly says he met?' Green asked Rollinson, his pen poised over his notepad.

'Oliver Statham. One of my officer's is attempting to obtain security videos of the airport check-in area showing Owen Sutton when he booked in. I intend to let Kelly watch the video. If they are one and the same man and he picks him out, then I think it goes a long way to corroborating his story.'

Brooke listened to the inspector's accounts about the robbery and the interviews he had conducted with Kelly so far, and agreed that it looked doubtful that he was involved with the murder of O'Connor.

'Do you think Kelly was given inside information about the building society?' Green asked.

'There's nothing to suggest that at the moment. There are only four people who work at that building society. It's only a small place. Three of them are part time and share the work, the fourth is the full time manager who was shot.'

'I'd like to have a word with Kelly myself, to get a better impression of the man,' Brooke suggested.

'Of course. His solicitor is Mr Roger Miles, who was appointed for him, and will want to be present at the interview. I'll let him know, and check to see if DC Smith has had any luck obtaining those videos.'

Kelly was brought from the cells to the interview room. A room in the centre of the police station that had no windows, which helped to induce a feeling of oppressiveness, as if it served to give suspects an experience of what life would be like in prison. Kelly sat next to his solicitor. He was quiet and solemn, like a man who knew that he was in deep trouble and was not able to cope very well with the situation. The interview tape was started and Rollinson stated the time and date.

'With me at this interview are DI Brooke and DC Green. They are from Special Branch and have some questions to put to Mr Kelly.'

Brooke went over the main points of the robbery and shooting with Kelly, who confirmed what was already known.

He then asked, 'Who gave you the name and telephone number of the man who sold you the gun?'

'I don't want to say.'

'Why not? It would help to confirm your assertion that you only received the gun a day before the robbery.'

'I don't want to get he … the person into trouble.'

Though Kelly's hesitation was slight, Brooke was aware of it, but said nothing.

The interview continued, until it was interrupted by DC Smith entering the room. He motioned to Rollinson that he wanted to speak to him in private and the interview was halted. Brooke and Rollinson left the room to talk with him. They stepped into the inspector's office, where DC Teal was waiting.

'No joy with that name, Sir, there no record of an Owen Sutton on file.'

'Okay, Ray. Try Oliver Statham and see if there's anything on him.'

'Okay, Sir,' he said, happy to leave the room and join PC Jordan again.

'Righto Smith, what have you got?' asked Rollinson.

'The airline companies do record the booking in queues for security purposes, especially after the September 11th attacks. I looked through the recordings and had quite a job trying to identify exactly which customer was the man we are looking for. The airline staff have been very helpful and we are pretty sure that we know which one he is,' asserted Smith.

'But not one hundred per cent?' asked Brooke.

'No, not at the moment. I asked the Liverpool police to fax me a photograph of Owen Sutton before I went to look at the video recordings. Apparently, he's quite elusive and they only have a rather fuzzy picture of him.'

'And does it look like the man on the video?' asked Rollinson.

Smith nodded. 'I reckon so. This is the photo,' he said, handing it to his inspector.

He and Brooke looked at it. 'Hmm, I see what you mean, it's not a very good photo. Let's take a look at the video and see if either of us can pick him out before we show it to Kelly,' suggested Brooke. 'How long does the video last for?'

'Eight hours each recording and four recordings covering all the booking-in desks.'

'What!'

'Don't worry. The airline's computer system, logs the time and desk number that each passenger uses to check in. It wasn't too difficult to find the approximate place on the recording and check the few people near the front of the queue at that time.'

'Thank goodness for that,' confessed Rollinson.

The group transferred to a second interview room where the DVD player and monitor were set up. Smith closed the blinds and ran the player, starting at five minutes before Sutton booked in. Brooke and Rollinson stared at the screen, scrutinising each passenger as they waited in the queue and approached the desks.

'That looks a bit like him,' Brooke announced, 'the man who's third in the queue.'

'Yes, I agree. He appears to be the nearest to the photograph,' Rollinson added.

'That's our man all right,' Smith announced. 'He can also be seen on the recording from the next desk, but is in the background and not so easy to identify.'

'Show us,' said Rollinson.

Changing the discs over, Smith fast forwarded it to the right time and pressed the play button.

'I see what you mean. There he is in the line at the back,' Rollinson stated, pointing at the screen.

Brooke nodded in agreement. 'Let's show this recording to Kelly first and see if he spots him,' he suggested.

'Good idea. Get the discs ready Smith, I'll have Kelly and his solicitor brought in.'

Roy Kelly, accompanied by his solicitor, was escorted into the room and sat in front of the television screen. DC Green followed him in after glancing at Teal chatting to the attractive PC, and sat at the back of the room next to the door.

'We are going to show you recordings of the booking-in desk at an airport,' stated Brooke. 'We'd like you to look at it and tell us if you recognise anyone. Is that clear Mr Kelly?'

Saying nothing, Kelly nodded. He looked pale and drawn, his shoulders hunched. In the last few days, he had been under more pressure than he had ever known before, including his last appearance in the dock, and it was beginning to show on his face and in his demeanour. Brooke nodded to Smith, who closed the blinds and pressed the recorder's play button.

Kelly's face was expressionless as he watched the line of

passengers slowly move forward and check in. Several minutes past without a movement or sound from him, before he sat more upright and stared at the screen more intently.

'Can you zoom in on the line at the back,' he asked.

'Why?' asked Brooke.

Pointing at the screen, Kelly said, 'That man at the back, he looks a bit like that Oliver Statham, the man who sold me the gun.'

'We have a recording of that queue. It'll show the man more clearly.'

'If it's him, I'll be able to tell you.'

The discs were changed over and when their suspect came into view, Kelly was out of his chair immediately.

'That's him! That's him! That's the man who sold me the gun,' he declared, prodding the screen with his finger.

Brooke and Rollinson looked at each other. Each knew what the other was thinking. It was looking more and more as if Kelly was telling the truth about when and where he had received the gun, and cast grave doubts that he was involved in O'Connor's murder. Smith opened the blinds, allowing shafts of sunlight to illuminate the room.

Standing, Brooke asked, 'If he's the man who sold you the gun, then who's the woman who told you about him? Was it Mrs Boyd?'

Kelly tried to look nonchalant at the comment, but he was surprise and flustered, it was written all over his face and clear for everyone to see.

'I … err … don't know what you mean … that is, I don't know who Mrs Boyd is. And who said it was a woman anyway?'

'You did. You're not a very good liar, Mr Kelly,' Brooke stated.

'I don't know a Mrs Boyd. Who is she anyway?' he stated, looking at his solicitor with a worried expression across his face.

Brooke continued, 'She is the woman teller at the building society. The person who suffered a few minor cuts from the flying glass, the same person whose condition you enquired about through Mr Miles to Detective Inspector Rollinson. Need I say more?'

'I don't know what you're talking about. I saw her taken into the ambulance with blood running down her face and simply enquired to make sure she was not badly injured by flying glass, and I refuse to say anything else,' Kelly asserted, again looking to his solicitor for guidance.

'I wish again to talk in private with my client,' Mr Miles stated.

Rollinson scratched his head. 'We'll talk again later Mr Kelly, after you've had time to consider your position and listen to the advice of your solicitor. Take him back to the interview room with his solicitor first, and afterwards back to the cells,' he said, nodding to DC Smith.

After Kelly had left the room, DC Teal entered the office. 'The computer's thrown up some information about Owen Sutton. He's been questioned several times about drugs and arms smuggling, but there's never been enough evidence to charge him.'

'Okay, Ray, thanks. That fits our man.'

Brooke turned to Rollinson and suggested, 'I'm now even more certain that Mrs Boyd is involved. I think we should bring her in for questioning before she does a runner, assuming she hasn't already disappeared.'

'Yes, I agree,' Rollinson stated.

'Have you run a check on her?'

'No, we've had no reason to, though Mr Wainwright's insurance company contacted us this morning asking what happened and what his condition was.'

'Why did they do that? How did they know about him?'

'It seems there is a large insurance policy on his life, and Mrs Boyd is the beneficiary. She informed them.'

'Really? Have you searched her home?'

'I'd need a court order if I wanted to ask my men to do that, unless she gave us permission, which if she's involved she's hardly likely to do.'

'How long will it take you to get the court order?'

Rollinson looked at the clock on the wall which showed the time as 1 p.m. 'At this time of day, I should be able to get one in about an hour.'

'I think you should do that straight away. If Mrs Boyd is guilty of helping Kelly, then she's not likely to voluntarily let us search her home. If Kelly visited her, then we might find his fingerprints there. That would suggest that she was involved in the robbery.'

'Hmm, yes, good idea. I'll organise that now, and have a check done on her,' said Rollinson lifting the telephone receiver and punching the buttons.

After the court order was applied for, Rollinson stepped into the main office and summoned DC Smith. 'Jake, get PC Jordan to accompany you to Mrs Boyd's house; she's the teller from Nelson's Building Society. Ask her to return to the police station to clear up a few points about the attempted robbery. Before that, get a team ready to search her place as soon as the court order arrives. We're looking for Kelly's fingerprints.'

'Okay, Chief,' the DC replied, grabbing his jacket.

It was not long before the fax machine in the office chatted out its message of replies to the enquiries about Mrs Boyd. The papers were collected by an officer and handed to Rollinson, waiting in his office for the court order to arrive, and taking the opportunity to chat with Brooke.

He read through the fax. 'There's nothing on Mrs Boyd in any of our files, apart from a parking ticket that was issued to her some months ago in Manchester, and she was divorced five years ago,' he told Brooke, dropping the fax in his 'papers to be filed' tray.

'She was a long way from home.'

'Nothing illegal in that. She seems to be clean.'

'That might simply mean she's careful. We'll have a better idea about our lady suspect after her house has been searched.'

11

GETTING THE PICTURE

Following DI Brooke's interview with Kelly and their subsequent decision to search Mrs Boyd's house for his fingerprints, two police officers were asked to visit her. Mrs Boyd was a little anxious when the police officers knocked at her off white painted front door with *The Red House* nameplate above it, and asked her to accompany them to the police station to answer yet more questions.

'I've already told you everything I know. It's all in the statement I gave to the policeman at the hospital,' she protested.

'We realise that Mrs Boyd, but there are one or two items that the inspector would like clarified. It won't take a moment,' DC Smith promised, as policewoman PC Jordan watched and waited patiently.

Mrs Boyd looked at the two officers standing on her front door step and sighed. She wondered if Kelly had told them about her involvement, and if he had, what sort of reception would really be waiting for her. They weren't arresting her, so she concluded that either they did not know or had not obtained any proof. Either way, she could hardly refuse without casting suspicion on her motives.

'You'd better come in and wait,' she conceded, opening the door wide. 'I haven't finished eating my lunch.'

'We'll wait for you,' DC Smith advised.

The two police officers stepped into the hallway and patiently waited while Mrs Boyd finished her lunch of scrambled egg on toast washed down with a cup of coffee. DC Smith was happy to wait there, knowing that it would give more time for the court order for a search warrant to be issued. He and PC Jordan spoke in low tones, in a house that had an eerie silence, which was broken only by the ticking of a clock in the hall and the clink of cutlery from the kitchen when Mrs Boyd placed the dirty crockery in a bowl of washing-up water. She disappeared upstairs and now, after keeping the officer's waiting for over fifteen minutes, appeared wearing a light beige coat and carrying her handbag.

She was driven to the local police station, and after a further wait in the reception area for ten minutes, was shown into the same interview room that Kelly had occupied only a few short hours before. The team was ready and waiting to receive the court order, and wanted to delay her for as long as they could without causing any suspicion.

'Would you like something to drink while you are waiting, Mrs Boyd?' asked DI Rollinson.

'Just a glass of water, please. How long are you going to keep me here?'

'Only a few moments more, then we'll be ready.'

To everyone's relief, the court order finally came through. DC Smith waved the paper aloft and Rollinson was informed. The team quickly dashed to Mrs Boyd's house to begin their search.

DI Rollinson returned with Mrs Boyd's glass of water and was followed into the room by DI Brooke. Rollinson started the tape, and gave the usual opening references.

'This is Detective Inspector Brooke from Special Branch,' he introduced.

'Special Branch! Why is he here?' Mrs Boyd questioned.

'He would like to ask you some questions. The interview is being recorded, so you may wish to have your solicitor present.'

Mrs Boyd was slightly alarmed at the comment. 'Do I need a solicitor?'

'That is not for me to say. The matter is entirely up to you.'

'Then, you can continue with your questions. I've nothing to hide,' she bluffed.

The comment only enforced Brooke's opinion that Mrs Boyd, in reality did have something to hide. In his experience, people did not usually make that type of comment unless they were concealing something. Rollinson motioned Brooke to begin the questioning.

'We have been listening to Mr Kelly's account of what happened at the building society last Friday, and asked him why he chose that particular one, and more importantly, where he got the gun from that he used. He informed us that he picked the society at random and bought the gun from a man in a pub,' Brooke began.

Mrs Boyd half-smiled and nodded to indicate that she accepted what she had heard. 'I presume that Mr Kelly is the man who tried to rob the society?' she asked, cleverly aware that she might not be expected to know his name as the local newspaper came out on Thursday, so had not yet printed details of the robbery.

'He is. Mr Kelly has refused to say anything further, though he did ask if you were all right after he'd noticed that you were hit by flying glass. We think that is a little odd, don't you?'

'I don't see why. He was obviously concerned that I hadn't received any nasty injuries.'

'Yes, but why should he ask that, while at the same time totally ignoring the condition of the man he'd shot and didn't even bother to ask if he was dead or alive, or even if he was likely to survive? It is a matter which means the difference between being charged with grievous bodily harm and manslaughter, a crime that would carry a considerably longer sentence.'

'I don't know. Perhaps it's because I'm a woman,' stated Mrs Boyd, who was starting to feel uncomfortable at the type of questions she was being asked, and shifted nervously in her seat. It was a movement that was not lost on either of the policemen, trained to pick up on such gestures that give a suspect's true feelings away.

'We have been looking into your background and have discovered that you have a good reason for wanting the other teller, Mr Wainwright, dead.'

'That's outrageous, and a lie,' Mrs Boyd protested, her face reddening with anger.

Brooke ignored the outburst. 'You are divorced and live on your own, I believe?'

'Yes, that's true. What of it. Many divorced women live on their own.'

'Perhaps so, though the house you live in is owned by Mr Wainwright I understand.'

'Yes, we were partners for a while, but that was a long time ago.'

'Doesn't that make things a little awkward, the two of you working side by side in a small building society, I mean?'

'No, not really. We still get along okay.'

'I understand that he now lives in a small flat above the building society office, which is owned by them?'

'Yes, so I believe.'

'And is it not true that he has been taking steps recently to recover his property from you; so far without success?'

'We have not yet come to an agreement about who is entitled to what percentage of the property, it's true. Our solicitors are sorting that out, but I don't see what that has to do with the building society robbery.'

'I'm coming to that. So, if Mr Wainwright were to die, you would be the sole beneficiary of the property you are living in.'

'Err, yes, I suppose that is so. I'm not really sure.'

'How much is the property worth, Mrs Boyd?'

'I don't know.'

'Approximately?' Brooke pressed.

'About £500,000 I believe.'

'Half a million pounds is a lot of money, especially when added to the one million pounds insurance policy that is payable on Mr Wainwright's death, which you are also the beneficiary of.'

'Jeffery took that policy out several years ago when we were together. I'd almost forgotten about it.'

'Almost, but not quite. The insurance company has told us that you informed them of Mr Wainwright's condition by email on Saturday.'

'I ... thought they should know. They will want to know details if the worst happens.'

'Yes, they will, which is why they contacted us this morning.'

Brooke paused for a moment and looked at Rollinson. He continued the questioning.

'Mr Kelly; have you ever met him?'

'No, I've never seen him – not before the robbery.'

'So you didn't give him any information about the building society or how much money it would be holding on the day of the robbery?'

'No, of course not,' said Mrs Boyd indignantly. 'We never hold much money anyway.'

'If you are as innocent as you say you are, then you won't object to us taking a look around your house.'

'Why do you want to do that?'

'Merely routine, Mrs Boyd.'

'I'm not happy about other people poking their noses into my belongings.'

'We could get a court order for a search warrant, if you insist.'

'Then you'll have to get your court order. I'm not agreeing to my place being searched by a lot of heavy handed policemen who will wreck the place.'

'I have to inform you that we anticipated your objections, and have already obtained that court order. Your house is being searched at this moment.'

Mrs Boyd's eyes opened wide with surprise. 'I protest! I should have been informed about this and should be there to see that nothing is damaged,' she complained, her face changing to one of anger with her cheeks reddening and her eyes ablaze with fury.

'I can assure you Mrs Boyd, that our men will be very careful not to damage anything at your premises, and we will gladly pay for any mishaps should they occur.'

'I'm not convinced, and if you've no more questions I'd like to go home now.'

Rollinson looked at DI Brooke. He had not heard back from his team yet. Brooke frowned and gently nodded. A signal Rollinson took to mean that there was no option but to charge Mrs Boyd or let her return home. As yet, they had only supposition and no evidence with which to charge her.

'You may leave now, Mrs Boyd, but we will be accompanying you to your home.'

A stern looking Mrs Boyd rose from her seat and was shown to the reception area where she was asked to wait.

'Perhaps you'd like to get a set of prints from that glass,' said Brooke, pointing to the tumbler that Mrs Boyd had used. 'They may come in useful.'

Rollinson nodded.

PC Jordan was called to accompany Mrs Boyd, and along with Brooke and Rollinson they set off for her home.

In the narrow, no through road where Mrs Boyd lived, curtains twitched as two more police cars joined the already crowded street where three other police vehicles were parked. Through the open front door entered Mrs Boyd and her police escort.

A man, holding a small fingerprinting brush came towards them.

'Found anything?' Rollinson asked.

'In the bedroom, on the bedside cabinet, one perfect fingerprint of Kelly's middle finger from his right hand,' the officer stated.

'Are you absolutely sure it's his?'

'Absolutely. There's no doubt about it. Kelly's fingerprints have long been on file.'

'What do you have to say about that, Mrs Boyd?'

'My house was burgled a week or so ago. It must have been Kelly. He's a thief, isn't he?'

'Why didn't you report this to us?' asked DI Rollinson.

'I was going to, but nothing of any value was taken and I didn't want to waste your time. If you look carefully, you will see that the kitchen window has been forced open recently.'

'Very well, we'll check it out. I'll ask Kelly and see if he confirms your story. Meanwhile, please be good enough not to leave this locality. I will want to speak to you again.'

Mrs Boyd gave him a half-smile of agreement.

'Okay lads, pack things up here and get back to the station,' Rollinson ordered.

The once bustling house was cleared of its occupants. Mrs Boyd watched them file out of her home, after they closed their case of inspection powders and brushes. The police vehicles drove away and she closed the front door with a sigh of relief. This was she knew, only a temporary lull. They would be back, they had guessed that she was involved in the attempted robbery and would pursue their investigation of her. How long would it be she wondered, before they found out the real truth from Kelly, or obtained the proof they were searching for.

At Brooke's suggestion, Rollinson asked one of the plain clothed policemen to keep an eye on the house and follow Mrs Boyd if she left. They realised that she might want to skip out on them now that she had been alerted to their suspicions of her.

On their journey back to the police station, Brooke suggested to Rollinson, 'It's too much of a coincidence that Kelly first burgled Mrs Boyd house, and then turns up at the building society she works at to rob it.'

'Yes, I agree. I'm sure they are both in this together.'

'Have you searched Kelly's place?'

'Yes, we found a few items that may have been stolen, but haven't been able to trace any of the owners as yet. House burglaries are what he's been to prison for, so it may be true that he broke into Mrs Boyd's house, and the kitchen window of her house was damaged.'

'What sort of state was Kelly's place in?'

'Very dishevelled. It looked as if he hadn't done any cleaning for weeks, except in the bedroom. That was tidy.'

'The bedroom, eh? That's where his fingerprints were found in Mrs Boyd's house. You don't think he could be having a relationship with her, do you?'

'What him, with Mrs Boyd? I wouldn't have thought so. He's a scruffy looking, insignificant thief. She's a good-looking, intelligent handsome female. Why would she want to entertain a man like him?'

'Manipulation?'

'Like getting him to do her dirty work, you mean?'

'Yes. Like robbery, or even murder.'

'It seems a bit far fetched, but I suppose it's possible.'

'Was Kelly's flat checked for fingerprints?'

'No. There didn't seem to be any need for it.'

'Could you get your fingerprint team to check if Mrs Boyd's

prints are there?' asked Brooke, as the convoy of cars pulled into the police station car park.

'Yes, can do,' Rollinson said, stepping from his car.

He walked over to DC Smith, who was parking his vehicle. He rolled the window down.

'Jake, I'd like you to take the boys to Kelly's flat and check for fingerprints there. We're looking for Mrs Boyd's prints this time.'

'Yes, Sir,' he stated. 'Do we have a set to compare them with?'

'Yes, we do now. They were lifted from a glass that she used.'

Smith collected Mrs Boyd's prints. 'Come on lads. We've got another job to do now,' he shouted, waving the team back into their vehicles.

While Smith and his fingerprint team checked Kelly's basement flat, Brooke and Rollinson discussed the case and pondered over various scenarios that would fit the facts they had before them.

Back at her house, Mrs Boyd was now pacing up and down in a state of panic and unsure what to do next. She knew that if she ran, it would be a sign that she was guilty of what the police were accusing her of, but she might escape though without the big payoff she was hoping for. Her friend's house in France was looking like a good hiding place. If she stayed, and they found no proof of her involvement she was in the clear, however, if she stayed and they found the proof she was in deep trouble. So much to ponder, so much to decide, and the man standing at the end of the street was still there. Was he a policeman waiting for her to make a run for it? It seemed likely. Mrs Boyd picked up the telephone and tried to ring her friend again for advice, without success this time, the telephone call remained unanswered.

Back at Chatham Police Station, the telephone on DI Rollinson's desk also rang.

'I think we've got it,' announced a jubilant DC Smith when his boss answered the call. 'It's a good job that Kelly doesn't bother to do the washing up very often. In among the dirty crockery in the sink, we found a cup with lipstick on. It looks like the same colour Mrs Boyd was wearing today. There was just one good fingerprint on the cup. It matches her prints, we've got her.'

'Good work, Jake. Get back here with that proof straight away.'
'And one other thing.'
'What's that?'
'We found a typed note with a telephone number on it. Guess whose number it is?'
'Mrs Boyd's?'
'Correct. Mrs Boyd's.'

Rollinson told Brooke the news. 'They've found a print that matches Mrs Boyd's and a note with her telephone number on. She's definitely tied in with Kelly, and the robbery.'

'We could charge her as an accomplice to the attempted robbery, but could we prove she had anything to do with the shooting?' asked Brooke.

'Probably not, but it's a start. I think Kelly is protecting her, and your suggestion that she is having an affair with him in order to get him to do her bidding is looking a lot more likely now. When he finds out that we've got proof she was involved in the robbery, he may crumble and tells us more.'

Smith arrived back at the station with the note and the fingerprint evidence, which was double-checked to make sure there were no mistakes.

'I think we got enough proof to arrest her on suspicion of being involved in the building society robbery, don't you?' Rollinson asked Brooke.

'Yes, I do.'

Nodding, Rollinson grabbed the telephone and barked out his orders. DC Smith and PC Jordan left to collect the policeman on duty outside Mrs Boyd's house and make the arrest. When they entered her house, they found that she was in the middle of packing her belongings.

'Not thinking of going anywhere were you, Mrs Boyd?' asked DC Smith, looking at the suitcase, partially hidden behind a settee.

He received no reply and read Mrs Boyd her rights, before placing her under arrest.

12

AN EVENING OUT

The Metropolitan Hotel in Cannes was a five star hotel where no expense was spared to look after the requirements of each of their guests. Only those who were in the millionaire bracket would normally consider renting a suite. Situated on the main coast road, guests had a panoramic view of the golden sands in front of the hotel. To one side was the marina, only a short distance away, for those who had arrived by seafaring means, which was majority of their guests. The marina boasted a plethora of yachts, most of which were in the million dollar bracket. At the hotel they offered all the amenities that were expected of a top class establishment, including shops, two restaurants, a heated swimming pool with a private swimming area attached, and gambling rooms where guests could choose from a range of activities that were all designed to relieve them of their money. It was an internationally renowned hotel, which boasted a clientele of rich and famous people, including many government ministers and movie stars.

The grand, glass fronted entrance was flanked by palm trees, regularly attended to in order to keep them looking their best. The thousands of windows were spotlessly clean, washed in a never-ending cycle that required the group of window cleaners to start again from the beginning once they had finally reached the end. The car park beneath the hotel, housed a prodigious number of Rolls Royce cars and other quality vehicles parked in its vast underground space.

Following Suzie's rescue from the local police station by Jeremy Pendleton after she had encountered an awkward police chief, his chauffeur drove them to *The Metropolitan Hotel*. One of the hotel's front door attendants, dressed in his smart outfit of top hat and white gloves, hurried to open Pendleton's Rolls Royce passenger door almost before Henry had brought the vehicle to a halt. Pendleton and Suzie stepped from the car into the warm early evening sun, entered the hotel and rode the lift to the Twelfth floor where they set foot in suite 1205, Jeremy Pendleton's apartment. Because of the dishevelled state that the police had left her yacht *Quester* in, Suzie had accepted an invitation by Pendleton to use his suite in preparation for an evening meal in which he had insisted she was to be his guest.

'You would be very comfortable here – if you wished to stay,' suggested Pendleton, gesturing to the lavishly presented suite.

Suzie smiled. 'Yes, I'm sure that I would but, like last time, Mike would not be happy if he found out that I'd stayed the night in your suite.'

'And like last time, if you didn't tell him then he'd never know.'

'But I would know. I wouldn't like it if he had secrets from me, so it would be unworthy of me to have them from him … unless it was for a very good reason and I thought it would do more harm than good if he knew.'

Pendleton's face relaxed a little and softened. He knew that Suzie was not completely shutting the door on his advances, merely keeping him on the hook. He wondered why for a moment, before his thoughts turned to the theft of his motor yacht stolen three days previously and due to be delivered the following day. He reasoned that the theft had something to do with her reluctance to give him a definite rejection. Time was short, so he knew that he would not have to wait very long for an answer, one way or another.

'Would you like to take a shower?' he asked.

'Yes, please, I would. I'd like to get rid of the smell of that police station cell and the jailer.'

'Of course. The shower is through here,' Pendleton indicated. 'You'll find spare towels and a dressing gown in an airing cupboard. And that is a spare bedroom where you can dress afterwards,' he stated, pushing a door open, 'and sleep if you change your mind about staying. And if you must tell Mike, you can say that you slept in a separate bedroom without lying to him.'

'Presumably, after I'd left your bedroom,' said Suzie.

'That would be your decision.'

Suzie gave a slight nod in acknowledgement to Pendleton's assessment.

'I'll ask the fashion department downstairs to bring up a selection of clothes for you to choose.'

'Thank you, Jeremy. Nothing too expensive please, though I do appreciate your help. I'd like to telephone Mike afterwards, to see how he's getting along.'

'Getting along?'

'I'll tell you about it later.'

Pendleton nodded. 'Feel free to make yourself at home and use anything that you require.'

Suzie took her shower and washed away the odour of the prison cell. While the warm water cascaded over her body, Pendleton opened the bathroom door a few inches and stared at Suzie's naked form behind the frosted shower glass. Suzie felt a slight draft and guessed what Pendleton was up to, but gave no indication that she knew he was there. He watched for a few minutes before returning to the main room. Suzie turned round and saw the door as it finally closed. She smiled at his infatuation with her body, and it reinforced her belief that it could provide the answer to their late delivery problem, if it became necessary.

Suzie pondered about the evening ahead and mulled over what she would say to her host. If Mike was unable to get the repairs completed and the yacht delivered as agreed, she thought it unlikely that Pendleton would be generous enough to relax the delivery time. If he would not, then she may have to resort to using the infatuation he had for her to persuade him to change his mind, even if that meant sharing his bed with him. If that happened, Suzie would have to trust that Mike would understand and be willing to accept that she had no choice if SMJ Boatyard was to survive by avoiding the hefty penalty that the late delivery clause provided.

Entering the vast, lavishly furnished main room in her fluffy white towelling dressing gown, Suzie rang Mike's mobile. Pendleton was nowhere to be seen.

'Hello Mike, where are you and how are you getting on?'

'I'm still in Gibraltar. Reg and George are close to finishing the repairs. I should be able to get moving again later tonight or early tomorrow morning.'

'Good.'

'How about you? Where are you?'

'I'm in Jeremy Pendleton's suite on the twelfth floor of *The Metropolitan Hotel*. I had a bit of trouble with the local police when I reported the dead body to them. They thought I might have killed him.'

'What! Did they think you are stupid enough to shoot the man, dump him in the water, then fish him out again and inform the police about the body?'

'Apparently so. I'll tell you all about it when you get here. I was stuck at the police station and it looked as if I might have to spent the night there, so I rang Jeremy Pendleton, he came to my rescue.'

'Did he now? So that's why you're in his suite. I'm sure he'll try to take advantage of having you in his debt.'

'Maybe. If you can't get here by noon tomorrow, I might have to keep Pendleton occupied in order to persuade him to relax the deadline so, you'd better get here on time to thwart his amorous advances.'

'In that case, I'm on my way now, whether the yacht's ready or not.'

Suzie smiled. 'Don't be silly. The yacht must be in pristine condition if we're to fulfil our part of the contract and get the final payment.'

'I guess you're right. I hate the though of you having to show favour to Pendleton's amorous intentions though.'

'I know, but we can't afford to pay that hefty fine, and have a delay in receiving the rest of the payment for the yacht. The two together would severely test our financial resources.'

'I understand that. You'll have to do whatever is necessary to persuade Pendleton to relax his deadline.'

'Get here as quickly as you can.'

'I will. Believe me, I will.'

'Give me a ring on my mobile the moment you enter the marina.'

'Okay.'

'I'll see you tomorrow then. 'Bye.'

The door opened as Suzie put down the receiver. Pendleton stepped in, followed by a smart well dressed manageress from the designer fashion department, who waved six of her female assistants into the room. Three were each carrying two dresses for Suzie to appraise and select; two were holding boxes of shoes and the last assistant was a make-up and manicure beautician. Four of the dresses had low, round necklines and two had plunging V-necklines.

'I see that you've chosen dresses for me which reveal a large amount of naked flesh,' Suzie remarked.

'I seem to recall that when you last dined with me, you wore a dress that was quite similar to the ones I've chosen, so I assume the style is to your liking,' Pendleton maintained with a wicked glint in his eye.

'That was because I needed your attention to get you to place your luxury cruiser order with our boatyard.'

'You certainly got my attention, and I very much hope that you will want to get it again tonight.'

Suzie knew that Pendleton's yacht, and its possible late delivery, were the object of both their interests. 'I think we both know what is happening here, Jeremy.'

'It should make for an interesting evening, Suzie. Don't you agree?'

Turning to enter the spare bedroom, Suzie remarked, 'I'll choose something appropriate to wear for this evening in that case.'

The manageress and assistants followed Suzie into the room where she rejected three of the dresses and tried on the remaining three. After careful consideration about the purpose of the evening, she chose one of the most eye-catching dresses to wear, which was made from silk, full in length, sleeveless and bright red in colour. The shoulder straps were narrow; the dress had no frills, with a straight skirt, a figure-hugging bodice and plunging V-neckline with criss-cross straps at the back. Suzie wore no bra as the neckline went down to her slim waist showing all of her cleavage, but just allowing her nipples to be covered. High-heeled red shoes completed the outfit.

The beautician applied Suzie's make-up, choosing bright red lipstick to match the dress and shoes. Suzie enjoyed being pampered and fussed over by the experienced assistants, a delight she rarely received. The beautician brushed her long black hair and tied it into a ponytail at Suzie's request. She liked to wear her hair that way and felt that it helped to keep her looking young, an opinion that most people agreed with, especially Jeremy Pendleton. When all the pampering was complete she returned to the main room, and was greeted by smiles of approval by him.

'You look gorgeous,' Pendleton gushed. 'All my friends will be very jealous when they see you with me but, you need something to show off your neckline,' he said, producing a box, which he opened to reveal a gold necklace with a diamond pendant.

Lifting it out, he slipped it around Suzie's neck. The pendant nestled between her breasts and Pendleton fastened the necklace, kissing the back of her neck as he did. She felt his moustache brush her and a tingle ran through her spine. It had been a while since someone had lavished such gifts and attention on her and she delighted in it. She and Mike had given most of their attention to the consolidation of their boatyard business and the building of Pendleton's motor yacht in the past year. They had little time to relax and socialise, though Suzie missed some of the more tender touches he once gave her, a sign that he was becoming accustomed to having her around and was starting to take things too much for granted. She would remind him of the tender touches that Jeremy Pendleton had shown her, and encourage Mike to take more notice of some of the other womanly needs she had, as well as great sex.

Pendleton turned Suzie around to face him. 'That gives the finishing touch to a beautiful, ravishing lady,' he enthused.

Fingering the diamond necklace, Suzie declared, 'You shouldn't have. It looks far too expensive a gift to dine out for one evening, or is it only on loan?'

'No, of course not. It is yours to keep, and I hope you will be able to wear it on other evenings for me.'

The inference that Pendleton was suggesting by his comment was not lost on Suzie. She was aware of his probing hints in trying to establish a closer relationship with her and was, like many others before her, finding it difficult to ignore his charming manor, and the lavish gifts that he bestowed on her.

Pendleton turned to the manageress and her assistants. 'Thank you very much, ladies.'

They smiled and left. The manageress was very happy to have made the sale and add the cost to Pendleton's already expensive bill.

'I've taken the liberty of booking a table for us in the hotel restaurant. I hope that meets with your approval?'

'Of course, Jeremy.'

He looked at his Rolex watch. 'It's almost time. Shall we go?' he said, lifting his arm for Suzie to hold.

The couple took the lift down to the first floor and strolled into the lavish dining room arm in arm. The lighting was subdued, and a trio situated on a small dais, played music quietly in the background. A gentle murmur of voices, communicating in quiet tones drifted from the room. Most of the tables were already occupied with groups of customers, mainly two or four to a table, chatting while they ate or drank, or waited to be served by one of the many smartly dressed waiters buzzing back and forth.

Suzie was guided by the headwaiter to their table. She noticed many of the customers glancing her way. Most of the men took longer to avert their gazes, while examining the contours of her body, and eyeing her bare cleavage and the shape of her protruding nipples, brought on by the smooth silk brushing against her, coupled with the tingle that she was experiencing by feeling extra special.

The headwaiter held Suzie's chair for her to sit down before handing her and Pendleton a menu.

He hovered asking, 'Would you like to order drinks first, Sir Jeremy?'

Pendleton looked at Suzie. 'What would you like to drink, Champagne?'

'Thank you, Jeremy, but no. I'd be just as happy with a glass of good red wine.'

'A bottle of you finest red wine then, Monsieur Dupont.'

The waiter bowed and left to fulfil the order.

'Are you going to order seafood, like we had last time?' Pendleton enquired.

'No, I don't think so. The menu is very comprehensive, but my French is a little rusty. I fancy a mixed grill.'

'Then you shall have a mixed grill. How do you like your steak?

'Medium, please.'

'Medium it is. How about a starter?'

'I think I'll start with a prawn cocktail. After all, I am a seafaring lass.'

'And a gorgeous one you are.'

'Thank you, Jeremy.'

'That's a good choice as a starter. I'll think that I'll join you, and have the sirloin steak, rare with all the trimmings for my main meal – it's delicious.'

Pendleton ordered the meals – in English; his French was also limited. The wine was brought and he was asked to confirm that it was acceptable. Pendleton took a small sip and nodded his agreement that the wine was good and could be poured.

The couple made small talk and sipped their wine until the starters were brought. Their dishes were overflowing with large succulent prawns on a bed of chopped lettuce and topped with a seafood sauce. When the pair had finished their starters, the empty dishes were swiftly collected and immediately followed by their main dishes.

As they ate, Pendleton asked Suzie, 'I trust that your meal is satisfactory?'

'Yes, thank you, Jeremy. It's delicious. All the meat is very tender and cooked just as I like it.'

'Good. So, are you going to tell me what's happened to my brand new, very expensive motor yacht? You know that I have been told that it's been stolen from your boatyard.'

'Yes, as you quite rightly say, the motor yacht was stolen, and our two employees guarding it were murdered.'

Pendleton looked up in surprise. 'I didn't know that, I am very sorry to hear it,' he said with genuine regret. 'It must have been awful for you.'

'Yes, it was. We'd completed building the yacht and recently showed it at the Southampton Boat Show. It was seen by a lot of people, and is what we believe encouraged someone to have it stolen. There was a great deal of interest in her.'

'Yes, I imagine there was. I was away on business at the time, otherwise I would have been there myself to see it. Mr Lassiter told me it was a star attraction.'

'When we returned to the yard at the end of the boat show, the yacht was completely refitted throughout. Many people had tramped through her on their visit to the show, and we wanted everything to be in pristine condition for the handover.'

'I would expect nothing less.'

'Of course, Jeremy. We'd recently finished all her trials, and were ready to make the delivery to you.'

'Then disaster struck.'

'Yes, then the yacht was stolen. As you are aware, she has a sophisticated electronic system installed, including a GPS tracker system hidden aboard, fitted to enable the motor yacht's position to be easily located should, as happened, the vessel be stolen.'

'I'm very pleased that it was one of the requests I insisted upon when drawing up the contract. Presumably, you are using the tracker system to locate it.'

'Not using, but used. Mike and I chased after your luxury yacht in our motor yacht *Quester*. It's not as fast as your boat, but after heading down the Spanish and Portuguese coasts, your stolen yacht stopped out to sea off the Portuguese coastline near Porto. We kept going day and night and were able to catch up with it.'

Suzie explained how Mike boarded Pendleton's yacht after they found a body in the water; a body they were sure was the pilot of the stolen yacht, an assumption, which turned out to be correct, and one that eventually landed Suzie in the police prison cell.

'Mike dealt with both guards after the second boat carrying the man who had hired the crooks, reached them and he and his men stepped aboard. You might be surprised to hear who turned out to be the mastermind behind the robbery of your property?' Suzie suggested.

'Presumably, it's someone who I know, though I can't think of anyone who would commit murder to steal my yacht. You've intrigued me, Suzie. Who is it?'

'Giles Harman.'

'Giles Harman! The wealthy boatyard owner, surely not?'

'The same. It seems that he was more than a bit sore at losing your motor yacht contract to us.'

'But, to murder three people …'

'Apparently, that wasn't his intention, so he claimed. He complained to his men for taking such drastic action. However, it was his idea to steal the boat and he engaged the men to do it, so ultimately it was his responsibility. And after being thwarted by Mike and losing the yacht, he boarded his craft and motored away. His man then let loose with a machine gun and put several bullet holes into the fuel tank of your brand new motor yacht to empty it, in order to stop us delivering it to you on time.'

'Did he now? That was nasty. If what you say turns out to be true, I'll have a few things to say about Giles Harman when I get back to England. He certainly won't be bidding for any more contracts from me, or any of my friends, I can assure you of that. Why did he want my motor yacht stolen? Surely his yard could have built one?'

'I believe for two reasons. One, to get our boatyard into trouble with you and … possibly to be fined for not completing the contract on time,' Suzie stated, trying to gauge whether Pendleton was sympathetic to the troubles they were in. 'This would put our yard in financial difficulties and be less of a threat to his business, and possibly put us completely out of business.'

Pendleton gave no reaction to her probing. 'And the other reason?'

'Simply profit. He had a buyer in the Gulf States who had seen the motor yacht when we showed it at the Southampton Boat Show. He wanted it straight away, and was willing to pay for it, and presumably turn a blind eye to how it was obtained.'

'So, my yacht was not only stolen, but is damaged and is unlikely to be delivered on time?' Pendleton questioned.

'Not necessarily. Mike has docked the yacht in Gibraltar and we've flown out two men from our boatyard to do the repairs and have it refuelled. I came on ahead to apprise you of the situation, and to ask if you could see your way to relaxing the delivery deadline for a short while, considering the problems we've had and how effectively we've remedied the situation,' stated Suzie, in her businesslike manner.

'Very eloquently put, Suzie. But I have organised a motor yacht naming party for tomorrow night and I have a lot of important and influential guests arriving. Not only would I look silly if the yacht is not there, and feel very foolish, but it will cost me a great deal of money for all the food, drink and entertainment that I have ordered and will go to waste if I have to cancel.'

'SMJ Boatyard would be willing to pay for any expenses you incur by the late delivery of your motor yacht, if you were willing to extend the deadline, and repair or replace anything that you are not satisfied with on the yacht, free of charge.'

'I'd really like to Suzie and that is a very generous offer, but I've also arranged to meet important men about a business venture that I'm hoping to conclude, which would almost certainly collapse if I have to cancel the party.'

'It's that word 'but' again. Business venture, I thought you were self sufficient in the wealth department?'

'I am, but I've found that I need a bit more excitement in my life as well.'

'I imagined you'd got that, by enticing beautiful women into your bed.'

Pendleton laughed. 'I do, but there are always more challenges. Some are for the buzz I get by closing a big deal that will earn me a lot of money, whether I need the cash or not, others are for persuading gorgeous, but reluctant women like yourself, into accepting the pleasure that I am able to give them.'

'You mean that you look on bedding women as a method of adding to your trophies.'

'No, I'm not quite as cold as that. I look on it as a mutual exchange of passion and excitement. We both receive pleasure, though I have to say that I get a great deal of satisfaction, seeing the women receive more pleasure that I do. To them, it's an experience they will never forget.'

'Really? I have heard that you have a reputation as a good lover.'

'That is true, and well justified. Many women have boasted that their experience with me has taken them to new heights. Perhaps you should consider experiencing this for yourself?'

'Perhaps I will – one day.'

Suzie was no nearer persuading Pendleton to relax the delivery deadline, but he was open about his intentions in trying to get her into his bed. This could be the one weapon in her favour.

Returning the conversation to the problem of the yacht's delivery, Suzie stated, 'I'm sure that Mike will arrive with your luxury yacht tomorrow afternoon in pristine condition, it's a question of exactly when.'

'My guests will start arriving at eight o'clock in the evening. It will take four or five hours to get the yacht ready and the food and drink aboard. So you see, that if the delivery is late, then I will have to recoup some of my losses and embarrassment by enforcing the late delivery terms of our contract.'

'Surely a few hours won't make that much difference?'

'Possibly not, however my financiers who drew up the contract will expect you to honour your part, or pay the consequences whatever the reason for the delay is.'

'I'm sure they would understand a little leniency on your part, considering the circumstances.'

'They may. I'll tell you what I'll do. As you are such a good friend and business partner, who I do not wish to upset, I'll extend the delivery to two o'clock. How's that?'

'The deadline is for noon, so you're not giving us a lot of leeway. How about making it four o'clock? That would give us a sporting chance to comply, after all Gibraltar is a long way off,' stated Suzie.

She was confident that her early reading of the likely response from Pendleton and her subsequent call to Mike meant that he was already hurrying to complete the repairs, and would be charging his way towards them at the earliest opportunity.

'Okay, Suzie. I'll tell you what I'll do. I'll agree to split the difference and make it three o'clock. Four o'clock would leave me with little time to get things ready for the party should there be a hitch.'

'Okay. I'll agree to three o'clock. That'll give you five hours to get your party ready. I'm sure that should be plenty of time.'

'Done. Three o'clock it is then, and not a minute longer,' Pendleton stated, shaking Suzie's hand to accept the deal.

With the business side of their meeting concluded, Pendleton moved on to asking more personal questions about Suzie. As in their first evening together, Suzie was cagey about giving him too many personal insights into her life. He had to be content mainly with small talk, while learning only a little more about his beautiful guest.

Following a sweet of ice cream topped with nuts and a wafer biscuit they completed their meal, finished the wine and ended with a cup of coffee. Pendleton signed the bill, thanked the head waiter and they headed for the restaurant exit. Eyes still flashed in Suzie's direction, mainly from the men, causing their partners to eye them with slight annoyance at the diversion of their attention. Wandering towards the lift, with Pendleton's arm resting gentle on Suzie's waist to guide her, they rode the car down to the ground floor.

'The hotel has a casino. Before you leave, would you care to take a look?' asked Pendleton, as the lift bumped to a halt and the liftman slid the doors quietly open.

'I'm not a gambler. And anyway, I can't afford to lose the money.'

'I can – up to a point, but I always set my self a target, and a limit that I won't go beyond, though I do like to win and I don't give up easily.'

'So I've noticed,' said Suzie, aware the comment had

connotations other than the gambling Pendleton was referring to.

He grabbed Suzie by the arm and propelled her towards the casino entrance. The doorway was manned by two heavily built guards, ready to deal with any problems that occasionally occur when a punter had lost a lot of money, often because it was more than they could afford to lose. The attraction for someone to make a quick and easy fortune was encouraged, and the hotel advertised that the casino doors were open to anyone who cared to enter. A smartly dressed attendant in an evening suit smiled, and gave a nod to Pendleton and Suzie, and opened the door for them to enter the casino.

The room hummed to the sound of croupiers calling the bets, chips clinking as they were collected and the low murmurs of those watching the tables, quietly discussing the fate of players who were losing heavily and those who were on a normally short-lived winning streak. Cigarette and cigar smoke drifted across the room, waiters hurried to fulfil the drinks orders and occasionally the one-arm bandits rattled as they disgorged their winnings into a noisy tray, to the delighted yells of the mainly female players.

Pendleton collected $1,000 worth of chips and gave Suzie half.

'I can't accept these,' she protested. 'It's far too much.'

'Of course you can. We'll play a little roulette when there's a space available, and we'll see how you get on. It's just a bit of fun. The minimum bet is $10.'

Suzie and Pendleton gained a place at the table and both played inside bets. Pendleton placed 'Line Bets' with an odds payout of 5:1, while Suzie played more cautiously and played 'Straight Up' bets on colours, paying out even money.

Both of them lost their first bets, but then Pendleton won and was in profit. Suzie stuck to her cautious betting, winning some and losing some.

The night wore on, and it was not long before Pendleton's pile of chips had all disappeared, while Suzie still had hers and had gained a few.

'You seem to be doing rather well,' Pendleton confessed.

'That's because I'm a lot more cautious than you, Jeremy.'

'So I've noticed. I like to take chances. It's what puts the spice into life. Don't you take chances sometimes?'

'Yes, sometimes. It depends whether the prize is worth the risk,' stated Suzie, glancing at him.

Pendleton smiled. Suzie was indeed good company, and a good challenge. She lost the next two spins of the wheel and was left with the same amount of chips she had started with. She slid them along the table to Pendleton.

'There you are, Jeremy. We are still even.'

Pendleton put the whole stack on one number and lost the lot.

'That was a bit reckless.'

Pendleton shrugged his shoulders. 'Unlucky in gambling, lucky in … who knows?'

Suzie looked at Pendleton's watch. 'It's time I was in bed.'

'I had similar thoughts,' he said, looking at her with a question written all over his face.

She ignored his veiled remark, pursed her lips to cover a smile, and the pair left the smoke filled gambling casino and headed towards the hotel entrance.

'Are you going to take me up on my offer to let you sleep in the spare bedroom?'

'No, thank you, Jeremy. It's been a lovely evening and I don't want to spoil it by vying with you about which bed I should sleep in. We'll talk about it again tomorrow if Mike doesn't get here on time,' Suzie stated, dangling the prospect of Pendleton fulfilling his wish - a remark that Suzie stated to keep him interested.

'Fair enough. Would you like a lift to the marina?'

'Thank you, but that won't be necessary. It's a beautiful, clear evening and the stars are shining brightly. I'll walk. It might help me to burn off a few of the calories that I've consumed tonight. I'll try and get rid of the rest tomorrow morning on my jog around the harbour.'

'Then, if you'll allow me, I'll walk along with you.'

The pair wandered the few hundred yards along to the marina.

'I must say Suzie that you do look stunning tonight. All the men's eyes were on you and I felt a wave of jealousy coming from them … and the women they were with.'

'Thank you. I enjoyed the meal, Jeremy.'

'I hope we'll be able to do it again soon,' he proffered.

Suzie's dark green eyes met his. 'Perhaps.'

He smiled.

They boarded *Quester*. Pendleton's men had cleared up the mess and departed, leaving one man on guard. He approached them.

'I think you'll find that everything is shipshape and in order now,' he stated, 'though some of the drawers and cupboards that were locked, were smashed open and will need replacing.

'Okay. Thank you very much,' smiled Suzie.

'The chief of police came aboard and personally brought your guns back. The handgun is unloaded, he left it on the table along with the shells,' he said, nodding his goodnight and leaving. Pendleton watched him step ashore, and then turned to Suzie.

'I'll see you tomorrow,' he said. 'About a quarter to three?'

Suzie gave Pendleton a kiss on the cheek. 'About a quarter to three,' she confirmed.

Henry was already waiting with the Rolls Royce passenger door open when Pendleton turned to leave. Suzie returned his wave and entered the cabin. She had a lot to tell Mike on the radio before she settled down for the night. Tomorrow could be a tense and exciting day, for more than one reason.

13

THE SEARCH

Suspicion had fallen on Mrs Boyd being an accomplice to the building society robbery where she worked. Kelly's fingerprints had been found in her bedroom, and her fingerprints had been found on a cup in his flat along with a note of her telephone number. This proved that they had met previous to the attempted robbery and gave rise to the idea they were working together, despite Kelly's attempts to keep Mrs Boyd's name out of the investigation.

At the same time, by correctly picking out the Liverpool arms dealer at the booking-in desk from the airline security video, Kelly had left his arresting officers with a problem. If Owen Sutton, or Oliver Statham as he called himself, was the man who supplied the weapon that killed the Irish politician Murphy O'Connor, then the police would be very anxious to question him. Their suspect had left the country on a flight to Nairobi, which made finding and questioning him almost impossible until he returned to England either voluntarily or in police custody.

DI Brooke, along with his two DC's and DI Rollinson returned to the inspector's office to assess this new piece of information.

'The first thing we need to do, is find out if Sutton has stayed in Nairobi or if he's taken a flight on to somewhere else,' suggested Brooke.

Rollinson nodded, lifted his telephone and pressed a button. 'Jake, see if you can find out if Sutton was booked on another flight when he reached Nairobi will you?'

'I think we can safely say that Kelly is not our political assassin,' ventured Brooke. Heads nodded in agreement. 'So, there's nothing more we can do here in connection with O'Connor's murder. I can pursue that matter back in London.'

Rollinson nodded his agreement.

Brooke added, 'I'll leave you to deal with the problem of Kelly and his botched attempt at robbery and murder. Now we've established that Mrs Boyd was a party to the robbery, I think you'll find that she was the one who gave Sutton's name to Kelly. You could try pressing her into telling you how she obtained that information.'

'Good idea, I will.'

'Let me know if you get any success there, or any further news on Sutton or his whereabouts. If you do, and you need more manpower, one of my DC's can return to help you.'

Rising to his feet, Rollinson extended his hand. 'Many thanks. I'm sorry that you've had a wasted journey,' he said, shaking Brooke's hand.

'Not at all. We've made good progress and can eliminate Kelly from our list of suspects, and we've now got hold of the murder weapon. The boys in our lab will make further checks on the gun to see if it holds any other clues. Tracking down Sutton is our priority now.'

Brooke and his team drove back to London. DC's Green and Teal returned to their office to check for any important messages left during the day, and with nothing that needed their immediate attention, they both went home. Brooke drove to Whitehall to report his findings to Sir Joseph, knowing that he rarely left his office much before seven o'clock each evening. Sir Joseph's secretary, Miss Wilson, had already finished for the day, so Brooke knocked on his door and was invited in to his office, where they discussed the case.

'If Sutton supplied the weapon, and it looks likely, then we are one step nearer to finding the assassin,' Sir Joseph suggested. 'The PM is keen to get a result on this. Anglo-Irish relations could benefit a lot if we can bring Mr O'Connor's murderer to justice.'

'The Chatham Police will inform me if any new leads turn up, and I'll make my own inquiries to try and locate him.'

'Good work, Colin.'

'If he did supply the gun to the assassin, or took it off him afterwards, do you think he's likely to tell us who that is?' questioned Brooke.

'Normally no, but if we can put pressure on Mrs Boyd to confirm that she gave Mr Kelly his telephone number in order for him to purchase the gun, then we can also implement him in the shooting of the building society teller.'

'Yes, that would be quite a good lever for us to get him to talk.'

'Exactly. I'll get Miss Wilson to contact Europol and Interpol tomorrow to see if they've got any further information on him.'

'Meanwhile, I'll be doing my own checks on Owen Sutton. I've asked the Liverpool police to send me copies of everything they've got on him.'

'Let me know how you get on, Colin.'

Brooke left Whitehall and drove home, immersed in thoughts about Sutton, Kelly and Mrs Boyd, wondering what the connection between them all was. Perhaps the Chatham Police would come up with some answers soon.

As a bachelor living on his own, when Colin Brooke reached his two bedroom mid-terrace house, he rummaged through the freezer to find something to cook for his dinner. He always kept a few ready-made meals there to microwave for his evening meal whenever he reached home late, which was much of the time. After the meal, he settled down to watch television, flipped through the channels and found nothing that interested him. He decided to do half an hour of exercises instead, followed by a shower and bed. He tried to settle down, but found thoughts about Mrs Boyd, Sutton and Kelly buzzing around his head. He tossed and turned until tiredness finally overtook him and he closed his eyes.

★ ★ ★

By the time that Brooke reached his office at Special Branch HQ in London the following morning, he found a message on his desk asking him to ring DI Rollinson.

'Good morning, Inspector. What news do you have for me?'

'We've managed to ascertain that Sutton took a flight on to Roseburgh, the capital of Karuna. It's a small central African country,' Rollinson stated.

'Yes, I know of it. I believe there's still a lot of unrest quite close to that area in the neighbouring country of Kitsulana, which is probably why Sutton has gone there. I imagine that weapons are in constant demand in that locality. It's an ideal situation for an arms dealer to make a lot of money.'

'And locating him to talk about Kelly's murder weapon is nigh-on impossible.'

'You're probably right.'

'I'll let you know if we hear any more,' promised Rollinson.

'Thanks,' said Brooke, replacing the receiver.

He recalled a previous operation in that area in which Sir Joseph was involved, and decided to contact him and get his reaction to the news. He rang the Whitehall office and was put through by Miss Wilson.

'Roseburgh! That's still a very volatile piece of Africa,' Sir Joseph declared. 'I'm sure you recall that Mike Randle and Suzie Drake had a tussle with The General, who tried to take over the neighbouring country Kitsulana with his rebel army only a few years ago.'

'Yes, though I seem to recall that at the time, I was busy dealing with another arms dealer and a gang of crooks who were shooting at each other.'

'That's right, and Jim was caught in the middle of all that.'

'Did things settle down in Kitsulana afterwards?'

'No, not for long. Members of the rebel army were scattered about, but soon got together again when there was no improvement in the running of the country, not quickly enough anyway – too much corruption in high places in my opinion. Other men took over as leaders, and are now fighting among themselves and the government forces for power. Nothing much has changed there I'm sorry to say.'

'Ideal territory for an arms dealer I would imagine. If Sutton remains in the area, it will be difficult to find him,' confessed Brooke.

'Almost impossible, especially if he's travelled into Kitsulana. If he's supplying guns to the rebels, they will want to protect their source of armaments.'

'Your daughter-in-law Jenny was an operative out there for a while, wasn't she?'

'She was, before she and Jim were married. She supplied us with good intelligence, though I'm not too sure what methods she used to obtain some of it, and frankly would rather not know.'

'Yes, I understand. Do you still have anyone in the area keeping us informed of the situation there?' asked Brooke.

'That sort of knowledge is strictly limited to those who need to know in order to keep it secure. However, I can confirm that we do not have anyone from the department there, but we have maintained contact with a local who occasionally passes on information to us,' Sir Joseph acknowledged.

'Can you find out if they've heard anything about Sutton?'

'I can ask. I'll also contact Mr Robert Weston at our embassy in Karuna, and see if he can provide any news. I'll give you a ring if I hear anything.'

Brooke returned the telephone to its cradle and continued to scrutinise the information he had received from the Liverpool Police about Sutton, while Sir Joseph started his own enquiries into Sutton's whereabouts.

Later that morning, Brooke had a further conversation with DI Rollinson and quickly passed the information on to Sir Joseph.

'I've just had a very interesting call from DI Rollinson of the Chatham Police. Because of the attempted robbery of Nelson's Building Society last Friday by Kelly, the auditors were called in to check the accounts. Although nothing was stolen during the attempted robbery, they've discovered that a considerable amount of money is missing.'

'So, the plot thickens.'

'Yes, and what's more, the dates that the money disappeared tie in with Mrs Boyd's part-time employment there. When she was confronted with this information, she admitted that she enticed Kelly to attempt the robbery in order to cover up those losses.'

'That at least gives us a motive for the robbery, and is an admission that definitely ties Mrs Boyd in with the attempt.'

'Yes, and there's more. Mrs Boyd also stated that she told Kelly about it, and mentioned that her other teller, Mr Wainwright, had found out about her pilfering and was blackmailing her. She suggests this may be why Kelly shot him.'

'Hmm, interesting. But it still doesn't explain how Mrs Boyd knew about Owen Sutton's telephone number, to give to Mr Kelly so he could receive the gun. Has Mr Kelly been questioned about this blackmailing suggestion?'

'No, not yet. He's probably finding out about it as we speak. DI Rollinson will give me another ring when the interview has finished and apprise me of the details.'

'Has he any idea where Mrs Boyd got Mr Sutton's contact number from?'

'No, I don't think so. That will be put to her this afternoon, after they've spoken to Kelly. DI Rollinson is being very cagey about how he conducts the interviews. He listens to what one of them is saying and then questioning the other to confirm it, which is gaining him more information that he can return to the first one with. He's playing them against each other, and slowly teasing the facts out.'

'Good. The loose ends in this case seem to be coming together nicely. Let's hope we have some luck and get the information we need to catch up with Mr Sutton.'

Shortly after lunch, Brooke was working his way through the paperwork he had received from the Liverpool Police without gaining much new information, when his telephone rang. On the other end of the line was DI Rollinson once more.

'Kelly denies knowing anything about Wainwright blackmailing Mrs Boyd. He seems to be getting disenchanted with her, which is good news for us. He is at last, starting to realise that she is using him for her own ends and is quite happy to shift the blame on to him and will let him rot in prison.'

'That should help us to get to the truth,' suggested Brooke.

'Yes, I agree. We are slowly prising all the details out of both of them.'

'Good work, Inspector. Keep me informed of your progress.'

No sooner had Brooke completed his call, than the telephone rang again. This time it was Sir Joseph.

'Colin, I've just spoken with Robert Weston, our embassy man in Roseburgh, and received some interesting news about our Mr Sutton.'

'Good news?'

'Difficult to say. I gather that when he arrived in Roseburgh on Sunday, he was arrested by the police at the request of the army.'

'The army! Why, what on earth's he been doing, trying to sell guns in Karuna?'

'Nothing's clear at the moment and nothing has been confirmed yet, but I am hearing stories that about a dozen men who flew into Roseburgh today have also been detained. Something to do with being mercenaries and an attempted coup it seems.'

'Surely not in Karuna itself?'

'No, in neighbouring Kitsulana I believe. It appears that government sources there found out about the coup and asked the Roseburgh authorities to intervene and arrest the men at the airport before they got the chance to disperse into their country.'

'Hmm. Maybe we could get Sutton back after all. Could we have him extradited?'

'That might be difficult. However, if it turns out to be correct that he's been arrested, there's nothing to stop me enquiring about having him flown back to England for questioning about the sale of the gun and the shooting.'

'True.'

'The problem is that we've still got no proof that he's involved with selling guns in this country, other than the word of a man who's an ex-jailbird, and is in custody for attempted robbery and attempted murder. Getting an extradition granted will be difficult.'

'Yes, I see what you mean. So what do you think are our chances?'

'I'd say doubtful, but there's no harm in me trying. This country sends a lot of money to the government in Karuna in aid, so it is a possibility that they won't want to upset us too much. I'll use that as a lever and let you know how I get on.'

While Brooke gathered more information on Sutton, Sir Joseph Sterling asked Weston to make enquiries about the arrests. Later that afternoon, after receiving confirmation that the rumours were true, he contacted Brooke.

'Mr Sutton and twelve other men have been arrested under terrorism laws. The men were charged with attempting to overthrow the government of Kitsulana, and Owen Sutton is charged with financing the coup and being the weapons supplier.'

'So, can we get him brought back?'

'Not a chance. The men were handed over to the president of Kitsulana, who has had them transferred to one of his prisons after parading them on local television. He's promised his people that all of them will be dealt with as terrorists. They face a long time in prison or could possibly even face the firing squad or be hung. It will be headline news on the television tonight.'

'So much for getting any information out of Sutton. Isn't there anything we can do?'

'Mr Robert Weston is the nearest diplomat at our embassy in Roseburgh, but there's nobody in Kitsulana. No country has an embassy there at the moment while there's fighting still going on. I've sent him a message and asked him to clarify the position with the president if he can, but I wouldn't hold out much hope if I were you.'

Brooke sucked in a lungful of air in a resigned gesture. 'Right. I've done some checking on our Mr Sutton. He's an elusive character with numerous aliases and it's taken me a while to track them down. However, I have been able to determine that he amassed, and then lost, quite a lot of money from his arms activities. He financed a coup in another small African country last year, but lost all his money when many of the rebels defected to the government side after they were given big promises. The rest of them were defeated and the arms seized. I can't see how Sutton was expecting to finance this coup, and he certainly doesn't seem to have enough ready cash to buy his way out of trouble.'

'That won't stop him, I'm sure he'll try. It's common knowledge that Kitsulana's President Mr Gorringa, likes his wealth. Much of the aid to his country seems to go straight into his pocket. He lives in a palace by all accounts, has several expensive cars, numerous wives and dozens of servants.'

'How democratic is the republic?'

'Not very. Mr Gorringa was once a rebel fighter and pronounced himself as President after The General was no longer a threat. There was an election of sorts a year later, and he won that comfortably, which is not really surprising as he was the only candidate allowed to stand. All opposition candidates either ended up dead, backed out of the election or disappeared and were never seen again.'

'In that case, I'll put the job on hold. It doesn't look as if I can get any further at the moment.'

'Okay, Colin. I'll let you know if anything changes.'

Brooke gathered up all the papers on the case and jammed them into a folder, which he dumped into a tray marked 'Pending' on his desk. With a soulful look at the 'In' tray, he turned his attention to one of the many other cases that were piling up in front of him.

14

DEADLINE

Following an evening with Jeremy Pendleton in the restaurant and gambling casino, and verbally sparring with him about the delivery of his yacht and the consequences if he activated the late delivery clause, Suzie returned to *Quester* to sleep in her own bed, much to Pendleton's disappointment. After a good nights sleep, Suzie rang Mike the moment she awoke. He answered the call and yawned.

'Good morning, sleepyhead.'

'Good morning, Miss Drake. I've been up for hours. It's time for you to get up,' he said, sounding in a joyful mood.

'I am up – well at least I'm awake.'

'And dressed?'

'No, not yet.'

'Ahh, I can picture you now, naked under a thin sheet, barely covering your …'

'Down boy. Fun later, after you get here,' interrupted Suzie.

'And are you alone?'

'Of course I am, though I had a lovely meal last night with Jeremy, before he took me into the casino.'

'Did he now?'

'Yes, and while he lost all his money, I won some and lost some, and ended up even.'

'No doubt he's still trying to get you into his bed?'

'He is, but so far he hasn't succeeded.'

'Hmm, I'm not sure that I like the words, so far.'

'It may depend on how long it takes you to get here, whether I can still say that tomorrow.'

'Enough of this serious talk. How are we this lovely, bright sunny Tuesday morning? It is Tuesday, isn't it?' Mike joked.

'It is – I think. Well anyway, whatever day it is, it's D-Day for us – delivery day. So, more to the point is, how are you doing?'

'I'm doing fine. The yacht repairs are finished and Reg, George and I are heading your way as fast as the engines will take us.'

'Good. And how fast is that? What time do you expect to arrive?'

'It's difficult to give you an exact time, but I would think between six and seven this evening.'

'What! Between six and seven! Do you realise how long that means I'll have to try and keep Jeremy Pendleton entertained to stop him activating that late clause in our contract?'

'Only kidding, Suzie! By my reckoning, we should get there about half past four.'

'You rotten bugger! You wait 'til I get hold of you.'

'Hmm, I'm looking forward to that.'

A smile crossed Suzie's lovely face, but she was determined not to let Mike know that she saw the funny side of his joke.

'I managed to get him to extend the deadline to three o'clock, but no later, so it still means that I'll have to keep him occupied for an hour or more.'

'That's good news. Well done! However, knowing his infatuation with you, I don't imagine that you'll find keeping him occupied very difficult. Just spare me the details of how you manage it.'

'You know there is only one man in my life that matters to me.'

'Oh yes, and who's that,' Mike joked.

'Be serious. I'll keep Pendleton at bay for as long as I can, but he seems determined not to let his financiers or business partners see him weaken and give in. In the end it may take more than words to persuade him to allow us more time.'

Mike's tone changed to one of reflecting the seriousness of the situation. 'I realise that. If that happens, then you'll have to use whatever charms you think are necessary to stop him. We can't afford a delay on the final payment and have an enormous bill dropped on us for late delivery.'

'We all realise that, including Jeremy Pendleton.'

'We'll get there as quickly as possible. I can't do more than that.'

'I know you will. Don't forget to ring me the moment you enter the marina.'

'I won't forget.'

After dressing in shorts and a T-shirt, Suzie took a gentle jog around the marina in the early morning sun, which was warm enough to make her perspire. She enjoyed her early morning jogs along the beach at home and missed not being able to take them in the same way. She was used to a quiet, undisturbed jog on an empty beach with only Mike for company, trailing behind as usual and being prompted to make a better effort. Here, there were many people taking an early morning stroll or booking their spot on the beach before it became too crowded. She received stares and wolf whistles on her run, from numerous locals who were out and about, cleaning the beach and pavements to maintain the area's reputation and keep the high paying guests happy.

On her return to *Quester*, Suzie had a shower and ate a light breakfast. Although her clothes had been cleaned and she had washed her knickers, T-shirt and shorts to wear on the jog, she still felt as if they were soiled after being sorted through and scattered everywhere by the police. To overcome this, Suzie decided it was time she had some new items to add to her wardrobe, and it gave her a good excuse to take a look at what the local shops had to offer.

With her designer sunglasses perched on her button nose and her credit card at the ready, she wandered down the Rue d'Antibes, taking in the vast array of perfumeries, jewellers, florists, confectioners and ready-to-wear boutiques and shops. After trying on numerous T-shirts, blouses, shorts and several complete outfits, the price of which she considered outrageous and could only be presented in an upmarket location like Cannes, Suzie made her choices. She also purchased an additional chiffon, almost see-through, blouse with Jeremy Pendleton and her afternoon meeting in mind.

A return to the marina in a taxi was the order of the day, with Suzie carrying more shopping bags than she was happy to struggle along with. After putting her clothes aboard *Quester* she went out to lunch in a small restaurant near the end of the marina. While she ate her light lunch of a plain omelette and salad with a glass of orange juice, she mentally prepared herself for the meeting with Jeremy Pendleton. Viewing their appointment in the same way as she would an important business meeting, Suzie was conscience of the need to prepare first, and had the added knowledge of having been in similar circumstances with Pendleton before. She was determined to approach the encounter by being prepared to consider whatever it took to get the result she and everyone who worked at SMJ Boatyard wanted. When her lunch was over, Suzie returned to *Quester* to shower and change.

For her visit to Pendleton, she wore white skimpy shorts, her pale pink wispy chiffon top with no bra, and white trainers. Suzie's trim, athletic figure and pert breasts were firm enough for her to discard her bra while still retaining her model like figure. Her all over suntan, gained by her topless sunbathing at every opportunity, added good looks to the natural beauty that she already possessed.

Suzie left the top four buttons on her blouse undone, showing any fortunate onlooker an enticing sight of her cleavage, along with a faint outline of her nipples that protruded, massaged by the gentle motion of her blouse as she glided along. Suzie was ready to meet Jeremy Pendleton and send his pulse racing.

With a glance at the wall clock, which showed the time to be nearly half past two, Suzie contacted Mike on the radio. 'How are you doing?'

'We're doing quite well. The lads are getting as much out of the engines as they can. I reckon we're about fifty kilometres away, but there's a bit of a headwind today. That'll slow us up a bit.'

'How much is a bit? What time do you now expect to arrive?'

'We ought to make it by about half past four still.'

'You can't make it any sooner then?'

'Doubtful, but we'll try. We're squeezing ever ounce of speed out of her that we can. I don't want to blow up the engines. That would be a real disaster at this time.'

'Yes, it would. I'm about to see Jeremy Pendleton again to try and persuade him to extend the three o'clock deadline.'

'Okay. Good luck. Take care.'

'Yeah, I will. See you soon.'

With their conversation over, Suzie collected her mobile phone, shoved it into her pocket and patted it. 'I hope you don't take too long to ring,' she murmured to herself.

Jumping ashore, she walked past the vast array of luxury yachts moored in the marina and strolled along the crowded, sunlit avenue to *The Metropolitan Hotel*. She gathered admiring glances and smiles from each of the men she passed – something she had become accustomed to since the day she turned into an attractive teenager.

In contrast to the outside noise and heat, the lobby of the hotel was cool and quiet. The doorman smiled and saluted to her as she entered the hotel. Suzie padded across to the lift and rode it to the twelfth floor. Stepping slowly along the luxuriously carpeted corridor, she stood outside the door to suite 1205 and looked at her watch – it was exactly a quarter to three. She took a deep breath and knocked twice.

Opening the door, Jeremy Pendleton's eyes lit up the moment he saw Suzie in her revealing top. He motioned her to enter the room.

'I've taken the liberty of ordering champagne, Suzie. I hope that is all right with you?'

'What's the celebration for?' she asked, wandering into the room and noting that Pendleton's bedroom door was wide open.

'Delivery of my yacht or …' he left any further comment unfinished.

Suzie could see his king-size bed was turned down and two dressing gowns were laid on the bed in readiness.

'Expecting company?' she asked.

'No, only you,' he replied.

Pendleton popped the cork on the champagne bottle and poured two glasses. He handed one to Suzie. 'Here's to a successful afternoon,' he pronounced.

'Successful for whom?'

'For both of us. I receive what I've been after for a long time and you get the second half of your payment to keep your business alive.'

Suzie was well aware of all the double meanings that Pendleton's rhetoric was full of. 'What makes you think we are that desperate for the money?'

'My financial advisers have kept an eye on your business; purely for professional reasons of course.'

'Of course.'

'We couldn't afford for your company to go bust and not be able to complete the order for my yacht. So, I know that your business is ticking over but not making a lot of profit at the moment. A delay in payment would make things difficult for you, and a delay coupled with a late delivery fine, could even sink your business.'

'As usual, you seem to have done your homework, Jeremy.'

'It's what keeps me one step ahead in business.'

Suzie wandered over to the window and glanced down at the sandy beach, crowded with guests and tourists alike, sunning themselves to get that rich 'we've been to the south of France' suntan. Further along was the marina with its scores of expensive yachts and motor yachts lined up side by side, vying for the attention of those whose pockets could not stretch to owning such a luxury. Instead, they loved to gaze at the rows of luxury vessels and dream of winning vast sums of money in order to purchase their own yacht and join the millionaire set lazing in the sun. Many yachts had owners and guests aboard, to show off their luxury toys, with drinks, nibbles and endless chatting that had no real interest for either party and was only intended to boost their egos. Suzie looked towards the marina entrance and wondered how long it would be before Mike sailed through to her rescue.

Pendleton approached her. 'It's a wonderful view, isn't it, Suzie?'

'Yes, it is.'

'Can you see that gap over there,' he pointed.

'I can.'

'That's my berth and where my yacht should be moored, right now.'

'You should blame Giles Harman for your empty berth. I appreciate you giving us more time Jeremy, but you have to admit, the circumstances of your vessel's late arrival are unusual to say the least, and totally out of our control.'

'Unless one could accuse you of not taking sufficient care to see the yacht was kept more secure?'

'That's a bit harsh. We had two men patrolling the boatyard every night, and they were killed, in case you'd forgotten,' stated Suzie in an admonishing tone, taking a sip of her champagne.

'No, I hadn't forgotten.'

'Normally, one would expect that to be sufficient to safeguard the yacht.'

'Yes, I agree all that, but ...'

'Business is business,' finished Suzie.

'That's quite right, and I have been more generous with you, than with any other business associate I've dealt with in the past.'

'I realise that and I'm very grateful. I'm sure your circle of rich close friends would frown at you sinking a small business such as ours, considering the circumstances and our response.'

'Very eloquently put, Suzie. I particularly like the inference that my friends would disapprove. That's a good ploy to tug at my conscience. The problem is ... I don't have a conscience. Not about business anyway, and even if my friends did disapprove, they wouldn't say so; not to my face. Business can sometimes be hard, and we all have to face the consequences of difficult times even if it may seem a little unjust.'

'That may be the way you do business, Jeremy, but it's not the way I would behave. I do have a conscience, and it wouldn't let me ruin someone's livelihood after they'd made a great effort to correct things, especially if I counted them as friends.'

'That's the difference between us I suppose. I can separate business from friendship, and business always comes first. Friends I can gather by the dozen.'

'With all your money I'm sure that you can, but how many of them are true friends?'

Pendleton shrugged, he looked at his watch. 'It's a few minutes to three o'clock. Is Mike going to make it in time?' he asked, glancing at the marina entrance.

'Possibly not, but he's charging here as quickly as he can. Let's wait and see, shall we? There's still a little time left.'

The minutes ticked by. Pendleton constantly checked his watch and peered at the marina entrance.

'Well, Suzie, it's past three o'clock now and there's still no sight of my yacht. I'm sorry, but I'll have to exercise my rights and ring the accountants. They will set the wheels in motion,' Pendleton said, moving towards the telephone.

He grasped the receiver. Before he could lift it, Suzie put her hand on top of his and undid the bottom few buttons on her blouse, allowing it to drift open.

'Surely there is some way that I can persuade you to delay making your call?' she asked.

Pendleton pulled her blouse open wide to see the full beauty of Suzie's statuesque body, a sight he had glimpsed before, but had failed to get his hands on.

'I suppose that a short delay in making the call won't be catastrophic,' he declared.

'Perhaps we should adjourn to your bedroom and reassess our business values.'

'I'm sure that a reappraisal of our assets and how to make best use of them would be an advantage to both of us.'

'In other words, if I go to bed with you, you'll delay making your telephone call?'

'Yes, that's right. The decision is yours, Suzie. What's it to be?' he asked, lifting the receiver.

She answered his question by kicking off her trainers, slowly stepping towards his bedroom, stopping to glance at him as she removed her blouse before disappearing into the bedroom. He gazed at her naked back as she vanished from his sight. She looked so enticing wearing only shorts. Pendleton replaced the receiver and followed, with a hint of a smirk on his lips, first picking up her blouse from the floor. He followed her into the bedroom and picked up her shorts and lastly her knickers.

Suzie was reclining beneath the single, red silk sheet on the bed, which clung to her body revealing the nakedness of her outline.

She placed her mobile telephone on the bedside table.

Pendleton looked at it. 'I hope that thing is not going to ring again in the nick of time.'

'This time I think it's doubtful. I can safely say that it's unlikely to ring for quite a while yet.'

'If it takes far too long before it rings, you could lose out both ways.'

'What makes you think that I consider sleeping with you as losing out?'

'Well, you have been avoiding this moment,' he declared, unbuttoning his shirt and removing it.

'Avoiding? Not necessarily. Let's simply say that I've been delaying it until the right moment arrived.'

'And this is the right moment?' Pendleton asked, stepping from his trousers and shorts, slipping beneath the sheet to press his body next to Suzie's.

'Yes, this seems to be the right moment.'

15

DELAY

Because the delivery deadline had passed and Mike had not yet arrived in Cannes with Jeremy Pendleton's yacht, Suzie had the task of trying to delay him from making a telephone call to his accountants asking them to activate a late delivery clause. Sharing his bed was a last resort, but was the one tactic she knew he was unable to resist.

Having at last achieved his initial quest to get Suzie Drake into his bed, Jeremy Pendleton pulled the sheet back to gaze at her naked body.

'You do have a wonderful figure,' he maintained, moving across to grasp one breast.

He put his lips over her other nipple and gently sucked, teasing the nipple to full protrusion, before moving across to repeat the act on Suzie's other nipple.

'Your nipples protrude a long way. That's a sign of a sexy woman and one that all men like to see,' he proclaimed.

'I had noticed the stares,' she admitted.

Pendleton continued to kiss and pet her, quickly becoming bold himself. He rolled over on top of Suzie and prepared to penetrate her, but was surprised by Suzie's strength, rolling him back and climbing on top of him.

'Not so fast, lover boy,' she said.

Pendleton was anxious to make sure that he was not interrupted by Suzie's mobile telephone, sitting ominously close by. It thwarted him on his first attempt to get Suzie into his bed and he was determined not to miss out again, and was prepared to hurry the start of his lovemaking with her. Time was what Suzie needed to gain, and had to prevent Pendleton from taking what he wanted and satisfying his sexual urges too quickly. She was unsure how long it would take Mike to reach them with his yacht, but knew that it could be an hour or more. She needed to prolong their time in bed together for as long as she could.

Suzie pinned Pendleton to the bed, grasped his member and began stroking him. He enjoyed her touch, grabbed a breast in each hand and started squirming with delight before trying to pull her away from him. She resisted, slid down his body and put his member in her mouth. Suzie began to massage him with hand and mouth slowly, watching the excitement grow within him. He spread his arms wide on the bed, arched his back and uttered groans of enjoyment in response to the glorious feelings that his body was sensing. Pendleton wanted desperately to penetrate her, but Suzie held him at bay and forced him to accept her control of the encounter. His breathing became faster and his groans of ecstasy louder. Suzie relaxed her massaging and put her thumb over the top of his member, holding on tightly. Pendleton almost reached a climax; he got so close, but felt cheated that he had not received the pleasure that ejaculation would bring him. His ardour calmed down and his body relaxed the excitement that had built up within him.

Before the ardour diminished in him too much, Suzie again massaged him with her mouth and brought him back to full boldness and heightened expectations. She squeezed his member between her breasts and continued massaging him as he watched her actions, exciting him even more. His breathing became faster and faster; he took short, sharp breaths until finally his pelvis thrust forward in small jerks as he reached the climax he sought and ejaculated, releasing groans of enjoyment and satisfaction.

Suzie rested beside him and both remained still and quiet for a few moments, allowing Pendleton's heart to return to its normal rate. Suzie knew that he would want more than an oral encounter and would not be satisfied until he had entered her in the traditional male way. She also knew that it would take Pendleton a while to recover before he would be able to respond again to achieve his goal, and this would buy her valuable time.

'You are a very clever woman, Suzie,' he declared.

She looked at him with a question written on her face.

'You know exactly what I mean. Even in bed, your clever delaying tactics are designed to give you more time.'

'I'm a business woman,' she declared, with a rye grin on her face. 'And business is business.'

Pendleton smiled. 'Touché.'

'You have not enjoyed our time in bed together?' she questioned.

'Of course I have. Seeing and touching you is a pleasure, but that episode was only the starter, I want to enjoy the main course and I am concerned that your mobile may interrupt us again and prevent that once more.'

'That's a gamble you'll have to take. You like gambling, don't you, Jeremy?'

'I like gambling when I have a good chance to control the stakes. With you, I have to accept what you are willing to let me take.'

'I'm not letting you take anything – I'm giving it to you of my own free will. I don't have to share this bed with you.'

'But you are.'

'Because it's my decision to be here, not yours.'

'Then I am pleased that you have decided to make, what to me is the right decision. Is it based totally on the circumstances?'

'Not totally,' admitted Suzie.

Pendleton smiled. He was pleased at that comment. To him it meant that she acknowledged his charms, good looks and reputation with women, and sharing his bed was not purely for business reasons.

Suzie glanced at the clock on her mobile. It showed the time as twenty to four. Mike could still be nearly an hour away. She was willing her mobile to ring, but it sat on the bedside table and remained ominously silent.

Pendleton began kissing and petting Suzie again. She responded, needing to keep him happy and interested. After a few minutes he started to show signs of his renewed energy and gradually became bold again.

This time he allowed Suzie to push him on to his back and she straddled him. He wanted to enter her straight away, but she made him wait. She pinned him down and put her left breast into his mouth. He kissed, sucked and licked his tongue around her nipple bringing it back to full protrusion. She then transferred her right breast to his mouth. He repeated the process, pleasuring them both and increasing the desires in him. Pendleton entwined his arms around her smooth body, pulling her breasts into his face and nuzzled them. He had waited a long time to get Suzie into his clutches, and was determined to enjoy every minute of his conquest.

Suzie pulled away, opened her legs, slid down his torso and impaled herself on his member. Pendleton gave an audible cry of pleasure as he entered her, his goal at long last had been achieved; now he needed to extract the glorious pleasure the union could bring him.

Despite his almost overwhelming urge to thrust straight away, Suzie prevented him from making any movement by squeezing him tightly with her legs. She kept him still, allowing him no room to move. She rested her head on his chest and he ran his hands down her back and over her small firm backside, clasping each cheek and pulling her on to him a little deeper, wriggling to try and gain what movement he could. Even with the lack of movement, the excitement and anticipation grew in both of them, increasing his hardness.

Pendleton ran his fingers up and down Suzie's spine, creating an enjoyable tingling sensation for her. He kissed her in the ear and inserted his tongue, which sent more shivers of ecstasy through her. She could feel his boldness growing harder within her as they both remained still, with a warm glow of enjoyment increasing in intensity as it encompassed them. Expectations of an ecstatic climax heightened as they came closer and closer to the point of no return.

Pendleton began groaning again and arched his back. Suzie clung on tightly to him as the culmination of their union became unstoppable, and in a final burst of action, Suzie released her grip and Pendleton thrust in and out with great voracity as they both cried out with a final yell. She could feel the bursts of throbs within her when the final moments of their sexual explorations exploded into the heady feelings of euphoria, and Pendleton reached his climactic finish with spurt after spurt until it seemed, he had nothing left in him and he collapsed on the bed.

Both felt drained of energy and remained motionless, with Suzie still lying on top of him.

After a few minutes Pendleton spoke. 'That, Miss Drake, was the best sex I've had in the last twenty-five years. Not since my father gave me a sixteenth birthday present of an evening with an experienced woman who was twice my age, have I enjoyed myself so much with a female in bed.'

'I'll take that as a compliment then.'

'Please do. Mike is a very lucky man to have you as his partner. I trust that you found the practical demonstration of the reappraisal of our assets to your satisfaction, and that I didn't disappoint you.'

'You didn't, though I have to say that sex with Mike is better.'

'That's merely because, over time he has learnt what your sexual fantasies are, and what turns you on.'

'That's certainly a part of it.'

'Now, if I got the opportunity to find out what your sexual turn-ons are, then we could have even more fantastic sex. What do you say?'

'This encounter came about because of exceptional circumstances, and is not likely to be repeated very soon,' she informed him, rolling on to the bed beside him, the sheet covering only her lower half.

Pendleton noticed that Suzie did not entirely rule out another occasion. 'Surely there must be some other way that I can entice you?' he asked, gazing at her firm pert breasts.

'Buying another luxury motor yacht from our boatyard perhaps, assuming that in the meantime we have not been bankrupted?'

Pendleton laughed. 'You are a special lady, and this has been a fabulous encounter for me and is something I'd like to experience again. If I don't get another opportunity soon, I can at least treasure the memory of this afternoon's exquisite union.'

'I'm pleased that you'll be able to dream about today.'

'I will be judging all my other activities against yours now, and if past experience is anything to go by, I know they will not come up to your standards.'

'Then you'll have to keep looking for someone who does – won't you?'

Pendleton looked at his watch. 'It's nearly twenty past four. I was enjoying myself so much that I almost lost track of time and the real reason we are both here this afternoon. You've managed to delay me with your wonderfully sexy tactics for more than an hour and a quarter.'

'Doesn't time fly when you're having fun?'

Rising from his bed, Pendleton donned his white towelling dressing gown. 'I'm very sorry about this, but I have to make alternative arrangements for my guests. Of course, that means enforcing the late delivery clause in our contract – as agreed.'

'Can't you wait another fifteen minutes? Surely that won't hurt?'

'I'm afraid not. You've taken a lot more time than I'd planned for already. If your business collapses and you find yourself without a job, I'm sure that I could find you something appropriate within my organisation.'

'I bet you could,' said Suzie. 'But, no thanks. I won't be requiring another job, I've already got one as co-director of SMJ Boatyard Ltd. That's not going to change,' she informed, knowing that she and Mike still had some diamonds left to sell, which they had acquired on a mission a few years previously. They had sold them over the past few years to build up their business, and disposed of them a few at a time in order not to attract too much attention.

'So be it,' said Pendleton.

He padded over to the window, looked down at the empty berth where his yacht should be tie up and took a last look at Suzie sitting up in the bed. He lifted the receiver, and had prodded the first few buttons on his telephone when Suzie's mobile rang. With a finger hovering over the last button, he delayed starting his call as she snatched up her phone and pressed the receive button.

'Mike, yes, great! I'll be down to meet you in five minutes. The empty berth four yachts past *Quester* is where you should berth Jeremy's yacht.'

Suzie looked at Pendleton. 'Your yacht is here and ready for you to take delivery,' she gleefully reported, jumping out of bed. She wandered over to the window and stared at the marina entrance, and saw nothing.'

'So where is my yacht? Has Mike rung you from miles away just to try preventing me from making that call?'

Around the marina entrance Pendleton's yacht sailed into view.

'There's your yacht, Jeremy,' Suzie pointed as it sailed into the marina, 'and it's only slightly late.'

A smile crossed Pendleton's face as he pressed the button to cancel his telephone call, and pressed a different set of buttons.

On board the yacht, Mike put his binoculars to his eyes and scanned the hotel. At the twelfth floor window he caught a glimpse of Jeremy Pendleton standing at the window making his telephone call. Appearing next to him was Suzie, naked. A feeling of jealousy engulfed him, seeing her with him.

Pendleton made his call. 'Henry. The yacht has arrived. Ring the caterers and confirm delivery of the food for tonight. Get the people aboard to clean and decorate the vessel and make sure the nameplate is fitted and covered over ready for the naming ceremony. After that, meet me outside with the car in ten minutes.'

'Poor Henry,' thought Suzie collecting her clothes. 'That's a lot to do in just ten minutes, and I bet Jeremy will not be happy if he's late.'

Pendleton turned to Suzie, who had dressed and was buttoning up the bottom of her blouse. 'In recognition of the valiant efforts of SMJ Boatyard Ltd, you are invited to join me at the naming ceremony tonight.'

The inference about the nature of their time together that afternoon was not lost on Suzie. 'Thank you, Jeremy. I assume the invitation is to all four of us?'

'Four of you?'

'Me, Mike and of course, Reg and George, the two men who flew all the way to Gibraltar to repair your yacht.'

'Why … yes, of course.'

'I'm sure we'll all be there. Eight o'clock isn't it?' she said, with a smile.

A confirmation grin crossed Pendleton's face.

'I must go. I'll see you later,' said Suzie.

'I look forward to it.'

Suzie grabbed her trainers, took the lift down to the ground floor and dashed barefooted along to the marina, arriving in time to see Mike manoeuvring Pendleton's yacht into his berth. She went aboard and gave Mike a hug.

'It's good to see you. Pendleton will be here in a moment to sign the papers for the yacht and take charge of it. He needs his people to get it ready for the party tonight.'

'And the late delivery clause?'

'He was about to make the telephone call to invoke it when you rang. A few minutes later and my delaying tactics would have been in vain.'

'So, Pendleton got what he wanted?'

'And so did we.'

'I saw him a few moments ago through my binoculars, making the call. You were standing beside him, wearing what looked like your birthday suit.'

'Oh, Mike! I'm sorry. You shouldn't have seen that.'

Mike smiled. 'No matter, it's over now, for the moment. So, we should get our payment soon?'

'Yes, hopefully sometime this week.'

'Then we can go out and celebrate tonight?'

'Pendleton has invited us all to his motor yacht naming party tonight.'

Mike nodded, though his face showed his disappointment. 'Oh, right. The boys will probably enjoy that; free food and drink.'

'What about us? Are we going? I told Jeremy we would.'

'Only if Pendleton doesn't gloat about his conquest this afternoon.'

'I'm sure he won't. He's still interested in being friends with us.'

'You mean being friends with you.'

'That could be good for our boatyard, especially now that Harman and his boatyard are likely to be *persona non grata*.'

'I guess so,' conceded Mike.

He and Suzie, along with Reg and George, stepped ashore with their equipment and transferred it to *Quester*. Mike looked at the damage caused by the police search.

'They didn't exactly worry about how they searched the place, did they?'

'You should have seen it before Pendleton's men cleared it up. Compared to that, this is tidy.'

'I hope the Chief of Police will be at Pendleton's party tonight. I want to have a word or two with him.'

'It's best not to get too involved with him, as I found out. He's not a very nice man. In any case, Jeremy is going to speak to the Mayor about what happened to me and our boat, so that should be the end of the matter,' declared Suzie.

Mike grunted and said nothing.

His dash to Cannes had been in time – if only just. The price Suzie had paid to keep Pendleton from trying to sink their boatyard was a price that he did not care for, but had to live with. If Pendleton or the Chief of Police upset him before his annoyance subsided, he was more than ready to respond.

16

THE DEAL

Tuesday October 17th was a day of more than usual activity in Sir Joseph Sterling's office in Whitehall. Most of the details concerning the attempted robbery and shooting at Nelson's Building Society on the previous Friday had now come to light. The gun used in the attempt was linked to a political assassination and Owen Sutton, the apparent supplier of that gun, had fled to Karuna in Africa. On his arrival at Roseburgh Airport he was arrested on espionage charges, and with twelve other mercenaries was transferred to a prison in the neighbouring country of Kitsulana at their president's request.

Many telephone calls went back and forth between Whitehall and the British Embassy in Roseburgh, before Sir Joseph received a call from Mr Robert Weston, a diplomat at the embassy.

'I've arranged to see Mr Sutton in prison later this afternoon.'

'That was quick. How on earth did you manage that?' asked Sir Joseph.

'I contacted the Kitsulana Government House in Jetuloo and was amazed to speak personally to the president, Mr Gorringa.'

'That's quite a coup for you. I see on the television that he's been making political capital out of the affair and stirring all his people up. Do you know where Mr Sutton is being held?'

'He's in a prison cell at Camp West, just outside Jetuloo.'

'Camp West! That's an army barracks. They've only recently finished rebuilding the place after it was burnt to the ground.'

'So I believe.'

'Well, good luck with your visit. I'm not sure that we can get

Mr Sutton's release and return to England now, even if he agreed to it, considering the circumstances of his imprisonment. Give me a call when you get back to let me know how you get on.'

At his Special Branch office, DI Brooke arranged for his telephone calls to be forwarded to Sir Joseph's office where he joined him to coordinate the information they were receiving.

'Good afternoon, Colin,' said Sir Joseph, when Miss Wilson showed Brooke into his office. 'Take a seat. I want to go over everything that we've got so far, to get a clearer picture in my mind of how all this hangs together.'

'Right, Sir. We seem to have several pieces of a puzzle that's getting bigger by the minute, and I'm sure there's more to come.'

Sir Joseph and Brooke reviewed all the information they had obtained over a cup of coffee and biscuits, brought to them by Miss Wilson.

'I was very surprised when Mr Weston rang to say that he'd made arrangements to see Mr Sutton this afternoon,' stated Sir Joseph.

'Why? Isn't that what you'd asked him to do?'

'Yes, it is; only these sorts of visits are usually the subject of delicate negotiations and take a while to organise at the best of times. Very often, the visit is totally denied to start with, and is only agreed to after lengthy talks and some sort of offer in return is made. This visit was not only agreed to straight away, but our Mr Weston actually spoke in person with the president, Mr Gorringa, to arrange it.'

'That doesn't necessarily mean there is a problem, does it?'

'No, not necessarily. I'm simply saying that it *is* unusual, and experience has taught me to be cautious about anything that is a departure from the norm.'

'I presume that Weston is going to ring you when his meeting is over?'

'Yes. If necessary I'll hang on here tonight to receive his call. What he has to tell us could be very important.'

Sir Joseph's telephone rang at that moment, cutting short any further discussion on that subject for the time being. The call was forwarded by Brooke's office for him, and came from DI Rollinson.

'We've had a further chat with Mrs Boyd and she now admits to giving Sutton's telephone number to Kelly so that he could obtain a gun from him. She said it was intended to be used only to frighten the other teller into handing the money over without a fuss and said she didn't know that it was loaded. She's also told us that she obtained the telephone number from a girl friend who used to go out with Sutton, though she's refused to give us her name because she doesn't want to get her into trouble. It's the sort of refusal that seems to be happening all the time in this case. Progress is slow, but we are getting there.'

'Yes, I agree, you are. Have you questioned Kelly about this?'

'Kelly confirms that Mrs Boyd did tell him about this at the time, and said the woman's name is Maggie, but didn't know her surname.'

'Good work, Inspector,' praised Brooke.

'We are checking on Mrs Boyd's friends, and I'll let you know how we get on. Kelly has also let slip that Mrs Boyd was apparently beaten by Wainwright, but this is the interesting thing; Kelly thought that Wainwright was Mrs Boyd's husband.'

'Her husband! But why?'

'I'm sure it's because Mrs Boyd used that to influence Kelly.'

'In order to get him to shoot Wainwright?'

'Possibly. We haven't got to the bottom of this yet. We've questioned the landlord of the pub where Kelly said he met Sutton, and he recognised both of them from the photos we showed him. He remembers, because he thought at the time they looked like an odd pair to be together, and Kelly's strong Irish accent stood out.'

'Okay, thanks very much.'

Brooke relayed the information to Sir Joseph and they continued to discuss the case as the minutes ticked past, and turned into hours. Brooke looked at his watch showing the time as past 6 p.m.

'No word from Weston yet,' he grumbled. 'Perhaps your concerns were right.'

'No. It's getting late. You might as well go home, Colin. I'll ring you in the morning if I hear anything important.'

Brooke collected his papers, said goodbye and left Sir Joseph's office. He locked the folders in the boot of his car and held his stomach as it began to gurgle. He had only been able to grab a quick sandwich at lunchtime and was now feeling hungry. A lot had been achieved in the last few days and the volume of work had left him tired as well as hungry. He had to make a decision whether to go out for a meal or go straight home, have a quick snack and go to bed. Sitting in his car, the decision was made for him when his stomach started to rumble again and his much loved Thai food beckoned him.

'It's time I saw Tho again,' he decided, and headed towards Soho and his favourite Thai restaurant.

★ ★ ★

The following morning, Brooke stepped into his office, slipped off his jacket, carefully placed it on a coat hanger and hung it on the wooden coat rack standing in the corner behind the door. The hands on his wall clock jerked their way past number five at a few minutes after nine o'clock. He dumped his paperwork on the desk and no sooner had he plonked himself down in his chair when the telephone rang. He snatched it up.

'DI Brooke.'

'Good morning, Colin.'

'Good morning, Sir,' he replied, to the familiar voice of Sir Joseph Sterling.

'How are you this sunny morning?'

'Fine, except that I ate too much last night. I'll have to stay a bit longer in the gym tonight to work it off.'

'I presume that you went to your favourite Thai restaurant here in town?'

'I did, and very enjoyable it was.'

'The reason I'm ringing you this early is because I heard from Robert Weston late last night.'

'What did he have to say? Anything interesting?' asked Brooke.

'As a matter of fact yes, very interesting. As I said yesterday, Mr

Weston was given permission to see Mr Sutton by the president himself, and almost straight away. I thought that was unusual, until Mr Weston enlightened me with an explanation.'

'Go on, you've got me intrigued.'

'He was able to conduct an interview with Mr Sutton in a private room, with no other officials present, which is not normal in itself, there is usually a guard. After his initial attempts to question him about the gun he'd sold to Mr Kelly, Mr Sutton revealed that he'd somehow persuaded the president to let him be repatriated, on receipt of $250,000, paid to him personally in cash. Mr Sutton, of course, does not have that amount of money, but has said he will return to England to answer our questions about the gun, if we agree to pay that sum for his release.'

'Phew! $250,000 is a lot of money to pay simply to hear what Sutton has to say about that gun. He might be trying it on to get out of the mess he's in,' suggested Brooke.

'That's exactly what Mr Weston said to him. He replied that he knows the name of the gunman who shot Mr O'Connor, and will only give it to us if we pay the money, get him out and agree not to prosecute him. And he wants it in writing from a top government minister, on government headed notepaper and delivered by a government official.'

'Hmm, does he now? That's quite an impressive list. Do you believe him?'

'It's hard to know. The whole episode is rather unusual, but all the facts we have appear to fit.'

'Which are?'

'Let's review them. One, forensic checks confirm the gun used by Mr Kelly is definitely the murder weapon. Two, Mr Kelly, Mrs Boyd and the pub landlord all agree that is was Mr Sutton who met Mr Kelly in the pub to give him the gun. Three, Mr Sutton admits to giving Mr Kelly the gun, knew what it was previously used for and is willing to name the assassin.'

'Did Sutton say how he came to have the gun in the first place?'

'Yes. He owned up to supplying it in the first place to the assassin, and was supposed to get rid of the weapon afterwards. But, he was greedy and thought he could make more money by selling it instead a few months later, not expecting the police to get hold of it and tie it in to the O'Connor murder.'

'But he didn't sell it. Kelly said that Sutton gave him the weapon.'

'Yes, curious isn't it? I've a feeling that there's more to this than we're being told at the moment, and the only way we are likely to get to the bottom of it is by questioning Mr Sutton.'

'So, are we going ahead with the deal?'

'I don't know yet. I'm trying to arrange a meeting later this morning with the head of MI5, Special Branch and the PM. I'm sure the PM will want us to do everything we can to catch this assassin.'

'If it's agreed, who will go out there to pay the money and collect Sutton, someone from MI5 posing as a government official?'

'That's the tricky part. The British Government can't be seen to be involved with a deal like this. The opposition would have a field day if they found out the government had more or less given in to blackmail. Mr Gorringa wants the money, but doesn't want his people to know he's profiting from allowing Mr Sutton to have his freedom. He wants to tell them he escaped, but we've got to be careful and not let him blame our government for getting involved in helping him to escape.'

'That could turn out to be a tricky situation. Do you have anyone in mind to make the exchange?' asked Brooke.

'Yes, as a matter of fact, I have; Mike Randle.'

'Randle! Is that wise? Surely it would be better to use a freelance agent?'

'Who do you suggest, Zenon Horak?'

'No, not even if he's alive, which we are unsure of.'

'Mike Randle is the perfect man for the job. He's ex-para, an ex-mercenary, he knows the area, is not directly connected with the British authorities, and he's worked for us before, or should I say he's been involved with us before.'

'I realise that, and I agree that he's a likable bloke, but can he be trusted with all that money?'

'I'm sure he can. He's a man with a fair degree of principles, even though he's a bit of a rogue and cannot be totally trusted, despite his past experiences. He's not that desperate for money, especially now that he and Suzie Drake have at last managed to deliver a very expensive motor yacht to Sir Jeremy Pendleton MBE, and are due a large payment for it.'

'Is that important?'

'Very. SMJ Boatyard Ltd stood to lose a lot of money if the boat wasn't delivered on time. After my son Jim, informed me that two guards were killed and the motor yacht, which was commissioned by Sir Jeremy Pendleton, was stolen, I've kept a watchful eye on the situation – from a distance without letting them know. The problem has now been resolved satisfactorily with more than a little help from Mike Randle and his past experiences, which I now wish to make use of. As I am aware of some … tactics he used to regain the yacht, he might find it a little difficult to refuse me if he's not keen on taking this job.'

'You seem to have got everything sorted out. Is there anything that I can do to help?'

'Yes. You could apprise your boss with the relevant details of this case, and encourage him to accept my assessment and back my suggestion of a solution.'

'Okay. I'll do that straight away.'

'Thank you, Colin. I'll be in touch with you again after I've received a decision on how we are going to proceed with this matter.'

'Good luck. I hope you realise what sort of mess you could be letting yourself in for.'

'I do. We'll speak again shortly.'

17

THE PARTY

The local church bell tolled eight times, sending its message ringing across the city of Cannes, and echoing throughout the bay. This signalled the start of Jeremy Pendleton's yacht naming party. His guests began to arrive in their chauffer driven limousines. Each one brought the men dressed in their immaculate evening suits and bow ties, while their wives paraded in their designer dresses and very expensive glittering jewellery, each vying to outshine the others in their show of opulence.

Pendleton's yacht, decked out with bunting and impressively lit from stern to bow with coloured lights, added to the already brightly lit marina, turning the water into a shimmering glow of reflected colours.

The vast cabin area had its furniture and carpet removed, revealing shiny wooden floorboards that turned the cabin into a dining and dance room. A quartet quietly played at one end of the room, and tables along two sides of the cabin held more sumptuous food than the guests could hope to devour. Along the remaining side was a bar where every drink one could wish for was available, and free. Tables and chairs were dotted around the centre of the cabin, waiting to be moved to one side when the eating was done, and it was time to allow guests room to dance to the music.

It was a little after half past eight when Mike, Suzie, Reg and George wandered along the marina to Pendleton's yacht. Suzie wore a more modest dress than the one Pendleton had purchased for her earlier in the day, though she still looked very chic in her new outfit and radiated sexiness. She arrived in a figure hugging, long, flowing dress with a scoop neckline that showed a hint of cleavage and was graced by a necklace made from one large and several small seashells. Her suntan was enhanced by the contrast it showed against her white dress.

Mike wore a suit, hastily bought for him that afternoon, and a bow tie, which he complained about, but was persuaded by Suzie to wear. He dressed casually most of the time and enjoyed the freedom of an open neck shirt and hated 'stuffy suits' as he called them, with ties. Reg and George were dressed in suits that Suzie insisted purchasing for them, as they had only brought work clothes with them. Both of them felt slightly uncomfortable, dressed in clothes they usually wore at christenings, funerals and weddings only.

The three men went straight aboard while Suzie, who had seen Pendleton's chauffer Henry standing nearby, spoke with him for a few seconds before joining the others. She caught up with Mike and whispered a few words to him as Pendleton approached them when they entered the dining room.

'Good evening Suzie, good evening Mike, I'm glad that you could make it,' he said extending his hand, which Mike ignored and Suzie smiled at. 'Please help yourselves to whatever food and drink you want, it's all free,' he stated, in a tone of voice intended to impress. 'The naming ceremony is at ten o'clock.'

'Thank you,' said Suzie.

'The repairs are satisfactory, I trust?' asked Mike.

'Yes, they are very good. If I didn't know, I wouldn't be able to tell that any repairs had been done from the outside.'

'That's thanks to Reg and George here,' said Mike, gesturing to the two men standing behind him.

Pendleton looked at them and gave a slight nod.

'Everything has worked out okay then,' suggested Mike.

'I think you can safely say that, today I got what I've been waiting for, for quite a long time, thanks to Suzie … and you.'

The double meaning was not lost on Mike, or Suzie. She saw him clench a fist and put a calming hand on his arm, knowing the comment raised anger inside him.

Mike changed the subject. 'Is the Chief of Police here? I'd like to have a few words with him.'

'Originally he was invited, but the invitation was withdrawn after the unfortunately incident at his police station involving Suzie.'

'That's a pity,' bemoaned Mike. 'I was looking for a good fight – it might help to get some of the frustration out of me and liven the evening up.'

Pendleton stepped back a pace with an uncertain look on his face. He knew that Mike Randle would be aware of what happened that afternoon between him and Suzie, and did not want to get him so annoyed that he might attack him for his unethical tactics in getting her into his bed.

'I am, however, pleased that the Mayor is a guest here tonight,' Pendleton quickly announced to deflect away from any aggressive thoughts Mike may have in mind, 'and I intend to make him aware of what has happened. In fact, Suzie, I'd like to introduce you to him. He's bound to want a few answers from you.'

Pendleton grasped Suzie's elbow and looked at Mike. 'If you don't mind I'll borrow Suzie for a few minutes,' he said, waiting for a nod from him before leading her away.

The evening was beginning to warm up. The room was buzzing to chatting and laughter, glasses were clinking and the musicians were playing mood music in a low volume. Guests were sat at tables or stood around chatting and eating. The women tended to group together as did the men, many of them smoking; mainly fat cigars. Most of their conversations were about the various businesses each of them owned or ran. It was a night to make new contacts, conclude existing business deals and sow the seeds for future ventures.

With a pint of beer in his hand, unlike most of the other guests who were drinking champagne, wine or shorts, Reg turned to Mike.

'George and me don't fit in here with all these toffs, Mr Randle. We're going back aboard *Quester* to see if we can do some repairs to those broken doors,' he said, pulling the collar away from his neck with a forefinger.

'Okay lads. I understand. Thanks for your help. Have you had something to eat?'

'We've nibbled a few bits, but I don't know what's in half of these minute sandwiches. There's a little place along the marina that does great fish and chips. We'll get something to eat there,' said Reg looking at George, who nodded in full agreement.

'Righto. We'll see you back on *Quester* later on.'

The pair dumped their glasses down on the bar, pushed their way through the guests and went ashore, pleased to be out of it. They had barely stepped off the yacht when both men pulled off their ties and undid the top button on their shirts.

'Thank goodness I can take this ruddy tie off,' murmured Reg.

'Yeah,' agreed George.

Mike gazed across the room and watched Suzie and Pendleton talking to the man with a large mayoral chain around his neck. The room was illuminated by flashes every few seconds as a photographer from a local upmarket gossip magazine, took pictures of the guests. A tall good-looking leggy blonde with long flowing hair and a buxom figure, much of which was on view from her bright red low-cut dress, approached Mike.

'Hello. Aren't you the man who built this boat?' she asked.

'Motor yacht,' corrected Mike. 'And yes, I am one of the directors of the company that designed and built this luxury vessel.'

'You must be a very clever man,' she purred, 'to make such a wonderful boat … motor yacht like this.'

'It was a joint effort. We have some good designers and builders who work for our company.'

'They must need someone to guide them?'

'Well, yes of course. I have to point them in the right direction and correct them when the design is not quite right. I've had lots of experience in leading others and showing them the way,' boasted Mike, enchanted at the attention this woman was showing him.

'You must know every inch of this yacht.'

'Yes, I do. Building it was a sizeable project, lasting more than a year.'

'Maybe you could show me around and give me a guided tour?

Jeremy is far too busy with his others guests at the moment.'

'It's not my vessel any more, and Jeremy might not like me wandering around his yacht without his permission.'

'Oh, I'm sure he wouldn't mind. He likes other people to be envious of his possessions. You could always say that I talked you into it.'

The buxom blonde pouted and gave Mike the 'little lost girl' look. A look he found hard to resist.

He thought for a moment before conceding. 'Okay, why not? Suzie's still busy talking to the mayor, and I don't know anyone else here, so I'm at a loose end. I feel a bit lost among all these well-dressed millionaires.'

'Billionaires some of them,' corrected the blonde. 'My name's Helgar,' she said, slipping her arm through Mike's and leading him from the room.

Mike gave her an escorted tour of the yacht. She took a cursory glance into the galley and other bedrooms until they came to the large, opulent master bedroom. She dashed into the room and threw herself on the bed.

'Isn't this fabulous. I don't think I've ever seen a more gorgeous bedroom,' she gushed, rolling back and forth on the Royal Blue silk sheets. She patted the bed. 'Come and lay beside me.'

'I'm not sure that's a good idea,' protested Mike. 'I've had a few drinks and things might get out of hand. I don't want to upset my partner, Suzie.'

'Nonsense! We're two adults and can decide for ourselves what we do. Jeremy told me that he spent the afternoon in bed with your woman. He said they had great sex together, so I don't see that you have any obligations to her.'

Mike was taken aback by the comment. He knew what method Suzie had used in order to prevent Pendleton from trying to sink their boat building company, but did not expect to hear it put so bluntly to him by a total stranger – even if she was a gorgeous blonde.

Helgar pulled the straps down on her dress and released her buxom breasts. She looked an inviting sight as she lay there on the bed with her breasts swaying. She beckoned him to join her with an obvious willingness to let Mike have his way. Mike smiled and approached her.

Back in the dining room, Suzie finished telling the story of her treatment by the chief of police to the mayor, who was most sympathetic to her problem. He attempted to entice this attractive female complainant into his office for further explanations; an invitation that Suzie declined. Nevertheless, he promised to look into her case, though after talking to him, Suzie was not convinced that he would do anything about it.

'I think we should have a drink to celebrate the successful conclusion to our business contract,' insisted Pendleton, collecting two glasses of champagne from the tray of a waiter he had beckoned.

Suzie sipped the drink and looked around the room. 'I don't see Mike anywhere,' she stated.

'While you were talking to the mayor, I saw him leave with a fabulous looking buxom blonde,' Pendleton stated.

Suzie looked at him with surprise.

'I don't want to worry you,' he added, 'but they looked to be getting very friendly together. Perhaps we should look for them,' Pendleton suggested, putting his arm around Suzie's waist and leading her out of the dining room.

'He's probably gone to the men's room,' stated Suzie, placing her glass on the bar as they left.

'Possibly, but as you are aware this is a large yacht with a number of rooms, including several bedrooms.'

Pendleton opened the doors and looked quickly into two bedrooms before coming to the master bedroom. He put a hand on Suzie's waist, opened the door and guided her into the room.

'What are you two doing ... in here,' Pendleton stated, his voice trailing off.

Mike and Helgar were sitting on the end of the bed, both fully dressed.

'Helgar had a bit of a headache, so I brought her in here to get away from the noise and have a little peace and quiet,' explained Mike, rising from the bed. 'I hope you don't mind?'

'No, of course not,' replied Pendleton, his face showing a look of suppressed anger.

'Good. I'll let you continue to comfort her then,' said Mike, with more of a smirk than a smile on his face.

He grabbed Suzie's hand as he left the bedroom, and they returned to the dining room.

Slamming the bedroom door shut, Pendleton exploded. 'What the hell are you playing at? You were supposed to get him into bed.'

'He wouldn't come to bed. I stripped off and he couldn't take his eyes off my tits. Either he's very devoted to his woman or he guessed what I was trying to do. Perhaps I was a bit too obvious.'

'Bah! Get out!' yelled Pendleton waving a fist towards the door.

Almost crying, Helgar left the room and made straight for the ladies powder room, where she could compose herself before rejoining the guests. Perhaps she would have more luck with one of the other wealthy men who may be generous, and would treat her better.

Back in the dining room Suzie confessed, 'I wonder what you would have done if Henry hadn't told me about Pendleton's cunning plan to try and prize us apart, so that he could step in and comfort me.'

'You know me. I wouldn't do anything to upset you.'

'Yes, I know you all right.'

'Well, after Helgar told me that you'd spent the afternoon in bed with Jeremy Pendleton and had great sex, it became a temptation.'

'Oh Mike! I'm sorry you had to hear it like that. You must have guessed what happened, but I didn't want to upset you by mentioning any details or dwelling on the matter. I realise that it is difficult for you accept what I had to agree to, and it wasn't great sex like we have together. I'll make it up to you.'

A broad grin crossed Mike's face. 'My feelings were really terribly hurt,' he said.

'Yes, okay, I get the picture. You don't need to lay it on that thick. I've already said I'll make it up to you.'

'When?'

'How about tonight when we get back to *Quester*?'

'We could leave right now,' Mike suggested.

'No, we couldn't. The naming ceremony is due any time now. I'd like to know what Pendleton is going to call this expensive toy of his.'

'Some daft female name I expect,' said Mike.

The time was approaching ten o'clock. Pendleton returned to the dining room looking smart and unflustered as ever. He moved to the centre of the room and clapped his hands two or three times. The musicians stopped playing and the room sank into silence.

'My Lords, ladies, gentlemen and Mr Mayor,' Pendleton began. 'The time is almost upon us, for what this occasion is all about – the naming of my new, luxury motor yacht.'

Gentle applause rippled through the room, to which Pendleton nodded his thanks.

He continued, 'The Mayor has graciously agreed to say a few words and reveal the name plaque on this cabin wall. At the same time, the name painted on the outside of the motor yacht will be uncovered for everybody to see. If you please, Mr Mayor.'

To generous applause, the mayor moved to the wall where the name plaque was hidden behind a curtain, grinning in appreciation to the response he received from the guests.

He grasped the cord and began, 'Sir Jeremy Pendleton MBE, my Lords, ladies and gentlemen. It gives me great pleasure to perform this naming ceremony. I'm sure you all agree this is a magnificent motor yacht, which I hope will visit our beautiful city of Cannes on many occasions.'

Pendleton nodded in agreement.

'May all who sail in her, have a safe and enjoyable journey in the luxury that this vessel affords.'

The mayor pulled the cord to reveal the motor yacht name as *'Julia'*, to more generous applause. Outside, a barrage of fireworks was lit as the name was revealed on the sides of the yacht. All the assembled guests continued to clap in approval to the sounds of whoosh, bangs and the brightly lit-up sky from the fireworks, whether they liked the new name or not – it was polite to do so.

Only two people in the room were surprised by the name of the new vessel.

'Is that a coincidence, or does Pendleton know it's your middle name?' Mike asked Suzie.

'I don't know. I've never told him, but it can't be that difficult to find out, especially if you're a Sir.'

'So, is this all a part of his master plan, a plan that he though would see you by his side this evening?'

'Maybe, I wouldn't put it past him. If so, he's miscalculated how much his wealth and influence carries with us, and how much we mean to each other, and I have to say, his reputation as a good lover is a little generous. He's not bad, but not half as good as you.'

'I'm pleased to hear that,' retorted Mike.

'And I told him so,'

Pendleton raised his hands to quieten the applauding guests. 'I would like to make one other important acknowledgement. This magnificent motor yacht could not have been built without the full help and cooperation of the management of SMJ Boatyard Ltd, especially the two guests who we have here with us tonight – Mr Mike Randle and the lovely Miss Suzie Drake,' announced Pendleton, gesturing towards them.

A startled Mike and Suzie acknowledged the applause they received with smiles.

'Do you think this is Pendleton's way of conceding defeat of his little plan, and is trying to smooth the waters with us?' asked Mike.

'Yes, I think you're right. Let's hope this unexpected announcement encourages others to consider our boatyard for their work.'

'Now, let us continue with the dancing,' said Pendleton, turning to nod at the musicians, who resumed playing straight away as the waiters quickly removed the tables and chairs.

Pendleton approached Mike and Suzie. 'I hope you approve of the name I've christened my yacht?' he asked.

'What made you choose that particular female name?' asked Mike, before he gave an answer.

'I've had many female companions, and have enjoyed their

company. It seemed fitting that I should name my yacht with a woman's name that I like the sound of.'

'So, this name has no particular significance?' pressed Mike.

'None, other than it is one that I like very much.'

'So, it's a pure coincidence that it happens to be Suzie's middle name then?'

'Is it?' Pendleton said, in a surprised tone of voice, raising his eyebrows.

Pursing his lips, Mike shrugged in apparent disbelief, grabbed Suzie by the arm and guided her to the other side of the room, leaving Pendleton standing on his own.

'Believe that if you will,' Mike muttered.

'Please don't let it bother you,' pleaded Suzie.

He looked into her eyes. 'Yes, okay. Would the loveliest lady aboard this bonking boat care for a dance?'

Suzie smiled. 'Thank you Mr Fixer, I would.'

The pair had a shuffle around the room with their arms tightly twisted around each other. Mike glanced at Pendleton watching them out of the corner of his eye with a stern look on his face, which only changed to a smile when another guest spoke to him.

'Let's have another drink and leave Mr Pendleton to his millionaire cronies,' suggested Mike.

'I'm with you on that.'

The church bells chimed eleven times as Mike and Suzie said goodbye to Jeremy Pendleton. They went ashore and wandered past the lines of chauffer driven cars waiting to collect their owners. Among them was Henry, standing by Pendleton's Rolls Royce. Mike winked at him and Suzie gave a slight nod. They knew it was unwise to talk to him because Pendleton may be watching them and guess that he had given away his plans.

They strolled back to *Quester*, watched from the balcony of *Julia* by Jeremy Pendleton, ruing the plan that had backfired.

Other guests danced, chatted and drank into the early hours of the morning before they began to drift away. It had been both a satisfying and frustrating day for Jeremy Pendleton. He had achieved his goal of getting Suzie into his bed, but may have ruined his chances of ever repeating his quest by misjudging her loyalty to Mike. It was an error that would make it a lot more difficult for him to further savour the exceptional delights that Suzie Drake had shown him she possessed in bed that afternoon.

18

AN OFFER

While Sir Joseph Sterling was in conference with the heads of MI5, Special Branch and the PM, to decide what action to take about Owen Sutton's proposition to return to England if a ransom was paid for him, Mike and Suzie were sunning themselves on the deck of *Quester*.

'I'm sorry that last night's lovemaking wasn't very good,' apologised Mike, 'despite your best efforts. A lot's happened in the last few days, and it'll take me a while to settle down again.'

'Don't worry about it. I understand. Once we get away from here and you get Jeremy Pendleton out of your system, there'll be lots more times when our lovemaking will be great.'

'I thought that seeing that buxom blonde's big tits would inspire me, but it didn't.'

'I thought it would as well,' smiled Suzie.

Mike gave her a sideways glance – which she ignored.

'We've had a lot of worries in the last few days,' she admitted. 'After a few days relaxing in the sun, I'm sure you'll be back to your old, sexy self again.'

'I certainly hope so. Now that Pendleton has signed the delivery acceptance on his yacht, we ought to think about heading home,' Mike suggested.

'I guess so,' agreed Suzie, lazing topless on a sun bed next to him.

'Are we going to fly back or take the slow route in *Quester*?'

'In *Quester*, definitely. I'll be able to top-up my suntan and Reg and George will be able to relax. After all, they gave up part of their weekend to fly out and do the repairs, and they've fixed the broken doors on *Quester*. They deserve a rest, and so do you.'

'I agree. We could leave this afternoon then?'

'No, tomorrow morning would be better,' stated Suzie.

'Tomorrow, why?'

'I'd like to do some shopping this afternoon before we go. There are some fabulous shops here.'

'Oh, I see. You told me that you'd already looked around the shops.'

'I have, but I didn't like to spend too much until the contract was signed and we were assured of receiving payment for the yacht.'

'So, you want to spend all our profits, eh?'

'Well, at least we've got some profit to spend, thanks to my delaying tactics with Jeremy Pendleton.'

'The less said about that the better,' said Mike giving another sideways glance at Suzie, which she again knew was coming, and again ignored.

The four of them had lunch in a local tavern, paid for by Mike as a celebration to the conclusion of their deal. With lunch over, Suzie set off to do her shopping, while the three men returned to *Quester*.

Pendleton's motor yacht *Julia*, with its new name painted in gold lettering, was having the last of its empties and leftovers removed by the caterers. Suzie stopped alongside on the quay. Pendleton, supervising the cleanup saw her and came ashore.

'I hope you enjoyed the party last night,' he enquired.

'Don't spout niceties to me, Jeremy. That trick you tried to pull last night was underhanded and despicable,' Suzie spat. 'And I believe this belongs to you,' she said, handing him the diamond necklace he gave her to wear in the restaurant.

'It's yours. I'd like you to keep it.'

'No, thank you. Mike would not like me wearing something you'd given me, especially after your behaviour last night, and neither would I.'

Pendleton's expression changed to one of 'a sorry little boy' look.

'And don't give me that sorry look. You knew exactly what you were doing, and it was a deliberate attempt to cause a breakup between Mike and me. I'm very annoyed at you.'

'Yes, you're quite right, and I'm very sorry. If you forgive me, I guarantee that it won't happen again.'

'So do I.'

Suzie looked at Pendleton's face. His expression was pleading with her to forgive him. It was one of many looks that he could conjure up immediately, and was used to good effect by him on any occasion that warranted it.

She relented. 'Oh, all right. But you make sure you never try that again.'

Pendleton's face broke into a broad smile. 'Scout's honour,' he said. 'Though you have to take part of the blame.'

'Why?'

'Because we had such a wonderful exhilarating time together in bed, and I naturally want to experience those heady heights again.'

'Like I said, that was a one off occurrence caused by exceptional circumstances that are unlikely to happen again.'

'Unlikely, but not impossible. I may get the chance to get together with you again.'

'That's not the way to go about it.'

'I realise that now. Are we still friends?'

'I guess so.'

'I'll save this trinket until you dine with me next time.'

'That might be a long time away.'

'I can wait. Did I see you speaking to Henry last night?' he enquired.

Suzie knew immediately what he was angling for. 'Only to say hello to him,' she stated. 'I felt sorry for him having to stand there waiting for you to finish your party.'

He nodded, not knowing whether to believe her or not, but feeling it was unwise to press the point any further.

'And where are you off to now, may I enquire?'

'Shopping for clothes, now that we are assured of receiving your cheque.'

'I have instructed my accountants to transfer the payment to your company's bank today.'

'Good. Thank you.'

'I hope you have an enjoyable time, especially if you are looking for dresses like the one you wore to the restaurant with me.'

'If I get one it will be to dine with Mike, not you.'

Pendleton smiled and nodded.

Turning towards the main street, Suzie waved goodbye and left to enjoy her shopping. She was now safe in the knowledge that payment for the motor yacht would be made today, and she had profits to spend on a few luxuries for herself. After all, she deserved it.

★ ★ ★

Back in London, at Sir Joseph Sterling's meeting with the top brass, the PM could only spare half an hour, so a decision had to be made quickly. DI Brooke had already briefed his boss at Special Branch, and although the female head of MI5 preferred to use one of her own men, Sir Joseph's persuasive powers and his impressive reputation with the PM meant that he was given the green light to proceed as he wished. Part of this was due to the fact that, the man he was suggesting for the job had an intimate knowledge of the area and was not a government employee. That was the clincher in the argument in Sir Joseph's favour. Funding for the project was agreed and was to be made available by the following day.

Once he had returned to his office, Sir Joseph rang DI Brooke and gave him the news. 'I've been given the go-ahead and I'd like you to go with Mike Randle to Roseburgh to escort Mr Sutton back to this country, please Colin. I'd like us all to meet at my office to discuss the details.'

'Of course, Sir.'

'When you meet him, see if you can persuade Mr Sutton to give you the assassins name straight away, as we will have kept our part of the deal in getting him out. I'd like to get the wheels in motion to find this man. Knowing his identity is one thing, finding him and bringing him to justice may be an entirely different kettle of fish.'

'Right. I'll do that as soon as he's in my custody.'

'Good. I've now got the job of ringing Mike Randle and persuading him to take this venture.'

'Good luck!'

★ ★ ★

In Cannes, while Suzie was buying clothes, shoes, jewellery and a present for Mike, so that he did not feel left out of it, aboard *Quester*, Reg and George were preparing the yacht in readiness for their journey home.

Mike was snoozing on deck, enjoying the sunshine and taking a well earned rest, when his mobile telephone rang. He propped himself up on one elbow, reached for the phone and sank back down into his sun bed as he answered it.

'Sir Joseph! This is an unexpected call. What can I do for you? Not another job I hope.'

'As a matter of fact …'

Mike listened to the Foreign Office diplomat's brief explanation of the situation before he came to the reason for his call.

'… and I consider that you are the perfect candidate to handle the exchange and help escort Mr Sutton back to this country.'

'I'm flattered that you should think so highly of me Sir Joseph, but after a difficult year at the boatyard and a rather more stressful last few days, I would prefer that Suzie and I took a short break. We need some time together to chill out.'

'Jim told me about your troubles at the boatyard with the theft of Sir Jeremy Pendleton's yacht. I was sorry to hear of the death of your two men.'

'Thank you. They were good men, and didn't deserve to be shot in the back.'

'I gather that DI Maidley was a little upset that you didn't confide in him, and set off on your own to find the men responsible.'

'Oh, right! He wouldn't have understood our reasons, and it

would only have led to a lot of red tape and lost us valuable time, we couldn't afford that.'

'I believe that you recaptured the yacht and have now delivered it to Sir Jeremy Pendleton in Cannes.'

'Err, yes, that's right, we have,' said Mike, wondering how Sir Joseph came to know all this.

'What happened to the men who stole it?'

'They've disappeared.'

'Disappeared have they? And what about Giles Harman?'

'Harman! How do you know about him? He's the one who organised the theft. What happened was his responsibility.'

'So, how did you manage to recover the yacht?'

'We located it sailing down to the Med with a tracking device that's installed. I boarded her and sailed to Cannes to deliver her to Pendleton.'

'And the thieves had disappeared?'

'Yes.'

'Was that before of after you killed them?'

Mike was taken aback. 'What makes you think that I killed them?'

'Giles Harman was forced to radio for help after you shot holes in his yacht and he lost all his fuel.'

'He did the same to us,' defended Mike.

'I'm sure he did. He radioed a full explanation in order to set up an alibi for himself, not realising that we monitor all radio calls. When yours and Suzie Drake's names were mentioned, I was informed about the call and sent a full transcript of his conversation.'

'So, you know that he was responsible for the theft.'

'I do. The transcript made interesting reading. I also have a transcript of a conversation between Miss Drake and a man named Reg at your boatyard.'

'He's our foreman.'

'Miss Drake also spoke about Mr Harman's tactics and gave him instructions about getting the repairs done in Gibraltar. She also mentioned that you'd killed both highjackers.'

'We were in international waters, so you can't have me arrested for murder,' suggested Mike.

'You were aboard a British registered vessel. That means you come under British law, so I *could* have you arrested for killing those men.'

'Right. So, is that what you intend to do?'

'Not if you agree to do this one, simple job for me.'

'I see; blackmail.'

'Let's call it a mutual agreement, shall we?'

'Is this going to turn out like the last simple job we did, the one that nearly got us all killed?'

'I sincerely hope not. This job is simply handing over a package of money in exchange for a man and escorting him back to England.'

'It sounds easy enough. Why don't you get one of your own people to do it?'

'The government cannot be seen to be involved in paying to have a man freed from an overseas prison.'

'You mean that unlike me, you cannot be seen to be giving in to blackmail?'

'Quite, something like that. You are an independent man, of wide experience, and you now owe me a favour to keep you out of prison for killing those men, even if they were robbers and murderers.'

'Okay, okay, I give in. I'll do it, providing you wipe the slate clean and see that a copy of the transcript finds its way into the hands of Jeremy Pendleton as proof of who arranged the theft of his yacht.'

'That's government property and copies are not allowed to be sent to a third party.'

'Then you'll have to arrest me for murder and I'll take my chances.'

Sir Joseph sighed heavily. He was committed to sending Mike Randle on this job and did not want to have his plans altered. He thought for a few moments.

'I tell you what I'll do. I'll speak personally with Sir Jeremy Pendleton and confirm to him that Giles Harman was the man involved with stealing his yacht, in confidence of course. How does that sound?'

'Good. What if he asks you how you know? What will you tell him?'

'You let me worry about that. Is it a deal?'

Mike took a deep breath through his nose and exhaled. 'Okay. What do you want me to do?'

'Fly back to England this afternoon. I'll make all the arrangements and we'll discuss details in my office tomorrow morning.'

'Okay, but I may not be able to get a flight today.'

'There's a ticket waiting for you at the BA reception desk in Nice Airport. Your plane leaves at 6:40 p.m., check-in time is a minimum of 30 minutes before, but if I were you, I'd get there a bit earlier than that.'

'Right, thanks. You obviously knew it was an offer that I couldn't refuse.'

'Let's just say that I knew I could count on your unswerving cooperation.'

'Unswerving cooperation my foot! You've practically blackmailed me into accepting this job. You realise that Suzie's not going to like this one little bit.'

'I'm sure that you can explain things adequately to her.'

'Hmm. I'll see you tomorrow.'

Putting down his mobile, Mike glanced towards the quayside to see Jeremy Pendleton's Rolls Royce pull up alongside their yacht, and Suzie holding more bags than she could easily manage to carry, get out of the car. Pendleton appeared and helped Suzie to bring the purchases aboard.

'I met Jeremy in town and he kindly gave me a lift back with my things,' she explained to Mike.

Pendleton smiled at Mike, but said nothing. He was unsure of the reception he would get.

Mike ignored him.

'While you've been spending our money, I received a telephone call from Sir Joseph Sterling. He wants to see me in his office tomorrow morning, so I'll have to catch a plane home from Nice this afternoon.'

'Oh, Mike! That's a shame. I was looking forward to a nice relaxing journey home. Do you have to go?'

'I'm afraid so. I'll tell you why later,' he promised, looking at Pendleton, not wanting him to know everything about their business.

'Okay.'

'You take the yacht and return with Reg and George. I'll see you when I get back from this little job. It should only take a couple of days.'

'When do you have to leave?'

'Right now. I've got to get to Nice Airport in a hurry.'

'Perhaps you'd allow me to offer you the use of my Rolls Royce. Henry could drive you to the airport,' Pendleton suggested.

Mike looked at him unsure of his motives. Pendleton recognised his hesitation and held up his hands. 'No strings attached. I'd like to make up for last night.'

'Make up?'

'Well at least make up in part.'

'Okay. I'll be ready in a few minutes.'

Pendleton returned to his car to inform Henry of his task while Mike went below with Suzie, grabbed a few things and jammed them into a holdall.

'What does he want you to do?'

'He wants me to escort a man back from Africa.'

'What part of Africa, and why you?'

'From Kitsulana, because I've been there and know the layout of the land.'

'There's still a lot of trouble out there. Do you have to go?'

'Sir Joseph didn't give me much choice. He's found out that I killed those two men who stole our yacht and has threatened me with a charge of murder.'

'But they were thieves who shot two of our guards, and anyway we were in the middle of the ocean.'

'Aboard a British registered yacht. That apparently makes it subject to British laws.'

'That's charming! After all the help we've given him, he resorts to this. It's blackmail, you know.'

'I know, and I know that I have little choice.'
'I agree. So, you be careful.'
'I will.'
Suzie handed him his passport. 'You'll need this.'
'Thanks,' he said, shoving it in his pocket.
Mike gave Suzie a hug and they kissed passionately. 'I'll see you in a few days,' he promised.

Suzie smiled. Mike said cheerio and had a few words with Reg and George before going ashore and climbing into Pendleton's Rolls Royce. He waved to Suzie as he set off for Nice Airport.

When the vehicle was out of sight, Pendleton turned to come back aboard when Reg and George appeared behind Suzie. He took one glance at the stern look on their faces, smiled and wandered back to his yacht. A grin crossed Suzie's face as she watched him disappear into the distance.

'And where did you two appear from?' she asked.
'Mr Randle warned us about him and his intentions, Miss Drake,' confided Reg.
'Did he now?'
'Yes, he told us to look out for you.'
'Very thoughtful of him,' smiled Suzie, returning to the cabin. 'We'd better get under way then.'

An hour later *Quester* slipped her moorings. Jeremy Pendleton was standing on the deck of *Julia* watching the yacht head for the open seas. He smiled as Suzie, wearing her skimpy bikini, waved goodbye to him and disappeared from view. He wondered if he had irrevocably damaged his chances of getting her into his bed again. He hoped not; only time would tell. *Quester* moved gracefully out of the marina and into the dark blue waters of the Mediterranean Sea, and headed for home.

19

LONDON

Sir Jeremy Pendleton MBE had tried to cause a split between Mike Randle and his partner Suzie Drake at his yacht naming party, and it had backfired. In an attempt to make amends he offered to let his chauffeur, Henry, drive Mike to Nice Airport. He had been persuaded by Sir Joseph Sterling to act as a courier in an exchange to bring Owen Sutton back to England from Africa. On Mike's unexpectedly comfortable journey to the airport to fly home for his meeting with Sir Joseph, he spoke to the chauffer.

'I want to thank you for warning us last night, Henry. It was just as you said. Pendleton had persuaded a sexy young female named Helgar to try and seduce me. She was a very enticing female; good looking, with big breasts, obviously willing to let me have my way with her, and she did everything she could to get me into bed. Pendleton then burst in on us with Suzie, after inferring that we were having a romp in his bedroom. He got quite a shock when he found us fully dressed sitting on the end of his bed.'

Henry let out a quiet chuckle. 'I bet he did. What explanation did you give him?'

'I told him that Helgar had a headache, and I'd brought her out of the noisy party into a quiet room.'

'I bet he was seething. I'd loved to have seen the look on his face.'

'He had a look of suppressed anger and frustration. I hope it doesn't get you or her into trouble.'

'Pendleton may suspect that it was me who informed you, but he won't do anything unless he is sure. He relies on me quite a lot these days,' Henry stated, checking each way at a junction before continuing the journey. 'And as for Helgar, I saw her leave with a 60-year-old millionaire Lord something-or-other who's a member of the House of Lords in England, so I'm sure that she's in better hands now.'

'Good. At least she's out of Pendleton's clutches, and I hope that teaches him a lesson.'

'We should be there soon,' Henry stated.

'I'm curious to know why you warned us.'

'I've been Jeremy Pendleton's chauffer for many years now. During that time he's treated me well, but demands more and more from me and now expects me to be his secretary and odd job man as well. I don't mind that so much, but I've seen him treat others badly, especially the women. He uses them for his own pleasures then discards them for someone new and starts another sexual challenge. He leaves many of them in tears at his treatment of them. Your Suzie is a lovely lady and I'd hate to see Pendleton break the pair of you up, which is what he was trying to do in order to add her to the list of temporary conquests. That would only have lasted until someone new came along for him to go after, and then, like all the others, he would ditch her.'

'We both appreciate your help.'

'I'm glad to be of service, Mr Randle.'

The Rolls Royce purred its way into Nice Airport where Henry pulled it into a parking slot outside the departure terminal. Mike shook Henry by the hand, thanked him for his help, grabbed his holdall and made his way to the BA desk, where he collected his ticket and booked in. After a forty-five minute wait, he boarded the aircraft and was on his way to London's Heathrow Airport.

By the time that Mike reached the concourse at his destination it was past seven o'clock in the evening. He caught a taxi to Victoria Railway Station and boarded a train heading for the south coast. Much of the journey was spent with Mike staring out of the railway carriage at the dark clouds and spots of rain that were falling on the window and were blown along a curved line until they flew off into the distance. He dreamt about the warm sunshine he had been obliged to leave behind, along with his sexy partner Suzie, and dreamt of taking a cruise to sunny climbs when this job was over, now that the company coffers had been topped up.

It was a little after nine o'clock when Mike reached home and was glad to get some rest. He rang Suzie before he retired for the night and slept a restless sleep in an unfamiliarly empty waterbed.

When he awoke the following morning, Mike decided not to bother with taking a jog along the beach, which he usually did to accompany Suzie. After a breakfast fry-up, which he would not get if Suzie had anything to do with it, he felt satisfied enough to begin the day.

Mike journeyed to London to keep his date with Sir Joseph Sterling on *Bonny*, his motorcycle, and parked it in the visitor's section of the Whitehall Foreign Office car park.

After security guards had confirmed his appointment, he was escorted to Sir Joseph's outer office where Miss Wilson greeted him and announced his arrival. She showed him into Sir Joseph's office. He rose from his desk, shook Mike's hand and motioned him to sit down on the waiting chair in front of his desk. Mike nodded a greeting to Brooke, who was already sat there waiting.

'Good flight home?' Sir Joseph asked Mike.

'Yes, fine thanks, though it was a shame to leave all that lovely sunshine behind and return to cloudy skies and rain.'

The comment brought no response.

'I see you've driven up here on your motorcycle,' he said, eyeing Mike's leathers and his helmet.

'Yes, I had to. Our car is still at the boatyard.'

Between Sir Joseph and Brooke, they related the main points of the investigation so far, ending with the need for a courier to deliver the money and collect Owen Sutton.

'It's a little worrying that things seem to be moving rather fast, that's a bit out of the ordinary isn't it?' Mike suggested to Sir Joseph.

'Yes, I agree. I had the same thought. However, we have to go with the information we have, and trust that things work out as we expect. That's not to say that we won't take every precaution necessary and try to anticipate any problems.'

'I hope so, after all, it's my neck that's on the line in a dangerous country.'

'Quite so. Colin will accompany you to Roseburgh. After that you'll be on your own. He can only go into Kitsulana with a diplomatic pass, which I've given him in case of an emergency. It is preferable that he doesn't have to use it. An unfamiliar diplomatic face would only cause questions about government involvement that we are trying very hard to avoid. He'll stay at a local hotel and will meet you to escort Mr Sutton on the flight back home.'

Brooke added, 'The trip itself should be straightforward. We'll fly to Nairobi and catch the internal flight to Roseburgh. When we arrive at about eight in the morning, you hire a car at the airport and drive across the border to the prison. You should have no trouble getting through as we've agreed a timetable with them, and they are expecting you around three in the afternoon. Once there, you will exchange the money for Sutton, ring me to confirm that everything is okay, drive him back to the airport and meet me there. We'll catch a plane home. We've already booked the tickets. The last connecting plane to get us to Nairobi for our flight home leaves Roseburgh Airport at five minutes to seven, so that should give you plenty of time to get Sutton there.'

'It sounds easy enough. Tell me again why you're not sending one of your own men to Kitsulana.'

'The government cannot be seen to be directly involved, and we want a man who's experienced in the field and who knows the area,' stated Sir Joseph. 'That's you.'

'Where is this prison?' Mike asked.

'It's at the newly built Camp West.'

'Camp West! I can't go back there. They'll hang me if they find out who I am. The last time I was there I had to shoot my way out, and they think that I'm responsible for the place being burnt down.'

'That's strange. When you returned, you told me that the camp was still in one piece when you left.'

'It was, but it was slightly alight.'

Brooke stifled a chuckle.

'I see. Slightly alight,' repeated Sir Joseph.

'Yes, that's why I can't go back. Someone may recognise me.'

'Highly unlikely. We'll be giving you a new name and a shiny new passport to go with it. I can't imagine that anyone at the camp will recognise you. It's been a couple of years since you were last there, and the whole place is run by a completely different regime.'

'Some of the soldiers may have returned.'

'That is possible, but if my memory serves me correctly, you didn't exactly stay long enough to be recognised.'

'That's very true, however in the short time I was there, I made quite an impact.'

'So I believe. And we can safely say that when you left, you burnt your bridges, so to speak.'

'Quite so,' replied Mike, mimicking one of Sir Joseph's favourite comments, which he raised his greying bushy eyebrows at.

'That's all decided then. Miss Wilson has your new passport, papers and ticket. You will be travelling as Mr Mike Eastmond, a company representative for a medical instrument manufacturer named Medinstman Incorporated.'

'Medical instrument manufacturer! What the hell do I know about that?'

'Probably nothing, but that doesn't matter. We will supply you with a catalogue and sample instruments. You must look at it and try to remember some of the salient items it contains, just in case anyone questions you about it, though I think that is highly unlikely.'

'Great!'

'We also need a recent photograph to go into your new passport. Miss Wilson will take one before you leave. Your plane departs on the next flight out at 4.30 tomorrow afternoon. Check-in time is 2.30.'

'When do I go to the prison to collect Sutton?'

'As Colin stated, you'll arrive in Roseburgh early on Saturday morning. You'll have plenty of time to get to your appointment at three in the afternoon with General Abotto, the camp commander. That gives you almost three hours to exchange the money for Sutton, ring Colin to let him know everything went as planned, and meet him at Roseburgh Airport in time for the flight home.'

'I'll go home and pack my bags and collect a firearm.'

'No firearms! You do not have permission to take one aboard the aeroplane, and a medical instrument rep would not carry a gun.'

'He might if he had to go into Kitsulana.'

'No guns. This is a straightforward exchange. You deliver the money and collect the man and escort him home.'

'When do I get the money?'

'Colin will meet you at the BA desk at London Heathrow Airport, and hand the papers and passport to you so that you can check in. When you arrive at Roseburgh, he will give you the package of money. Keep it with you at all times. I'm sure I don't have to emphasise that you'll be carrying a large sum of the department's hard fought for budget, and you are responsible for looking after it. It must not go missing under any circumstances. Do you understand?'

'If it does, you can take it out of my next pay cheque,' suggested Mike.

'Very amusing, Mr Randle, but I'm not laughing. You will be responsible for a lot of money and this is a serious matter.'

'I'll hang on to your precious money, provided there are no hitches and no surprises in store for me. How much will I be carrying anyway?'

'$250,000 in used notes,' replied Sir Joseph.

'Phew! That is a lot of dough to carry around.'

'And we'd rather you did not lose it.'

'You must want this Sutton guy back pretty badly to pay a hefty sum like that for him. What's he done?'

'That is our concern. All you need to worry about is delivering the money to General Abotto and returning with Mr Sutton.'

'Do you have a photo of him? I wouldn't want to give away all your hard earned cash for the wrong man,' Mike said.

Sir Joseph took two photographs from a folder and pushed it across his desk. 'This was taken from a video, shown on television when all the men were paraded before the cameras. It's reasonably clear. The second one is from the security cameras at Heathrow taken when he booked his flight. Neither are brilliant, but they are the best we've got at the moment.'

Mike picked up the pictures and looked at them. 'These should be good enough. The bloke looks like a hard-headed character.'

'He was in and out of trouble when he was a teenager. However, he has managed to steer clear of the law since then, and has avoided a prison sentence until now.'

Putting the photographs in his pocket Mike asked, 'Will there be anyone out there to help me?'

'Not in Kitsulana, you're on your own from the moment you land. We cannot be seen to be helping you. If you get desperate for help, you could try ringing Mr Robert Weston at the British Embassy in Roseburgh. He's our diplomat in Karuna. He set up the meeting and exchange, so he is able to venture into Kitsulana. His telephone number will be with the papers you receive. Colin will be waiting at his hotel for you to ring him on his mobile. His telephone number will also be with your papers. If there's any delay, ring him to get the flights rearranged. Is there anything else you need to know?'

Mike stood up. 'No, I guess not. That just about covers it.'

Sir Joseph stood and shook hands with him. 'Good luck. Keep your wits about you and bring our man back.'

Miss Wilson took Mike's passport photograph before he left the office and gave him the medical instruments and the catalogue. He stepped outside into the London street and took a deep breath. This was a job he had no interest in doing and had an uneasy feeling about the speed with which it was set up, and the country he was obliged to return to. Despite this, he knew that Sir Joseph left him with little option but to go along with it, however he was not going to leave all the planning arrangements solely to him. A few telephone calls, and a rummage through some of the items he had kept from his mercenary days were definitely called for.

20

ARRIVAL

At London's Heathrow Airport, Sir Joseph Sterling and DI Brooke were waiting for Mike at the BA reception desk. Brooke was to accompany Mike to an African country where he was to act as a courier in an exchange. Mike took the train to Heathrow and bustled through the crowds of mainly holiday travellers and joined them. Brooke handed him his papers.

'I didn't expect to see you here,' Mike remarked to Sir Joseph.

'I wanted to make sure the package was safe.'

'Right. Who's got it?'

Brooke pulled a small package part way out from his zip-up bag.

Mike grabbed it. 'It's hard to believe there's so much money in such a small package,' he said, tossing it in the air and catching it.

'There is, so we don't want to lose it,' said Brooke, snatching it back and replacing it in his bag.

'Stop worrying,' said Mike.

Brooke passed him a small attaché case. 'Here take this. It contains a nicely pressed and folded suit for you to wear to the meeting.'

'A suit!' exclaimed Mike.

'Yes, a suit. We want you to look the part, and I guessed that you'd turn up in something casual,' Sir Joseph remarked.

'I like casual,' maintained Mike.

'But not when you are representing Her Majesty's government.'

Mike shrugged. 'I though the government weren't supposed to be involved in this swop.'

'They aren't to outsiders, but will be to those involved in the exchange.'

'Don't forget that when we get to Roseburgh, we're not to speak to each other in case Sutton has someone watching the airport,' reminded Brooke.

They nodded their goodbyes to Sir Joseph and passed through customs into the busy waiting lounge, amid barely understandable Tannoy calls every few minutes announcing the departure of a flight to some far off country. Mike and Brooke headed straight to one of many snack bars, coffee bars and other shops that populated the waiting lounge, to have a cup of coffee. Here amongst the vast array of shops, almost anything could be bought, ranging from a newspaper to a motor car or cheap watch to a diamond necklace, at a price that was advertised as Duty Free and cheaper than if purchase outside the airport.

Mike whiled away the time thinking about his last trip to Africa and wondering how Suzie was getting on. He rang her on his mobile.

'Hello love, how are you doing?'

'Fine. We're taking it easy, not rushing. I'm soaking up the sun and relaxing. I could get used to this lifestyle.'

'So could I, if I got the chance. Are you topless?'

'Of course. We're out in the middle of the ocean, away from the thronging crowds.'

'But not from Reg and George.'

'They are busy looking after the yacht, not ogling at me.'

'Hmm. I wish I was there with you.'

'You will be, soon. We could have a nice relaxing holiday when you get back.'

'Sounds good, as long as we can be together – alone – with no Jeremy Pendleton to worry about.'

'Okay, that's a date,' Suzie smiled. 'Where are you?'

'I'm at London Airport waiting to board the plane to Nairobi.'

'Be careful when you get there. I don't like the sound of what you're getting into. It all sounds too easy.'

'Yeah, I will, my thoughts exactly. I'll give you a ring when I arrive.'

'Okay. 'Bye love.'

After finishing their coffees and passing the time sauntering through some of the shops, their flight was eventually announced. Mike and Brooke grabbed their bags and wandered down the long corridors to where they boarded a coach, which transferred them to the aeroplane.

It took nearly thirty minutes for everyone to get aboard, jam their bags into the overhead lockers, settle down and fasten their seatbelts ready for takeoff. The Boeing 777 taxied on to the main runway, stopped for a few seconds before it shuddered as the engines were boosted to full power sending it charging down the runway and lifting into the air, watched by Sir Joseph from the visitor's gallery. While the stewardesses went through their ritual of explaining the emergency procedures, Sir Joseph whispered a silent 'Good luck' to them, nodded to his guard and chauffer, and returned to his London office.

★ ★ ★

The flight was long – nearly nine hours, and both men dozed much of the time. Mike watched the in-flight film, which he had already seen on DVD and spent the rest of the time trying to calculate how Suzie and the boys were doing on their journey home in *Quester*. Thoughts about Jeremy Pendleton pushed their way into his mind, and he wondered how much more trouble he would cause trying to get Suzie back into his bed. His tactics at the motor yacht naming party proved to Mike what type of man he really was, and guessed that his ego would encourage him to try again once he thought the episode was past and forgotten. Past it may be, but forgotten – not on Mike's part, he had a long memory for such unscrupulous things. It was hard enough knowing that Suzie had to agree to his advances, without him trying to split them up so that he could satisfy his craving for possessing all things sexy that he cast his eyes upon.

Mike's thoughts also turned to Helgar. Under different circumstances he would have been tempted to take her up on the enticing offer she made. She was very attractive and had wonderful, big round breasts. Jeremy Pendleton looked unflustered when he reappeared to start the naming ceremony, but Mike imagined that a few words were said between them before he emerged from the bedroom. Did Helgar get into trouble? He thought it likely, and wondered how she managed to get involved with such a man deeply enough to agree to attempt something like that. Perhaps she was besotted by his charms, and his money? He was glad that she had found someone else to charm.

Eventually the flight landed at Nairobi Airport. It was 4:30 a.m. local time and the temperature had dropped very little from the 32°C it reached during the day. The airport itself was old, outdated and had nowhere open where they could get a good cup of coffee, let alone something to eat. Tramping to the holding lounge, Mike and Brooke sat on uncomfortable seats in a small room and waited. More than an hour passed before they were able to board the Airbus A320 for their connecting flight to Karuna.

The plane arrived at Roseburgh Airport bathed in early morning sunlight, and the outside temperature was already climbing. From inside the air conditioned cool cabin, Mike stared out of the window as they came in to land. He noticed many new buildings, which had been constructed in the intervening years since he was last in the country.

At 8 a.m., after Brooke had handed Mike the valuable package, they stepped through the cabin door. For Mike, it was into the familiar heat and smell of the country; bringing back memories of the last time he trod this soil. He recalled how glad he was to get out of Africa and back to terra firma in England. It felt as if history was repeating itself, and he needed events on this trip to go more smoothly and be a lot less hazardous than before. For Brooke, it was his first time in Africa and he was surprised at the wall of heat that hit him when he stepped outside, losing the comfort of the air conditioned cabin.

They joined the long queue that progressed slowly through passport control. When he reached the front of the line, Mike's passport and his features were carefully scrutinised, more than he had expected. He began to wonder if there was something wrong.

Had somebody recognised him? The last thing he needed was to be searched. Explaining why he was carrying $250,000 in cash would be hard to do, and he may even have the money confiscated. He glanced around and saw several armed policemen, so fighting his way out would be difficult.

After what seemed an eternity, Mike's passport was handed back to him and he was instructed to step through a metal detection doorway, while his bag went through an X-ray scanner. He wondered if they would see the cash, but to his relief nothing was said, though the attendant was busy chatting to the other officials and appeared not to be watching the screen very carefully. Mike was allowed to proceed and stepped into the main arrivals area. Brooke, who stood a few places behind him and watched the proceedings, sighed with relief when Mike was allowed through.

The airport was busy with passengers and visitors alike standing under the information board, staring at the arrival and departure times. Mike and Brooke stayed apart and did not speak to each other as agreed, though they managed a few quick glances in each other's direction.

Mike found a vacant seat, dumped his holdall on the floor and rang Suzie to see how far they had travelled on their journey home.

'How's the trip going?' Mike asked.

'It's going great. The sun has shone all the time and the water's calm and smooth. I'm enjoying myself relaxing, sunbathing and winding down. How about you? Where are you now, Roseburgh?'

'Yes, we arrived a few minutes ago. It's bloody hot and sticky out here, the way it always was.'

'I wish you didn't have to go back there. I'm constantly hearing of problems in the news about that area, and the fighting that still goes on.'

'I'm not happy about it either, but it should be a straightforward job, and if all goes to plan I should be out of here by tonight.'

'Yes, *should*. I hope you're right.'

'Our friend Sir Joseph didn't give me any choice. It was this or face a possible prison sentence for killing those two blokes who stole the yacht.'

'I'm sure he was bluffing. I don't believe he'd do that. Jim would never speak to him again.'

'Perhaps. How far have you travelled?' asked Mike changing the subject.

'I reckon we're about two thirds of the way home, maybe a little over that. We're making steady progress, but there's no point in us rushing. With any luck we should get back to England about the same time as you.'

'Okay, that's good. Got to go now. Things to do.'

'Give me a ring before you leave.'

'Will do. 'Bye love.'

Mike turned off his mobile and looked around the lounge. Armed policemen patrolled in pairs and the new airport building boasted a few shops, a café and a restaurant. His eyes landed on the desk he was looking for – a car rental company. After sweet-talking the attractive sales lady into giving him a good deal, Mike hired a four-wheel drive car for two days, and paid for it with his new credit card, courtesy of Sir Joseph. He collected the car and set off for his first destination.

Colin Brooke was nowhere to be seen; however he was close by and watched Mike leave before taking a taxi to his hotel.

The city of Roseburgh, capital of Karuna, was situated ten miles from the airport. The main highway from the airport, wound through mostly barren scrubland at first, before arriving at an urban sprawling city that had seen many changes during the previous few years. Mike approached the outskirts of the capital and saw the dramatic changes all around him that were taking place. The city showed signs of the prosperity it was now enjoying as a democracy, encouraging the influx of major corporations. The country was growing to meet their needs, with new found wealth that was generated by so many companies eager to establish their businesses there, in what was a fast emerging economy.

Gone were many of the corrugated roofed shanty homes located around the city perimeter, replaced by modern brick dwellings. Driving through the heart of Roseburgh, Mike marvelled at the expanding city, with new construction work in abundance. The streets were thronging with people and vehicles, enjoying the trappings of a bristling society that an end to the civil wars had brought them. Many high-rise buildings were in evidence, or under construction. New street lighting and an abundance of traffic lights, constantly flashing their signals, had appeared since his last visit.

Not that the whole country was as fortunate as Roseburgh. Having the nearby airport was crucial in encouraging many of the overseas businesses to this location. All were hoping to cash in on the flourishing city that had citizens with money in their pockets – many for the first time, and many who were eager to acquire the possessions that those in the rich western countries took for granted.

Passing through Roseburgh towards the outskirts on the far side, the buildings again became the older type and Mike motored on, approaching the pub he was looking for.

Paul's Bar had the same battered pub sign hanging from the first floor balcony as it had when he left nearly two years earlier.

Paul O'Connor was Mike's army buddy who originally owned the pub, but he got involved in gun running and drugs, and was killed. The pub was left to Mike and Suzie who did not want an African pub, so they left it to the barman, Manny, who was very grateful and was determined to make it a success to honour the memory of Paul.

Mike parked his vehicle in the yard at the rear of the pub, as he had done before, and wandered in through the open back door. He stepped into the shaded main bar area, which like most pubs had an aroma of stale cigarette smoke and beer. A movement on the left caught his eye, and he turned to see an old friend wiping and stacking glasses behind the bar.

'Manny! How the devil are you?' Mike asked, stepping towards him.

A broad grin crossed the local man's face, his teeth showing bright white against his dark features. 'Mr Randle, how good to see you again.'

The two men shook hands vigorously and eyed each other up and down. Mike thought that Manny looked exactly the same as when he last saw him, still boasting a wiry frame and not an ounce of fat on him. Manny thought Mike looked older and a little heavier than when he last saw him, but was courteous enough not to say so.

'I was delighted to get your telephone call,' said Manny. 'What brings you to this part of the world again?'

'Business. I've got a business meeting to attend and thought it would be a good opportunity to see you again while I was in the area.'

'I'm glad that you did. Please sit down,' he said, pointing to one of the empty table and chairs sitting lifelessly in the bar area waiting for customers to occupy them. 'Would you like a drink?'

'Just cool water, thanks. It's a bit early for me to start drinking alcohol,' Mike said, wiping the sweat from his brow. 'I'd forgotten quite how hot it gets out here.'

Manny smiled and poured him a drink of water from the refrigerator.

'The bar area is smaller now,' observed Mike glancing around.

'Yes. After you left, the rebel soldiers stopped coming to the bar and I needed to do something to attract more customers. I put a partition up and turned the other half into a restaurant. I have been lucky enough to get a good chef, and business has picked up nicely since he started working here. We are fully booked most weekends and are well attended for lunch and evening meals during the week.'

'Good, I'm glad you've made a go of things here.'

'I'm sure it's what Paul would have wanted,' suggested Manny.

Mike smiled. 'Do you still have a large safe in the office?'

'Yes.'

'Would you look after a package for me?'

'Of course, I'd be happy to. Is it valuable?'

'It is, there's nothing illegal in it and it's not mine, but it's very important that you give it to no one but me – no one, do you understand?'

'I understand.'

'If anyone calls, or tells you that I sent them, deny having the package and don't give it to them.'

Manny looked a little surprised at the stern request, but agreed. 'Okay. When is your business meeting?'

'Not until later this afternoon.'

'Good. Then you can be my guest for lunch. I've extended the hours and now open at twelve o'clock to attract the lunchtime customers. We don't get as many in here as we do in the evenings, but there's enough to make it worthwhile.'

'Okay. I'd love to stay and sample your cuisine, thank you. Tell me, do you have a gun that I can borrow? I have to go into Kitsulana, and I hear there are still a lot of bandits around.'

'Paul's old revolver is in the safe, you can have that. I clean and check it regularly, just in case of trouble, though I'm thankful to say that I've never had to use it. I'm sure it still works okay.'

'That'll be great. Thanks.'

Following an enjoyable lunch of fish, rice and vegetables, prepared by Manny's new chef, Mike asked Manny to secure the package of money in the safe. He was curious to know what the package contained, but refrained from asking any questions about it as it was obvious that Mike wished the contents to remain a secret.

With the time approaching three in the afternoon, Mike thanked him, changed into the suit Brooke had given him to wear to the meeting, felt hot and uncomfortable in it and changed back. He shoved his medical catalogues into the attaché case and said goodbye to Manny. Dumping the case on the passenger's seat, Mike hid the old wartime revolver under the parcel shelf and started his eight mile journey to the border with Kitsulana.

The dirt road had changed very little. Mike glanced at the turn-off into the jungle path that bypassed the border crossing on the road, and wondered if anyone still used it, as he had done in the past. It looked more overgrown now and less obvious as an established path through to the jungle.

He approached the border checkpoint, manned by two guards carrying sub-machine guns. In the nearby guard hut a third man stood by, watching the proceedings. Mike's passport and papers were carefully scrutinised. While he waited, Mike casually glance around, but was studying the guard's weapons and the area carefully, a legacy of his army training that had taught him to automatically assess each location and its potential for danger. After a telephone call to General Abotto confirming his appointment, the guards allowed Mike to enter. He continued with an army Jeep as an escort the fifteen miles to Camp West.

'Security at the border is certainly tight,' he muttered inwardly. 'I hope there's no problem when I bring Sutton out. The guards have automatic weapons and the area is very open, getting past them could be tricky. If there's a problem, I may have to resort to the old jungle route again and hope that it is still passable.'

Following the Jeep, he bumped along the unmade heavily used dirt road, which the traffic had compressed down into an underlying surface as hard as concrete with a light sprinkling of dust on top. The month of September had past, when the heavens opened and the heaviest tropical rain fell, but even then, the rain failed to penetrate the hard baked surface. Heavy as the rain was, it either rested in the dips as puddles or rolled off the top as if it was waterproof. Within an hour of the rain ceasing to fall, the road returned to a dust-strewn track and looked as if the sky had never opened and the deluge had never fallen from above.

The road cut a path around the outer edge of the dense jungle, which masked the difficult track that Mike used on his last visit to the country when he needed to arrive at Camp West unannounced. This time, his arrival was by arrangement and he travelled by the normal route, with his escort covering him in case they met any bandits or rebel soldiers.

Camp West loomed into view before him. The location was the same, but the camp was unrecognisable to Mike. It had undergone a dramatic change; rebuilt by rebel prisoners who were captured during the fighting. The barbed wire fence and wooden huts had disappeared, replaced by a stone perimeter wall and brick buildings. Only the brick built prison remained from the original camp, the only building to survive the fire that demolished the rest of the site.

The outside camp barrier was raised to let the Jeep escort pass, before closing again. Braking to a halt, Mike was approached by one of the duty guards.

'I am Mike Eastmond. I have an appointment with General Abotto,' he informed him.

'Passport,' the guard barked.

Mike handed his passport over. The surly looking guard checked the photograph and without speaking turned, stepped into his guardhouse and picked up the telephone. Mike sat in his car, brushing flies away from his face while he watched the guard speaking to someone without taking his eyes off the visitor, continuing to stare at him. Finishing his telephone call, he raised the inner barrier to let Mike pass, handed him his passport and pointing to a building at the far end of the camp.

'The commander's quarters are in the last building,' he stated in an accent so strong that Mike understood only a few words, but gathered the meaning of them.

He drove into the camp, passed a few soldiers wandering around and glanced at the padlocked metal grill by the side of the road.

'So, the dreaded solitary pit in the ground is still there,' he murmured to himself. 'I wonder how many poor buggers have had to endure the sweltering heat in there like I did. At least the guard didn't search me or the car.'

The layout was much the same as before, with the new brick buildings erected on the identical place of each original wooden hut. Driving past the prison block, Mike glanced in through the open door and noted that no guards were in evidence. He grabbed the gun from below the parcel shelf and tucked it in his belt at the back.

Parking his car next to a Jeep outside the commander's office, the door opened and a soldier beckoned him inside. Mike picked up his attaché case, was led along a dim but cool corridor, and shown into a small almost empty room, brightly lit by a scorching sun blazing through a closed picture window. Inside, a bare wooden table and four chairs were all the room contained.

'General Abotto will be with you in a moment,' the guard assured him, closing the door as he left.

The room was stiflingly hot, cooled by a fan that hung from the ceiling and turned so slowly that no discernable movement of air in the room was generated.

After a few minutes, three men entered the room – two white Europeans in civilian clothes, one wearing a smart suit, and one black local man in a military uniform. Mike recognised Sutton immediately from the photographs, and alarm bells started to ring loud and clear. Something was not right.

'I am General Abotto,' the military man stated.

'Mike Eastmond,' declared Mike, extending his hand.

'Would you like to sit down?' the general said without shaking hands, pointing to a chair.

Mike sat in the chair, nearest to the door, and stood his case on the floor. The other two men grabbed a chair each. The smartly dressed man, who Mike did not recognise, pulled the chair next to him aside and sat at the end of the table; all three with stern expressions faced him.

'This is Mr Sutton,' said the general, 'and this is Mr Weston from your embassy.'

Mike said nothing. He was trying to gauge the situation. Why was Weston there?

'I expected an important Whitehall diplomat to look a lot better dressed than you are,' stated Sutton. 'Your Mr Weston here wears a smartly pressed suit, you are dressed much more casually,' he stated nodding to Weston.

'So I see. Well, we don't all wear pin striped suits,' Mike replied.

'Even so, you don't much look like an important Whitehall diplomat to me,' Sutton complained.

'And you don't much look like a prisoner to me,' replied Mike.

'I'm not,' said Sutton, producing a gun from his pocket and pointing it at Mike. 'This whole exchange business was concocted to get an important government official out here so that I could do an exchange of my own.'

'And repay our President Mr Gorringa with a tidy sum of money for allowing you to do it,' stated the general.

'As well as a nice sum for me, for helping to set the whole thing up,' added Weston.

'So, that's what this is all about. This is a kidnapping not an exchange?' said Mike, gauging whether he had time to grab the gun he was hiding. With Sutton's gun already pointing at him, he decided it was prudent to wait for a better opportunity.

'No, it's still an exchange, but not the one that you were expecting.'

'I don't understand. Who are you expecting to exchange me for?'

'The Chatham Police have a woman in custody who I want released. Her name is Mrs Katherine Boyd,' stated Sutton.

'Mrs Boyd! I recall seeing something in the newspapers about her. Isn't she the woman who assisted in that building society robbery?' asked Mike.

'That's the one, and I want her back.'

'I see. So, you and Mrs Boyd are … how shall I say it … an item?'

'You could put it that way. She was stealing money from the building society to help me in my business before that interfering man Wainwright got wind of it and not only did he put a stop to it, but he was blackmailing her to keep it a secret. If she didn't pay up he threatened to expose her, and we couldn't have that.'

'So, you devised a robbery to steal more money and get rid of him at the same time.'

'I'd pre-booked a flight here for the day following the robbery, and expected to bring the stolen money with me.'

'And what about Mrs Boyd? What would happen to her?'

'She was to join me in a couple of weeks time, after things had cooled down. It would have all worked out okay if that Irish idiot Kelly hadn't messed things up and let slip that Katie was involved.'

'Now she's in prison and you want to exchange me for her?'

'That's about it.'

'And you expect British Government officials to lose a lot of money and participate in this blackmail?'

'Of course. They have no option if they want to see their man get home safe and sound. Where's the money you were supposed to bring? Is it in the attaché case?'

'You didn't think I was stupid enough to bring it with me to a bandit filled country like this, did you?' insisted Mike, his mind racing to concoct a plausible explanation to help his situation.

Weston jumped up grabbed Mike's case and dumped it on the table. He flung it open. 'There's only a lot of medical instruments and papers in here,' he complained, rifling through and throwing the case on the floor.

'Just tell me where the money is,' Sutton threatened waiving his gun at Mike.

'So that each of you can have his share? It won't be that easy. I was simply told that it would be handed over at the airport, when I confirmed that you were ready to fly back to England with me.'

Sutton looked at the general. 'Do you believe him?'

'I don't know. It seems reasonable that a few precautions would be taken to ensure the deal went as planned. After all, we are talking about a great deal of money. Perhaps he is telling the truth.'

'Brooke must be looking after the money in that case,' Weston stated.

'Whose Brooke?' asked Sutton.

'He's the London copper who's come along to escort you back to England.'

'Has Brooke got the money?' Sutton asked Mike.

'I don't know. I was simply told that it would be handed over when I get you back to the airport in Roseburgh.'

Waving his gun at Mike, Sutton declared. 'You'd better not be lying to me or I'll blow your fucking head off.'

Mike was not fazed by threats he knew to be hollow and sat unflinching at the swearing bluster, giving Sutton a cold stare. He was a man of many words and few actions he gauged; a man who paid others to do his dirty work; a man who even got his woman to steal for him. Until the money was secured and the exchange deal agreed, he needed Mike alive.

'I'll get the money off Brooke,' declared Weston. 'He's likely to try contacting me at the embassy now that he's arrived. If he doesn't want to hand it over quietly, then I'll have to kill him.'

'If you do, you'd better make it look like an accident. We don't want more British coppers coming out here to investigate,' Sutton stated.

'Okay.'

'And make sure you return here with the money,' threatened Sutton, 'or else …'

'Yeah, okay. We're all in this together. I'd better get back and find out what our London copper is up to. He'll be wondering where I am.'

Sutton nodded. Weston looked at Mike with a disbelieving scorn on his face. 'I'll see you later,' he said, leaving the room.

Mike was concerned about Brooke. Like him, he believed that Weston was on his side and will not imagine that he is a traitor. There was no way that Mike could warn him unless he got the chance to use his mobile, which he knew was unlikely.

'Exactly what is your job in the government?' the general asked.

'I work in a department that has a lot of financial dealings.'

'It sounds as if we've got hold of the right man then.'

'We target unsuspecting individuals to make them hand over lots of cash.'

'Really? What's the department called?'

'The Inland Revenue,' smiled Mike.

'Very funny,' scoffed Sutton. 'We'll soon wipe that smile from your face. Until Katie gets out here, you'll be spending you time in the camp prison. It's not a very comfortable place and the food's probably not up to the standard you're used to, so you'd better hope that your government responds quickly.'

'I'm sure they will, especially if you kill a London copper. They're unlikely to believe that it was an accident.'

'Guards,' shouted the general.

Two armed soldiers entered the room and grabbed Mike.

'Take this man to the prison cells. Search him, I want him stripped of everything he has including his belt and shoe laces, and lock him up tight.'

'You won't get away with this,' Mike proclaimed, as he was ushered towards the door by prods from the guards rifle barrels.

In the corridor, to move him more quickly one guard shoved Mike hard in the back with the tip of his rifle.

Mike stopped and turned to face them. 'If you do that again, you'll be sorry,' he threatened.

The two men looked at each other and smiled. They stood with the barrel of their guns a few inches from Mike's chest.

'Shut up and get moving,' the guard said, prodding him again.

In one quick movement, Mike grabbed a rifle barrel with each hand and pulled them sharply towards him. Both guards were caught off balance and stumbled forwards. Mike's foot came up sharply, giving the first guard a hefty kick between the legs. He screamed, releasing his grip on the rifle, which Mike used to swing round and crash the stock against the head of the other guard, propelling him into the wall.

Both guards were rolling around the floor nursing their wounds when Sutton, hearing the commotion opened the door. Mike threw the rifles to the floor, but before he could grab his revolver Sutton stepped from the room and thrust his gun in Mike's ribs.

With his finger on the trigger he threatened, 'Not so fast, if you don't want a bullet in your gut. Back off.'

Mike took two paces backwards.

'And raise your hands,' demanded Sutton.

Raising his arms, Mike watched the guards stagger to their feet.

'Search him,' demanded Sutton.

The revolver, tucked in Mike's belt was discovered and handed to Sutton, along with Mike's mobile telephone, wallet and passport.

'Not the sort of weapon I would expect a diplomat to carry,' he said, weighing the weapon in his hand. 'It's old and heavy, but I bet it still works.'

'Like I said, I was told this was bandit country,' retorted Mike.

'How did you get this past airport customs?'

'I didn't. A local man sold it to me.'

'Do you know how to use this thing?'

Mike said nothing.

'You seem to know how to handle yourself, more like a soldier than a diplomat.'

'I did a spell in the army a while ago,' admitted Mike.

'I thought so. Well, don't try any more army tricks or you'll end up dead!'

Mike stared at Sutton with contempt written over his face. 'We'll see about that,' he warned.

Two more armed guards were summoned, and between them they escorted Mike to the prison hut where his belt and shoelaces were removed.

'Sod!' mumbled Mike. He was hoping to keep his belt, which had a lock pick concealed inside it; an item he had kept from his mercenary days.

Many faces appeared at the other cell windows when Mike was shoved into a cell. The door was banged shut and locked. He had been in this prison before; this indeed was déjà vu.

21

THE UNEXPECTED

After his annoying discovery that the British Government's envoy Mike Eastmond had not brought the ransom money for Owen Sutton with him to Camp West, Robert Weston hurried back to the British Embassy in Roseburgh. He was the embassy contact man who had turned traitor for a share of the ransom, and wanted to tackle DI Brooke, the London policeman who had accompanied Eastmond to Africa. He now believed that Brooke had charge of the ransom money. To keep his co-conspirators happy, he needed to obtain it from him – even if it meant killing Brooke to get it.

When he arrived back at the embassy, Weston discovered that Brooke had telephoned him earlier, and left a contact number with the receptionist. Weston rang him.

'DI Brooke?'

'Yes.'

'I'm Robert Weston from the British Embassy. I'm sorry that I was unable to meet you when you arrived, but I had a few urgent things to attend to,' he confessed.

'They must have been very important for you to be unavailable for most of the day. After all this is a crucial exchange that we are dealing with, and you are our contact man.'

'Yes, I agree. I'm very sorry. I'd like to come over and discuss a few things with you, if that's okay.'

'Can't we speak on the telephone? I'm expecting an important call and may have to leave any time now,' said Brooke, glancing at his mobile to confirm it was turned on.

'It's wisest not to. In this country you cannot be sure of absolute privacy on the telephone,' Weston insisted.

Brooke thought that a strange comment to make, but agreed. 'I'm in room 105 on the first floor of *The Ambassador Hotel*.'

'Right, I know where that is. I'll see you in about ten minutes.'

Weston replaced the receiver and wandered over to his desk. From a drawer, he took out a gun and checked the clip. Satisfied that it was loaded, he slammed the clip back in with the palm of his hand and stuffed the gun in his pocket.

He informed the receptionist where he was going and hurried along to *The Ambassador Hotel*. Ignoring the lift, he took the stairs two at a time and marched along the corridor to room 105. Outside the door, he checked that his tie was straight, ran his hands down his light grey suit to smooth it out and knocked on the door.

'DI Brooke?' he asked when the door was opened.

'Yes, you must be Robert Weston. Come in,' Brooke said, opening the door wide.

Weston wandered into the room and turned to face Brooke. 'Has your important telephone call come through yet?'

'No, not yet. I'm a bit worried. The exchange will only take a few minutes to conduct and Mike Eastmond should have contacted me by now to say he's on his way back with Sutton to the airport,' he stated looking at his watch.

'Do you think there's been a problem with the exchange?' Weston probed.

'I hope not. There's no reason why there should be, unless you know anything different,' Brooke stated, motioning Weston to sit down.

Sinking his young wiry frame into the armchair he replied, 'No, I don't see why there should be any hitches, though your Mr Eastmond is dressed a bit casually, perhaps they are suspicious that he's not really a government representative.'

'I suppose that's possible,' Brooke agreed. 'Would you like a drink?'

'A scotch and soda water would be nice, thank you.'

Brooke moved to the drinks cabinet, turning his back on

Weston. The embassy man saw this as his chance and pulled the gun from his pocket.

Brooke kept his back to him and asked, 'Would you like some ice with it?'

'Yes, please, then you can tell me where you've hidden the ransom money,' Weston declared, pointing the gun at Brooke's back.

Turning swiftly with the soda siphon in his hand, Brooke sprayed it at Weston, catching him full in the face. He closed his eyes for a second as the water hit him, and when he opened them again, the siphon, thrown by Brooke, was an inch away from his head. It caught him on the bridge of the nose, breaking it and sending him crashing to the floor. By the time he regained his senses, Brooke was standing on his wrist and he yanked the gun from Weston's grasp.

'Perhaps you'd now like to tell me what is really going on?' he threatened, pointing the gun at him. 'I presume that you are in league with the general, or Sutton, or both.'

'How did you figure that out?'

'I though something was wrong when you disappeared for such a long time when you knew this important meeting was taking place. Then instead of using the telephone you insisted in seeing me, suggesting the telephone call may be bugged. Nobody knows who I am or why I am here, so why would the telephone be bugged? It's just no plausible.'

'I didn't think of that.'

'And when you said that Mike Eastmond was dressed casually, I knew something was definitely wrong. How could you possibly have known, unless you were there to see him arrive.'

'A silly mistake on my part, but it won't do you any good. The general and Sutton have Eastmond locked up in the prison cells, and won't release him until you pay the ransom and let Mrs Katie Boyd go free,' stated Weston, getting to his feet and taking a handkerchief from his top pocket to stem the blood running from his nose.

'Mrs Boyd! Are you talking about the woman involved in the building society robbery in Chatham?'

'She's the one.'

'What on earth has she got to do with this?'

'She's Sutton's woman, and you've got her locked up. He wants her back.'

'I see. Things are becoming clearer now.'

'So, you can tell your masters that unless we get the money, and the return of the lady, Eastmond will get a bullet in the head, and quite soon.'

'I'm not sure than Sutton is up to adding murder to his list of crimes just yet.'

'Huh! That's because you don't know what sort of man he is. He's impulsive and anyway, there are plenty of people at the camp who are willing to pull the trigger for him. He won't be very happy if you stop me from delivering the money to him, so you might as well give it to me and let me go. It's the only way you're going to see Eastmond alive again.'

'You're not going anywhere. I'll see to it that you are shipped back to England to face conspiracy charges, and if Mike Randle or anyone else dies, we'll make that accomplice to murder.'

The though of returning to England on a murder charge frightened Weston, and his face showed it.

'Who the hell is Mike Randle?'

'He's the man you know as Mike Eastmond. He's freelance, and not a government official at all, so there's no chance of anyone getting that ransom money for him, or having Mrs Boyd released from prison.'

The knowledge that they had all been duped by the London authorities angered Weston. He made a sudden rush at Brooke and grabbed the gun. The two men grappled for the weapon, crashed to the floor and rolled over and over as they both struggled to gain possession of it.

Weston fought like the young tiger that he was, but Brooke was an experienced copper whose progress through the ranks had taught him how to take care of himself. He was a fitness fanatic, and strong.

Both men had a finger on the trigger, and Weston grabbed the gun barrel and did his best to turn it towards Brooke. For a few strength-busting moments he started to force the weapon in his direction. Flexing his muscles to resist the movement, Brooke suddenly released his grip for an instant, and the pressure that Weston had built up, swung the weapon past Brooke to point at the floor. Trying to jerk the weapon back, the young man only succeeded in forcing the barrel past his intended target and towards his own body. With the pressure of both men's fingers on the trigger, the weapon fired a muffled shot, sending a bullet tearing into Weston's stomach.

With screams of agony, his eyes opened wide in terrified realisation of his fatal miscalculation and impending death. He grabbed hold of Brooke's arm as his mouth opened and the stifled groans of intense pain gurgled to the surface. With a final shaking of his body, he went limp, released his grip and exhaled for the last time. Brooke lowered him to the floor. He checked his pulse, but there was none; he closed the man's eyes.

Shoving the gun in his pocket, Brooke picked up the telephone and rang Sir Joseph's home number. It was three o'clock on a Saturday afternoon in England, and he guessed that Sir Joseph would be at home, which he was, and working in his study.

The events of the day were relayed to him by Brooke '... and of course that means Mike Randle is in serious trouble and presumably has hidden the money somewhere for safe keeping.'

'This is very disturbing, Colin. I must think what is to be done about it. I'll ring you later when I've sorted things out in my mind. Meanwhile, I'd better arrange for Mr Weston's body to be brought home. Can you get him back to our embassy without being seen?'

'Yes, I think I should be able to manage that. I noticed a fire escape at the rear of the hotel. I'll use that, and get an embassy official to meet me out back with a car.'

'Good. Once you get him there you'll technically be on British soil, and there is no need for the local police to be involved. Tell them he died of a heart attack and get our embassy doctor to supply the death certificate to confirm it.'

'Okay, Sir. I'll hear from you later.'

Replacing the telephone in its cradle, Brooke looked at the body of Weston and inhaled a deep breath. His career as a policeman had made it necessary for him to kill before, but he always regretted taking someone's life. His task now was to get the body back to the embassy, and sort out the details to get Weston returned to England.

As well as this dangerous turn of events, Mike Randle was in a bad situation and they were all relying on Sir Joseph to come up with a solution – and quickly; it had not been a good day.

22

A NASTY SURPRISE

With the events at Cannes, and Jeremy Pendleton's yacht *Julia* becoming a distant memory, Sunday morning dawned with a clear sky and a light wind as *Quester* was sailed up the English Channel towards her berth on the River Hamble.

Suzie stood on deck; an orange sun was rising in the eastern sky and the wind slipped through her hair. She was pleased to see the English coastline and knew they were almost home. The trip had been both exhilarating and worrying, but the outcome was all she could have hoped for, now that Jeremy Pendleton had received his yacht and payment for it was secured. Now all she wanted, was to see Mike home safely from his sojourn to Africa. On that, she was about to get a nasty surprise.

After doing her exercises and preparing breakfast for herself Reg and George, Suzie lazed on deck, enjoying the final hours of their trip home. The familiar ring tone of her mobile grabbed her attention. She hurried down the steps to the cabin where it lay on the L shaped seat positioned around the dining table. She was expecting Mike to give her a call.

'Hello.'

'Good morning, Suzie. I hope you are experiencing a pleasant trip,' announced the familiar voice.

'Yes, thank you, Sir Joseph. We're nearly home.'

'When do you anticipate arriving at your boatyard?'

'Probably some time later this morning. Why?'

'I'd like you to come and see me at my home in Woking, after you've docked.'

'What! On a Sunday! That's very unusual! What's the problem? Has something happened to Mike?' she asked, settling down on the seat.

'The situation out there is more complicated than I'd hoped for, and I need to speak with you about it.'

'Something's wrong. What's happened to Mike? Is he all right? Tell me,' demanded Suzie in a frustrated tone of voice, rising to her feet.

'Mike is okay. I don't want to say too much on the telephone. It's better that we should speak face to face,' suggested Sir Joseph, trying to be as diplomatic and calming as he could.

'You're worrying me,' stated Suzie.

'There's nothing to worry about. Things are not that bad.'

'Not that bad, but obviously not that good either. Is he hurt?'

'No, he's not hurt. Ring me when you get ashore and let me know what time you expect to arrive.'

'I'll be there as quick as I can.'

Switching off her mobile, Suzie bellowed out to Reg who was piloting the yacht, 'Full speed ahead, Reg. Mike's in trouble and I need to get back quickly.'

'Very good, Miss Drake, we'll be home before you know it.'

The sails were dropped, the engines on *Quester* were revved up to full speed and the motor yacht surged forward cutting a path through the water, racing towards her berth.

Suzie telephoned Jim. 'Your dad has just rung me and asked me to meet him at his home this afternoon. Something's happened to Mike, but he won't tell me what it is until I get there. I'm worried, Jim, will you try and find out what's happened?'

'I'll try, but you know my father, he's not likely to tell me either.'

'Do try.'

'I will. I'll ring you back after I've spoken to him.'

Suzie paced up and down in the cabin until her mobile rang again a few minutes later. She snatched it up straight away. 'Hello, Jim'

'I couldn't get anything out of dad either. He did say that Mike is unharmed and not to worry unnecessarily.'

'That's what he told me. It's fine for him to say that, but it doesn't really help. Thanks for trying.'

'How long before you berth?'

'I'd guess about two, two-and-a-half hours or so, around lunch time.'

'Okay. Jenny and I are at the boatyard today. We'll wait here for you to arrive, and drive you to dad's house.'

'Okay, Jim, thanks.'

It was a frustrating two-and-a-half hours before *Quester* finally tied up at the rear of SMJ Boatyard Ltd. Suzie had explained the situation to Reg and George and asked them to look after the boatyard while they were gone.

'You leave things to George and me. We'll handle everything.'

'Thanks, Reg. I don't know what the boatyard would do without the pair of you.'

Jim and Jenny were waiting for Suzie on the jetty as she jumped ashore before the yacht had finally come to rest.

'I'll drive,' stated Jim, the three hurrying towards his Rolls Royce Silver Cloud. 'You can tell us what has happened so far while we're on the way.'

Accelerating out of the boatyard, Jim headed the Rolls towards his father's Surrey house. 'I tried hard, but couldn't get any information from my father,' he said. 'All he would say is that Mike is doing a job for him. What's this all about?'

'Your father *persuaded* Mike to go to Africa to handle an exchange for him.'

'Persuaded?' asked Jim.

'That's a courteous way of putting it.'

'You meant that he put pressure on Mike to go?'

'He did.'

'So, what sort of an exchange is it?'

'It's to exchange money for a man in Africa who your father wants to interview. Mike was to hand over the cash and escort the man back to England with Colin Brooke. A simple job, said your father.'

'Whereabouts in Africa has he gone?' asked Jenny, sitting in the back seat next to Suzie.

'Kitsulana, would you believe?'

'Kitsulana! Why on earth has he returned there?'

'Sir Joseph wanted someone to go out there who knew the area, he said.'

'But it's very dangerous for Mike out there. If anyone recognises him, he could be shot,' Jenny stated.

'He's travelling under an assumed name, and hoping that nobody there realises his true identity.'

'Which part of Kitsulana is he going to?' Jenny asked.

'Near Jetuloo, Camp West.'

'No! Not Camp West. Surely, he wouldn't go back there?' Jenny stated in amazement.

'He thought he had no option.'

'But why?' asked Jim. 'What sort of pressure did my father put on him?'

'Try blackmail.'

'What! Blackmail? From my father? Are you sure?'

'I'm sure that you heard from Reg about the way we got the motor yacht back, and how Mike killed the two blokes who murdered Pete and Barry?'

'Yes, we did. He could hardly contain his delight at the news, but told us not to mention it to anyone else.'

'Well, Sir Joseph found out about the killings and suggested to Mike that he might have to stand trial for murder, unless he carried out this job for him.'

'What! That really is blackmail,' asserted Jim. 'You wait until I see him. I'll tell him a thing or two.'

'It's no use having a go at your father. That won't help the situation.'

'I thought Camp West was destroyed,' said Jenny.

'That's right, it was. It burnt to the ground, but it's been rebuilt since we were last there.'

Leaving the M27, Jim turned the car on to the M3 and sped up to 90 mph on the outside lane. Other cars moved out of the way to let the Rolls Royce flash past.

'Be careful Jim. You don't want to get a ticket.'

'Sod the ticket. I can afford lots of them.'

'But, you might lose your licence. Then what would you do?'

'Get Mr Charlie to chauffer me. He loves driving this car. I'm sure he would be very pleased if I lost my licence and had to rely on him to drive me everywhere.'

Jenny and Suzie looked at each other and smiled. Suzie's smile hid the apprehension she felt at not knowing what was happening to Mike. She was soon to discover the truth.

They drove into the London suburb of Woking, and at the end of a private road, Jim steered his car into the driveway of his father's house and parked it in front of the doors to his garage. The house was an Edwardian, detached four-bedroom residence that backed on to fields and had a small wooded area nearby. It was private enough for Sir Joseph's needs and allowed him the space he wanted to take his dog for a walk whenever he returned home early enough; which was not very often. Generally it was left to his housekeeper, Mrs Brown, to exercise the dog.

The front door was opened by Sir Joseph before the trio had reached it. 'Come on in you three. I thought you'd all be turning up to hear what I have to say. Would you like a drink?' he asked, as they entered his tall hallway, typical of that style of turn-of-the-century houses.

'Not for me, I'm driving,' stated Jim.

Jenny and Suzie both shook their heads.

'I'd rather hear what you've got to say straight away,' declared Suzie.

Sir Joseph led them through to the dining room. A large oblong room with a dining table and eight chairs was situated at the far end and overlooked the garden. A settee and two armchairs surrounded the fireplace at the front of the room where visitors could gaze through the wooden framed, sash windows.

'This is DI Burgess, from Chatham police station,' Sir Joseph advised. 'He's here to give us some help on one aspect of this case.'

The inspector stood from his armchair and nodded his greetings.

'Please sit down,' Sir Joseph said, motioning to the settee.

Oliver, his German shepherd dog, came lolloping into the room and sniffed around each of them and ended up putting a paw on Jenny's lap asking to be fussed, which she obliged giving his face and neck a hearty rub.

'I imagine that Mike told you what I'd asked him to do?' said Sir Joseph, looking at Suzie.

'Yes, and I've told Jim and Jenny as much as I know.'

Taking a deep breath, Sir Joseph began, 'It was supposed to be a simple job handing over a package in exchange for a man who has flown to Africa, then escorting that person back to the airport, meeting Colin Brooke and everyone flying home to England.'

'So what went wrong, Dad?'

'The man we are after is wanted for questioning about a gun used in a robbery and a murder, which is why I need him to return to this country so that I can speak to him. The police in Chatham have two people in custody for that robbery, and one of them is a woman. What we were unaware of is that she is familiar with the man we want to question.'

'Familiar? Do you mean that she is his partner?' asked Suzie.

'Yes, that's exactly what I mean, and is what has complicated matters, and is why our suspect wants her released.'

'I don't see the connection,' said Jim.

'I'm coming to that. This man flew to Africa and was apparently put in jail for financing an attempted coup against the government of Kitsulana, along with several other security consultants, otherwise known as mercenaries.'

'I recall seeing something on the television news about it,' said Jenny.

'That's right. Our embassy man out there, Mr Weston, managed to get an interview with our suspect and informed us that he'd agreed to return to England if we negotiated his release, and would then speak to us about the gun used in the murder. For that release we had to pay a sum of money, delivered by a government official.'

'That sounds fairly straightforward,' said Suzie. 'So, what's happened?'

'We now know that the whole plan was simply a ruse in order

to get a high-ranking government official to deliver the money. What their real plan turned out to be, was for them to hold that government man in order to exchange him for this woman who was arrested for the robbery, with the money going to corrupt officials for allowing our suspect to escape.'

'So, Mike is a prisoner of this man in … where? Camp West?'

'So we believe, Suzie. We understand that he is being held in the prison block there.'

'That's not a nice place to stay. I've seen it.'

'Yes, we realise that, which is why we wanted to talk to you about a possible solution to the problem.'

'The solution is obvious. Pay the money; send the woman back and get Mike released.'

'It's not as easy as that,' stated DI Burgess. 'She is in custody for participating in a robbery in Chatham and the shooting of a man, with the same gun used in a political murder. The man who was shot is still critically ill, and may yet die.'

'We cannot simply release her,' said Sir Joseph.

'Why not?' Suzie asked, raising her voice in frustration.

'It would cause a scandal if anyone found out we'd released her and given in to blackmail, and the government wants to avoid that.'

'Sod your scandal; you've already agreed to pay for the man's release.'

'Only unofficially, which is why we asked Mike to handle it. We cannot accede to blackmail.'

'Sod your blackmail as well! Blackmail's something you know about, Sir Joseph, isn't it?'

'I know what you are referring to, but it isn't quite like that,' he countered.

'Oh, yes, and what is it like? Mike and I have assisted you on several other occasions when you needed help, and it's about time you returned the favour now he's in trouble because of doing your dirty work.'

'We appreciate that Suzie, and we want to do all we can to resolve this situation with a minimum of fuss,' stated Sir Joseph.

Suzie leapt to her feet. 'Minimum of fuss, my arse! You sound just like a bloody politician – all talk and no do. You're happy to break the rules to send unauthorised people out on so-called safe missions by blackmailing them into doing it, but when things go wrong, all of a sudden the rules are sacrosanct and can't be broken to help them.'

'That's unfair, but I understand your frustration. Let me offer you a solution,' calmed Sir Joseph.

Sitting back down, Suzie was fuming and already considering her own solution.

'Mr Sutton, that's the man in Africa we wish to speak to, is expecting his woman, a Mrs Boyd, to be allowed to fly out to him. So, we'll send a woman out there, but not the one he's expecting.'

Suzie looked hard at Sir Joseph. 'I intend to go. I imagine that is what you were going to ask me anyway?'

'Quite right; it is. We'd like you to go in her place.'

'Of course,' said Suzie in agreement, with a slightly condescending nod of her head. 'When is this arranged for?'

'It isn't yet, not completely anyway. We had to make sure of your consent, before we could proceed with plans to agree to Mr Sutton's demands, though we have organised the flight arrangements. I felt sure that it would be almost impossible to prevent you from going after you were apprised of the situation, so it seemed sensible to use your involvement to our advantage.'

'Too right. What does this woman look like? I mean, is Sutton going to mistake me for her, even for a moment? Have either of you seen her?' asked Suzie.

Burgess replied, 'We brought her to Chatham Police Station when the investigation into the building society robbery first began. She's not unlike you, about your age, a little shorter, fuller figure, but I don't think that needs to concern you.'

'That's right,' interrupted Sir Joseph. 'Mr Sutton almost certainly won't see you until you arrive at Camp West.'

'Almost certainly?'

'We can't be absolutely sure, but it's a fairly safe bet.'

'Really? About as safe a bet as sending Mike on a simple job?'

'Quite so.'

'Why won't he be at the airport to meet his woman?'

'Technically, he's supposed to be under arrest at the camp with the other imprisoned mercenaries. He is unlikely to chance being seen out and about in public; awkward questioned would be asked. We are hoping that with your skills, you'll be able to elude Mr Sutton when you reach Camp West and contact Mike.'

'This is all an assumption on your part, I presume?'

'Yes, it is, but based on good logic. He will send someone to collect you from the airport, I'm certain of that.'

'They may have a photograph of Mrs Boyd and realise I'm an impostor.'

'Possibly. I'm hoping that when, whoever is sent to collect you, sees a woman ... who he is expecting ... dressed in the way he is expecting, he will assume you are the right person.'

'Let's hope so.'

'We will be giving you an aid to that end at the airport before you leave.'

'What sort of aid?'

'You'll find out later.'

'How did Sutton manage to arrange all this if he's in prison?' asked Jenny.

'I can't divulge that piece of information, but I can tell you that he's had help from higher places.'

'How high. I mean, that when I go in there, who have I got to look out for?'

'To be safe - just about everybody.'

'That's great!' exclaimed Suzie. 'And how much help can I count on?'

'Not a lot, I'm afraid. Diplomatically this is a sensitive area, we have to be careful.'

'At least I know where I stand; on my own.'

'Not entirely, Colin Brooke is already out there and will be nearby to give any assistance that he can, though for the moment, you will have to pretend that you don't know him. I have to say that things are a lot more delicate than I thought they would be.'

'Why?' inquired Suzie.

Sir Joseph hesitated for a few seconds before replying and glanced at DI Burgess who gave a slight nod. 'Mr Weston, our representative at the British Embassy in Roseburgh, was the man who set up this deal with Mr Sutton. I was a little suspicious that things moved rather faster than I'd expected.'

'Yes, I remember Mike saying was also a little worried about that.'

'I found out the real reason last night. He was in collusion with Mr Sutton for a share of the ransom money.'

'Was? How did you find that out?' asked Jenny.

'He tried to kill Colin Brooke to get the ransom money, because he thought that he was holding it. Fortunately Brooke was too alert and he didn't succeed.'

Suzie, Jim and Jenny all looked amazed at the revelation. 'He wanted the ransom money from him! I thought Mike had that, so that he could deliver it,' said Jim.

'That was what he was supposed to do. I don't know what happened there, or what's happened to the money.'

'Mike's no fool,' suggested Suzie. 'He wouldn't be so stupid as to take the money in with him. He probably hid it before going to Camp West, just in case something went wrong. He's got a nose for trouble.'

'That's what I am hoping.'

'What happened to Colin?' asked Jim.

'He was too strong for Mr Weston. They got into a fight and Mr Weston was unfortunately killed.'

'Does Sutton know this?' asked Suzie, a more worried expression crossing her face.

'We've no way of knowing at the moment.'

'He might shoot Mike just for the hell of it, when he finds out his man has been killed.'

'I don't think so, Suzie. Mr Sutton is desperate to get his woman returned to him and is unlikely to do anything to jeopardise that.'

'I hope you're right. Will Colin Brooke venture into Kitsulana?'

'That's doubtful, especially if there's any trouble. The British Government …'

'I know,' interrupted Suzie, 'can't be seen to be involved.'

'Quite so. Well, if that's all clear, then I'll let DI Burgess complete the picture. He has agreed to meet you this evening at eight o'clock by the BA desk in Heathrow Airport.'

Sir Joseph looked at DI Burgess and nodded. He took up the conversation.

'I've instructed my DC to tell Mrs Boyd that she is to be set free by this agreement, and escorted to Heathrow. Along with prison officers and a woman PC, she will be taken to her home first to let her dress and pack. When she's done that she'll be driven to Heathrow. I'll meet you there and ask you to change into her clothes before you board the plane.'

'Why? Is it necessary to go to all that trouble?'

'Yes, I'm afraid it is. We believe that one of Sutton's accomplices has been told to keep an eye out and check that she is put on the plane. He's been spotted sitting in a car outside the prison, and will no doubt, follow her to the airport,' Sir Joseph reported.

Burgess added, 'He won't be able to get through customs control, but if you dress in Mrs Boyd's clothes, he will be able to see you walking along the departure corridor towards the plane, from a distance. We are sure that he will be fooled and will confirm to Sutton that Mrs Boyd is on her way, and will probably relay what she is wearing so that the man meeting her at the other end can identify her.'

'Probably! Okay, whatever it takes,' said Suzie, frustration showing in her voice. She preferred direct action, but needed their help to get out to Africa where she could assess the problems first hand and decide what action she wanted to take.

'I think that just about covers everything,' said Sir Joseph.

Suzie nodded. 'I'll be at Heathrow Airport at eight o'clock then.'

'Have a safe journey and take care,' he told her.

DI Burgess and Sir Joseph stood by the doorway as Jim and Jenny drove Suzie back to the boatyard where she collected her car and drove home.

'I hope she'll be okay,' Burgess said to Sir Joseph.

'She's a resilient lady, and very skilful, I'm sure she'll manage.'
'I hope your right.'
'So do I. This is turning out to be a lot more troublesome than I had anticipated, and I wouldn't want either of their deaths on my conscience.'

23

FOLLOWING ON

Suzie said goodbye to Jim and Jenny, as their Rolls Royce crunched over the gravel driveway at the front of her house, and disappeared through the wrought iron gate. They had driven her to the boatyard to collect her car and followed her home. They discussed their meeting with Sir Joseph and DI Burgess before Jim and Jenny drove home. Suzie now had a clearer idea of the sort of problem that Mike was caught up in, and what she needed to do in order to help him escape. Jim had insisted on returning in the evening to drive her to Heathrow Airport for her journey to Africa.

Many thoughts were buzzing around Suzie's head as she went on a five mile jog along the nearby beach in an effort to make sure she was fit and ready for the task ahead. She used the time to prepare her thoughts and consider what obstacles might be in her way and plan a counter measure to deal with them. When she returned to the house, she made a telephone call to Paul's Bar in Roseburgh.

'Hello Manny, it's Suzie Drake.'

'Miss Suzie, this is a pleasant surprise. Is something wrong? I saw Mr Mike yesterday. Is he okay?'

'I can't tell you much about that, but I am coming to Roseburgh on the flight which lands tomorrow at around two in the afternoon, and I'd like you to do me a big favour if you will.'

'Of course, I am pleased to do anything for you.'

'When I arrive at Roseburgh airport, I'd like you to …'

Suzie finished her telephone call and went to bed. Sleep eluded her for much of the afternoon; it was the wrong time of day to be in bed, but with a long journey ahead of her she knew it was best to get some rest. She tossed and turned, while she dreamt vividly in the few hours of her snatched sleep.

Rising at five o'clock, she had a light meal of toast and orange juice followed by a cup of coffee and declared herself ready for whatever was in store. She packed a few belongings, including hers and Mike's genuine passport.

'He made need this if they've confiscated his fake one,' murmured Suzie, waving the passport in the air.

Jim arrived in good time and they set of on the journey to London's Heathrow Airport.

'This feels a bit like déjà vu, only the roles are reversed. This time I'm charging off to Africa to help Mike, instead of the other way round,' commented Suzie.

'Yes, I see what you mean. Let's hope the outcome is as satisfactory as last time.'

'Amen to that.'

In a little over an hour-and-a-half they arrived at Heathrow Airport. Jim brought the Rolls to a stop outside the departure entrance.

'Are you coming in?' asked Suzie.

'No, I'll get back to Jenny, if you don't mind.'

Suzie nodded. 'Okay. Thanks for the lift.'

Jim took her holdall from the boot and handed it to her. 'You're not taking much with you,' he suggested.

'I don't anticipate staying very long.'

Suzie gave him a kiss on the cheek.

'Good luck. Keep in touch. We'll be anxious for news,' said Jim, lingering long enough to see Suzie push her way through the glass entrance doors.

At the BA desk waiting for her to arrive, was DI Burgess, smartly dressed in his police uniform. He smiled a greeting and took Suzie's bag from her.

'This way. Mrs Boyd has already been taken through to a holding room.'

'Have you seen her? I mean, does she know yet that she's not going to be set free?'

'I haven't seen her, no. Prison officers escorted her here. I travelled up separately to keep out of the way. As we suspected, Mrs Boyd's police van was followed by the man who was watching the prison from his car. I didn't want him to see me; he might suspect something was not right if he saw too many policemen involved.'

'I understand. Has he seen what she's wearing?'

'Yes, he watched Mrs Boyd come out of her house and enter the airport before parking his car, so he's taken a good look at her clothes. At the moment he's sat opposite a screen in the main hall, waiting to see a gate number for the flight. We've got men watching him.'

Burgess handed Suzie's bag and her new passport, which showed her photograph against Mrs Boyd's name, to a waiting attendant who nodded. He put a label through the bag handle and inserted the boarding pass into the passport and returned it.

Suzie opened the passport and looked at the photograph. 'Where did this photo of me come from?' she asked. 'It's a few years old.'

'But you're still easily recognisable. I believe Sir Joseph had a copy in a file he has on you.'

'Oh, yes, the files he has on us. I should have guessed.'

Leading Suzie to the departure area, Burgess flashed his identity card at the man in the checking desk, escorted Suzie into the lounge and headed for the holding room.

'Exactly how well will this minder be able to see passengers getting on to the plane?' asked Suzie.

'Not very well. He'll only be able to see you from a distance, as you walk along the corridors to get on to the departure bus. He's got a pair of binoculars with him, but it will be difficult for him to see you clearly.'

'It still might be tricky.'

'I don't think so. He'll only be able to see you mainly from the rear and will really only be able to identify you by your clothes, so I shouldn't worry.'

They approached a door and Burgess knocked. The door was opened a few inches, just wide enough for a pair of eyes to see who was standing there, before it was fully opened. Suzie and Burgess stepped inside.

'Has she been told?' he asked the plain clothed policeman.

'She has, and what a commotion she's caused. When she was told to undress, she refused, went wild and fought like a tiger. She had to be restrained and undressed by three policewomen. Not an easy task. She's in the adjoining room,' he pointed.

Burgess took a deep breath and looked at Suzie. 'Right, shall we go? You'll have to change in there I'm afraid. We've no other rooms and they can't take Mrs Boyd back to prison until after the flight's departed, and our spy has made his telephone call and left the airport.'

'I understand. That's not a problem.'

Suzie entered a small, twelve foot square room with plain walls, a central light hanging from the ceiling and no windows. The room contained a table and three chairs. On one chair by the table sat Mrs Boyd, now wearing prison overalls and with a furious scowl on her face. She had expected to board a plane to her freedom, and now discovered that someone else was to take her place. On a chair by the corner, in a neat pile, sat her clothes. A policewoman stood by the door and two others stood behind Mrs Boyd, all with their hands behind their backs.

Looking up Mrs Boyd declared, 'Who are you? Are you the one who's going to try and impersonate me?'

'So they tell me.'

'I hope you've enjoyed your life, because it's not going to last much longer. Owen will kill you as soon as he realises what you're up to.'

'I might have something to say about that.'

The anger rose in Mrs Boyd, she smashed a fist into the table and declared, 'Bitch.'

Shoving the chair away, she pushed the policewoman aside and thrust herself towards Suzie with fingernails ready to scratch her eyes out. Swivelling on her left leg, Suzie threw out her right leg and hammered it into Mrs Boyd's chest above her breasts. She was catapulted back into the chair, tipping it over and spread-eagling her on the floor with a heavy thump. The wind was knocked out of her as the three police women dashed forward to end the affray.

One grabbed Suzie by the arm. She turned to stare at her with a blaze of anger in her eyes. The policewoman saw the anger on her face and released her grip.

'She is in our custody. We are responsible for looking after her,' she said.

'Then you should make sure that she's not able to attack me, shouldn't you?'

The policewoman turned and asked the other two, who were picking Mrs Boyd from the floor, 'Is she all right?'

'Yes, I think so, she just a bit winded that's all.'

Suzie grabbed the clothes from the chair and stripped to her knickers and bra. Mrs Boyd was sat back on the chair and stared at her.

'Owen likes a woman with some meat on her, you're skinny and you've got no tits, there's nothing there to grab. He'll suss you out straight away.'

'I might have a more athletic figure, but at least I'm free to have my tits fondled. Who's going to fondle yours, another woman prisoner?' Suzie countered.

Mrs Boyd's face dropped. With her hopes of freedom hanging in the balance, the realisation that she could spend a long time in prison was becoming more of a reality. She was trying not to think about it, hoping that somehow things would work out; a hope that was fading fast.

'We have a larger, padded bra for you to wear,' explained one of the policewomen, handing it to Suzie.

'Huh! It'll take more than a padded bra to fool Owen,' spat Mrs Boyd.

Suzie was getting fed up with all the jibes that were aimed at her. 'Why don't you shut up about Owen? He pissed off to Africa and left you in this predicament to face the authorities on your own, so he can't be that wonderful.'

Mrs Boyd fumed. Suzie completed dressing and looked at the, below-the-knee length skirt and cotton blouse. 'Do you always wear such cheap, old-fashioned clothes?' she asked, to bait Mrs Boyd.

Anger again rose in her; her nostrils flared as she took the bait and started to rise from her seat. A hand clamped her on each shoulder and pushed her back down. Suzie picked up the hat, pinned her long black hair on top of her head and jammed the hat in place.

'It's a good job you wear an awful hat, or I'd never be able to hide my hair otherwise,' she complained, donning Mrs Boyd's dark green anorak.

Mrs Boyd stared at her and said nothing.

'If you've finished in here it would be better if you left us to look after our prisoner,' stated one of the policewomen opening the door.

Shoving her clothes in the holdall and taking one final look over her shoulder, Suzie turned and slipped from the room, leaving behind a seething Mrs Boyd.

'How do I look?' Suzie asked Burgess.

'Good enough to fool anyone at a distance. Shall we go?'

They emerged into the departure lounge and were joined by two uniformed policewomen.

'These two ladies will escort you on to the plane, the same as we would if it had been with Mrs Boyd.'

Suzie nodded. 'Okay.'

Looking at his watch, Burgess asked, 'Would you like a coffee while we wait? We've probably got at least a half-hour before the announcement to board the aircraft.'

'Good idea,' said Suzie. 'I feel strange dressed up like this with a big pair of boobs. I keep thinking that everyone is staring at me.'

'You look fine. No one is staring at you, unless they're admiring your beauty.'

Suzie smiled. 'You say the nicest things.'

Trooping into the coffee shop, Suzie sat at a table in the crowded establishment while Burgess lined up in a queue to get their drinks, and the two policewomen waited near the entrance. Returning, Burgess slid the tray on to the table; Suzie took her cappuccino coffee and smiled her thanks. They sipped their coffees, but spoke very little. Both were aware that what Suzie was trying to achieve was difficult and dangerous. If things went wrong, she and Mike could end up in serious trouble, and the British Government would then have the tricky situation of deciding whether to bail them out or not.

The Tannoy system constantly rang out its barely distinguishable messages, until finally an announcement was made giving the departure of their flight to Nairobi at Gate 51.

'This is it. How do you feel?' asked Burgess.

'Strangely nervous. I'm not quite sure why. It may be because I feel uncomfortable in theses clothes and I've never tried to impersonate anyone before.'

'You'll be okay. Walk slowly and steadily along the corridor, so that Sutton's man can see you. Our men will be watching you all the way.'

'Okay,' said Suzie, rising from the chair. They were joined by the two escorting policewomen.

Burgess handed Suzie a newspaper. 'Sir Joseph asked me to give you this. He said you may find it useful when you arrive.'

She looked at the newspaper. It was *The Chatham Chronicle*, a local newspaper with a main headline about the building society robbery. Alongside the article was a photograph of Suzie with a caption stating that she was, 'Mrs Boyd - the terrified teller who worked at the building society and who had witnessed the robbery and shooting.'

'The article is genuine. The editor was asked to substitute your photograph in place of the one of Mrs Boyd, which was printed on the original copies.'

'Very clever. This looks like it's the same photo that's on the passport.'

'It is. I believe that Sir Joseph asked his son for it. The police photographic whiz-kids added the building society in the background'

Suzie acknowledged it with a slight nod of her head. 'Let's hope it works and they haven't got a copy of the original newspaper.'

With her escorts walking either side of her, Suzie wandered along to the corridor, which led to Gate 51. Burgess watched from a distance. In the visitor's gallery, a man stood by the window with a pair of binoculars scanning the corridor that led to the departure gate. He too, had heard the call for the flight and was now scrutinising all the passengers as they walked, or rode the moving walkway, towards their aircraft. DC's Teal and Green were lurking nearby. Teal also watched the passengers and saw the man stiffen when Suzie came into view wearing the green anorak. He moved closer to the window as if another two inches nearer would confirm what he saw. Suzie and her escorts moved along the corridor and disappeared from view. A few seconds later, the two policewomen wandered back and the man lowered his binoculars with a hint of a smile crossing his lips.

He walked smartly from the visitor's gallery while punching the buttons on his mobile. Teal and Green stayed close behind and heard him relay his message.

'Tell him she's on, and everything's okay. She wearing a green anorak,' was all he said, before closing his mobile and making his way to the car park, totally unaware of the men watching him.

'So far, so good,' declared Green to Teal. 'We've got to trail him, see where he goes and pick him up later on, after they've arrived.'

'Okay. Do you want to follow him on the first leg?'

On the plane, Suzie settled into her seat. The onboard safety regulations were announced as the plane taxied to the end of the runway and halted for a few moments. Suddenly, the engines increased in power, bursting into a cacophony of vibration and noise, and the plane slowly gathered speed. It trundled down the runway gathering more and more speed until it blasted into the air. Smoothness took over and the noise abated. Stomachs turned over as the massive chunk of metal climbed gracefully into the sky.

★ ★ ★

Back in Africa at Camp West, Sutton received the message that Mrs Boyd was on the plane and winging her way towards him. He was elated that his plan to free her was working, but was annoyed at his inability to contact Weston and was getting anxious about his disappearance. Eventually, he was told by an embassy official that Weston had died naturally of a heart attack. It was the excuse that almost everyone in the embassy had been given to protect Brooke and the ongoing problem surrounding Sutton's exchange.

Neither the general or Sutton were concerned about Weston's death, but were no nearer to getting their ransom money – and that did concern them.

'Maybe that London copper killed him when he tried to get the money from him, and they're covering it up,' suggested Sutton.

'That's possible,' agree the general. 'There's nothing we can do about that, but we still have Mr Eastmond, and the British government will want him back, and without a fuss. And for that they will pay the ransom, I'm sure of it.'

'I hope you're right. Katie's on her way here. At least I've achieved that much today.'

★ ★ ★

On the plane, travelling towards them at great speed, Suzie closed her eyes and silently prayed that she would be able to help Mike escape from Sutton's clutches.

Meanwhile, she had a long journey to make, and a lot of time to think about the problems that would confront her when she arrived, and what she could do to counter them. She too was familiar with the area, but that did not help Mike. Suzie hoped that this time, she had the element of surprise and would be able to use that to good advantage.

24

CAMP WEST

The long and tiresome journey, first to Nairobi and then on to Roseburgh, was almost over. Suzie yawned and stretched as she gazed from the window at the airport below bathed in bright sunlight, with the A320 circling round to make the landing approach. The plane quickly dropped towards the ground, and a final bump when the tyres gave a slight bounce and squealed on contact with the runway, was followed by the feeling of rapid reduction in speed with the roar of the reverse thrust of the engines when the brakes were applied.

The aircraft slowed to a crawl and taxied into its allocated space, guided by the marshal waving the bats, and finally came to a halt with a whistle from the engines winding down to a stop. The journey was over and Suzie had arrived. Her quest in the guise of Mrs Boyd, was to rescue Mike from the prison cell in Camp West where he was being held.

Passengers released their seat belts and rushed to get their belongings out of the overhead lockers, even before the plane had come to a complete halt. They all had to wait while the steps were trundled up to the plane, before they could begin to file out through the doors one by one, with the stewards and stewardesses smiling a goodbye to each one of them.

It was past midday, the temperature was hot, nearly 30°C, and was much as Suzie expected. She had been here before and was not surprised by the blast of heat that hit her. She slipped her sunglasses on and stepped through the aircraft doorway into sunshine that was so bright, it hurt your eyes and made them water if sunglasses were not worn. Suzie trundled to the baggage area, collected her holdall and joined the single queue waiting to pass through customs.

In the arrivals hall, a sea of faces jostled to see those who emerged through the exit, eager to greet their friends and relatives. Among the crowd was Colin Brooke. He kept to one side and gave a slight nod as his and Suzie's eyes met, giving no recognition to anyone. Suzie, biting one arm of her sunglasses, held the green anorak over her arm and *The Chatham Chronicle* in front of her. She peered over the top, and observed the waiting crowd. One local man looked at her and the newspaper more intently. She walked towards him.

'Mrs Boyd?' he asked.

Suzie opened the newspaper, showing the picture of her, and lowered it to show her face. The man looked at the newspaper, quickly took in the meaning, compared the photograph to the woman in front of him and smiled. He took Suzie's bag and they headed for the exit.

Suddenly a group of young local children surrounded Suzie, all of them with arms outstretched and open hands begging for a handout. A local man rushed up and shooed them away.

'I'm sorry about the children,' he apologised.

'That's quite all right,' explained Suzie.

The man said his thanks and quickly shook her hand. Their eyes met, he bowed a further apology and left. Sutton's man, who had stopped to stare at the intrusion, turned and pushed his way through the exit door and strode towards his car, leaving Suzie to follow, with Brooke watching the proceedings. Suzie had made contact with Sutton's man and all appeared to be okay.

Walking out into the bright sunlight from the shaded airport terminal, Suzie donned her sunglasses and followed the man to his car, a shining black Mercedes. He threw her bag into the car boot and held the rear door open for her to enter.

In the limousine, Suzie gazed through the window as a silent chauffeur drove her through the city of Roseburgh. Because of his silence, she was beginning to think that he may have realised she was not the real Mrs Boyd, but he seemed relaxed and Suzie was more than prepared for trouble, she was expecting it.

In a little more than half an hour, the vehicle drew to a halt at the border in Karuna. Suzie was asked to produce her passport for scrutinisation, as was the driver. They were quickly allowed to pass and stopped a few yards further on at the border check into Kitsulana. Suzie was again asked to produce her passport, but not the driver. He was well known to the guards at this checkpoint and spoke to them quietly for a few seconds, while they shared a light for their cigarettes. The driver chatted while he smoked, then dropped his cigarette end on the ground, stubbing it out with his foot before returning to the car. The barrier was lifted and they were on their way again.

The route towards Camp West, along the dust filled road that was first carved out many years before, had deteriorated badly in the intervening years. The Mercedes bounced along the road where there was little to see other than scrubland and trees in a country that because of its continual fighting, had not yet modernised. Camp West drew near and looked a much more daunting sight to Suzie than it had previously, now with brick walls and buildings.

Their car passed straight through the entrance gates with a wave by the guards, and moved into the heart of the camp. Suzie's pulse began to race. Until this point, events had been worrying, but posed little risk. With her arrival at the camp, all this had changed and the scent of danger sharpened her awareness with the adrenaline that was coursing through her body. She glanced at the prison block as they passed by and could almost feel Mike's presence. She knew he was locked in there, and wanted desperately to let him know she was nearby.

The car drew up outside the general's quarters and the driver collected Suzie's bag from the boot. She followed him into the building and was shown into Sutton's private office.

Placing her bag on the floor he smiled, 'Mr Sutton will be here in a moment,' and closed the door behind him.

The room was comfortable; decorated and furnished in a simple style with practical rather than exotic fittings. A painting of an America western scene with cowboy's guns blazing hung on one wall.

'Perhaps Sutton's love of firearms,' murmured Suzie to herself.

Wandering around the room, Suzie glanced at several African carved objects stood on an ornament shelf along with a photograph, which showed a motor yacht named *Elude*. Mrs Boyd and Sutton posed on deck for the photograph, with their arms around each other's waist.

'The love birds,' thought Suzie, 'well one of them is in for a big surprise, and very soon.'

She deliberately stood with her back to the door when it opened.

'Darling, you're free at last,' Sutton declared, stepping into the room.

Suzie turned to face him. 'Darling, you're in for a surprise.'

Sutton stopped in his tracks and stared in disbelief. 'What! Who are you? You're not Katie!' he proclaimed, pulling a gun from his belt.

Taking one step towards him, Suzie swivelled, and shot out her right leg. It slammed into his chest and sent him crashing to the floor. It was a move that she had practised and perfected, and one that had come in useful on several occasions. Taking a small gun from her pocket, she thrust it in his face, grabbing his gun hand at the same time.

Snatching the weapon from him Suzie declared, 'And there I was, thinking you wouldn't know the difference, especially as I've gone to the trouble of wearing a nice big pair of boobs for you.'

'Where did you get that gun from? Customs screens everybody with a metal detector. You must have had help.'

'Little friends.'

Sutton screwed up his face; he had not understood. 'What do you want?' he demanded, staring uncomfortably at the gun barrel, hovering a few inches from the end of his nose.

'How about an exchange? You like exchanges, don't you?'

'What sort of exchange?'

'Your life, for that of Mike Randle's.'

'Who the hell is Mike Randle?'

'A would-be diplomat.'

'Aah, things are become clearer now. So he's not a diplomat. I though he didn't look the type. He was dressed too casually and almost too much to handle for the guards. He might have escaped if I hadn't intervened. Who is he?'

'He's my partner; an ex-mercenary, just like me, and he kills people, just like me. In fact, he killed a couple of unsavoury men only last week, which is the reason why he was obliged to take this exchange job and come out here. If you don't play ball, I'll have no hesitation in putting a bullet through your brain; if you've got one. Do you understand, perfectly?'

Sutton nodded nervously. A woman with a gun worried him. A woman with a gun who had already shot other people, worried him even more. He rose from the floor slowly.

'Where is Mike being held; in the prison block?'

'Yes.'

'Is there a guard present?'

'Yes.'

'Then we are going to walk over there in a moment, quietly and calmly with no fuss, and you are going to tell the guard to unlock Mike's cell.'

'He'll think that's strange and want to know why. What am I going to tell him?'

'I don't care, tell him anything you like, as long as it doesn't arouse his suspicions,' warned Suzie. 'Now get back and don't try anything,' she said, waving the gun at Sutton to usher him into the corner of the room.

Keeping a watchful eye on her adversary, Suzie put the guns down on the table beside her and took out her top and jeans from her bag. She removed the blouse and skirt she had been obliged to wear and divested herself of the padded bra that gave her Mrs Boyd's buxom figure. Wearing only her knickers, Sutton gazed at her sylph-like figure and though he admired the model type of shape she possessed, he did not care to admit it.

'At least Katie's got a decent pair of breasts, something to get hold of, not like the skinny tits you've got,' he said, trying to vent the anger within him at the predicament he now found himself engulfed in.

'She said almost the same thing, and maybe it's so, but who's going to enjoy hers now – another female prisoner perhaps?'

Anger and frustration crossed Sutton's face. 'She won't be in there long, I'll see to that,' he boasted.

'You'd better get her the best legal representative you can afford then, because the case against her is strong,' said Suzie, throwing on a blouse and fastening the belt on her jeans. She put on her sunglasses and pushed them to the top of her forehead.

She tucked Sutton's gun into her belt at the rear, covering it with her blouse. 'It's time to go. My gun will be in this pocket with my finger on the trigger, so no funny stuff; I will shoot you,' she warned, grabbing her small gun and pocketing it.

They left the building and stepped into glaring sunlight beaming down from a clear blue sky. Suzie pulled down her sunglasses and they made their way to the prison hut. A slight breeze whipped up a cloud of dust that swirled past them. Sutton looked at Suzie, hoping the dust would blow in her face and distract her for a moment. He was wrong. She had encountered much stronger mini dust storms on her previous visits, and was well aware that they occurred. Her green eyes watched him carefully from behind her sunglasses.

Opening the prison block door, they entered the gloomy central corridor with cells either side. The building was stiflingly hot with the brick walls radiating heat. The guard heard the door open and emerged through a doorway at the far end grasping a rifle. His guard's room, converted from a cell to enable him to relax when there was nothing else to attend to, remained a few degrees cooler, the temperature lowered by two whirring fans blasting the air into circulation around the room.

'What can I do for you, Mr Sutton?' he asked.

'My … partner and I would like a word with our government official.'

The guard looked at Suzie a little suspiciously, before jamming a key in the lock and opening the cell door.

Suzie pulled the gun from her pocket and was about to thrust it at the guard when Sutton yelled out, 'Lookout,' and swung his arm at her.

He caught Suzie in the face, knocking her to the far wall, propelling the gun from her grasp. The guard, eyes wide in amazement at the sight before him, took a moment to react. He lifted his rifle and aimed it at Suzie as she snatched the gun hidden at the back of her waistband. Her fast reactions were quicker than his and she fired first. The bullet hit the guard squarely in the chest, catapulting him into the cell door, bursting it open and sending his body crashing to the floor.

Sutton lunged at Suzie, grabbing her gun with one hand and her throat with the other. He kept her pinned against the wall with his weight and was squeezing hard, choking the life out of her and pushing her down to the floor. Suddenly his head snapped to one side, his grip eased and he sank to his knees. Standing over him, holding the guard's rifle, butt end towards her, was Mike.

'Am I glad to see you,' said Suzie, shoving Sutton aside and nursing her bruised throat.

'Not half as glad as I am to see you,' replied Mike. 'How the hell did you get here?' he asked, grabbing her hand and pulling her to her feet.

'It's a long story. I'll tell you about it later.' They embraced and kissed, before Suzie pulled away. 'Someone might have heard that shot.'

Mike picked up Suzie's gun. 'It's quite well insulated in here – to mask the screams of the prisoners they torture. Perhaps we'll get lucky.'

Sutton slowly returned to life and rubbed the lump on the back of his head.

'What hit me?'

'Never mind that,' said Mike, grabbing his collar and hauling him to his feet. 'If you don't get us out of here, that'll be nothing to what you'll get next time,' he said, putting the end of the gun barrel against his nose. 'Understand?'

Sutton nodded. He was getting quite used to being threatened.

'Where's your car?' Mike asked.

'Outside my quarters.'

'It's a Mercedes, Mike. Nice and comfortable, but not very

good to escape in if we're being chased.'

Mike shook Sutton. 'Got any better vehicle?'

'My Jeep's there as well.'

'That's the perfect vehicle to escape in. You can tell the guard we are going for a drive to show your lady friend the territory.'

'I'll go with him to collect the Jeep,' said Suzie. 'You'd better wait in here in case anyone sees you.'

'I'll put on the dead guard's shirt and hat. It'll look as if I'm accompanying you both to give you protection.'

'Good idea.'

Mike slipped on the guard's shirt over the top of his own, grabbed his hat, keys and rifle. The arrested mercenaries and captured rebels faces appeared at the prison cell windows, all wondering what was happening. Mike asked them to be quiet and wait until he was safely away before trying to escape, and passed them the keys.

General Abotto, in smart full military dress, was about to enter the prison hut when Suzie stepped through the doorway with Sutton.

'Ah, Sutton. I though I heard a shot fired.'

'It was the guard, keeping one of the prisoners in line who tried to attack him.'

'I see. And I presume this is your woman?'

'This is General Abboto, the camp commander,' Sutton informed Suzie.

'I'm Katie Boyd,' said Suzie, smiling at him. 'Owen was about to show me some of the countryside around here.'

'Huh, countryside! There's not a lot of countryside to see in this war torn territory. Most of it is either jungle or scrubland, with a few small villages dotted here and there. We are a poor country, which is why we have so many rebels to deal with. Don't venture too far from the camp, it might be dangerous.'

'Thank you for the warning. I'm sure Owen will look after me.'

'What are you going to do with the diplomat now that your lady has arrived?' he asked Sutton.

'I haven't decided yet. I'm sure they'll pay the ransom for him, and then we'll probably send him home.'

'Good idea. We don't want to antagonise the British unnecessarily. I hope to have the pleasure of your company at dinner tonight.'

'Of course, General. We look forward to it, don't we Owen?' Suzie smiled.

Sutton nodded and gave a slight smile. 'Yes, dear.'

With a salute of his baton, the general walked smartly away.

'Well done, Mr Sutton. If you continue to behave like that, you might come out of this with your life intact. It's a good job the general hasn't taken a lot of notice of the photograph in your room of us, or we might have been in trouble. Shall we go?'

The camp was quiet, with few soldiers wandering around; most of them were taking a siesta. Sutton collected his Jeep and Suzie picked up her bag. She sat beside him as he drove to the prison hut and pulled up outside. Mike, carrying the guard's rifle, got into the back seat and held the weapon across his lap.

They drove to the main gate and were approached by a guard. Mike pulled his hat down to cover much of his face and rested his finger on the trigger.

'Where are you going, Mr Sutton?' the guard enquired.

'We are going out for a short run, to show Katie some of the country.'

The guard looked at Suzie with suspicion; something about her didn't look the same. 'This is your woman?'

'Yes, it is.'

'She looks different.'

'A change of clothes makes all the difference,' Suzie stated.

He looked at her face. It certainly looked familiar. 'I suppose so.' He glanced at the man in the back seat. 'I see you are taking a guard with you.'

'Yes, it was a precaution General Abboto suggested,' said Suzie.

The guard raised his eyebrows in surprise; he was not going to argue with his commanding officer's suggestion. He turned and signalled for the gate to be opened. Sutton accelerated the Jeep through the gateway of Camp West and motored along the road towards the border, creating clouds of dust that swirled into the air behind them.

The three occupants were jolted up and down as the Jeep bumped along the crater ridden track, devoid of any traffic other than the occasional military vehicle.

'Once we get past the border we're home and dry,' suggested Suzie.

'You've both forgotten one thing,' smirked Sutton.

'Oh! And what's that?' asked Mike.

'Only the camp guards know I'm not a prisoner, and nobody gets through the border without a passport or a letter from the general. My passport is back at the camp,' he gleefully related.

'Shit! I forgot about that in our haste to get away,' said Mike.

Suzie pulled two passports from her bag. 'I've got mine, and the one I brought for you. Owen here, is the only one without a passport.'

'Stop the vehicle,' demanded Mike.

Pulling off the road, Sutton brought the Jeep to a halt.

'We are supposed to escort him back to England. Should we go back to get his passport?' asked Suzie.

'Not a good idea,' suggested Mike. 'They might have discovered the dead guard by now, and I hope they do not have to deal with escaped prisoners yet. I asked them to wait an hour before trying to get out, but they may be anxious to escape as soon as possible.'

'Escaped prisoners?' Sutton queried.

'I gave them the keys before you collected me.'

'So, what do you suggest we do?' Suzie asked.

'Dump Sutton and make our way home. I've just about had enough of this exchange caper.'

'Good idea, me too,' she said, putting her foot against Sutton and heaving him out of the vehicle.

He crunched to the ground, picked himself up with a scornful look on his face, shook his fist and declared, 'You haven't seen the last of me.'

Mike pointed his gun at Sutton.

'No, Mike,' said Suzie, putting a hand on his arm, 'he's not worth it. When the general finds out that his exchange plan has not worked and he won't be getting his share of the cash, he could be in more than enough trouble.'

'I hope we have seen the last of you, for your sake. The next time I see you, I'll shoot first and ask questions later,' maintained Mike.

'And in case you're wondering exactly what happened to your accomplice Mr Weston – he let the whole plan out of the bag before he tried to murder Detective Inspector Brooke. The trouble is – he wasn't good enough and ended up dead, so you won't be getting any more help from the embassy,' stated Suzie.

Mike threw the guard's hat and shirt away and climbed into the driver's seat. 'It's about five miles to the border, and a few more back to the camp,' he told Sutton. 'I hope you enjoy your walk,' he smirked, revving up the engine, leaving him to choke on the trail of dust they left behind.

25

PASSPORT HOME

Following Mike and Suzie's escape from Camp West, they shoved Sutton out of the Jeep, because his passport was missing and they were not prepared to go back for it. They headed towards the border checkpoint in the stolen vehicle.

'Better get ready in case we have to fight our way through,' suggested Mike.

Suzie checked their guns and handed one to Mike, who hid it on the seat under the top of his leg. She tucked a gun into her belt, which was hidden by her loose fitting blouse.

They approached the border, the barrier down, blocking their path. A guard emerged from his hut and walked towards them holding one arm aloft, while keeping his other hand on the gun holstered around his waist. Mike slowed the vehicle to a halt.

The guard looked at them suspiciously. 'Passports,' he demanded, in a gruff voice, holding out his hand.

Mike grabbed their passports and was about to hand them to him when a loud explosion was heard in the distance behind them. All three turned to stare in the direction of the sound and witnessed a cloud of black smoke rising into the sky.

'That looks like it's coming from Camp West,' announced Suzie.

The guard turned and ran for the guard hut. He grabbed the telephone, banged frantically on the lugs and spoke with animated gestures before slapping the handset down. Mike guessed that the prisoners at Camp West had not waited very long before they decided to make an escape, and the camp guards had been alerted.

More border guards appeared and stared at the plume of smoke rising into the sky, pointing and giving their opinions about the cause of the explosion. After a frantic word from the man in charge, they piled into a truck and sped off towards the camp.

Mike moved the Jeep forward and held up their passports. The guard, more concerned about the explosion, saw the passports, lifted the barrier and waved them through. They were after escaped prisoners, and they did not have passports.

Accelerating the Jeep across the border, Mike flashed their passports at the Karuna border guards and drove on towards Roseburgh. 'That was easy. Letting those men go proved to be very helpful after all.'

'I wonder what that explosion was.'

'I don't know, and don't much care. At least it got us out of a potentially difficulty situation without having to resort to violence,' he maintained, passing his gun to Suzie.

'Amen to that. Are we going to stop at Paul's Bar and see Manny? I'd like to thank him for his help at the airport this morning.'

'Yes, I've got to ring Colin Brooke to get plane tickets organised, and I've something to collect. What help did Manny give you?'

'He passed a gun to me. I couldn't have got the drop on Sutton without it. What is it that you want to collect from Manny?'

'Just a small package that I asked him to look after.'

'Not the money? You haven't still got the ransom money, have you?'

'What makes you think that?' Mike said defensively.

'I know what you're capable of. Sir Joseph said he didn't know what had happened to it and was hoping you'd hid it before you went to Camp West. Are you going to give it back to him?'

'It was hidden in my car. Sutton found it after he'd locked me up.'

'Are you sure?'

'Well, that's what I'm going to tell Sir Joseph. He'll have a job to prove otherwise. It's about time we were rewarded for risking our lives for him.'

Arriving at the outskirts of Roseburgh, Mike steered the Jeep into the back yard of Paul's Bar and drew the vehicle to a halt. Stepping into the pub, bathed in its usual gloom, they approached Manny, standing behind the bar, chatting to a few early customers who had adjourned to the bar after lunch.

'Miss Suzie, and Mr Mike, it's good to see you,' he effused, stepping out to meet them. 'I'm so glad that you're both okay.'

'Thanks Manny, so are we. I'd like to have the parcel that I gave you to look after,' Mike said.

The expression on the man's face changed. 'A man came in asking about you. He said he wanted the parcel you'd left here. I didn't know what to do.'

'I explained that I would collect it myself and you were not to give it to anyone else.'

'I know, but he was an official.'

'Official? What sort of official?'

'He was a policeman from London; I think he said he was a detective inspector.'

'A detective inspector! Did he say what his name was?'

'No, but I asked to look at his credentials, just to make sure. There are still a lot of con men around here and you can't be too careful.'

'Yes, yes,' said Mike. 'What did he say?'

'He showed me a card with his name on … I can't remember what it was. I think it was … something like … river, or stream …'

'How about Brooke?'

'Brooke! Yes, that was it, Detective Brooke.'

'That means Colin was here,' said Mike in an exasperated tone.

'How did he know about this place?' asked Suzie.

'The information about this pub must be on file, thanks to Jenny. She worked here – remember?'

'Jenny!' exclaimed Manny. 'Jenny Jones? Are you still in contact with her?'

'Yes. Yes, we are. She married a friend of ours and is now Mrs Jenny Sterling. She's a partner with us in our boat building business,' explained Mike.

'So, she is doing well?'

'Yes, she is.'

'Good for her. Please give her my regards when you get home.'

'Of course, but what happened to my parcel?'

'The man demanded it, so I had to give it to him. He said he would tell the authorities and get my licence revoked if I didn't.'

'Sod!' exclaimed Mike.

'But …'

'Never mind, Manny. You had no choice, I realise that,' dismissed Mike. 'I'd like to use the telephone, if I may.'

'Of course. It's upstairs in the office,' he said, in a deflated tone of voice, annoyed that he'd not been able to fully explain his actions.

'Okay, I remember,' said Mike, making for the stairs.

While Mike rang Brooke's mobile, to sort out a ticket for them to fly home, Suzie chatted with Manny and thanked him for slipping her the gun at the airport.

'Where did all the children come from?'

'From a local orphanage. Many of them lost their parents because of the fighting in Kitsulana. A local Christian society looks after them as best they can, but they desperately need funds to keep them going.'

'Perhaps Mike and I can help.'

'All donations are gratefully received, no matter how small,' said Manny.

Mike returned to the bar after his ten minutes call.

'I've spoken to Colin. He's disappointed that we haven't got Sutton with us, but understands why. He'll sort out the tickets and meet us at the airport with them at six tonight. The flight leaves just after seven.'

'We've got just over an hour to kill then. Did he say anything about the parcel?' asked Suzie.

'No, the least said about that, the better.'

'Right.'

'Have you eaten lately?' Manny asked.

'No, we've been a bit too busy for that,' explained Suzie.

'Then I'll get the cook to prepare something for you before you go.'

'Thank you, Manny' said Suzie. She turned to Mike, 'Do you think Sutton will try to stop us leaving.'

'I doubt it. We'll have Brooke with us at the airport and he's not likely to make a fuss in Karuna. He might get arrested again.'

After a welcome meal of chicken and rice, deliciously cooked by Manny's chef, it was time to leave. The pub was starting to buzz as it gradually filled with customers.

'You've done a good job here, Manny,' Mike praised.

'Thanks to you and Jenny for letting me keep the pub. I think Paul would be proud of what I've achieved.'

'I'm sure he would.'

They said goodbye to him and promised to keep in touch. Mike drove to the airport where they met up with Colin Brooke.

'Thanks very much for all you've both done,' Brooke said.

'I'm sorry that things didn't work out quite as we'd all hoped,' Mike stated.

'Maybe we'll get another chance at Sutton some other time. You're both safe, that's the most important thing, and his exchange ruse didn't work,'

'I hear that you had a bit of trouble to contend with as well,' stated Mike.

'Yes, it's not been a very successful trip for either of us, has it?'

Mike looked at him and shook his head. They were all pleased to be going home.

The trio went through passport control and boarded their flight to Nairobi. It was the beginning of a long journey back to London after Mike had been successfully rescued by Suzie, but disappointed that they were leaving without their prime suspect, Owen Sutton. Sir Joseph Sterling would not be happy with the outcome. The failure to return Sutton to England meant that he was no nearer discovering who murdered the Irish politician.

26

ESCAPE

With the failure of their mission to return home with Sutton now behind them, Mike, Suzie and Brooke stared through the aircraft window at London's Heathrow Airport. The journey from Roseburgh had taken a gruelling thirteen hours.

Mike and Suzie were met by Jim and Jenny, who drove them home. Despite the early hour of six o'clock, they had a renewed surge of energy, and chatted to them during their journey. Jenny was pleased to hear that Manny was doing well and had sent his regards. Mike explained about the events that had transpired in Africa, filling in the few gaps that were needed for them to have an almost complete picture of their quest to bring Sutton home. He deliberately left out the part about trying to ensure that, if things went wrong, he and not Sutton would end up with the ransom money.

Opening the front door and stepping into the hallway gave them a heightened appreciation of their home. It was a good feeling to be back. Mike dumped the letters he had collected from the mailbox by their front gate, on the hall table. After Jim and Jenny had said goodbye and motored home, Mike and Suzie took a shower together and put on their dressing gowns.

While Mike was having a shave, Suzie declared, 'I'm going to ring Manny. I promised to let him know that we've arrived home safe and sound, and again to thank him for all his help.'

'Okay.'

After the telephone call she returned to the bedroom. While Suzie was brushing her hair in the dressing table mirror, she asked,

'What are you going to tell Sir Joseph about why you left the money at the pub? He's bound to ask you.'

Mike sat on the edge of the bed watching her.

'I'll tell him that I wanted to make sure it was safe before going into Camp West as I was suspicious about how quick the exchange was set up. I left the money with a friend, and arranged that I would pass it to the general's man at the airport when I left with Sutton. That's what I told Sutton, so that sounds plausible – doesn't it?'

'I guess so. The only trouble is ... the package that Manny gave to Colin didn't contain the ransom money.'

'What! You're kidding me, aren't you?'

'No, it's true.'

'What was in the package?'

'Paperback books.'

'Books! How on earth did that happen?'

'Manny knew that you didn't want anyone else to have the package, so he gave Colin a different one. He, apparently, shoved it in his bag and left without looking at it, assuming it was what he was after. He didn't mention it on the plane, so I imagine that's how he'll give it back to Sir Joseph.'

'What a laugh! I bet he'll get a surprise when he opens it. What happened to the real package?'

'It's probably still in Manny's safe, where you left it,' explained Suzie.

'What! Why didn't he tell me about this?'

'He tried to, but you wouldn't give him the opportunity. You cut him off in mid sentence, as I remember.'

'I was annoyed because I thought I'd lost all that money.'

'It showed.'

'How do you know all this?'

'Manny told me when I rang him half an hour ago.'

'We'll have to go back and get it.'

'Not on your life. I've had enough of Africa for the moment, thank you.'

'Drat!' exclaimed Mike, pacing up and down. 'There must be some way I can get hold of it. I know ... I'll get Manny to post it to me.'

'Too late!'

'What do you mean, too late?'

'I told Manny to hand it in to a local Christian orphanage ... because he said he didn't want to be accused of holding on to British Government money. They might take away his licence if they found out.'

'What! You mean to tell me that you've given away all that cash?'

'Never mind. We've got the money from Jeremy Pendleton for the cruiser, and we're both home safe and sound. You should be satisfied with that.'

'I guess so,' sighed Mike, sounding as if he did not really agree.

The pair decided to catch up on a few hours lost sleep. During the journey, they had both dozed on the plane, but a meaningful sleep had eluded them and they felt a little jaded. They slipped under the duvet cover of their water bed. Mike, grateful at getting out of Camp West so easily, started petting Suzie.

'We're supposed to be getting some shuteye,' she reminded.

'Yes, but we'll both sleep better afterwards,' he suggested, drawing his tongue over her nipples, making them hard and protrude.

He cupped both her breasts and kissed them lovingly. Suzie responded and soon they were kissing and petting. Suddenly the telephone rang.

'Who the hell's that at this time of the morning?' Mike growled.

He looked at the bedside clock. It showed the time as half past nine and he grabbed the receiver.

'Yes, who is it?' he grunted.

Suzie could hear a tinny voice on the other end, sounding as if they were not pleased with the manner of Mike's tone of voice.

'Miss Wilson, do you know what time it is? ... Yes, I know, but we've had a long journey and only just got home and gone to bed ... When? ... Tomorrow? ... Yes, okay,' Mike said, slamming down the receiver.

'Sir Joseph would like to see us in his office at ten o'clock sharp tomorrow morning,' he told Suzie.

'At least that'll give us a day to rest and get over the jetlag.'

'I would have preferred an invitation from Sir Joseph, rather than an un-refusable order from his secretary,' moaned Mike.

'Perhaps he's not happy with us for not bringing back Sutton.'

'Hmm, perhaps. More likely that he wants to know what's happened to his precious ransom money,' suggested Mike.

'That's okay. You've got your story worked out.'

'I'd better ring Jim and let him know that he and Jenny will have to look after the business again for tomorrow. At least we can blame our non-appearance on his father again.'

Mike and Suzie made love and grabbed a few hours sleep. Despite feeling weary, they found it difficult to fall into a deep sleep during the day, even though their waterbed was very comfortable.

They rose shortly after lunch, had a bite to eat and spent most of the afternoon walking hand in hand along the nearby beach, while they discussed the events of the past twelve days since the boatyard was robbed. Much had happened to them since then, and the nature of their dangerous tasks had given them an even greater appreciation of each other and brought them closer together.

'Isn't it about time you asked me to marry you, so that we can stop dashing around the world on dangerous missions for Sir Joseph that might get one of us killed one day? This isn't the first time I've mentioned it,' Suzie suggested.

'Yes, okay, I realise that. I guess it's about time we tied the knot and made everything legal.'

'Is that your only reason for getting married, to make it legal?'

Mike blustered a little, 'No, of course not. The past few weeks have been … testing, and has shown me that we have a good partnership and a good relationship … you're a gorgeous looking woman, and you're good in bed.'

'Thanks for the compliment. I wondered when you'd get around to the sexy bit.'

'It's true. You are a sexy woman, and I don't want to share you with anyone.'

'Yes, and …'

'Okay, I don't want you jumping into Jeremy Pendleton's bed

again. He's too smarmy, and I'm sure he'll boast about it to his friends.'

'Then marry me, and I'll have a cast iron excuse to refuse him and anyone else who thinks I'm available because I don't wear a wedding ring.'

'Don't you think an engagement ring would have the same effect?' asked Mike.

'Are you trying to get out of marrying me already?'

'No, it's just that it's a big step to take and I don't want to rush into anything.'

'Rush? We've known each other for more than five years now, and have been together for most of that time.'

'Is it really that long? I remember when we first met. It was …'

'Stop changing the subject,' demanded Suzie. 'Are you going to marry me or should I be on the lookout for somebody else?'

'Somebody else? You wouldn't … would you?'

'I might. Jeremy Pendleton's available. He likes me a lot and he's very rich.'

'Nice try, but Pendleton's not the marrying sort. He'd rather get you, and all the other females, into his bed for sexual pleasure, but not for marriage.'

'Maybe so, but there are other available men around.'

Mike stopped walking, kicked the sand and faced Suzie, while still holding her hand. 'I know you are only suggesting that it's time I made a decision, and I want to spend the rest of my days with you …'

'But …'

'But, I'm a little afraid of committing myself. Let me think about it.'

Suzie gave Mike a kiss. 'All right. I'll give you a week to think about it, then I want a decision, one way or another. Okay?'

'How about two weeks?'

'One week!'

'Okay.'

They wandered along the beach and climbed the wooden steps from the beach to the top of the cliffs, walked through the trees and across the dead end pathless lane to their house.

The following day, after their regular early morning jog along the beach, which as usual ended up with Suzie having to wait for Mike to catch her up, they took a shower. During breakfast, they listened to the morning news in their dressing gowns, before getting ready for their journey to London.

They travelled to Whitehall in their DB7, and parked it in the visitor's area of the Foreign Office car park. Following instructions given to them by a security attendant, keen to do his duty by allowing visitors in allocated areas only, they joined Colin Brooke in Sir Joseph's office.

After the usual greetings, Sir Joseph stated, 'Perhaps, between the three of you, you will explain to me what has happened in this case - from the beginning if you don't mind, I'd like to get the complete picture.'

DI Brooke began by relating details of the building society robbery, and his involvement when the gun that Kelly had fired was matched with a weapon used in the murder of the Irish politician, Murphy O'Connor. This had eventually led to the arrest of Roy Kelly and Mrs Katherine Boyd. The supplier of the weapon was traced to Owen Sutton, who had fled to Africa, and was supplying the rebels with arms. He was caught by the local army and arrested, but agreed to return to England for questioning, if a ransom was paid to free him.

Mike took up the story and related how, when he arrived at Camp West posing as a diplomat to escort Sutton home, he discovered that Sutton's imprisonment was false. It was all a ploy used to detain an important diplomat in order to exchange him for Mrs Boyd, who they had now discovered was Sutton's woman.

Brooke continued by saying that the Roseburgh embassy employee, Mr Robert Weston, was working with Sutton and believed that he, Brooke, had the ransom money. During his visit a fight ensued and Mr Weston was killed.

Suzie then completed the explanation by relating how she impersonated Mrs Boyd, flew to Africa to free Mike, was successful, but they were unable to bring Sutton back to England.

Suzie was about to add something when Sir Joseph's telephone rang.

'Excuse me,' he apologised, lifting the receiver.

He listened to the caller and replied, 'Thank you, DC Green. I'll let DI Brooke know.'

Sir Joseph pressed a button on his intercom and spoke to his secretary. 'No more calls now Miss Wilson, unless they are very urgent.'

'Yes, Sir Joseph.'

Brooke looked up in anticipation of the comment. 'Good news, Sir?'

'Good news indeed.' He looked at Mike and Suzie who were wondering what the call was about. 'Mrs Boyd appeared in court today. Her solicitor tried desperately to get her released on bail. I am pleased to say that he failed. If he had achieved it, I have no doubt that she would have absconded, and we would not see her again.'

'I agree,' stated Brooke. 'What exactly was the outcome?'

'She was ordered to be detained at her majesties pleasure, and to appear in court again in three weeks time on charges of assisting in a robbery and of inciting others to commit murder. She is fortunate that the other teller, Mr Wainwright, has survived, though it looks as if he may be crippled for the rest of his life.'

'Where has she been taken?' asked Suzie.

'She is being driven back to Holloway Prison as we speak.'

'Sutton won't like that when he hears about it,' said Mike.

'I'm sure he won't,' agreed Sir Joseph. 'Please continue with what you were about to say, Suzie.'

'I was about to say that we were lucky to get out of Kitsulana so easily. Only because the other prisoners, freed by Mike, caused a stir, did it enable us to get over the border while the guards were more interested in chasing after them.'

'I understand from other sources in the area, that the prisoners broke into the armoury to get guns, and found explosives there as well. When the soldiers started shooting, they lobbed sticks of dynamite at them. During the fighting, it seems that more explosives caught alight, and several of the new buildings were blown sky high,' Sir Jeremy stated.

'That must be what we saw when we reached the border,' suggested Suzie.

'You do seem to be making a habit of destroying much of the camp after you leave,' said Sir Joseph.

'Nothing to do with us. If the explosion hadn't happened when it did, we might have had to fight our way to get across the border,' Suzie suggested.

'With or without Sutton?' Brooke asked.

'Either way wouldn't have mattered,' added Mike. 'We left in such a hurry that we forgot to take his passport with us, so the guards would not let us take him across the border, which was heavily guarded; shooting our way out would have been very difficult.'

'I kicked him out of the vehicle and we drove to Roseburgh,' Suzie stated.

'Sutton swore that he'd get his revenge on us and said we hadn't seen the last of him. He was very angry.'

'I see,' Sir Joseph said, looking at them over the top of his glasses. 'And what happened to the $250,000 ransom money? Tell me why Mr Weston though that Colin had charge of it?'

'I didn't want to take it into the meeting with the general, in case something went wrong. So I hid it in my rented car. When I didn't produce the ransom money, Weston jumped to the conclusion that Colin was looking after it, because he knew that he'd accompanied me to Roseburgh.'

'Why didn't you tell him where the money was hidden, when you knew that he was going to confront me about it? You must have realised that it would be dangerous for me,' asked Brooke.

'If I had given him the money he may well have decided to shoot me.'

'I don't think so. He still wanted to make the exchange for Mrs Boyd.'

'I didn't realise that he was going to take a gun to shoot you with,' lied Mike. 'I know that you are a capable man and can take care of yourself. It also meant that it would enable you to discover what Sutton's real reason was for the exchange, and would know that I was in trouble, though I was still hoping to escape with him and the money.'

'I see,' said Sir Joseph. 'So what happened to the money?'

'I checked my car before we left and the money was gone, so Sutton must have searched it and found the ransom. I imagine the general has stashed it somewhere safe.'

Suzie had to stifle the inner smiles she felt at all the lies Mike was telling in order to abrogate the responsibility he had for ensuring the money was kept safe.

'It's a good job that Colin was able to deal with Mr Weston,' Sir Joseph added.

Mike and Brooke's eyes met. The detective was unsure whether Mike Randle really thought he was capable of taking care of the situation, or if he simply decided to leave him to his fate in order to try and keep hold of the ransom money and protect himself.

★ ★ ★

While Sir Joseph listened to the events of the past few weeks, a stolen white van with darkened windows was parked in a side street off Camden Road. Inside, four men waited patiently; two in the front and two in the rear.

The driver answered a call on his mobile telephone. 'Okay. We're all ready and waiting as agreed,' he confirmed, closing his mobile and pocketing it. 'Everyone get ready. It's on, and we go into action any time now. Get covered up.'

The four men grabbed balaclava hoods, pulled them over their heads to cover their faces, and adjusted them.

'Remember now, no unnecessary violence. We don't want the police after us for killing anyone, it'll only make them more determined.'

Heads nodded and a couple of grunts were issued in agreement.

In a stolen Volvo estate car, parked behind the van, sat a driver, also patiently waiting.

Among heavy traffic along Camden Road, drove a police motorcycle escort, riding ahead of the prison van holding Mrs Boyd, returning her to Holloway Prison.

Suddenly the stolen van burst into life, lurched from the side street and headed straight for the motorcycle escort. Crashing into him, it sent him sprawling across the road and blocked the route of the prison van, which shuddered to an abrupt halt with tyres squealing.

Four men jumped from the stolen van. Two from the cab and two through the rear doors who dashed to the back of the prison van. One man smashed the prison van driver's window with a sledgehammer and the other thrust a shotgun into his face.

'Put the radio down and just sit tight and nobody will get hurt,' he demanded, covering him and his passenger. 'Tell your man in the back to open the doors.'

The guard hesitated. The barrel of the shotgun was pressed into his face. 'Now,' screamed the hooded man.

The motorcycle policeman staggered to his feet and was met by the second man crashing the stock of his shotgun against his helmeted head, knocking him unconscious. Nearby shoppers looked on in horror at the events, but stood rooted to the spot and were unwilling to get involved with armed gangsters waving shotguns in the air.

At the rear of the van, a worried prison guard opened the doors. He was grabbed by his lapel and thrown to the ground. 'Stay there and don't get up if you value your life,' he was told.

The doors were flung open wide, and a worried female prison officer looked at the hooded man holding a shotgun. Fear was etched across her face. She was shoved back into the van and the handcuffs between her and her prisoner were cut. Mrs Boyd was free.

With tyres spinning furiously, burning rubber on the road, the Volvo car sped out of the turning and screeched to a halt behind the open prison van doors. Mrs Boyd jumped from the van and climbed into the passenger seat, and the car accelerated away.

The four masked men dashed back into their van, and almost cause an accident as they blasted their way down the high street and disappeared in the distance, leaving behind them four relieved prison guards and one badly injured police motorcyclist.

★ ★ ★

Back in Sir Joseph's office, the conversations continued.

'Do you know what happened at Camp West after we left? Did

the soldiers catch the escaped prisoners?' asked Suzie, anxious to steer the conversation away from the questions about the missing money.

'I haven't heard. Information is sketchy, but it seems that some prisoners and guards were killed before a number of the prisoners escaped. You seem to be making a habit of doing that as well.'

'Right,' Mike said, turning to Brooke. 'I understand that you collected a small parcel of mine, from Manny at Paul's Bar?'

'Yes,' he said sheepishly. 'I gave it to Sir Joseph.'

'I had a thumb through the contents. Very interesting,' Sir Joseph said.

'I hope there's nothing missing,' Mike stated, trying his hardest to embarrass the pair of them.

'I'm sure you will be able to confirm that the contents are untouched,' Sir Joseph retorted, as the telephone rang again.

Mike half-smiled at the remark, but said nothing.

'Excuse me,' Sir Joseph said, lifting the receiver. 'This must be urgent to interrupt our meeting.'

Listening to the caller, Sir Joseph's face showed no change of expression, nor did his voice give any hint of what he was hearing, either good or bad. These cultivated qualities had helped him earlier in his career and led to his success as a diplomat, and later as a troubleshooter.

He responded, 'Was anyone hurt? ... Yes, he is ... Yes, I will ... Goodbye.'

'Bad news this time?' enquired Brooke.

'Yes, the police vehicle and escort rider taking Mrs Boyd back to prison was attacked by an armed group with shotguns.'

'And Mrs Boyd?'

'She was set free, and has escaped.'

27

SMASH AND GRAB

Mike, Suzie and DI Brooke had returned from Africa without Owen Sutton, and were in Sir Joseph's London office explaining the circumstances of their failed visit when he received an urgent telephone call. Sir Joseph replaced his telephone receiver and informed the trio that Mrs Boyd had been set free by an armed gang while she was being escorted back to Holloway prison.

'How on earth did that happen?' asked Brooke.

'A van knocked the policeman off his motorcycle and blocked the prison van. The guards were threatened by armed men with shotguns and were forced to open the doors. A car whisked Mrs Boyd to freedom.'

'Anyone hurt?' asked Mike.

'The motorcycle policeman was injured, but not too seriously, thank God. He was knocked unconscious and has been taken to hospital, but fortunately no shots were fired.'

'That's very audacious. I suspect that it was planned by Sutton. His man was probably watching the court proceedings and saw that she wasn't granted bail, and the plan to free her must have been set up in advance if that happened,' maintained Brooke.

'I should have anticipated this,' Sir Joseph confessed.

'Why? There's no reason for you to think that he would go to these lengths to get Mrs Boyd out,' suggested Suzie. 'And I don't suppose you even knew he was in this country, assuming he has returned to mastermind this breakout.'

'I don't agree. A man who is willing to try conning the British Government into paying a ransom for his release, in order to capture a diplomat to exchange for his woman, is likely to go to almost any lengths to get her back. I should have realised this earlier and put out an alert at the airport to watch out for him.'

'What's the next step?' asked Brooke.

'I'd like you to handle the investigation, Colin. I suggest you start by taking a look at the prison van to see if you can gain any clues from the scene.'

Brooke stood up. 'I'm on my way. Where did it happen?'

'Not far from the prison on the A503, Camden Road. Roadblocks have been set up, but I'm not hopeful that it will stop them getting away. They have planned this very carefully, and are certain to have changed vehicles quickly.'

'I'll contact DC's Teal and Green to help me. I'll telephone you if I find out anything useful,' Brooke stated.

He nodded to Mike and Suzie, opened the door and hurried from the office.

'I imagine the major ports and airports have now been alerted,' said Mike.

'Yes, but there are so many small sailing clubs where a person can slip out on a small boat and sail away. We've no hope of covering them all. This may be how Mr Sutton slipped into this country unseen.'

Suddenly, a thought occurred to Suzie and she stiffened.

'What is it?' asked Sir Joseph. 'Has that rung a bell with you? Do you remember something?'

'Yes, I have. While I was waiting for Sutton to arrive in his office at Camp West, I took a look around the room. He had numerous mementoes and a photograph of himself and Mrs Boyd. They were standing on the deck of a motor yacht, arm in arm. The name of the boat was visible in the photo, and I remember thinking that the name was rather appropriate.'

'What was it?'

'I can't remember.'

'Think, Suzie. It could be very important.'

Suzie put her head in her hands and closed her eyes. 'I can almost see it now. It meant something like … getting away … disappearing …'

Mike and Sir Joseph made suggestions.

'Err, vanish?'

'No.'

'Escape?'

'No.'

'Depart?'

'No.'

'Evade?'

'No, but that sounds close. It's something like that. I've got it!' exclaimed Suzie. 'It's *Elude*. *Elude* is the name of the vessel.'

'Great! That's an unusual name. It shouldn't be too hard to trace if the vessel is moored in the south. Well done,' praised Sir Joseph, snatching up his telephone. He rang Special Branch and passed the information on. 'They will organise a search of all the south's yachting clubs, marinas and harbours.'

'That's quite a job,' announced Mike.

'Yes, but it's a lead, the best lead we have at the moment, unless Colin comes up with something from the incident site.'

'If you've finished asking your questions, we ought to be getting back. We've had to leave Jim and Jenny to look after the business while we've been away,' said Mike, anxious to depart before more questions about the money arose.

'Yes, of course. I've got more important work to do at the moment now. We can finish our conversations later.'

The comment perturbed Mike, though he tried hard not to show it. He and Suzie said goodbye and returned to their car.

London traffic was heavy as lunchtime approached, and it took Mike and Suzie a while to reach the M3. Once on the motorway, Mike was able to make better headway. As they neared the M27, Suzie's mobile rang.

'Hello, Sir Joseph.'

'Suzie, Special Branch has traced a yacht named *Elude* to a Littlehampton Marina club, named *The Mainsail Yacht Club*.'

'*The Mainsail Yacht Club*. Gosh! That was quick!'

'Yes, we tasked a lot of people to ring around the south's yacht clubs and it looks as if it may have paid dividends. Can you get there easily?'

'Why, yes we can. We're approaching the M27 turnoff. We can be there within about half an hour,' Suzie said, tapping Mike's arm and pointing to the sign which lead to the eastbound turnoff. 'Take the road to Littlehampton,' she told him.

Mike nodded, signalled left and moved into the nearside lane ready to pull into the approach road leading east.

'Good. You've seen both Mrs Boyd and Mr Sutton, and can recognise them. The local police are on their way, but I've instructed them only to watch the yacht unless it starts to leave the harbour. I'd like you and Mike to check it out for me.'

'Do we know if Sutton is part of the gang?'

'Yes, we do. Colin rang to say the video camera in the rear of the rammed police van, clearly shows Sutton, through the open rear door, driving the car that picked up Mrs Boyd. He obviously hired a gang of thugs to carry out the raid for him. We found the stolen Volvo dumped a few miles away, so they've transferred to another vehicle.'

'Right, so he really meant it when he said we hadn't seen the last of him.'

'I'm afraid so. Ring me when you get to the marina and let me know what you find.'

'Okay,' said Suzie, turning off her mobile. 'Did you get all of that?' she asked Mike.

'More or less. I gather Sutton is behind the ram raid and might be heading for Littlehampton,' he said, moving into the outside lane of the M27 motorway and accelerating fast.

'That's about the gist of it. The police have located a yacht named *Elude* in a yacht club there. We've been asked to check it out to see if it's Sutton's escape boat.'

'And if it is, and we see him, what then?'

'I guess we tackle him again, with caution, he's bound to be armed.'

'We'd better be ready for him then,' Mike suggested.

Suzie opened the glove compartment, released a false back and extracted two handguns and two spare clips. She checked and loaded them. 'I wish we had our protective vests,' she remarked.

'They're in the boot,' informed Mike.

'You think of everything,' she praised, kissing him on the cheek.

'Having survived as a soldier and a mercenary, I don't want to get shot by some tinpot crook.'

'Quite right. I'd have no one to browbeat into running faster along the beach, and to suggest buying me a particular type of ring.'

'Are they the only reasons you don't want to see me shot?'

'No, they're not the only reasons. I don't want to live in a big house on my own either. I want to share it with my hubby.'

'Hmm ... thanks for the vote of confidence,' Mike said, in a deliberately hurt tone of voice.

'I want you to occupy the house as well, so that we can enjoy each other's company, and things.'

'It's the things that I enjoy mainly.'

'I know that, Randy. That's part of our good relationship.'

'True.'

'So, when are you going to ask me to marry you?'

Mike spluttered and nearly lost control of the car. 'I ... don't know ... I've been thinking about it ... really.'

Suzie opened her mouth to speak when Mike suddenly interrupted her, 'Oh look! We're here,' he said, pointing to a sign that conveyed a welcome to all who past it, and confirmed that they were now in the seaside town of Littlehampton.

Following the signposts, Mike and Suzie found their way to the marina where the yacht was moored. Police cars surrounded the entrance, to prevent anyone getting near. After stating who they were to a local bobby, who rang the police superintendent in charge of the operation to confirm that it was okay to let them past, Mike was allowed into the marina. He drove along the approach road and parked their car in a secluded spot. Suzie took off her blouse while Mike took off his jacket and they grabbed their protective vests from the boot, donned them and dressed.

'Does the vest show?' asked Mike.

'Not unless you look carefully.'

'Good. I don't want the police suspecting that we're armed. They might not like it,' said Mike, stuffing the gun in his belt beneath his loose shirt and pocketing the spare clip.

Suzie did likewise, as they were approached by the superintendent. He was a gangly man, with a long, thin moustache, an ex-RAF man who looked and sounded typically like one.

'I'm Superintendent James Hadley,' he introduced. 'Please follow me.'

The trio scurried towards the mooring area on foot.

'If this is Sutton's yacht and he's here, the police might as well have given him a phone call and informed him who they were,' complained Mike. 'There are policemen everywhere, and they're not very well hidden,' he whispered.

'Ssh, he might hear you. Yes, it's true. Let's hope it's not Sutton's yacht or that he's stayed below and hasn't seen them.'

'He's a cautions man and would have to be almost blind not to see them,' suggested Mike.

They reached the river and peered around the corner of the wooden clubhouse belonging to *The Mainsail Yacht Club*. Ahead of them were the pontoon moorings for visiting yachts with several tied up on each side.

'*Elude* is the large yacht, second boat along on the left,' informed the superintendent, pointing in the general direction.

'Yes, I can just make out the name. I notice the entrance to the moorings is barred by a gate with a security code lock. Do we have the code number to the gate, in case we have to get in there in a hurry?'

'Yes, it's 124.'

'Right. Take a look, Suzie. Does the vessel look like the one in the photo you saw in Sutton's office?'

Suzie peered around the corner. 'I'm not sure. It's difficult to tell, the photo only showed a part of the yacht. It could be the same one, it looks about the right size, and it's an unusual name, I can't imagine there are many vessels called *Elude*.'

'No, I agree. Do you know how long has it been tied up here, Superintendent?'

'I've spoken to the yacht club secretary. He tells me it arrived here on Sunday the eighth, just over two weeks ago.'

'That was a few days before the building society robbery,' said Mike.

'What building society robbery? I haven't heard about that,' said the policeman.

'Nothing to do with this, it's what the woman we're after was accused of.' Mike turned to Suzie. 'I bet they were planning to take the money from Kelly, once he'd done the job, and quietly slip out of the country aboard their boat.'

'And, no doubt, fit him up to take the blame. He was probably their fall guy,' suggested Suzie, 'and Mrs Boyd's sexual attractions were the bait.'

As they watched, a sailor appeared on deck. He looked around, looked at his watch and disappeared below.

'That's not our man, and he looks as if he's waiting for someone. I wonder if Sutton and Mrs Boyd are yet to arrive. They had to dump their getaway car, pick up another one and drive here carefully, in order not to attract any attention,' Mike speculated.

'If that's true, the obvious police presence here would scare them off,' suggested Suzie.

'Right. I think you should ask your men to let the traffic flow normally and keep their vehicles out of sight, Superintendent. We don't want to scare our love birds off if they haven't arrived yet.'

'Righty-ho. I'll see to it straight away,' he promised, scurrying off to see his men.

Mike and Suzie scampered into the clubhouse for *The Mainsail Yacht Club*; a building that was constructed of cedar wood and in need of a coat of preservative. Access was through a central front door, situated at the top of four wooden steps, enclosed by a hand rail. They stood in a poorly lit corridor, full of photographs and diplomas, disappearing into the gloom, hanging on both walls along its full length. Alongside them near the front entrance was a room on each side. Walking in through an open doorway, they entered a room where they could see *Elude* at its moorings through the window. Pulling up a chair each, they waited. Mike put his feet up on the desk, pulled the gun from his waistband and checked the clip.

'It's loaded and ready,' stated Suzie. 'You should put it away before that policeman sees it. He may take it away from you otherwise.'

Mike slipped on the safety catch and stuck the gun back in his waistband. 'If Sutton doesn't show up soon, then I reckon he's rumbled what's going on here, assuming that's his yacht.'

'There isn't anybody walking around. The police must have told everyone to leave. It looks deserted, and may frighten Sutton off if he's suspicious.'

No sooner had the words parted from Suzie's lips, when a black VW Golf vehicle drew up and stopped outside the clubhouse beneath the window where they were spying on the yacht. Mike and Suzie ducked down quickly.

'Did you see who was in that car?' asked Mike.

'No, I was too busy ducking out of the way. I saw two heads though. One was a man and the other a woman. Do you think it's them?'

'Don't know. I'm going to find another window to take a look. Watch out in case they come in here,' said Mike, scrabbling across the room, keeping low.

He crossed the corridor and entered a room on the far side. Gingerly, he raised his head above the window sill and peered out. The front of the car was visible, with no sign of the occupants. Suzie joined him.

A woman hurried towards the security gate, pressed the code to open it and glanced back. Sutton stepped from the rear of the car and looked around. It was very quiet – perhaps too quiet. He was starting to get suspicious.

'That's Mrs Boyd,' whispered Suzie. 'Sutton must be close.'

No sooner had she spoken than they heard the clubhouse front door open and they turned to see Sutton appear in the open doorway.

'I thought something was wrong. It's all too quiet. I might have guessed it was you two up to no good again,' he said, pulling a gun from his waistband.

Mike grabbed the pistol from his belt and the pair of them fired at each other and ducked simultaneously. Both shots missed their target. Sutton fled from the room and crashed through the front door. He ran for all he was worth towards the moorings.

Mrs Boyd had almost reached the yacht when she stopped and turned at the sound of gunfire. The sailor jumped ashore from the boat and beckoned her aboard.

'Get in the boat,' yelled Sutton, turning to fire a volley of shots at Mike and Suzie as they emerged from the clubhouse.

Back at the main gate, the superintendent exclaimed, 'They're jolly well shooting at each other!'

He and his men jumped into their cars and dashed towards the sound of gunfire.

The sailor ushered Mrs Boyd on to the boat, untied the line and fired up the engine. Sutton furiously jammed the code in using the barrel of his gun, opened the gate and slammed it shut behind him, firing two more shots into the security lock pushbuttons before turning to run for all he was worth.

The motor yacht was pulling away from the moorings slowly when Sutton leapt across the gap on to the deck. The yacht's revs increased as it chugged away from the berth, gathering speed and heading down the river towards the open sea.

Mike grabbed one of the bars on the gate and yanked it back and forth. The gate was stuck fast and the security locking mechanism was shattered, making it impossible to enter the code. He stood back, fired two shots into the lock and kicked the gate hard. It crashed open, allowing him to race down the pontoon to the fast disappearing yacht.

Suzie, meanwhile, was running as hard as she could along the riverside road, making for a bridge where the river narrows, and the yacht would have to pass beneath. *Elude* was approaching the bridge as she clambered over the parapet and stood on a narrow ledge above the centre of the river.

At the moorings, a speedboat was pulling in to dock, close to where Mike stood. He dashed to the boat and shouted at the owner, an elderly man wearing a blazer and a seafaring cap.

'Jumping into the boat, Mike stated, 'I need to borrow your boat. I'm chasing a fugitive.'

'I'm not sure that I want you to do that,' the man protested.

'I haven't got time to argue,' said Mike, giving him a gentle shove.

He fell backward, yelled and disappeared overboard, hitting the water with a resounding splash that drowned his protests. He waved a fist at Mike who started the engine and roared the speedboat away in pursuit of Sutton's vessel.

Watching the yacht as it passed below her underneath the bridge, Suzie jumped on to the cabin roof and landing in a crouch above the pilot house. Standing up, she made a grab for her gun, tucked in her belt at the back. Sutton, standing at the controls, heard her land on the roof, snatched up his gun, dashed out and fired three shots, point blank at Suzie, hitting her in the centre of her body before she could grasp her gun. The blast knocked her off her feet, propelling her from the roof and into the river.

Mike, charging towards them in the speedboat watched this with horror and yelled out, 'Suzie! Suzie!'

In anger, he let loose with a volley of shots, emptying his gun at the yacht. Sutton and Mrs Boyd dropped to the floor as a fusillade of bullets peppered the pilot house, smashing windows and digging into the woodwork. *Elude* continued to speed her way towards the open sea.

Mike pulled back the throttle controls and brought the speedboat to a halt near where ripples in the water fanned out where Suzie had fallen in. He threw his gun down, ripped off his jacket and protective vest, took a deep breath and dived into the water.

An eerie wall of silence greeted him below the surface as the water enveloped him and he searched the murky river for Suzie. Frantic, at not being able to see clearly, he thrashed around, finding it difficult to swim with his trousers clinging to his legs. Mike felt real terror for the first time at the though he might lose her. He swam back and forth, searching for any sight of Suzie, but saw nothing. His lungs were getting close to bursting point and he knew he would soon have to surface for air, and that meant Suzie must be almost out of air as well. Then, from the corner of his eye, he caught a glimpse of a dark shape in the deep.

Swimming towards it, the water cleared and he saw Suzie, her limp body drifting downwards towards the bottom, her cumbersome bulletproof vest dragging her down. Small bubbles of air seeped from her mouth and nose, her long hair swirled about in the water, her arms and legs drifted helplessly. Mike snatched out and caught her wrist. He dragged her towards him, wrapped an arm around her body and clasped her under the armpit. He headed for the surface as fast as he was able. His lungs were on fire and it seemed as if he would never reach the top. The murkiness of the water began to clear, the sunlit surface beckoned and was agonisingly close, but time felt as if it had almost come to a stop and distance to the surface appeared no closer. After what seemed an eternity, Mike burst from the water, rising like a phoenix from the river, taking in great gulps of air.

The superintendent and two policemen were gingerly edging their way down the embankment. Mike swam to the edge and they grabbed Suzie and pulled her out of the water. Mike scrambled out and turned Suzie on her back.

'Come on Suzie, breath,' he pleaded, cupping her face and blowing air into her lungs five times before pressing down on her chest in a calculated steady rhythm.

There was no response. Mike continued to press hard on her chest.

'Come on Suzie, please,' he pleaded.

The three policemen stared in silence, unable to help.

Suddenly, she began to cough and spat out water. Mike turned her on her side. She coughed again as more water was brought up and dribbled from the corner of her mouth. Suzie opened her eyes, rolled on to her back, looked up at Mike and half smiled.

'Thank goodness you're alive. I thought you were a goner for a moment,' Mike said, wiping the straggles of wet hair from her face.

Suzie put a hand on the side of his face. 'You still haven't asked me to marry you, so you can't get rid of me yet.'

He grabbed her hand and kissed it. 'Thank goodness for that.'

'If it hadn't been for all the exercise I do keeping fit, I don't know if I would have survived.'

'You have, that's all that matters.'

The superintendent looked up to see a rather ancient, police launch chugging past in pursuit of the fleeing motor yacht. Mike fingered the powder burns on Suzie's T-shirt.

'He must have shot you at point blank range. It's a good job you were wearing your protective vest.'

'The force of the shot knocked me out. My ribs hurt like hell.'

'I think we should get Miss Drake to hospital for a check-up,' stated the superintendent.

Mike nodded. 'Good idea. Could you see to that?' he asked.

'Yes, of course. What are you going to do?'

He looked at Suzie, smiled, turned and ran back into the river. Mike swam to the speedboat and climbed aboard. He revved up the engine, and the boat roared away in pursuit of Sutton, leaving a trail of churning river behind him that rolled to the water's edge.

Changing the clip on his gun, Mike's fast speedboat caught up with the police launch quickly and motored past, leaving them rocking from side to side in its wake. *Elude* had disappeared around a bend in the river and was out of sight. Mike rammed the throttle wide open to gain as much speed as he could. The speedboat leant over at an angle, blasting its way around the bend in the river. To his surprise, Mike caught sight of the almost stationary motor yacht, bobbing up and down in the water less than 250 yards in front of him.

Pulling the throttle lever back, he approached cautiously, watching the yacht which had slowed down almost to a stop. Mike wondered why, spun the wheel and brought the speedboat level, but wide of *Elude*. Keeping one hand on the throttle, he was ready for a quick getaway if, as he suspected, it was a trap.

The sailor appeared on deck. Mike pointed his gun at him and he threw up his arms and yelled, 'I'm not armed.'

'Where's Sutton?'

'He's below with his woman. She has been badly wounded by your bullets. He is very sad, and very angry with what you've done to her.'

'But has no compunction in shooting my woman at point blank range,' defended Mike.

'She was armed and would have used her weapon on Mr Sutton. It was self defence.'

'I saw what happened. He shot her before he could see if she was armed. He's a cold blooded killer and I want his hide.'

As Mike uttered the last few words, Sutton emerged from the cabin clasping a gun. 'No chance,' he shouted, blasting away at Mike.

Dropping smartly to the deck, Mike jammed the throttle wide open as bullets smashed the windscreen and dug into the framework. A few seconds later, he raised his head to peer over the edge and check that he was not on a collision course with another craft. His speedboat was now well ahead of Sutton's yacht in the river.

Throttling back, Mike turned his boat around in a wide arc and headed back, gathering speed as he went. Sutton was at the wheel of his motor yacht and stared at the oncoming vessel. It was like a modern day jousting tournament with two opponents charging towards each other. Sutton let loose with more shots as his yacht and the speedboat closed in on a collision course at a high rate of knots.

The two craft came closer and closer with ever increasing speed, as the power of the speedboat reached its maximum. The wind blew past Mike's face, his hair whipped about in a swirl, his teeth gritted in anger at Sutton's actions in shooting Suzie, and his determination to seek revenge for his cowardly act.

Sutton watched in horror at the speedboat charging towards him like an arrow, speeding death and destruction closer by the second, not wavering or deviating from its course. In a final desperate attempt, Sutton wrenched the steering wheel round, in a last second bid to steer the yacht away from the path of the incoming missile, but he had left it too late. When the vessels were only a few yards apart, Mike threw himself over the edge leaving the racing speedboat to smash into the side of Sutton's motor yacht.

The fuel ignited, exploding both boats into a fireball of fragments, shooting high into the air with thick, black smoke bellowing from the burning shells of both vessels. Mike surfaced to see the Sutton's yacht engulfed in a fireball with its centre section blown clean away. It keeled over on its side and sank quickly into the abyss of the dark, all-consuming river.

The police patrol boat chugged around the river bend and slowed to a halt among the debris of charred and splintered wreckage of the two boats. The men aboard searched for survivors, but Mike was the only person they picked up.

'What happened?' one of the policemen asked.

'He went out with a bang.'

After circling the area for almost half an hour, much to Mike's frustrations at wanting to return to see how Suzie was, the police gave up hope of finding anyone else alive and headed back to the marina. The superintendent was waiting by the landing strip for news, after hearing the explosion. He was trying hard to pacify the sailor who was complaining voraciously about his speedboat being stolen and demanding the culprit be arrested. Mike was only interested in knowing that Suzie was okay.

'Where's Suzie? Is she alright?'

The superintendent nodded. 'She's fine. The ambulance took her to Littlehampton Hospital for a check-up.'

'He's the man,' pointed the sailor. 'He the one who stole my speedboat, he should be arrested.'

'He was on police business and you will be compensated for your loss,' stated the superintendent.

'What loss? Where's my speedboat? What has he done to it?'

'My sergeant will sort things out with you,' said the superintendent, grabbing Mike's arm and leading him away as quickly as he could.

'Can you show me the way to the hospital?' asked Mike.

'I'll take you there. You can tell me what happened on the way,' he said, hearing the angry shouts from the sailor fading into the distance.

On their journey to the hospital, Mike related his story to the superintendent, but made a slight alteration, changing it to make it seem as if Sutton had rammed his boat and come off worse.

'My men didn't find anyone, so I guess that's the last we'll see of him, alive anyway. His body should surface pretty soon, and the others on the boat. You say that Mrs Boyd was injured?'

'So the sailor man said.'

'Then it's unlikely that she survived. Sutton must have been pretty mad to ram into you like that.'

'The sailor said he was angry at seeing her hit by my bullet. It must have tipped his mind, coming all this way to rescue her, only to get her shot.'

'I guess so. There will be an enquiry in a few weeks time and you'll have to attend to give your version of what happened, especially as you were armed, and strictly speaking that is against the law, as I'm sure you know.'

'Are there likely to be any problems?' Mike asked.

'I don't think so, though you might be reprimanded for having the firearm and discharging it.'

'I did it to try and protect Suzie.'

'Yes, I realise that and I'm sure it will be taken into account.'

'Great!' mumbled Mike. 'Perhaps a word from Sir Joseph Sterling on my behalf would help?'

'Yes, I'm sure it would. We're here,' the superintendent said, pointing at the hospital as they motored through to the main entrance.

Mike dashed to the reception and was told that Suzie had been examined by a doctor, and taken afterwards to 'Birch Ward'. Mike was given directions and hurried along the corridors to the ward. The familiar hospital smell of disinfectant, and the off-white corridors reminded him of a time when he was badly hurt, and grateful for all the attention the staff gave him in nursing him back to health.

Mike entered 'Birch Ward', which held five other beds, all occupied by women. He spied Suzie in a bed by the window, pulled up a chair next to her bed and held her hand.

'How do you feel?' he asked.

'Okay. I'm a bit drowsy. I think they've given me a sedative to ease the pain and help me relax.'

'Any bones broken?'

'I've had an X-ray, and it showed that I've got a couple of cracked ribs as well as slight concussion. They've strapped me up and said I can go home tomorrow after the doctor has seen me, as long as I'm feeling okay.'

'That's good.'

'What happened to you? Did Sutton get away?'

'He's keeping the fishes company.'

'He's dead?'

'Yes, at least I think so. We'll know for sure when the police find his body.'

'And Mrs Boyd?'

'She's keeping him company, and the sailor.'

'What happened?'

'I'll tell you all about it when we get home. Meantime, you're looking a bit tired, so get some rest and get your strength back, or I'll be leaving you behind on our early morning jog.'

'Not a chance!'

Mike smiled and kissed Suzie. He had a word with the doctor and promised to pick her up the following morning.

It was a lonely drive home and Mike thought more about whether the time was right to buy Suzie the ring that she deserved. Life would certainly never be the same if he ever lost her, and today that nearly happened. It made him realise how much he loved and counted on her, and could not imagine life without her.

At home, he rang Jim and Jenny to bring them up to date on the day's events.

'She is alright, isn't she?' asked Jenny.

'Suzie is. She's a bit battered, but she's a fighter and will be okay. Don't worry. I'm collecting her from the hospital tomorrow morning.'

'It must have been awful.'

'It was. It made me realise how much I want her.'

'You mean love her, don't you?'

'I guess so. That's a word I find hard to use.'

'So I've noticed, and so has she. If you don't do something about asking her to marry you soon, you may find her straying from you.'

'She wouldn't – would she?'

'She might. Suzie is a very attractive woman. She's nearing the age where she wants to have more permanent roots, and I'm sure she'd not go short of admirers. If you don't buy her a ring, somebody else might.'

'Do you really think so?'

'Anything's possible,' Jenny said, trying hard to convince Mike that it was time for him to pop the question, even though she knew that Suzie had told her she would never leave him.

Mike ended the telephone conversation deep in thought. Jenny had given him something very important to think about. Jim rang his father to pass on the information about Sutton, but he'd already heard most of it from the police superintendent.

The following morning Mike dashed back to the hospital to collect Suzie. She was already dressed and waiting for him, and he gave her a bunch of flowers he had bought at a local petrol station.

'Thank you, Mike. That is very sweet of you,' said Suzie, giving him a kiss on the cheek.

'I'll have to take it a bit easy for a while,' she said, lowering herself gently into their car seat. 'I'm still heavily strapped across my middle.'

'You take it easy and don't worry about a thing. I'll take care of everything.'

'Does that mean you are going to do the cooking as well?'

'I'm a dab hand at baked beans on toast.'

'So, is that all we're going to live on for the next few days?'

'There's a great Pizza shop opened in town and they do deliveries as well,' Mike replied.

Suzie smiled. 'I thought as much.'

Mike revved up the car and drove them home.

28

FINAL FLING

On the last Saturday in October, Mike collected Suzie from Littlehampton Hospital, after her bulletproof vest had saved her from certain death when Sutton shot her at point blank range. Cracked ribs and concussion were the worst that she suffered from after Mike had rescued her from the murky river.

The iron gates of Mike and Suzie's home by the sea parted, allowing their DB7 to pass through. The car crunched over the gravel driveway, and Mike brought it to a halt in front of their dark green double garage doors.

Helping Suzie from the car, she linked her arm in his and they walked in small steps to the house. Mike pressed the button on the remote to shut the electronic gates while he helped Suzie to climb the three steps to their front door. With his back to the gates, he was unable to see the shadowy figure slip into the garden before they clanged shut.

Throwing the keys on the hall table, Mike punched the code into the beeping alarm console to turn the intruder alarm off.

'How do you feel?' he asked.

'A bit achy. I think I'll have a rest.'

'You go and lie down on the settee. I'll make us a nice cup of tea.'

'That sounds good to me,' said Suzie, gingerly wandering into the living room and gently stretching out on the settee.

Mike stepped into the kitchen, opposite their living room at the front of the house, filled the kettle and depressed the 'on' switch. As he prepared their drinks, they were unaware the intruder was busy forcing open the door at the rear of the house.

'We've got to start preparing soon for the London Boat Show in January. I hope you are not going to be out of commission too long,' shouted Mike, across the hall from the kitchen.

'It's a couple of months away yet. I'm sure that Reg will already be making plans for the show.'

'Yes, I guess so. He's usually got those sort of things planned well ahead.'

'I've got a wonderful surprise for you in the bedroom.'

Mike's eyes lit up. 'Great! I didn't think you were up to it yet.'

'Not that kind of surprise, Randy! You'll have to curb your sexual instincts for a few days until I'm feeling a bit better. And anyway, I couldn't take your weight on top of me at the moment.'

'That's okay. It's your turn on top this time.'

'That's not what I meant, and you know it.'

While the kettle boiled and Mike made the tea, the intruder glided into the living room through the double doors and crept up to the back of the settee where Suzie was resting. Mike filled the teapot, placed it with the cups and milk jug on a tray, and wandered into the living room. He was confronted by a man leaning over the back of the settee, with an arm around Suzie's neck and holding a gun against her head.

Mike stopped in his tracks. 'So, Mr Sutton, you are not feeding the fishes in the river after all.'

'No, but my sailor friend is and my wife Katie is dead, thanks to you.'

'Your wife! I thought you were partners, I didn't realise you were married.'

'We were married in South Africa a short time ago. And now you've killed her, shot her then drowned her, with your gung-ho ramming tactics. She didn't deserve to die.'

'Neither did Suzie, but you put a gun into her ribs and pulled the trigger several times without any compunction or thought about killing my woman,' said Mike.

Mike slowly wandered into the room and carefully put the tray down on the coffee table, watched closely by Sutton. He cautiously sat down in the nearby armchair, facing them.

'I don't know how she survived that,' admitted Sutton.

'I'm only alive because of a protective vest that I wore, and Mike's heroic efforts to save me from drowning afterwards,' remarked Suzie.

'Lucky you! Unfortunately I wasn't able to do the same for my wife after the explosion almost knocked me unconscious for a short time. And you won't be quite so lucky this time. I intend to make you both sweat for a while, before I shoot you in front of your partner. That way, Mr bloody Randle, you will suffer in the same way that I had to, seeing my wife after she'd been shot and drowned, and watching her die moments later in my arms.'

Suzie groaned and wriggled, shifting her weight as she lay on the settee. Sutton stiffened and thrust the gun at her.

'No sudden movements or I'll kill you right now,' he threatened.

'I'm not going to spring at you. Previously I might have attempted it, but your bullet cost me several broken ribs. The slightest movement is very painful,' Suzie stated, exaggerating the discomfort.

A furrowed brow of disbelievement crossed Sutton's face.

'We've only just got back from the hospital. I'm heavily bandaged all across my middle. Look, I'll show you,' she stated, unbuttoning her blouse from the bottom.

The heavy bandaging around Suzie's middle was clear for Sutton to see as she continued to undo the buttons.

Sutton tapped her ribs with the barrel of his gun. Suzie screwed up her face and was in obvious pain. Mike started to rise from his seat, but sat back down when Sutton pointed the gun his way.

'So, the little lady is in a bit of pain. That's good.'

With only the last two top buttons still fastened, Suzie ripped opened her blouse wide. She was not wearing a bra and her nakedness was in full view for Sutton's eyes. The sudden sight of her breasts, within touching distance of him, distracted his attention for a split second.

That spit second was what Mike was waiting for, and knew that Suzie would somehow manage to find it. Suddenly, he tipped up the coffee table in front of him and wrenched free a gun, taped to the underside. Sutton reacted quickly and the living room echoed to the sound of gunfire.

For the second time in two days, he and Mike fired at each other simultaneously. Mike's aim was better this time, and his bullet ploughed into the centre of Sutton's body, sending him crashing to the floor, whilst the bullet from Sutton's weapon glanced through the edge of Mike's shoulder, knocking him into the armchair.

Mike got to his feet, clutching his right arm as blood seeped between his fingers. He padded around to the rear of the settee, with his gun poised to shoot, and saw that Sutton was mortally wounded and in no shape to put up any resistance. Mike kicked the gun away from Sutton's hand and gave his to Suzie, who had got to her feet. Mike knelt by Sutton, lifting his head.

'It's just not your day, is it?' he stated.

'Not with people like you around,' choked Sutton, blood seeping from the corner of his mouth.

'Care to tell me the name of the gunman, who everyone was so anxious to discover?'

'Couldn't do that. If I told them who it was …' Sutton stopped, coughed up more blood and breathing heavily continued, 'If I told them, they'd be after me.'

He half-smiled, stiffened for a second before his body went limp, and his head rolled to one side. Mike laid him down on the floor.

He rose to his feet. 'So, it was Sutton himself who shot the Irish politician.'

Suzie peered over the back of the settee. 'Unless he was lying to protect someone else. I presume he's dead.'

'Yeah, he's dead this time all right. I don't think he was lying. It answers a lot of questions and is plausible that he was the trigger man. When you think about it, it doesn't make sense that the gunman should give him back the weapon to get rid of. He'd never be sure that he'd done it, and that nobody else could get hold of it.'

'So why do you think he gave it to Kelly then?'

'To have him arrested for both shootings. That way it lets him off the hook for the political assassination.'

'I guess so.'

'That was a neat trick to get his attention,' said Mike, staring at Suzie's nakedness as she pulled her blouse together and buttoned it.

'It's a good job we're on the same wavelength and you reacted quickly.'

'I always act quickly when seeing you undress.'

'So I've noticed. How's your arm?'

'The bullet went right through and missed the bone. It's a nasty flesh wound, but I think that's all it is, thank goodness.'

Suzie gave Mike a kiss. 'There have been several close shaves for both of us in the last two days. We might as well go back to being mercenaries; I think it was safer,' she joked.

Mike smiled. 'We'd be a lot safer, refusing to do so-called simple tasks for Sir Joseph Sterling.'

'You could be right. You'd better ring him and let him know what's happened, and tell him this is the last time we do a favour for him.'

'Until the next time,' whispered Mike.

'He might find it more difficult to ask us if we were married,' suggested Suzie.

'Hmm ... possibly, but somehow I doubt it.'

Less than an hour later, two men arrived to collect Sutton's body.

'That was quick,' remarked Mike, watching them bundle him into a body bag and zip it up.

'We aim to please,' the red headed, boiler suited man replied.

Mike watched the gates clang shut after the van roared away. He returned to the living room where Suzie was once more resting on the settee.

'I'll have to get the carpet thoroughly cleaned now. There's tea and blood everywhere, and I don't like the idea of knowing there was a body in here. I wonder how he got in. I though we had a good security system to stop intruders,' she complained.

'He must have been waiting outside and sneaked in before the gates were shut. I turned the alarm off when we arrived and didn't reset it. I normally only do that when we go to bed. He's buggered up the back door lock getting in, so I'll ring our maintenance man and get him to fix it.'

'We'll have to watch out for that in future.'

'Now that we are alone again, what's this surprise that you have for me in the bedroom?'

'Help me up. I'll show you.'

Holding on to Mike's arm, Suzie climbed the stairs and they entered the master bedroom. She opened the bedside cabinet drawer, took out a parcel and handed it to Mike. He recognised the package and tore the paper off to reveal $150,000 in used notes.

'Where on earth did you get these from? You told me it was left in Africa and you'd given the money away.'

'Manny gave it to me while you were upstairs making your telephone call to Brooke at the pub. I gave him $100,000 to pass on to the local orphanage where the children came from who helped me at the airport.'

'Why didn't you tell me, instead of letting me think I'd lost the money forever?'

'I wanted to keep it as a surprise, and I needed to make sure that you were convincing when telling Sir Joseph the cash was lost in Africa. If you knew I'd got the money, you might have accidentally given the game away.'

'Have you checked them to make sure they're not bugged in some way or covered in some obscure dye that only shows up under an ultraviolet lamp?'

'Are you kidding? I think you've been watching too many espionage films.'

'But have you checked them?'

'No, should I? Do you think Sir Joseph would do that?'

'Too true,' stated Mike. 'Where are your kitchen gloves?'

'In the kitchen, where else? You're not going to get them now, are you?'

'No, I'll sort through the notes later. Sir Joseph would have said something before now about it, if there was a bug in the parcel.'

'And you should ring Manny and thank him.'

'Yes, okay. I'll ring him later,' said Mike, unbuttoning Suzie's blouse. 'After you've shown me the same luscious body that you enticed Sutton with, and taken your rightful place … on top,' he declared, lowering Suzie on to the bed.

'Okay, Randy. I guess you've earned it … saving my life. I'm still a bit fragile, so be gentle with me, but make it good.'

'Good! It'll be worth $150,000.'